WHEN ANIMALS ATTACK:
THE 70 BEST HORROR MOVIES WITH KILLER ANIMALS

Edited by Vanessa Morgan

TABLE OF CONTENTS

Special thanks to

Sandro Mastronardi
Olivier Bernard
Ton van Rooij
Gilles Vranckx
Kurt Debaillie

INTRODUCTION

"Why a book on animal attack movies?"

This is the question many people ask when they hear about this guide.

Animal attack movies have become a genre unto itself, and like any movie genre, it's one worthy of study. One of the most interesting aspects is how it has evolved over the decades in conjunction with trending angst.

In the 1920s and 1930s, it was the lingering colonial fear of foreign lands that drove audiences to panic in front of rampaging wild beasts. For

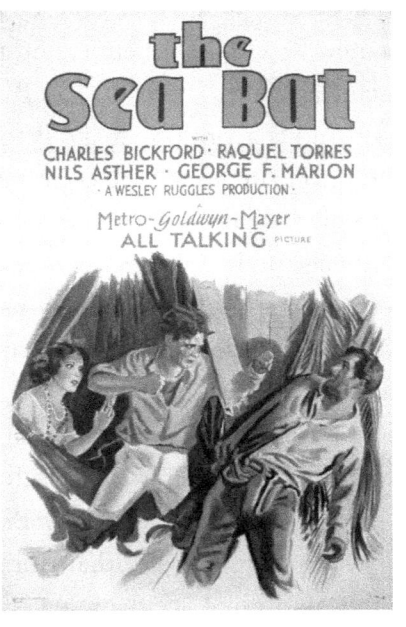

example, in the Mascot film serial *The King of the Kongo* (1929, Richard Thorpe), a giant gorilla guards a temple in the jungle and menaces those who dare to approach it. Many of this era's animal

attack adventure movies took place at sea, like *The Sea Bat* (1930, Wesley Ruggles and Lionel Barrymore), about a giant manta ray attacking sponge fishers near the West Indies, or the silent film *The Sea Beast* (1926, Millard

Webb), based on the novel *Moby Dick* by Herman Melville.

The animal attack movie flourished in the 1950s. In the post-war period, with the nuclear genie released from its bottle, it was the impact of atomic radiation that led us to cower from mutated animals the size of freight trains, reflecting our hubris back to ourselves. "When man entered the atomic age, he opened a door to a new world," a scientist intoned at the conclusion of the 1954 giant ant film, *Them!* In *The Black Scorpion* (1957, Edward Ludwig), enormous scorpions make it to the earth's surface after a volcanic eruption and attack the countryside. Leeches have been mutated by atomic radiation in *Attack of the Giant Leeches* (1959, Bernard L. Kowalski). In *Beginning of the End* (1957, Bert I. Gordon) locusts turn gargantuan after eating radiated giant vegetables. In *Earth vs. the Spider* (1958, Bert I. Gordon), an abnormally large spider attacks a rural community. And in *Tarantula* (1959, Jack Arnold), a laboratory experimenting with size enhancers creates a monster tarantula. Humans weren't safe from giantism either. In both *The Amazing Colossal Man* (1957, Bert I. Gordon) and *Attack of the 50th Foot Woman* (1958, Nathan Juran) people grew to over 50 feet tall after an atomic accident. So do otherworldly and extinct creatures in *The Beast from 20,000 Fathoms* (1953, Eugène Lourié), *Godzilla* (1954, Ishirō Honda), *The Cyclops* (1957, Bert I. Gordon), *The Monolith Monsters* (1957, John Sherwood), *Kronos* (1957, Kurt Neumann), and many more.

Much like its zoological counterpart, atomic radiation was a

Blood Freak (1972)

danger that was out of proportion and difficult to control. Killing the hulking beast therefore quite literally meant saving the planet and staving off the possibly disastrous effects of the atomic

Max Mon Amour (1986)

bomb for yet another day. Luckily, the monster movies of the atomic age always had a team of visionary scientists and heavy artillery at the ready to solve or exterminate the problems man created.

This reassuring dynamic faltered by the 1970s, worn away by grueling images of Vietnam and the disillusionment of Watergate. The authority figures could no longer save or protect us. Filmmakers portrayed them as ruthless politicians more interested in preserving their own image, and willing to sacrifice lives rather than lose money during tourist season. People also realized that *they* and not just the government were interfering with nature as the detritus and pollution from our consumption-crazed society was turning nature against us, one animal at a time or all at once. In this age, killer-animal rage was stirred into action by human interference in the environment. For example, pollution in the swamps rouses violent animal behavior in *Frogs* (1972, George McCowan), fishing with dynamite and drugs cause a man with a turkey head going on a slasher spree in *Blood Freak* (Brad F. Grinter, 1972), and a hole in the ozone layer affects the behavior

Komodo vs. Cobra (2005)

of the animals in *Day of the Animals* (1977, William Girdler).

Though the viewer can still spot a few movies with ginormous animals (the oversized ants who menace and brainwash icon Joan Collins in *Empire of the Ants* or the rats and chickens in *The Food of the Gods*), the majority of these films now focus on animals of average proportion. One of the stronger entries in the eco-horror genre, the "Ozploitation" independent *Long Weekend* (1978, Collin Eggleston), bears witness to the fact that the beasts of the 1970s did not have to be huge anymore to pose a genuine thread. We angered them, and they turned against us.

Keeping in mind that these films tell a story about man vs. the environment, and warn us against an apocalypse of our own making, this type of film rarely concentrates on a singular character. If and when they do, they tabulate the differences and similarities between species, with simians in particular. In *Monkey Shines* (1988, George Romero), Ella's behavior is a direct reflection of her master's thinking, and in *Link* (1986, Richard Franklin), Terence Stamp and an orangutan try to outsmart each other. These movies teach us that critical misunderstandings will occur between species, whereas movies outside of this genre try to prove that creatures of different species can even fall in love, as seen in *Max*

Octopus (2000)

mon amour (1986, Nagisa Ôshima) and *Tanya's Island* (1980, Alfred Sole).

At the same time, censorship in the 1970s was relaxed and the gate to excess thrown wide open. The 1970s became the decade of intense development and extremity.

In the late 1990s, animal attack movies got a turnaround. After a few made-to-entertain features such as *Arachnophobia* (1990, Frank Marshall), *Deep Blue Sea* (1999, Renny Harlin), or *Lake Placid (1999, Steve Miner)*, the animals got bigger again. But, this time, they did not scare us anymore. On the contrary, the giant creatures were meant to be laughable. Look at luridly-titled wonders like 3 Headed Shark Attack (Christopher Douglas-Olen Ray, 2015), *Beasterday: Here Comes Peter Cottonhell* (Snygg Brothers, 2014), *Zombeavers* (2014, Jordan Rubin), *Mega Shark vs. Crocosaurus* (2010, Christopher Ray), *Komodo vs. Cobra* (2005, Jim Wynorski), or *Scorpius Gigantus* (2006, Tommy Withrow), and you'll understand that many of the recent animal attack films have been made ridiculous on purpose. The emphasis shifted from survival and resistance to cosy reassurance that humanity can cope. The colossal beast looks foolish with cheap CGI. More often than not, a group of imbeciles serves as a counterpart. It's easy to feel comfortable if even "losers" can survive. The animal attack film becomes a "can do" lecture. What was once a painful confrontation has now become the feel-good subgenre of horror.

But let's not forget the main objective of this book: fun.

Rise of the Animals (2011)

When Animals Attack is mainly a book about guilty pleasures. While the subtitle states, "The 70 Best Horror Movies with Killer Animals" no one could make the claim that all of the titles included herein are qualitative. Sift through this compendium and you'll find a few acknowledged classics and underappreciated gems but also a good deal of animal attack movies that could be categorized as "so bad they're good." Even readers who are not into the genre will have a blast as they leaf through these pages to find silly killer animals, themed drinking games, and hilarious stories about guerilla filmmaking and censorship.

As this is one of the most varied horror subgenres, both in terms of animals and tone, adding different voices to the fore reflects these variations. The contributors for *When Animals Attack* are a mixture between film historians, horror fiction authors, film critics, authors of movie reference guides, film directors, film festival programmers, actors, screenwriters, and bloggers. That means some of the essays are serious and informative in nature, while others are clearly meant to entertain. In a few cases, the writer discusses a movie he or she worked on: Beverly Gray (*Piranha*) was a former employee of Roger Corman and Jeff Lieberman wrote and directed *Squirm*. However, most authors chose an animal attack movie they feel passionate about.

These opinions don't always line up with the critical consensus. I asked each contributor to write about an animal attack movie that's dear to him. I made it clear from the beginning that it didn't matter what other people thought. If the writer considered it to be a fun or cleverly wrought man vs. animal horror, it must hold something good in the first place. I wanted to discover the passion for that particular movie through the writer's voice. I don't always agree with everything. Some of the movies in this book I wouldn't personally recommend, while several of my favorites are not included.

The creatures, too, are diverse. As long as the animal exists and is still alive today, it could be discussed in this book. That means vertebrates (birds, mammals, amphibians, reptiles, fish), molluscs (octopuses, squids, snails), arthropods (insects, spiders, scorpions, crabs), annelids (earthworms, leeches), and jellyfishes are all joining the party. Since dinosaurs are extinct, aliens have not been proven, and mushrooms are neither animals nor plants, they don't count. However, the animal could be genetically modified or gigantic.

Because of the nature of this book, you won't find every single animal attack movie ever made in here, nor will you find every single animal. But you'll find the most fascinating ones that are worth discovering. Some of them have cultural or historic importance, some are touching, some are repulsive, and some are plain silly. Yet they all have one thing in common: they have made the heart of at least one writer beat faster with excitement.

ALLIGATOR (1980)

By Kevin Matthews

Urban legends. They often provide rich source material for fun movies. Whether it's the babysitter being pestered on the telephone by someone hiding in the house, the vengeful spirit of Bloody Mary, or alligators that have grown large and fierce in the sewers of New York after being flushed down the toilet. As you may have already guessed, *Alligator* uses that last urban legend as a basis for its thrills.

There has been, in recent years, a resurgence in the killer croc movie: *Rogue*, *Lake Placid*, *Black Water*, *Primeval*, *Alligator X*, *Croczilla*, and even one or two movies from The Asylum. Tobe Hooper even tried his hand at this particular subgenre with *Crocodile*, a film released in 2000 that could easily be mistaken for something made ten years previously. Even that inferior film was given a sequel, alternately titled *Crocodile 2: Death Swamp*

and *Crocodile 2: Death Roll*, depending on when and where you saw it. But none of those movies had the benefit of a fun-filled script from John Sayles. Or even a winning lead performance from Robert Forster.

Alligator is the daddy of them all. Equally inspired by the "big bug" movies of Bert I. Gordon and the simple brilliance of *Jaws* (or, perhaps more accurately, *Piranha*, which remains arguably the best film to come along in the wake of Spielberg's thrilling classic), this is a movie that mixes sly humor with genuine thrills, and features an imposing and highly impressive central creature.

While some moments highlight the fact that this was a movie made at the lower end of the budgetary scale, such as a slightly wobbly depiction of the alligator breaking through paving to cause havoc on the streets, there are plenty of times in which numerous tricks cover up the slight failings. It also helps that there are some unexpected shocks that remind us that this is a horror movie, despite the levity. I'm thinking about one swimming pool sequence involving playing kids while the creature waits beneath the waterline, or the reptile gate crashing a garden party in spectacular fashion, ensuring a third act that constantly ups the ante until reaching the inevitable "face off" finale.

Aside from the titular beastie causing havoc, *Alligator* focuses on the aforementioned Robert Forster (playing a cop named David) and a reptile expert named Marisa, played by Robin Riker. Both end up putting the pieces together until they come to the inevitable conclusion that a giant alligator is killing people in their city. Of course, it becomes harder and harder to jump to any other conclusion as the reptile is seen by more and more petrified eyewitnesses. Meanwhile, a hunter (legendary Henry Silva) decides to try and claim a major trophy.

Eschewing the typical alpha male role normally put forward as the hero, Forster is a self-deprecating charmer, constantly aware of his own limitations, especially the fact that he's prematurely balding and not the most handsome man in the area. Yet those exchanges with Riker make him all the more likable and render the developing relationship between the two believable. The scenes that don't actually feature the alligator zip by pleasantly enough thanks to the way the central characters are developed and the reality that they seem to be grounded in. We have Forster to thank for that, as it was he who decided to comment on his own hair, an idea that Sayles loved and subsequently wrote into the script. But we also have exchanges like the following to raise a smile:

"We got a big toe in the ward once. Nothing else just a big toe."

"Yeah?"

"Never found the rest of him. But we figured out who it was.

Had a funeral, and everything."

"Must've been a pretty small casket."

Aside from the writing and acting, it also helps that the 1980s were *the* decade for director Lewis Teague, a man who knew how to stretch a dollar and how to make the best use of talented actors who weren't always up there on the a-list. *Alligator* kick-started a run of movies that would also include *Cujo, The Jewel of the Nile, Cat's Eye,* and others (including *Collision Course,* which stars Pat Morita and Jay Leno). In fact, *Navy Seals* and *Wedlock* in the early 1990s left Teague with a run of genre hits that will probably include at least one minor favorite for any b-movie fan. But none of them rival *Alligator* for the blend of sheer fun and sly intelligence.

It may start with a baby alligator being flushed down a toilet, but the film is just as much a comment on chemical pollution, and, separately, the ability of people to make a buck from any newsworthy event as it's a simple monster movie. One could even argue that it's an interesting look at the constant nature vs. nurture debate, due to the fact that Marisa is the grown-up version of the little girl who lost her pet alligator all those years ago. Although she's unaware of this fact throughout the movie, her life has been defined by the actions of her parents, themselves reacting badly to a young girl who was already developing an interest in a subject that would lead to her future career. Is it too much of a stretch to think of the movie unfolding under the shadow of the ouroboros (the serpent/dragon eating its own tail) when considering the way the main characters are affected and changed by others? David, Marisa and the alligator are the obvious subjects to focus on, but there's also an interesting story strand that leads to a cynical news reporter capturing the alligator on camera during a violent death scene. The reporter was following the story developing around David, which then led to death, which subsequently led to the proof of life required to step up the hunt. See?

Or maybe it's just about nothing more than a dangerous, oversized alligator on the prowl. The beauty of the film is that it's everything above and also none of those things. Like a number of the best monster movies, you can transfer a lot of meaning onto the onscreen events, or you can just sit back and watch the chaos unfold with a satisfied smile. But DO watch it.

Kevin Matthews

Kevin Matthews lives in Edinburgh, Scotland, a city that he loves boasting about to anyone who will listen. He's a Sagittarius, who doesn't believe in horoscopes unless they promise something good on the horizon.

Kevin writes for Flickfeast.co.uk, has only recently stopped serving up a movie a day on his online blog *For it is Man's Number*, and has been involved in the books *Dr. A.C. Presents Horror 101* and *Hidden Horror: a Celebration of 101 Underrated and Overlooked Fright Flicks*, alongside many other talented writers/fans.

The things he likes most are watching movies, writing, embarrassing loved ones, and watching more movies. The things he dislikes most include increasingly rude cinema audiences and writing about himself in the third person.

Favorite films include *Jaws, Some Like it Hot, Sunset Blvd, An American Werewolf in London, Goodfellas, Re-Animator, Halloween,* and *Gremlins.* Favorite creature features include those already mentioned in this bio, plus the likes of *Ticks, Empire of the Ants, Tremors, Grabbers, Arachnophobia, Wild Beasts,* and *Squirm.* And *Alligator,* of course.

ANACONDA (1997)

By Russ Hunter

Any film that opens with a sweaty Danny Trejo desperately crawling up a ship's mast to escape from an unseen menace and then promptly shooting himself in the head grabs your attention. From then on *Anaconda* is the kind of cheesy, camp, raucous absurd piece of fun that guarantees it a place in the pantheon of cult horror films. After that bedazzling coda, the film starts conventionally enough, setting up the story of documentary filmmaker Terri Flores (Jennifer Lopez) and her crew (Ice Cube, Owen Wilson, Kari Wuhrer), who, under the guidance of Anthropologist Dr. Steven Cale (Eric Stoltz) and spiky English presenter Warren Westridge (Jonathan Hyde), are searching for a

legendary lost Amazonian tribe, The People of the Mist. Heading down river on an old barge they encounter a stranded snake hunter Paul Serone (Jon Voight), who harbors a not-so-secret desire to capture a live "giant" Anaconda. Things quickly escalate as Serone takes over the boat and forces the crew to hunt for the gigantic anaconda that he promises will be worth "millions." What follows is a fast and furious mixture of horror, good old fashioned adventure film and action extravaganza that sees various crewmembers gulped, crushed and slowly digested by a monstrously large snake. By the time the ship's captain, Mateo (Vincent Castellanos), has his head engulfed inside a ginormous anaconda, it's clear that what you're viewing is going to be delirious fun.

Subtlety is certainly not king in *Anaconda*, but that's part of its charm. The film's flaws are also its main strengths and what rapidly marked it out as a cult property. The joy of *Anaconda* is precisely that it isn't trying to be the *Citizen Kane* of monster movies. It wants to make you smile, it wants to make you laugh, and it wants to give you some good old fashioned scares, too. There are jump scares, tilted camera angles to add a general sense of unease, crushed bodies and heads swallowed whole, and even a scene where a tiny baby anaconda rather comically attempts to consume Westrdige's index finger. Badly realized in places, more convincing in others, the snakes are a mix of animatronic, CGI and real live serpents, all of which lends the titular anaconda an oddly uncanny feel.

The cast are what you might get if you invented an automated cast-generator and set it to random. Mathematicians will tell you how difficult it is to create random pairings, that human design and a desire for structure inevitably plays a part in ordering apparently random elements. It's almost as though the producers defied all laws of moviemaking (and mathematics) and put together the most unlikely combination of actors ever seen on film. The central enjoyment of *Anaconda* revolves around the campy fun that Jon Voight appears to be having as its (very) arch villain. In perhaps the worst pairing of actor with back-story, he's a South American snake hunter. His performance is a joy to behold as, replete with a comic interpretation of some form of "South American" accent, for most of the film's runtime Voight looks like he might have been given the acting cue of "look menacing, then grimace... a lot." When he isn't delivering killer lines of dialogue such as, "Please, people, don't make me out a monster. I didn't eat the captain," he spends much of his time staring off into the middle distance looking sinister. As such, he steals the film. Some of the other performances have perhaps been unfairly maligned. Ice Cube provides solid support as the crew's stoic cameraman and Jonathan Hyde, in particular, as neck-time wearing, wine-guzzling Englishman, who plays golf on deck, is clearly having an immense amount of fun.

Critical reaction to the film was not good, symbolized most obviously by it six Razzie award nominations (most notably for the Worst Couple for Voight and the animatronic anaconda). If not for the magic of Kevin Costner's *The Postman* then *Anaconda* might have swept the board. Regardless, for the major part, the film was viewed as an expensive piece of schlock – the budget was rumored

to be close to $50 million – and dismissed as a poorly executed, poorly acted genre mistake. But as time has passed it's clear that the film was a slow-burning cult phenomenon. You don't watch *Anaconda* for the stellar acting, for the intricacies of its plot or its piercing social commentary. You watch *Anaconda* to celebrate all the absurd fun that genre cinema can bring us.

The film is very clearly the product of a number of cinematic predecessors. A pre-opening credit sequence, for instance, evokes Italian cannibal films of the 1970s and 1980s, baldly stating, "Tales of monstrous, man-eating Anaconda have been recounted for centuries by the tribes people of the Amazon Basin, some of whom are said to worship these giant snakes…" But the influence of high-profile films like *Apocalypse Now* is obvious here too. Coppola's film, a loose adaptation of Joseph Conrad's *Heart of Darkness*, whilst iconic in its own right, also helped to popularize the "dangerous jungle journey" subgenre that was typified by ludicrous exploitation fare like *Massacre in Dinosaur Valley* (1985). Looked at in this way, *Anaconda* is *Apocalypse Now* with enormous snakes instead of Vietcong and a crazed homily-spouting Jon Voight instead of a crazed homily-spouting Marlon Brando.

Its relative box office and particularly home video success ensured that, whatever the critical reaction, three increasingly vapid sequels eventually followed: the theatrically-released *Anacondas: The Hunt for the Blood Orchid* (2004), and two cheap made-for-television films, *Anaconda 3: Offspring* (2008) and *Anacondas: Trail of Blood* (2009). The final breath was squeezed out of the franchise with an attempt to make an absurd crossover film, *Lake Placid vs. Anaconda* (2015). A number of films based around animals or insects systemically attacking humans can end up taking their central premises far too earnestly. The resultant films can end up as either too worthy to really enjoy or too serious to poke fun at. No such fear with *Anaconda*, a film that slithered into our collective cult consciousness in 1997 and embraced us all so tightly we feared our bones might break (if we didn't die laughing first). As Owen Wilson's soundman Gary Dixon says after a moment of profound realization in *Anaconda*, "You don't know shit about the shit we're in out here, and neither do I."

Russ Hunter

Dr. Russ Hunter is a Senior Lecturer in Film & Television at Northumbria University. He has published widely on Italian genre cinema, the work of film critics, and European horror cinema. He has recently published an edited collection (with Stefano Baschiera) entitled *Italian Horror Cinema* for Edinburgh University Press and is writing a book entitled *A History of European Horror Cinema*.

Russ has spoken at a number of film festivals, including Abertoir Horror Festival and Offscreen, and his work has been included in *101 Horror Films*, *101 Sci-fi Films*, *101 Action Films*, *101 Gangster Films*, *101 War Film*, *510 Movie Directors*, *501 Movie Stars*, and *This is Cinema*. Despite all of this, his favorite film is still *Cinema Paradiso*.

ANTS (1977)

By JP Wendel

Thanks to both the box office success of *Jaws* and the eco-movement hitting the mainstream after being considered a fringe issue in the 1960s, the "animal attack" film exploded in the mid to late 1970s, with every animal from bear to barracuda, snake to rat, roach to rabbit snagging their own movie. Ants, however, thanks to their abundant numbers, reasonably predictable behavior, and the simple fact that even PETA doesn't raise that much of a stink if a few don't make it through the production, made them one of the most popular of this revitalized subgenre. This brings us to the subject of this little essay, the 1977 TV movie *Ants*, or if you prefer it's wonderfully ambiguous original title, *It Happened at Lakewood Manor*.

I first came across this little gem when I was somewhere around seven years old. Despite living in what at the time was a very rural part of Mississippi, we had a tiny - roughly the size of your average walk-in closet if memory serves - video rental place

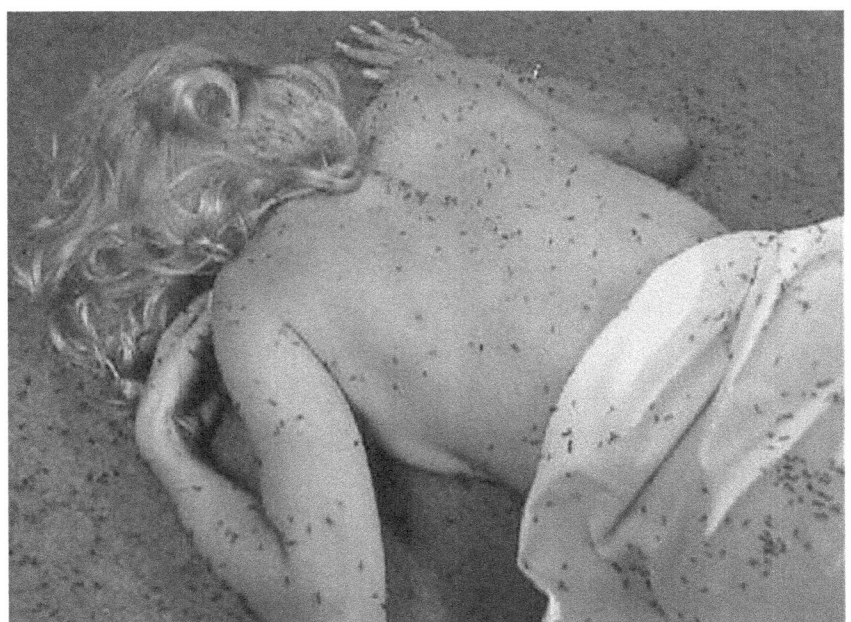

that was attached to a feed-and-seed store and a storefront that was a gas station in the loosest sense of the term (it had one pump and only occasionally gas in the tank). Always hotter than a nutsack in the tropics no matter what the weather was like, the walls of the building were completely crammed with VHS tapes, only their spines visible, while two long double-sided, shoulder-high shelves of the type common to only video stores and seedy adult bookstores, took up the majority of floor space. A tiny checkout counter, the top usually cluttered with some kind of horrible off-brand candy, manned by a teenager who could be described ambivalent at best, was tucked away in a corner in front of the only window.

I was there with my parents one balmy summer day, the humidity level so high it felt more like breathing soup than air. Doing whatever it is that children do when bored and not particularly interested in what's happening around them, one VHS cover caught my eye. It featured the image of a bare-chested young blonde, ubiquitous gold chain draped around her swanlike neck, her face partially obscured by some glorious bangs, her ample bosom covered in tiny black specks. Upon further inspection the dozens, nay hundreds, of black dots were revealed to be little bitty ants, which should've been obvious to me as the word "ants" was scrawled across the top in big bold letters, punctuated by a generous exclamation point no less. I immediately snatched the box from its perch and held it up to my mom and dad for their approval. Since these were people who allowed a 6-year-old to watch *Child's Play*, they responded with an enthusiastic "yes."

Our story takes place entirely at the titular Lakewood Manor (depending on which title you go off of), a beautiful old B&B run by the wheelchair-bound Ethel - played by Myrna Loy, a woman whose acting career stretches all the way back to the era of silent film and includes roles in such classics as *The Thin Man*, *The Great Ziegfeld*, and the original *Cheaper by the Dozen* - and her daughter Valerie, played by the gorgeous Lynda Day George whom you may remember for her roles in another classic animal attack film called *Day of the Animals* and the ultra-gory Spanish slasher film *Pieces*. Valerie has been pressuring her invalid mother to sell the old place to possibly the least sleazy real estate magnate ever portrayed in film, Anthony Fleming, who wishes to bulldoze the entire property to build a casino, and she has finally agreed to sell. The surprisingly non-sordid agent and his assistant/paramour, Gloria, played by Suzanne Somers right before she became a household name thanks to *Three's Company*, have come for the night for Ethel to sign the contract and to have sick, nasty hotel sex.

Meanwhile, construction being done on the property, lead by a deliciously hirsute Robert Foxworth, who's also having an affair with the owner's daughter, comes to a screeching halt when two workers are accidentally buried alive in a pit. Little does everyone know those men were dead long before their bodies were uncovered, not from asphyxiation, but the über-deadly stings - infused with DDT no less, a common plot point of insect related

animal attack movies of the era - of some very pissed off arthropods that are now on the move, and the charming B&B with the tranquil lake views is squarely in their multifaceted sights. The tiny terrors soon have our coifed protagonists besieged inside, forcing them to keep climbing levels (sort of like the disaster films, like *The Poseidon Adventure* and *The Towering Inferno*, that were still popular at the time) until only a few are left, and they must endear a more aggression-free way of dealing with them until the cavalry arrives.

Ants is one of those films that's so stuffed to the rafters with star power it's practically *The Lawrence Welk Show*. In addition to the heavyweights mentioned above, *Ants* features performances from Bernie Casey (*In the Mouth of Madness, Revenge of the Nerds, Dr. Black/ Mr. Hyde*), Anita Gillette (*Moonstruck, Trapper John MD*), barrel-chested silver daddy Brian Dennehy (*First Blood, Cocoon*), and Stacy Keach Sr. (practically every movie ever made). As if that weren't enough, writer Guerdon Trueblood was also the man behind *Tarantulas: The Deadly Cargo* and *The Savage Bees* and its sequel;

director Robert Scheerer lensed several episodes of some of the most popular TV shows to hit the small screen, including *Dynasty*, *The Love Boat*, and both *Star Trek: The Next Generation* and Voyager.

By this point, I'm sure you're wondering just where in the hell I'm going with all this. I'm not here to convince you *Ants* is the best dang animal attack film out there. Hell, it's really not even the best made-for-TV flick. What it excels at, however, is being such a perfect time capsule of the era, one that this writer will always remember with fondness and not a little bit of Pavlovian-style sweating.

JP Wendel

JP Wendel is a massage therapist by trade, while writing is a hobby. When not rubbing strangers (appropriately), knocking back whiskey like it's water, or suffering through Fred Olen Ray movies, he writes for his own horror movie review site *Death Blog: The Blog That Eats People*. He currently lives in Mississippi with his partner.

ARACHNOPHOBIA (1990)

By Declan Lynch

My brother, Cyril bought Empire magazine every month. When he was finished reading it cover to cover, it was my turn. But for the time it took him to read, he was effectively the source of all up to date movie knowledge. In our house, Cyril was the closest thing we had to the Internet. It was the beginning of a new decade, and the web was where spiders hung out.

Arachnophobia was Hollywood Pictures first film. The company was set up by Disney to intensify its position among adult cinema goers and spawned over 70 films of varying quality over the next decade. Directed by Frank Marshall and co-produced with Amblin,

Arachnophobia has the strong thumb print of Steven Spielberg throughout. Marshall, more known then and now for his producing duties (with his wife Kathleen Kennedy and Spielberg) made his drama directorial début. It's a forgotten and some would argue forgettable tale, but not for me.

The film was released in Ireland on the first Friday in 1991; I remember that weekend as I spent it almost entirely on a VHS marathon of *Twin Peaks*. That Sunday, with my sister Fiona and two brothers (Cyril and Pio) I made a failed trip to the recently opened UCI cinemas in the Square shopping center in Tallaght, Dublin. It was sold out. A week of heavy snow, college work, and attempts to stick to my new year's resolutions passed. The following Sunday night I took the bus into the city center paying the newly raised fare of 85p and made my way to O'Connell's street. *Arachnophobia* was screening in the Savoy 3, and I had pulled together a group of misfits. I did this using a small notebook with phone numbers in and a telephone - connected to a wall. 1991 kids, 1991! Ten of us in all; Ciara, Anne, DOC, Gillian, Mango, Gar, Helen, Ciaran and Clare met outside the Savoy, a perfect mess of nerds, Goths and jocks. Brief introductions for those who hadn't yet met; tickets and popcorn bought, in we went.

The credits sequence lets us all get comfortable, but that was pretty much it for the evening. The very visceral reaction of the audience on that night is still vivid in my mind. Like horrors and comedies, *Arachnophobia* is a film to be seen with a crowd. As it happens, it's kind of neither.

The film quickly establishes its premise tracking a photographer Jerry Manley (Mark L. Taylor) on a visit to a scientific research team led by Dr. James Atherton (Julian Sands) in deepest Venezuela. Some overdubbed plot pointers follow and when the group's Amazonian guide dares not proceed, we know there's danger here.

In the jungle; bugs and creepy crawlies abound, Trevor Jones' soundtrack underscores some mini scares, spider tiptoeing, hisses and jumps with great aplomb. The film set-ups its arch villain with a series of comic notes before we get to see its fangs; predictably sinking into Manley, whose death confirms that this will be spun in the entertaining traditional of Hollywood morality tales. Manley kills a spider and thereby disrespects Mother Nature - ye can't do that, ye can't be doing that!

Cut to: a hearse driving Manley's body back to the town of "Canaima" (little script writers joke there) where the rest of the action is to unfold. A clever sequence takes the audience and our eight legged Venezuelan friend from the local mortuary to the Jennings family's first day in their new abode. It's a perfectly set scene, the American dream home complete with shadowy barn, dark basement; all good spots for the creepy scenes to come. All the more creepy as it's soon evident that Dr. Jennings is mortally afraid of spiders. "Can you blame me for being a spiderphobe?" he asks his wife as they enter the spooky barn. "Arachnophobe," she replies. De-da-daaah!

Building tension is what the film is all about, and the key player here is the central character of Dr. Jennings. Jennings is played by a fresh faced Jeff Daniels, likely not the producers first choice but a very effective one. Promoting the film Marshall claimed: "I really

wanted a polished actor rather than a box office star." Daniels had proven his drama chops in the box office smash *Terms of Endearment* and followed up with further critical acclaim in films such as *The Purple Rose of Cairo, Something Wild, Heartburn, Radio Days,* before a mini career stall in the late 1980s. I suppose what I'm trying to say is that back then; he was bringing credibility to the role. And it's by enlarge to his credit that key sequences and scenes work. Daniels sells the often incredible plot-turns with ease, marking insignificant moments with human and comic touches. If acting is about reacting Daniels gives his insect co-star Big Bob (named after Marshall's friend Robert Zemickis) a master class in the films' final scenes.

A less subtle but not ineffective performance comes with the introduction of John Goodman's Delbert – a kind of cartoon-like insect exterminator. Goodman treats this as an opportunity to stamp his arachnid stained boots on every scene. Inevitably Doc Atherton is called back in to help to sell some plot enhancing science. Sands' depiction of Atherton is fit only for the attention of termites. His performance and indeed his character's most important decision was a subject of some sarcastic guffaws in the cinema that night. For the most part the audience screamed at and laughed with the film, not so when Sands lumbers in. His inevitable death raised a victorious cheer from a Dublin crowd happy to switch sides and back the spiders for a kill.

But Marshall's *ode to octopod* never quite killed, at least not in terms of box office. "When the movie was being screened and tested, people were going wild. It was being predicted as the sleeper of the summer, the biggest hit for years, and then it

opened, it opened OK, but never really took off," claimed Marshall. "So now we're trying to overcome the immediate negative response that this film is about spiders, because it isn't about spiders..." Spinnerets engage! The unavoidable truth is *Arachnophobia* is about spiders, killer spiders, lots of them, with a very big one reserved for a final fun, ridiculous showdown. Marshall avoids any real character conflict, instead favoring building tension for each of the attack set-ups. Could Spielberg have done both? I suspect not, how much realistic tension can be got from a grown man, however fear-struck, fending off the multiple attacks of a large but by no means giant spider? It's to the director's credit that he plays loose and light with the plot and keeps his tongue firmly pressed in cheek. And within this context, the film doesn't disappoint.

For me, this is easily Marshall's best work as a director. It's fun, sometimes scary but never truly terrifying - unless like one of our number that night, you actually do fear the little critters. Otherwise, it's a popcorn movie - with spiders, so check every mouthful. We were college friends in our first year of studying broadcast journalism. We'd blag tickets from distributors on the promise of landing a film review in local print. We were starting out, outsiders to a media industry yet to find its feet.

Revisiting the film, I'm struck by how refreshing the combination of live action and animatronics used to bring the terror works. It's the fact that you believe both actor and badass spidy are in the same room at the same time; that your brain never questions the eye line of an actor and the knowledge that *"that thing"* is "real" even though it's not. Add to that, pace perfect editing by Spielberg's longtime collaborator Michael Kahn, and you have a film that goes for every shock and gets it. At a reported cost of over $30 million, it was far from a low-budget movie back then, but it's rooted in the best traditions of the b-movie genre. If you want to give logic a break, eye some pretty terrible fashion and listen to the optimistic chords of the beginning of a new decade, watch this film. I loved it then and still do now. Back then, after exiting the cinema, I remember being in the minority (I most likely still am). Almost everyone thought the film was "crap." Mango, looked the worst for wear, having belatedly admitted to suffering from the titular condition. And, of course, it was entirely my fault. Those of us who wrote reviews, didn't get them published, but we had a few more years of college left to hone our skills. I returned home and told Cyril what I thought of the movie; a rare chance to be the first with the news. Later we got the Internet, and my brother finally had a competitor.

Declan Lynch

Declan Lynch is an Irish writer, television editor, and film producer. Declan is the son of Justin and Patricia Lynch from Co. Cavan, Ireland. He grew up in Knocklyon, Dublin. He studied broadcast journalism and media studies and has worked in film and television since 1994. In 1995 he co-produced and directed *25 Years of Solitude*, an environmental documentary about the effects of US foreign policy in Colombia, South America. His television work includes editing credits on BBC's *Panorama* and *Spotlight* current affairs series in addition to documentary work for RTE & TV3. In 2002 he set up Unity Productions to handle independent production projects. His background is documentary filmmaking though he has more recently explored drama projects.

Lynch is the founder of FollowGent, a voluntary experimental filmmaking project based in Ghent, Belgium. The project has led to a number of films screening at world-renowned festivals. Lynch is also writer of the *Orlok* comedy/horror series. His film credits include *Dublin: The Movie (2008)*, *Hotel Darklight* (2009), *The Nixer* (2011), *Meeting on the Stairs* (2012), *Follow* (2013), *Follow: Tall Tales from a Small City* (2014), and *Love, Life, Ghent* (2015). He's currently writing *the political satire Gone Metric*.

Declan is interested in the space between traditional narrative fiction and user interaction online and can be found largely talking to himself on twitter @lildec.

ATTACK OF THE CRAB MONSTERS (1957)

By Noah C. Patterson

During the 1950s, monster movies were extremely popular. Drive-ins during that time period would fill to capacity with teenagers who were all trying to see the latest scary movie and get some nookie in the process. It could easily be said that creature features are the equivalent of what slasher movies are for teenagers today. They represent cheap cinema that's quick to film and easy to sell.

During the 1950s, fear of unknown worlds, unknown species, and fear of nuclear testing were like tinder for the cinema's fire. Filmmakers took up these ideas and exploited them. Over and over again there came new movies about mutated animals or new

species from beyond our mind's reach. Films such as *Creature from the Black Lagoon* (with an unknown animal species), *Them!* (with giant mutated ants), and *The Fly* (with a man merged with a fly's DNA) all contributed to cinema wide exploitation of our animalistic fears.

Many films of this type have, over the years, ended up in the public domain or other similar Internet archives. However, one film, Roger Corman's *Attack of the Crab Monsters* — due to its cult status — has been retained under copyright and has therefore received a fancy DVD style release with new commentaries and interviews.

It's that exact DVD copy of *Attack of the Crab Monsters* that I excitedly picked up to re-watch this bizarre creature feature classic once again.

All my life I have indulged in classic b-horror and b-science fiction films from the 1950s and 1960s. On any given warm summer day in Colorado, the days of laziness, boredom, and youthful relaxation, my mother would drive me out to the local video rental store. Once there I would peruse the horror section with a trained eye, looking for movies that looked scary while still appropriate enough that my mother would let me watch them.

On this particular summer day, I picked up a VHS triple feature pack. My 10-year-old mind realized this meant I could rent *three movies* for the price of one. It was an opportunity I wasn't going to pass up. The collection included George A. Romero's *Night of the Living Dead* (1968), *The Devil Bat* (1940) and *Attack of the Crab Monsters* (1957). These three films seemed to have little in common besides being all three horror movies. The packaging on the VHS box seemed sketchy at best, with pixelated artwork haphazardly slapped on the front. (Back in the 1990s there was less chance of the copyright offices catching up with you if you recorded a couple of movies on tape and sold it on a small scale.)

Once I had arrived home I immediately pulled out one of the

tapes and plopped it into the VHS player. The movie was *Attack of the Crab Monsters*. The film told the story of a scientific expedition to a remote Pacific island. A previous expedition had been sent out and disappeared. This new crew were intended to uncover what happened. But, instead of people, they encounter a supernatural

force of mutated giant crab monsters that are attempting to rip the island apart.

While the film itself didn't necessarily scare me, I was really surprised at the gore. Within the first 10 minutes, one of the crewmembers falls from the boat. When they pull him back on board, his head is missing. Later on in the movie we see one of the scientists get their hand smashed off with a rock. For such an old movie this was a shock to me. On top of all the gore, the element that really stood out to me as a kid (and honestly confused me at the time) was the sentient nature that the crabs took on after killing one of the crewmembers.

Now as an adult (and as a horror film critic and journalist), re-watching the film, much of the violence is tame. However, the sentient nature of the crab monsters means more to me now than it did then. As I have written multiple essays on the development of the horror genre, it's apparent that much of the elements of *Attack of the Crab Monsters* spawn from pre-existing fears of the time period.

As I mentioned before, there seems to be a universal fear of the unknown. During the 1950s there were all kinds of new scientific developments. Because so much of what was being studied was still unknown there was significant fear surrounding science. Explorations of unknown parts of the world, new species, space, and nuclear power were all elements that added to the American nation's fear.

Attack of the Crab Monsters combines many of these concerns into one succinct package. Many different people, even today, fear animals of one kind or another — particularly strange looking animals such as insects, spiders, or crabs. It's my opinion that the point of the horror genre is to explore our pre-existing fears. In order to embark on these types of explorations the creators of horror fiction and film explode our fears into larger proportions. In the case of *Attack of the Crab Monsters* the creators and writers quite literally explode the crab. They make the crabs gigantic. The effects of nuclear radiation cause the crabs to grow to disproportionate size.

The combination of radiation and mutated animals wasn't anything new. However, the fact that the crabs absorbed the human mind and could speak, move, and solve problems like a human is what made the movie's concept original — despite the poorly explained science behind it all. One reason we may fear animals is because we may be like them. In many ways, the pride of the human race has caused us to believe ourselves better, smarter, and more entitled to our place at the top of the food chain. However, if we truly believe we came from animals, then we may not be so different from them.

The crabs absorb their victims' thoughts, feelings, and experiences once they eat the brain. They become us. And ultimately that makes us the true horror, the animals we so fear in these types of animal attack films. Many people are afraid of animals, and these movies delve into this fear. *Attack of the Crab Monsters* explodes it to a level rarely seen in other creature features of this caliber. But, ultimately, with the combination of science, advancement, and exploration, we're truly showing the fear of the animal within ourselves. And what better way to utilize the horror genre than to look within and see the potential animalistic nature we all hold in our genetic past?

Attack of the Crab Monsters is a goofy and fun romp into 1950s b -horror. But, we can also look at ourselves, the culture of the time, as well as our modern civilization, all based on the low art that was then created. *Attack of the Crab Monsters* is a movie to remember for more reasons than one.

Noah C. Patterson

Noah C. Patterson is a professional writer, editor, journalist, and blogger.

He's the lead writer and editor for *A Slice of Horror* where he works with horror authors, filmmakers, production companies, and artists to review and promote upcoming horror news. Noah is also the editor-in-chief and owner of the print horror magazine *WitchWorks*, the eBook publisher *Splatter Chronicles Publishing* and the children's book publisher *Spook Chronicles Publishing. He has previously worked for LDS.net, Sanitarium Magazine,* and Horror-Asylum.com. He has written and published two books, multiple short stories, as well as a variety of dissertations on the relevance and importance of the horror genre.

Noah graduated with a Bachelor of Art in creative writing and publishing from Brigham Young University, Idaho.

BATS (1999)

By Ton van Rooij

Not least thanks to the movie industry, many people have come to associate vampires with human-shaped bloodsuckers rather than with the bats they're named after. Although there have been countless film productions in which humanoid vampires are seen turning into a bat, movies in which bats play a pivotal role are quite scarce. A good example of the latter is *Bats* (USA, 1999), directed by Louis Morneau.

Before discussing *Bats*, let's take a closer look at the titular animals. Bats, the only mammals that can fly, belong to the order of Chiroptera, which comes from the Greek words *cheir*, meaning "hand," and *pteron*, meaning "wing." Of the more than 1,100 different species of bats, only three, as far as we know, feed on blood. Vampire bats live in Latin America, and in contrast to movie vampires, they do not use canines to bite, but incisors. And while count Dracula and his soul mates prefer to bite their victims in the neck, real-life vampires would rather go for the legs, also because they usually strike from the ground.

In body size, most bats aren't much bigger than an adult person's index finger. The smallest of them is the Kitti's hog-nosed bat or bumblebee bat, of which the body measures 2.9 to 3.5 cm (1.14 to 1.38 in). Designated the world's smallest mammal by skull size (by mass, the Etruscan shrew holds that title), it weighs just 2 g (0.07 oz) and has a wingspan of 15 to 16 cm (5.91 to 6.30 in). The largest bats flying, sitting and hanging around belong to the suborder of mega bats or flying foxes. They can be found in Southeast Asia, have a body size of about 60 cm (2 ft), weigh up to

1.2 kg (2.65 lb) and can reach a wingspan as wide as 1.7 m (5 ft 7 in).

In many countries, bats are legally protected – even in Dracula's home country Romania. And for good reason. Because almost three quarter of all bats are insectivores, consuming hundreds of bugs in just a few hours, they're of inestimable value for pest control. Hence, they're of the utmost importance to our ecosystem. Without bats, the number of insects would grow disconcertingly high!

Bats opens in classic horror movie fashion: with a teenage couple being gruesomely killed – in this case by extremely aggressive bats. Later on, in Gallop, Texas, Dr. Tobe Hodge (Carlos Jacott) of the Centers for Disease Control and Prevention (CDC) and bat specialist Dr. Sheila Casper (Dina Meyer) inspect the corpses. As unlikely as it seems, the two youngsters appear to have been assaulted by a bat. Sheila and her assistant Jimmy (Leon) then hear from a scientist, Dr. Alexander McCabe (Bob Gunton), that six days earlier, two genetically-altered, virus-carrying flying foxes have escaped from his research laboratory. The two "super bats" have infected a considerable number of bats in the region. With the help of Sheriff Emmett Kimsey (Lou Diamond Phillips), Sheila and Jimmy must not only find the bats' roost(s) but also prevent these fluttering menaces from harming more people by either capturing of

killing them.

Shortly afterwards, zillions of these ferocious and ravenous creatures head for Gallup. Although the residents had been strictly advised to stay in their homes with doors and windows firmly locked, the majority of the population ignores this.

When arriving in Gallup, the bats, in a *modus operandi* reminiscent to Alfred Hitchcock's *The Birds*, soar through the streets and into houses, bars and shops, injuring and killing hundreds of people (as a wink at vampire movies, the makers at one point let a car crash into a theater with the sign "Now showing – *Nosferatu*"). Some villagers try to defend themselves with fire arms, but these fast-flying predators are virtually impossible to shoot. Police officers do what they can, but no matter how big the track record of some of them may be, they're now fighting adversaries that are unlike any others that have ever crossed their path. In other words, it's a war zone!

And what do you frequently see in motion pictures when citizens lack the resources to cope with a warlike situation? Armed forces come into action! Likewise in *Bats*. To tie in with a cliché, the solution the military leaders come up with only threaten to

make things spiral out of control even more, putting Sheila, Emmett and Jimmy under extra pressure to think up an alternative. As often used as this paradigm is, it incontestably is an effective instrument to raise the tension and thus hold the viewer's attention.

It's not all too surprising that the makers chose to set the film in Texas during the summer for Texas is known – and popular among tourists – for its bats in this season. Every summer, the Congress Avenue Bridge in Austin, Texas, becomes the temporary residence of more than 1.5 million Brazilian free-tailed bats, the largest urban bat colony in the USA. And in Bracken Cave, central Texas, no less than 20 million of these bats have their roost. Also mind-blowing: in a single midsummer night, they devour over 200 tons of insects!

Granted, the flick has its flaws here and there. *Bats* is fairly formula-ridden and somewhat campy, in close-ups the bats don't always look overly convincing, and how only two flying foxes managed to infect thousands, if not tens of thousands of bats in a matter of days remains a mystery. But all this does not invalidate the fact that it's a fast-paced, alternately amusing and thrilling smorgasbord of action, horror, comedy, and drama. Truly awe-inspiring are the bat attack scenes, with the absolute highlight being the spectacular invasion of Gallup.

Bats is popcorn entertainment at its very best. As easy as it may seem to concoct something like this, it definitely is not – it's a craft in its own right that must not be underrated. After all, still a vast majority of people just want to have a jolly good time when watching a movie. And if you're a filmmaker who has the quality to give viewers exactly that and surround yourself by similar creative minds, you can rest assured you will deliver the goods and are here to stay. And that's a quality Louis Morneau and his team most certainly have.

Ton Van Rooij

For about 30 years, Ton van Rooij, residing in Eindhoven, the Netherlands, writes about film, for both magazines and websites. Additionally, as a freelance journalist, he reports on the most diverse topics, albeit often related to art, business and technology, for domestic and foreign media.

He served as co-organizer of the first and second installment of the BUT Film Festival, assisted in realizing the 2009 and 2010 edition of Duistere Openbaringen (Dark Revelations), organized The Amsterdam Tromathon in 2010 together with Amsterdam film museum EYE employee Ronald Simons, was part of the feature and short film jury of the 9th BUT Film Festival, and co-judged short films for the Méliès d'Argent (Silver Méliès) at the 7th Razor Reel Flanders Film Festival.

As co-screenwriter, co-producer and publicity assistant, Ton Van Rooij contributed to the Dutch zombie film *Horizonica* by Ramon Etman. He also acted as associate producer on the Australian short thriller *Crazy in the Night* by Jason Turley.

For Troma, he intermediated the distribution of two Australian films: the philosophical vampire film *A Nocturne* by Bill Mousoulis, and the quasi sci-fi film *Purge* by David King. He was also a middleman in the screening of the short Dutch films *Copy Paste*, *I Wish I Could Share the Happiness of Being Alone with Someone Else* (aka *I Wish*), *Fight Seeing Eindhoven*, and *Suiker* (*Sugar*) at *Short Cut*.

BAXTER (1989)

By Daphnis Olivier Boelens

Based on the Ken Greenhall novel *Hell Hound*, *Baxter* was the first film directed by Jérôme Boivin and one of the earliest works of Jacques Audiard as a screenwriter (who became famous years later with *Un Prophète* and *De rouille et d'os*). Also note that *Baxter* was produced by Ariel Zeitoun, who became a film director with *Saxo* and several Luc Besson productions.

Do not think that *Baxter* embodies the French version of Stephen King's *Cujo*. In this case, man is depicted like a predator,

probably even more monstrous than any other animal because he's acting intentionally. The particularity of this feature film is obviously the intellectual approach and the constant narrative. The narrator is the heart of the story. Baxter the dog is the voice of the authors, materializing their thoughts on the unlimited cruelty of man and the potential danger of a dog.

"I always thought humans teach me a lot," Baxter says just after the opening credits, which will justify, all through the film, its need to get closer and closer to the human species, multiplying emotional experiences that will confront him with fear, sweetness, sexuality, and eventually with tyranny and death.

The art of soliloquy, so striking in Albert Camus' novels (to name but one writer among so many authors in French history who write in the first person singular), articulates here around a desperately dark and bloody enterprise, lead by a dog the same way it could be hosted by a person. While watching it again 25 years after the film was shot, I found myself making a parallel with the character of Philippe Nahon in Gaspard Noë's *Seul contre tous*, the story of a man who, narrating his own actions and mental convolutions, opts for the ultimate solution to give his life meaning: crime. Same situation here: killing seems to be the only option for Baxter to get rid of undesirable masters and to find his way in a world that, at his birth, welcomed him with hostility (he mentions the kennel where he was raised before being adopted and where he became aware of power relations between individuals).

Baxter's personality oscillates between courage (he dares to

attack a big wild dog and eventually kills him) and cowardice (he kills an old woman and tries to kill a baby). However, Baxter is unable to kill his last master, a young sadistic boy fascinated by the Third Reich. When faced with physical and mental violence, he finds himself acting like a slave, as if only violence could master violence. As if the only possible winner of this game were the most brutal one. Isn't that a simple illustration of the so-called "survival of the fittest?"

One could put to question the relevance of the authors' position: did the screenwriters successfully express the dog's point of view, or did they fail at verbalizing the mind of an animal by deciding to have him talk like a human being? While Cujo thinks and plots as silently as a stone, Baxter meditates aloud and elaborates a strategy of war in a scheme of self-defense and survival, comparable to John Rambo's attempts to stay alive when all the police forces are chasing him. This produces a strange effect on the audience: familiarity on the one side, but on the other side a total uncanniness. There's a sense of evil at the beginning of the film, even when nothing bad happens. Is evil contained in the act of speaking? Does language corrupt the eye and instill in one's heart the biblical "temptation of the wicked one?" One thing is sure: from the moment you hear Baxter think, you cannot help but feel uncomfortable. Words feed the uneasiness, probably because of the density of the dog's speech, contrary to what emerges in cute animal films like *Babe*.

The self-awareness that characterizes the dog's stream of consciousness gives the suspense a climactic psychological dimension. Like an analyst, Baxter unveils the sex drive and

obsessions that riddle him and have him attracted to women, more than to female dogs. Isn't *Baxter*, basically, the story of a dog who wanted to be a man and who takes revenge on his (feeling of) inferiority by killing the weakest human creatures?

Another quite remarkable feature of the film is the voyeurist angle, reminding of the camera's point of view in Alfred Hitchcock's *Psycho*. Like Norman Bates, who peeps through the hole in the bathroom wall, Baxter scrutinizes his neighborhood through his slanting eyes, sunken eyeballs, almost impossible to decipher. Impenetrable like a cave, he's always watching before catching.

The most striking aspect of the film is definitely the last part, where, in the hands of a young kid who's obsessed with the life of Adolf Hitler, Baxter experiences humiliation, ill treatments, subjugation, and finally death. The core of the authors' message lays in the portrait of this kid whose cruelty beats Baxter's, who asserts when Charles orders him to kill one of his friends: "I only killed when I had reasons to. I killed when my situation was unbearable, or when I was threatened. I will not kill for nothing." Like in *Apt pupil*, one finds out that the child, whose initial intention is to blackmail the former Nazi general, behaves as cruelly as the Nazis in the 1940s. The thesis is established here that a human being can be more bestial than an animal. I could not end this paragraph without mentioning the obvious parallel with Alain Jessua's *Les chiens*, starring Gérard Depardieu and Victor Lanoux, where dogs become bad and aggressive only because men raise them that way. The same conclusion was established in Romain Gary's *White Fang*, where a dog is trained to slaughter colored people only and who eventually kills everybody, colored and white people as well, because what ultimately fills his heart is the thirst for blood.

Baxter establishes the parallel between humanity in animals and beastliness in humans. In both cases the stream of consciousness brings to light an inner violence that seems to originate from remote times, betraying a primeval nature specific to every living creature, either human or animal.

Daphnis Olivier Boelens

Daphnis Olivier Boelens (Daph Nobody) was born in 1975 to an Italian painter and a Belgian photographer. Influenced by the violence and loneliness of the poor Brussels' neighborhoods in which he grew up, he published his first short stories in specialized magazines and through writing contests where he got several awards. During his studies at the ULB, he released two collections of short stories: *Les ténèbres Nues* and *La Lumière des Au-Delà*. He later published two novels in France: *Blood Bar* – nominated for the Prix Chimère and the Prix des Futuriales in Paris – and *L'Enfant Nucléaire*.

He wrote and directed several plays in which he also worked as a comedian *(De la Mouche à l'Hameçon, The Fatman's Fate)* and drafted an open-air show based on famous cartoon character *Yakari*, created by Derib and Job *(Yakari at the Labyrinthe de Barvaux)*.

In film, he acted in different feature films *(Mauvaise Réponse, Le Singe Roi, La Liste Noire...)* and was the co-author of *A Broken Life* (starring Tom Sizemore, Ving Rhames, Saul Rubinek) and of a multitude of award-winning short films.

He was a member of the jury for Fun Radio, Title Films, Festival du Film Indépendant de Bruxelles, BIFFF, etc, and gave lectures at book conventions in France and Belgium.

BEAKS: THE MOVIE (1987)

By Fawn Krisenthia

In the pantheon of animal attack horror movies, killer birds might be one of the most difficult to pull off. One can imagine being stalked and torn apart by a shark, bear, or Australian razorback hellbent on your destruction. Even without seeing *Jaws*, people have a fear of being devoured by sharks because attacks already happen in real life. A movie about killer birds (or frogs, slugs, shrews), however, can never really rise above the inherent schlockiness of the idea because the director is tasked with creating a fear that does not naturally exist. The only thing to fear with birds is parking underneath a tree. Birds are not scary. It's hard to take seriously.

In 2010, I caught a Nature documentary about the creepy, secret life of crows, aptly titled *A Murder of Crows* in which biologists had recently learned that crows could remember people by facial recognition for over two years and would actually use this information and communicate with other crows on how to "handle" the individual.

It's in remembering this scientific highlight that I try to suspend disbelief for the 1987 bird attack movie, *Beaks: The Movie.*

Released in Italy as the sequel to Hitchcock's *The Birds* (1963), *Beaks* is an obvious homage to Hitchcock's definitive animal attack horror - most notably the reporter's last name Cartwright and the mirrored attack on the children's birthday party. *Beaks,* directed by Mexican writer, director and producer René Cardona Jr., tells the story of a news reporter Vanessa Cartwright (Michelle Johnson) and her cameraman boyfriend Peter (Christopher Atkins of Blue Lagoon), who are begrudgingly covering a fluff piece on chickens attacking a farmer in Spain. Vanessa and Peter soon learn that the mysterious bird attacks are occurring worldwide. They hop from one country to another to interview several victims of bird attacks, including a couple that witnessed birds wiping out a town 30 years ago. The blonde duo works to warn audiences about an impending aviary up rise.

Hitchcock created a sense of dread in *The Birds* by employing a bait and switch – focusing on a mother afraid of losing her son to another woman while slowly dropping hints throughout the film that something is wrong with the birds. The actual attacks only begin when Tippi arrives as a stranger in Bodega Bay, and the attacks rise concurrent to the increased intimacy between Tippi and Mitch. It's a masterful stroke; this buildup is also used in the king of all animal attack movies *Jaws.* Don't show the monster, make the audience beg for it. The horror is expertly muted until the final act, and it allows the viewer to wonder if the film is a simulacrum to the manifestation of a mother's psyche or the townspeople's fear of outsiders. In fact, if you take all the mommy issues out of the two hour film, you would probably be left with less than 30 minutes of actual bird attacks (resulting in only two directly related deaths) and with no real explanation to the cause.

With *Beaks,* however, director Cardona Jr. forgoes any tension or mystery by weighing the film down with soapbox exposition through the news reports of a lackluster journalist and repeated footage of an innocuous flock of birds. The most terrifying idea of a killer birds story is that billions of them can be organized into a unified attack on mankind. And, unlike being chomped whole by a great white or sewer alligator, you would be pecked slowly to death with what must feel like a thousand papercuts. Yet this fear is not bastioned by experiencing it through any sympathetic characters in *Beaks*, but rather shoved down your throat. There's no deeper psychological layer to the film; instead, it's a tedious formula that can be reduced to a cavalcade of monotonous scenes, one after another - news story, non-inventive bird attack, flock footage. The movie plays like a made-for-TV movie that takes itself too seriously and doesn't quite cross over into the "so bad it's good" territory. Though any real suspense is absent, Cardona Jr. attempts to artificially create fear by upping the body count: a hawk gouging out the eye of a hunter, birds purposefully taking down a plane, a hawk plucking an eye from a hang glider and wearing it like a badge of honor, birds pecking out the eyes of a farmer and his wife, etc. The resulting scenes are ambitious and not completely without entertainment value.

My favorite scene early in the film is the news report on the farmer in La Mancha, Spain who believes that chickens are launching a personal assault on him. In Poe-like gravitas, Mr. Neilson describes how "the chickens got together, like they were following some kind of orders." His dubbed voice has the air and tragedy of a 1970s detective rehashing the most traumatic moment in his harsh career on the street beat: "Any bird that sees me, jumps on me, just like that." When Vanessa brings out a cage with a canary to test his claims, he eyeballs the small bird like it's his mortal enemy. She pulls the canary out, and it flits and tweets around the church for the longest 30 seconds, before it flies at the farmer causing a small scratch under his eye. This scene is posed as a serious moment but turns out to be one of the few unintentionally funny gems in the movie.

The dialogue is save for the curious use of profanity. When Vanessa shouts to her producer, "a story about attacking chickens? I won't do it! I majored in journalism in college, not animal husbandry!" The line would have been better suited if it had been delivered by a cult favorite like Linnea Quigley who could embrace the absurdity of the story, rather than the tone-less, straight-playing Michelle Johnson who stumbles her way through most of her lines. Since filming spanned several countries in Peru, Spain, Mexico, Italy and Puerto Rico, the supporting actors were all dubbed in English, giving the dialogue a pleasant giallo feel.

It should be noted that birds were definitely harmed in the making of this film. Cardona Jr. copied a trick from Hitchcock's classic *The Birds* by tying birds to the actors clothing to make it appear that they're attacking when in reality they're just frantically trying to fly away. But while Hitchcock was reportedly sensitive to the harming of birds, Cardona Jr. flaunted it. In fact, within three minutes of Beaks, pigeons are being shot out of the air repeatedly. In a later scene, birds are thrown through a glass window of a plane by stagehands. Cardona Jr.'s other trash epics *Tintorera* (1977), which piggybacked off the popularity of *Jaws,* and *Night of a Thousand Cats* (1972) are similarly tinged with flagrant animal harm. With *Beaks*, there's a sense of duplicity with a movie that admonishes mankind for its transgressions against nature while causing harm to the very animals it warns about in the special effects. Cognizant viewers may be shaken out of watching a didactic fantasy film about birds attacking man, when clearly the opposite is happening.

Beaks is a popcorn movie best enjoyed with low expectations. If you can power through the repeated exposition of why birds are killing (i.e. fighting against contamination and pollution, revenge on hunters, restoring the balance in nature, etc), then the movie can be enjoyable for its bird attack scenes – that is, if you can move past the violence against animals. Ultimately, though, the chief contribution of *Beaks* is to make viewers appreciate the genius of Hitchcock's *The Birds* that much more.

Fawn Krisenthia

Fawn Krisenthia is an artist, writer, horror fan, and slave to her 15-year-old cat Diffy.

She has written on *Henry: Portrait of a Serial Killer* in the book *Horror 101: The A-List of Horror Films and Monster Movies*, and on *The Tenant* in *Hidden Horror: A Celebration of 101 Underrated and Overlooked Fright Flicks*. She has recently contributed to an upcoming horror trivia book from the Dr. AC presents series.

She has also written several reviews for *Cult Reviews* and *WildClaw's Blood Radio*, and horror podcasts and reviews for female-fronted horror blog *Dreams in the Bitch House*.

She's currently working on several projects, including a book that's more in keeping with her bachelor of science degree in criminal justice and forensic psychology and her love for true crime trash. She's also posting art, horror projects, and fiction on her website HeadNotFound.com.

Her favorite "when animals attack" horror films are *Long Weekend* (1978), *The Alligator People* (1959), and *The Boneyard* (1991).

BEGINNING OF THE END (1957)

By Ken Begg

Every year the Entomology Department of the University of Illinois in Champaign-Urbana holds its Insect Fear Film Festival. In 2003, I made the trek downstate from suburban Chicagoland to attend. The draw was two-fold. First, they were showing three classic big bug movies, a genre for which I maintain an abiding passion. Second, the director of all three of that year's featured films, Bert I. Gordon, attended as their guest star. I had been watching Gordon's films since I was a tot, and the chance to see him was too good to pass up.

In person he proved a somewhat grumpy old man. I can't really blame him, though. For example, during the Q&A one blasé young lady asked him if he had always meant his monster movies to be funny. Gordon has suffered from having his work, made during an era generally lacking in irony, now being viewed by the terminally snarky. Given this, his spleen was entirely understandable.

The first feature shown at the Insect Fear Film Festival was *Beginning of the End* (1957). The film's climax features gigantic grasshoppers attacking Chicago and doing nearly as much property damage as the Blues Brothers. Even better, the film opens in rural Champaign-Urbana, where the Insect Fear Film Festival takes place. Needless to say, the U of I crowd greeted all mentions of the location with cheers. I also remember the explosion of laughter, which greeted the sight of mountains in the background, a geological feature for which Illinois is not especially well noted.

The movie follows the template laid down by *Them!* Things

kick off with a "series of mysterious events" (such as two teens "necking" in a parked jalopy and getting killed off-camera), followed by the "astounding reveal" that atomic monsters are at large. We then watch as the government mobilizes to fight the menace, wrapping up with man's narrow victory over a foe who literally threatened to destroy human civilization.

At least the film's title fails to foreshadow the solution. I mean, half of hour of mystery is pretty silly when your movie is called *The Deadly Mantis* or *The Black Scorpion*.

Meanwhile, the nearby small town of Ludlow - a real place, by the way - is destroyed literally overnight, its entire population completely vanished. Luckily, an attractive female war photographer just happens to be in the neighborhood. Smelling a scoop, she enlists hunky scientist Peter Graves, stationed nearby and performing atomic experiments for the Agriculture Department, involving gigantic tomatoes and strawberries. Although the experiments were humanitarian in intent, insects ate the irradiated fruit, and, well, you can take it from there.

Soon the grasshoppers are on the march, overcoming tanks and artillery and flamethrowers. They head north until they threaten Chicago, so apparently unstoppable that the military considers using a nuclear device to kill them. "You can't drop an atomic bomb on Chicago!" an aghast Peter Graves replies. I mostly agree with him, although if they had done it right after the White Sox won the World Series I probably wouldn't have minded quite as much.

The climax of the film, featuring hordes of bus-sized bugs razing Chicago, is probably too ambitious. Nearly all of Gordon's 29 films dealt with some manner of gigantism, but he often strove to do too much with his paltry budgets and technical skills. Traveling mattes, in particular, were an ongoing issue. *The Amazing Colossal Man* was often transparent, a fact that continues to inspire chortles today, though it's anchored by a good tragic performance from the actor playing the titular role and Stan Lee clearly ripping off *The Colossal Man*'s origin, as it's exactly what befell Bruce Banner five years later when he became the Hulk. As a result, Gordon is best known to modern viewers as a serial victim of japing on Mystery Science Theater 3000. Wikipedia, for instance, asserts that *Beginning of the End* "is generally recognized for its

"BEGINNING OF THE END" starring PETER GRAVES, PEGGIE CASTLE, MORRIS ANKRUM. With Thomas B. Henry, Than Wyenn and James Seay. An ABPT PICTURE, DISTRIBUTED BY REPUBLIC PICTURES CORPORATION.   Printed in U.S.A.   57/380

atrocious special effects and considered to be one of the most poorly written and acted science fiction motion pictures of the 1950s." That's a bold assertion considering competition like *Robot Monster* or *Cat-Women of the Moon* or even Gordon's own *King Dinosaur*. More to the point, it's an unfair one. Gordon's script and direction are admittedly stolid, but they're also clean and get the story told with minimum fuss. There are as well a couple of genuinely good ideas in there, like replicating the grasshoppers' mating call to lure the monsters to a watery grave in Lake Michigan.

As for the acting, the film is top-lined by a solid cast of professional actors. Peter Graves and Peggie Castle ably perform the drab lead roles. The film's military brass, meanwhile, are played by Morris Ankrum, Thomas Browne Henry and James Seay. These guys alone probably appeared in half of all the decade's sci-fi films.

I should also mention instantly recognizable voice actor Paul Frees. He supplies any number of voiceovers, and if anything, his voice is too distinctive. When the film features a radio news report, it's Frees. That police radio call? Frees. The PA warning issued by a stock footage helicopter pilot? Frees. His vocal appearances would make a good drinking game.

The film is blessed with a short running time. At 76 minutes it doesn't have time to bog down or overstay its welcome. Things move along at a pace that seems blistering compared to the turgid Syfy "original" movies seen today. Make *Beginning of the End* 15 or 20 minutes longer and it's far more of a slog.

Gordon's traveling mattes continue to be an issue. I'm not even talking about the quality of them, I mean just as a general issue. I have always preferred monsters realized via props and practical effects. You can interact with props. Here the actors are clearly acting against monsters not actually sharing space with them. The illusion isn't irksomely bad, but it never really fools the eye, either

All that said, the thing people most usually talk about after seeing the picture is the sight of the monster grasshoppers veering off the skyscrapers they're purportedly scaling and walking out onto thin air. However, this appears to have been largely an aspect ratio issue. The DVD for the movie presented it in a letterboxed version. With the top of the image masked off to create the widescreen image, the bugs engage in far less aerial perambulation.

This is a film for people who love this sort of story. Yes, it has goofy moments, but hey, who'd want it any different? I know Gordon's oeuvre will be well represented in this book. Hopefully I won't be the only reviewer to have some kind words for his work. Gordon made my childhood — now chugging along into its fifth decade — a lot happier. For that I thank him.

Ken Begg

Ken Begg is the founder and proprietor of *Jabootu's Bad Movie Dimension*, the site dedicated to examining films on the bottom the bell curve. His advice to would be film buffs? Watch the really good stuff and the really bad stuff, and you'll learn something. Stay away from the great mass of mediocre films, however, it'll kill you.

As a young lad in the suburbs of Chicago, Ken grew up watching classic Universal horror films on WGN's *Creature Features*. With equal enthusiasm he watched horrendously cheap 1950s sci-fi schlock on WFLD's *Screaming Yellow Theater*, as hosted by the original Svengoolie. From this he learned his most valuable life lesson; good or bad, if it has a monster in it, it's Jake with me. Big bugs and sea monsters were and are his favorites, though.

When not working at his clerical job or spending way too little time writing (or way too much time writing, some might argue), he mostly watches old movies. He has attended Evanston's Northwestern University's annual 24-hour B-Fest for close to 30 years now, and flies to Texas twice a year to watch movies with his pals down there. If you ever want to tag along, you'd be more than welcome.

BIRDEMIC: SHOCK AND TERROR (2010)

By Johnny Zontal

I hate birds. I'm too old to remember if I have always hated birds, but the fact that I hate them remains. I guess if we're being honest

here, it's more accurate to say that I'm scared shitless of birds. They're unpredictable, disease spreading, flying balls of feathers, claws, and beaks. I can never shake the feeling that every bird that flies over my head is going to land on my face, and claw out my eyeballs. I'm not exaggerating here. I have taken crap from friends countless times about this matter. It's pretty embarrassing, but I'm bringing it up because it's relevant to the topic at hand.

I'm sure a lot of you are at least familiar with *Birdemic: Shock and Terror*, even if you haven't seen it. I was first made aware of it by seeing the now famous "conference room" scene on one of those green screen shows that makes fun of pop culture. As somewhat of a connoisseur of terrible movies, I immediately knew that this is something I had to see. It didn't disappoint. *Birdemic: Shock and Terror* really is one of the most woefully inept things ever committed to film. Everything about it is wrong. The pacing... The acting... The script... The editing... The sound design... The special effects... All of it makes you bury your face in your hands and question the decisions you've made in your life that led you to the moment you decided to watch this.

If you've seen this movie, you know exactly what I'm talking about. If you haven't, here's the basic premise. *Birdemic* is the story of Rod, a software salesman who has a raging boner for the environment. He has a creepy meet-cute with an up and coming lingerie model, and they start to date. Somewhere along the way, birds decide to go bat shit crazy and start murdering people, and our heroes are locked in a desperate struggle to survive the attacks. Sounds pretty bland, right? Well what makes this movie unique certainly isn't its plot. It's the details. And oh man, there are details.

Let's start with the alleged birds. Some movies that contain animal attacks use real animals. This can be a good way to provide realism to the production, although it isn't always practical due to either morality or logistics. So you can't get real animals? Maybe you'd try animatronics. They can provide a reasonable facsimile of the animals, and you don't have to worry about training or injuring them. Well, maybe you don't have the budget to pay for realistic animatronics. That's understandable with low-budget productions.

Computer software has come a long way in the last couple decades. As long as you're not pushing for Oscar caliber realism, this can be a cheap, and reasonably effective way to put those critters on the big screen. Or, you could do what *Birdemic* did and use poorly rendered animated .gif files of birds. Completely flat, unrealistic clip art birds. While you're at it, you could use equally terrible sound design and loop the sound of a squeaky toy being raked up

and down a chalkboard for their majestic calls. The birds in *Birdemic* are the single worst combination of special effects and sound design ever put in a movie. Ever.

Oh, another thing about the birds. They don't even show up until 45 minutes into the movie. The first half of this thing is basically a romantic comedy that's neither romantic nor a comedy... At least intentionally a comedy. It's just two slack-jawed imbeciles with nothing at all in common starting a romance and eventually screwing. Somewhere in there, there's a guy singing a song about hanging out with his family, but other than that, not a whole lot of action. This is really a Frankenstein's monster of garbage. It's a mish mash of two terrible movies pieced together with all the skill and subtlety of a toddler driving a garbage truck through a fireworks factory. In other words: it's pretty great.

A few years ago, a group of friends and I decided to form a monthly Bad Movie Club, where we'd meet up, watch a few films, and get wildly drunk. The first night we met up, we started nice and breezy with the Patrick Swayze epic, *Roadhouse*. It's a crowd-pleaser, to be sure. It's a dumb and cheesy, but it's fun. It's not what everyone would call a "bad" movie. When that ended, I took the temperature of the room and tried to figure out how deep down the rabbit hole this group of people was willing to go. I decided to show them *The Room* next. People got very upset at me. They had never seen this movie before, and I guess they had differing ideas of what the point of a Bad Movie Club was. I should have known this would be upsetting since I had serious requests to screen things like *Magic Mike* at one of our get-togethers. At any rate, everyone was in agreement that *The Room* was the absolute worst movie they had ever seen and probably the worst movie ever made. Then I told them that I had something worse.

I felt like Pinhead in the *Hellraiser* movies, and these foolish drunkards had just solved the puzzle box. I had such awful things to show them. They flat out did not believe that I had another movie that could be any worse than what they had just seen. I repeatedly asked them if they were SURE they wanted me to put in this movie. I warned them what they were in for. They didn't believe me. So I put in *Birdemic*, and then the fireworks started. I have been watching low-budget garbage horror for most of my life. I'm used to it and even appreciate it for what it is. I admit that sometimes I take for granted that not everyone shares my sensibilities and that showing a bunch of drunk people something this offensively inept might not be the most appreciated idea in the world. Half the people left after the first 15 minutes. The ones who stayed were very upset with me. No one enjoyed the experience. No one other than me, I guess. I admit I had fun watching people squirm. It's a rare occasion when something so innocuous can make people so unnerved. I think I could have put on something like *Martyrs* or *A Serbian Film*, and people would have left the gathering less traumatized. We had to amend the rules for the next movie night, and future screenings were decided by a group vote. *Birdemic* ruins people's lives.

In the end, the scariest thing about this movie isn't the carnage. The cheap birds and one dimensional performances don't put forth any particular sense of dread. But sitting in a room with people you care about and subjecting them to something so uniquely and bafflingly terrible and watching as one by one they realize what they're in for? That's the stuff out of nightmares. It isn't the birds in the world we should worry about. It's the people who make these movies and the friends who torture you with them.

Johnny Zontal

Johnny Zontal has been writing for DrunkInAGraveyard.com since September of 2013. Since then, he has been tackling the enjoyably bad, the random, the stupid, and whatever other garbage the webmasters don't feel like watching.

He hails from Pittsburgh, PA, which is notable for being the home of the *American Zombie* heritage, and a place where they put french fries on salad. It's unclear which is scarier.

BLACK SHEEP (2006)

By Kate Larkindale

The first time I heard about *Black Sheep*, I wasn't allowed to see it. I was running a boutique cinema in downtown Wellington, and the filmmakers hired our 60 seat theater for a test screening. Because test screenings happen before the final cut is locked, filmmakers are strict about not allowing media or exhibitors into test screenings.

It's only human to want something if you're told you can't have it.

So I wanted to see *Black Sheep*.

My wanting to see it was totally irrational. I don't really like horror movies. Especially not splatter movies.

Never underestimate the power of denial!

For decades New Zealand was best known as a country with 3 million people and 18 million sheep. Kiwis the world over suffered through "sheep-shagging" jokes everywhere they went. It was inevitable that someday, someone would imagine a world in which those 18 million sheep used their numbers to their advantage.

Jonathan King understood this is "the New Zealand story that had to be told."

And tell it he did.

Henry Oldfield is terrified of sheep. And not without reason — his father died when he fell from a cliff trying to rescue one of his woolies that got itself into a pickle. It's with great reluctance that he returns to the family farm to sell his share to older brother, Angus.

Alongside a small group of scientists, Angus has been experimenting with genetic engineering on the sheep. He's about to launch his new, genetically modified über-sheep to a crowd of interested potential investors.

Meanwhile, a pair of environmental activists, Grant and the oddly named Experience, are sniffing around. When Grant gets his hands on a modified fetus, he thinks he's hit pay dirt. But before he can get off the property with the sample, the scientists start chasing him and he trips, dropping and breaking the jar.

The mutant fetus turns out to be very much alive and with a bite that turns sheep into bloodthirsty predators. Now Henry has a very real reason to be phobic about sheep.

Even more so, when he discovers that humans bitten by these sheep turn into vicious, bloodthirsty were-sheep.

If it isn't already apparent, *Black Sheep* is not a straight horror movie. While there's plenty of blood and gore and intestine ripping, above all else this is a comedy. Just the idea that sheep - mild mannered, gentle, wooly creatures - could become vicious killers is hilarious. When you add in humans sprouting hooves and pelts, it gets even funnier.

The film skewers stereotypes left, right, and center. No one is safe. Farmers, environmentalists, and city-slickers are parodied with equal abandon. There's something very satisfying about watching tree-hugging greenies splattered with gore and wielding weapons to disembowel the mutant lambs.

That's not to say there isn't a more serious subtext to the film. With genetic engineering still a new and uncertain science - and something New Zealanders were very concerned about at the time the film was released - the film plays on a very real fear many people harbor and pushes it to nightmarish levels. But this is not supposed to be a serious film or even a satire. It's a splatter flick. One with a lot of splatter.

The best horror movies work if they have a recognizable emotional heart, and at the center of *Black Sheep* is a story about brothers. Sibling rivalry and the drive to protect inheritance are the universal themes that drive the film. While Henry doesn't want the farm, he doesn't want his brother to have the whole thing either. Getting his share of the money the property is worth is what drives him to face his fears and set foot on the farmland he swore he'd never see again.

Like all the best horror movies, *Black Sheep* wears its influences on its sleeve. There are distinct homages to such classic horror films as *An American Werewolf in London* and *The Howling*, particularly in the transformation scenes. This is most evident in the filmmakers' choice to use practical effects for these scenes, rather than relying on CGI.

Effects were done by Peter Jackson's Weta Workshop and are quite excellent. While no one is going to mistake the animatronic sheep for real ones, they blend nicely into the herd until they're needed to explode or gnaw enthusiastically on human flesh.

There are some genuinely funny lines, and the actors spout them with great relish. Even the obligatory sheep-shagging joke is delivered with both verve and humor:

"What about the sheep?"
"Fuck the sheep!"
"No time for that bro. Go, go, go!"

As the down-to-earth farmhand, it would have been easy to give Tucker all the best lines. But this isn't the case, with all the leads given a chance to play for laughs. One of my favorites is almost a throwaway line in an argument between the two brothers:

"You fucker!"
"Actually, it was a sperm sample."
"You wanker!"

As in many New Zealand films, the landscape plays a character. Here the lush green farmland, rolling hills, and wide expanses of blue sky promise something almost bucolic. So when the limbs start flying, and the arterial spray starts... well... spraying, it's all the more horrific. This is not the quaint, beautiful country we've seen in other New Zealand films.

In many ways, this could be seen as the most New Zealand of

any New Zealand film. It uses every well-worn cliché and stereo-type about New Zealand and delights in exploding them. Often quite literally.

Kate Larkindale

Kate Larkindale is a writer, mother, and marketing executive for the New Zealand Film Commission. With this much going on, she doesn't find much time to sleep and can usually be found with an espresso in hand.

Her short stories have appeared in *Halfway Down The Stairs*, *A Fly in Amber*, *Daily Flash Anthology*, *The Barrier Islands Review*, *Everyday Fiction*, *Death Rattle*, *Drastic Measures*, *Cutlass & Musket*, and *Residential Aliens*, among others.

Her debut novel, *An Unstill Life*, was published by the now closed Musa Publishing in January 2014. She's represented by Jackie Lindert and Suzie Townsend at New Leaf Literary.

She blogs at *Fiction and Film*.

BUG (1975)

By D.M. Anderson

Bug was originally released just days before a certain great white shark came along to scare the bejeezus out of anyone with a pulse. While tens of millions showed up in droves to catch *Jaws* in the summer of 1975 (and subsequently stayed out of the ocean forever), *Bug* came and went virtually unnoticed.

Animals with nasty dispositions were suddenly all the rage, and slews of similar films followed in *Jaws'* wake (no pun intended): *Alligator, Dogs, Squirm, Piranha, Prophecy, Day of the Animals, Mako: The Jaws of Death, Tentacles, Orca,* ad nauseum. One of the more successful *Jaws* rip-offs at the time was *Grizzly*, a low-budget scare fest released in 1976, with a plot so similar it could almost be considered plagiarism. As an impressionable 12-year-old recently stricken by *Jaws* fever, I couldn't resist.

Back then, theaters often offered double features for your

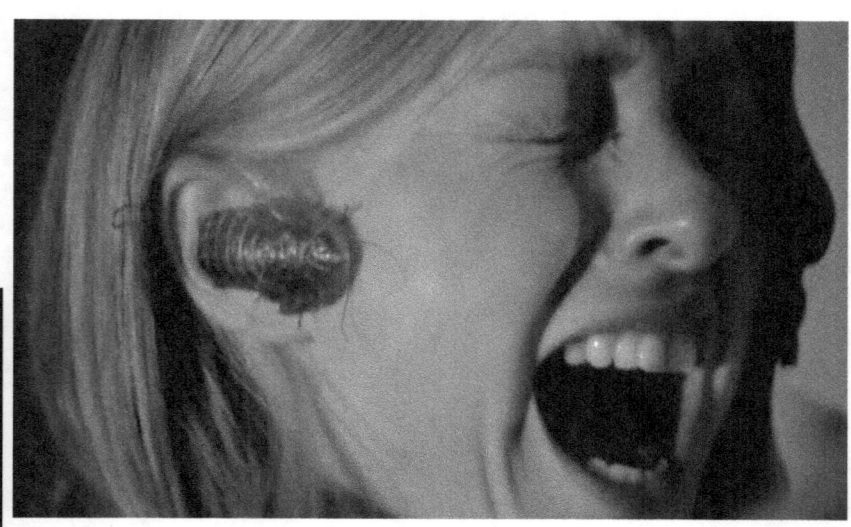

ticket, where new movies were accompanied by older ones of the same genre. Hence, *Bug* was back on the big screen as a co-feature (even if no one was pining for it).

Grizzly didn't leave much of an impression. It was fun, but mostly because it followed the *Jaws* formula almost verbatim. *Bug*, however, was a different story, especially for a kid whose exposure to horror was still fairly limited. The violent deaths in *Jaws* and *Grizzly* were suitably graphic for 1970s PG movies, but *Bug* featured the most disturbing death I'd ever seen up to that point, when one of the title creatures barbecues a cat alive. I felt sickened and appalled as this unfortunate feline howled and thrashed about, trying in vain to detach this burning roach from its head.

Man, I was *days* getting over that.

Aside from depriving a kid of a few nights' sleep as he wondered if they actually killed a cat for the sake of a shot (even today, that scene is pretty unnerving), *Bug* is mostly notable for being William Castle's last hurrah as a filmmaker. In the 1950s and 1960s, Castle was one of many prolific producers of low-budget horror schlock. But unlike the Cormans and  Arkoffs of the day, he's best-remembered for the gimmicks he came up with in order to sell more tickets, such as offering fright insurance policies for patrons of *Macabre* and rigging theater seats with makeshift buzzers for *The Tingler*. Obviously, this wasn't high art, but a lot of fun. Castle even managed to accidentally crank out a bonafide classic, *The House on Haunted Hill*, featuring his most gloriously-goofy gimmick, "Emergo," in which a wire-tethered, red-eyed skeleton hovered over the audience.

As the 1960s wore on and moviegoers grew more jaded,

Castle's tacky tricks seemed kind of quaint, no longer planting butts in seats like they used to. He made one noble stab at respectability (he's responsible for getting *Rosemary's Baby* off the ground, though Paramount refused to let him direct it) before relegating himself to churning out b-movie drive-in fodder - sans gimmicks - for the remainder of his career, with diminishing results. *Bug* ended up being Castle's final film, though at this point he was apparently content to write and produce, leaving the directorial chores to Jeannot Szwarc, who'd go on to make a name for himself as the best guy available to helm *Jaws 2*.

Based on the 1973 novel, *The Hephaestus Plague* by Thomas Page, *Bug* begins with an earthquake, which rocks the inhabitants of a small California farming town. As if that isn't bad enough, a previously undiscovered species of cockroach emerges from the fissures in the Earth. They're attracted by combustion engines and capable of creating enough internal heat to ignite fires, resulting in the flaming deaths of a few locals and the aforementioned cat. Fortunately, they're unable to survive very long above ground (something to do with atmospheric pressure). But *unfortunately*, college professor James Parmiter (Bradford Dillman) decides to play God and crossbreed them with domestic cockroaches, even though one of these firebugs just killed his wife by setting her ablaze. One would think any recently-widowed, right-thinking guy would prefer to ensure these critters' total extinction. Instead, Parmiter becomes increasingly obsessed and unhinged. Retreating to a cabin, he isolates himself from the outside world in order to conduct his breeding experiments.

Meanwhile, each new generation he breeds becomes smarter and more indestructible, to the point they can gather en masse to literally spell out threatening messages on Parmiter's wall... a laughable plot twist to any free thinking adult (how the hell did these bugs learn to spell?), but fairly ominous to 12-year-old kids in the 1970s who were generally unaccustomed to noticing plot holes.

Like most horror films prior to *Jaws*, *Bug* tries for a dark, oppressive tone with the usual ominous resolution. Whether or not it succeeds is subjective, but for a dated film with a ridiculous premise, budget-conscious production

values, and "oh-come-on!" story turns, *Bug* works on a visceral level. It's unlikely anyone watching this film will walk away thinking they've seen something great or groundbreaking, but there are many moments that are suitably unnerving, effectively exploiting our fears of creepy crawlies hiding in places we always dreaded they would. Aided immeasurably by clever camerawork and a weird-ass music score by Charles Fox (mostly known for *Killing Me Softly* and some TV theme songs), *Bug* gives us some truly hateful, malevolent creatures.

Additional kudos must go to Bradford Dillman, who was always a decent character actor, though never particularly memorable. In a rare leading role, he portrays Parmiter with over-the-top gusto, treading a fine line between scientific curiosity and total insanity. He's forced to utter some inane expositional dialogue, but he does it with enough conviction that, at least in the moment, we buy into his delirium.

Bug hasn't aged particularly well, nor does it display any unique directorial skill. Still, despite some unintentionally humorous moments, the film provides a surprisingly bleak - even nihilistic - suggestion that humankind's dominance (and arrogance) as a species could be usurped at any given time. Of course, it's unlikely William Castle had such a lofty message in mind at the time. He apparently still had a bit of the old huckster left in him as well, coming up with an idea to rig theaters with brushes that simulate bugs crawling up the audience's legs. Unfortunately, this cheeky gimmick never happened. Too bad... it would have been a nifty capper to an endearing legacy.

Finally, here's a bit of trivia for anyone who grew up in the 1970s... if Parmiter's kitchen and living room stirs strong feelings of déjà vu, that's because it's the same iconic set used in all five seasons of *The Brady Bunch*.

D.M. Anderson

D.M. (Dave) Anderson lives, writes, and works in Portland, Oregon. His blog, *Free Kittens Movie Guide*, features essays, reviews, interviews, and humor related to films past and present, classic and not-so-classic. He has also contributed articles to such websites as *WhatCulture* and *Moviepilot*. Decades after it gave him nightmares as a kid, Dave still considers *Jaws* the greatest film of all time.

In addition, Anderson is the author of two young adult novels (*Killer Cows* and *Shaken*, both published by Echelon Press). He has also had numerous stories featured in various magazines and anthologies such as *Strange F**king Stories, Zombiefied Reloaded: The Search for More Brains, Infernal Ink, Night Terrors,* and *Perpetual Motion Machine*.

CHOSEN SURVIVORS (1974)

By Doug Lamoreux

I love animal attack films but rarely find them scary. Wolves and bears really want nothing to do with humans and, annually, ten times more people are killed by falling coconuts than by sharks. Also, most "nature strikes back" pictures, by definition, take place in the open, and horror works so much better in isolation. That's why my favorite animal attack flick is *Chosen Survivors*, a claustrophobic horror treat with real monsters.

Director Sutton Roley intrigues from the opening as a helicopter drops ten disoriented people in a New Mexico desert. Shot from odd angles, in slow motion, the characters stumble through a gauntlet of soldiers into a futuristic elevator. Down they go, with a pause for what seems to be an earthquake, to a bio lab 1,758 feet below ground. The group, selected by a computer as the best in science, business,  the military, sports, politics, and literature, soon discover they (along with 168 others in identical facilities in 12 U.S. locations) have been chosen to survive a nuclear disaster. They also learn a nuclear war has begun and is, at that moment, devastating the earth.

Our traumatized characters hit the sack wondering to what world they'll wake. We, the audience, linger to see something is amiss in this subterranean paradise. A panning shot through the dark facility, heightened by the eerie score of composer Fred Karlin (*Westworld*), ends at a large built-in bird cage wherein the poor things flutter and dart in unexplained but obvious panic.

Morning finds the birds slaughtered and the film shifting into high gear. A vampire bat is caught in their sealed environment, and, not long after, circumstances bring two secrets to everybody's attention. One, a team member is forced to confess their situation is a hoax. There's no atomic war. All have been gathered as guinea pigs in a behavior stress test. And two, their lab – their prison – has apparently been built beside a cave of ravenous vampire bats. Oops! The flying blood suckers soon squeeze, flit, and flood their way into the facility. The stress levels of the chosen survivors and the audience are about to hit record highs.

The screenplay by H.B. Cross (Harry Spalding, who wrote the classy Don Sharp films *Curse of the Fly* and *Witchcraft)* and Joe Reb Moffly gives us exactly what we need: archetypes, characters we know immediately played by actors we know immediately. Their stories are not important, the situation is, and we must feel a part

of the group to experience their terror. To that end, the filmmakers give us Jackie Cooper (*Superman - The Movie*) whose character, Ray Couzins, is a stock corporate villain, a drunk, and a rapist, but he's also right when he smells something rotten in Denmark. We're at ease with Richard Jaeckel (*The Green Slime, The Dark, Grizzly*) and his Major Gordon Ellis maintaining the facility. We know Bradford Dillman (a legend in animal attack films; *The Swarm, Piranha, Bug*) and his psychologist will require watching. It's the same down the line, Barbara Babcock (*Star Trek*) as a Nobel Prize winning doctor who gets a quick refresher in bat bites and hysteria. Alex Cord (*Genesis II*) and Diana Muldaur (*Star Trek: The Next Generation*) as a novelist and Congresswoman who team up for the least motivated romance in film history. Lincoln Kilpatrick (*The Omega Man*), inconspicuous for 80 minutes, who climbs into the Horror Hall of Fame in the nail-biting climax. The rest of the cast follow suit, good actors playing two-dimensional characters who, ultimately, are there to scream, run, and bleed. They do, with relish. *Chosen Survivors* works not because of faux human drama; it works because of bats!

The flying monsters are realized, despite the budget, in numerous ways including, optical effects by the Westheimer Company and Van der Veer Photo Effects, practical effects by Federico Farfan, and bat puppets by Tony Urbano. But the sequences that deliver the cringes are those using real vampires. No CGI here, kids. Nothing is as freaky as the shots of live bats slithering in through cracks in the walls, flying at the screaming actors, and shinnying up the beds of sleeping victims on folded wing stalks. Care to wake up to a vampire bat sitting on the pillow by your face? Here, you do!

Dr. G. Clay Mitchell and his Mexican counterpart naturalist William Lopez Forment trained the bats. Mitchell, of the Denver Wildlife Research Center (later an advisor on *Nightwing*), and Forment, a vampire and fruit bat expert, were busy with the

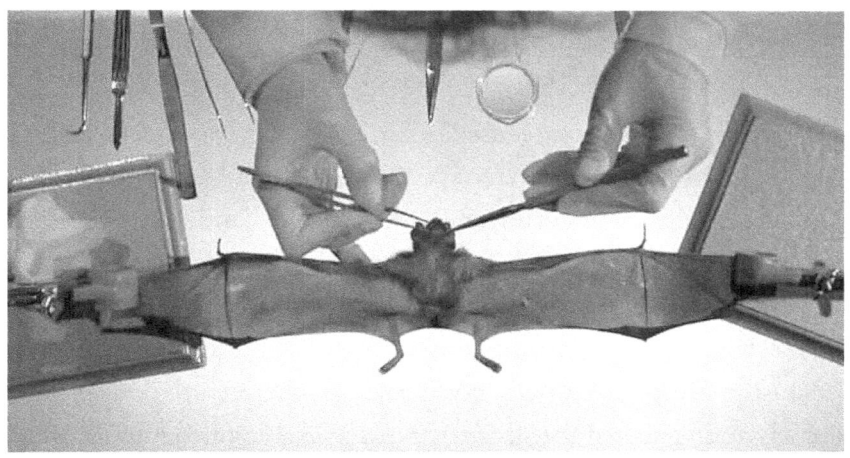

biological control of bats when Hollywood called. Mitchell spent the previous year conducting vampire control workshops in eight Latin American countries where ranch herds were losing over five gallons of blood a night, with upwards of 40 cattle a week dead from rabies. Controlled, bats are vital to their ecosystems. But in South America at the time, vampires were a plague; real life monsters destroying economies. As a precaution, the entire cast and crew of *Chosen Survivors* were inoculated against rabies before shooting began.

Producers Leon Benson and Charles W. Fries, for Alpine Productions and Metromedia Producers Corp (who backed Amicus' *Tales from the Crypt*), aware that the setting, paranoia in general, and fear of bats in particular, would generate the terror necessary, wisely skipped hiring a horror film director. Roley had one previous made-for-TV horror outing, *Sweet, Sweet Rachel*, to his credit and would go on to only two more, *Satan's Triangle* and *The Curse of Dracula* episodes of *Cliffhangers*. His forte was action adventure and drama, the areas where this film needed a lift. He and cinematographer Gabriel Torres provide it with skewed camera angles, carefully filtered stark white lighting, quick switches to brilliant red, green, and (during bat attacks) blue; aiding the claustrophobia. Like Pavlov's dogs, we're trained that when the lights fail, and the blue emergency lights come on... the vampires are coming.

Chosen Survivors was lensed in Mexico City at the legendary Estudios Churubusco Azteca S.A., home of the classic *The Magnificent Seven,* wonderful crap like *Brainiac,* and the delightful monster films of wrestling hero Santo. It was released in May of 1974 by Columbia Pictures, who ought to be ashamed of themselves. The theatrical trailer was awful and the release lackluster. Despite receiving good reviews, the picture disappeared quickly and vanished for decades. Now available on a 20th Century Fox Midnite Movie DVD with Terence Fisher's *The Earth Dies Screaming* (1964), *Chosen Survivors* has a chance to find the audience it always deserved.

The film is a collision of genres, nature strikes back, gothic horror, science fiction, and apocalyptic disaster, with the dormitory feel of a modern day reality show. It received a PG rating from the MPAA but delivers enough blood to make its point. *Chosen Survivors* is all anyone could want in "animal attack" horror: isolation, suspense, and the threat of real danger.

Doug Lamoreux

Doug Lamoreux is a father of three, a grandpa, a writer, and actor.

A former professional firefighter, he's authored six novels, including the Amazon #1 best sellers *Apparition Lake* (the spirit of an American Indian defends Mother Earth in Yellowstone), *Dracula's Demeter* (the vampire king's stunning sea voyage to England), and *When the Tik-Tik Sings* (a Philippine demon is unleashed upon a modern American tourist town). He's been nominated for a Rondo Award, a Lord Ruthven Award, a Pushcart Prize, and is the first-ever recipient of The Horror Society's Igor Award for fiction.

Lamoreux appeared in the radio/audio book series *Left Behind* and *Left Behind: The Kids*, starred in the 2006 film *Infidel* for writer-director Peter (*Tales From the Darkside*) O'Keefe, and appeared in the Mark Anthony Vadik horror films *The Thirsting* (aka *Lilith*) and *Hag*.

CUJO (1983)

By Maxim Stollenwerk

"A fucking Saint Bernard?"

It's a phrase that certainly crossed the mind of many people stumbling upon this film. Who can blame them? Saint Bernards are the Ghandis of canines. They're giant balls of cuddliness best known for waggling their cute neck barrels through avalanches, pouring some brandy down the throats of people in distress (although I'm not sure how that would help except accepting your impending snowy doom with more ease). *Cujo,* however, delivers hugely, and passing on this gem would be a huge mistake since it's not only immensely entertaining but also contributes to the genre by offering a different perspective on the heroine in distress.

The story takes place in Castle Rock, Stephen King's favorite playground for bad things to happen. And bad things do happen.

Cujo, the beloved family dog of the Cambers, gets bitten by a rabies-infected bat and turns into the homicidal killing machine we're all hoping him to become. Unlike the book, however, the film has no supernatural element to it. The book suggests that besides rabies, the evil spirit of a dead police officer is haunting the dog, but director Lewis Teague opted to cut everything otherworldly in favor of clarity. And rightly so.

In earlier scenes, Teague plays with our supernatural expectations by giving us a subjective view of Tad, a little boy who's scared of a monster in his closet. This is our way inside the Trenton family, where we mainly follow Donna Trenton around, played by Dee Wallace, a mother who tries to end an affair with a family friend. Meanwhile, Vic, her husband, is having a huge setback at work and puts their marital problems lower on his to-do list. In a scene illustrating how incompetent he's in solving their issues, he suggests they should have another baby to make things better, which means he believes the root of their problems is Donna having too much time wasted on things not involving baby making. That officially makes him "kind of a prick."

It's established early on that the father is the authority figure in the house. Donna is unable to scare away the imaginary monster in the closet, and it's only when Vic raises his voice that he listens, something that bothers Donna and serves as a dramatic arc throughout the film. This is highlighted with scenes from the Cambers family who are experiencing the same relationship imbalance. The wife there is so keen on her weekend away with her son that she conceals Cujo's rapid decline from her husband so he wouldn't use that as an excuse for them to stay.

One of the many things *Cujo* does right is its structure. The tension builds as the storyline of poor old Cujo losing his mind intertwines with the marital affairs of the Trenton's.

Cujo is clearly influenced by *Jaws*, even references it when a character hums the shark's famous leitmotif. In *Jaws,* the underlying theme is Sheriff Brody's role as a father figure. Here, it's our heroine as a mother who is central to the narrative. However, *Cujo* does differ from *Jaws* in a significant way. The shark in *Jaws* is set up as a bloodthirsty monster while we witness Cujo's slow transformation from a kid-loving family dog into the family-munching monster. In three scenes, Cujo's irritation with loud noises shows through the dog's perspective, which allows us to empathize with him, something rarely seen in animal attack films. You don't feel bad for the shark when his insides explode, and you don't feel bad for the birds who smack into the windows of Bodega Bay.

After killing a few rednecks, Cujo focuses his attention on Donna and Tad who find themselves trapped in a stalled Ford Pinto. From then on, most of the action revolves in and around the car. This very tight arena makes for some exciting cinema as Donna is now forced to protect her child from a real monster whereas he didn't allow her to confront the imaginary monster in the closet. This is intercut with scenes of the husband setting up a classic last minute rescue, though, in the end (spoiler), he arrives way too late, proving that Donna doesn't need a man to protect her child. For Teague, the monster attack and the final shot of them as a family unit signifies how trivial their marital situations are when confronted with real danger.

Stephen King wanted Lewis Teague to helm the picture after seeing *Alligator*. He was clearly the right man for the job, after first choice Peter Medak had to quit late in pre-production. Besides the discarding of the paranormal, Teague opted to have Tad survive the doggie terror. The book is much bleaker and lets him die of dehydration, making the mother's efforts fruitless.

In his memoir, King said this is the only book he doesn't remember writing because he was battling an alcohol addiction (which should make you question your productiveness when drunk). He regrets having let the boy die and is glad this is corrected in the film. He further praised Teague's film of having the most effective jump scare of all his filmography thanks to the scene where the dog first attacks the protagonists.

The perfect combo of Teague and cinematographer, Jan de Bont, creates not only a gripping narrative but also a sweaty visual atmosphere typical of de Bont's oeuvre (*Die Hard, Speed*). De Bont used five different Ford Pinto's, which he cut up to make full use of the space to get the claustrophobic feel he wanted. That all comes together in an iconic climax with a terrific shot of Donna passing out in the car while Tad is manically crying as the camera spins faster until it sweeps us into the next scene. It's especially impressive when you know temperatures during shooting were actually freezing, and they had to stack the car full of heaters that had to be turned off during each take because of the immense noise they made.

At least five Saint Bernards were used on set, each trained for different actions so they could believably simulate the attacks. As the Saint Bernards weren't fear-inducing enough, they also had a Rottweiler donning a Saint Bernard suit at hand. It looked just as ridiculous as it sounded, and the crew refrained from using it, possibly avoiding the first canine suicide. They did however have a stuntman in a dog suit, an image that will haunt you at least once during your viewing experience.

The great pace together with the incredible performances of both Dee Wallace and newcomer Danny Pintauro make for a film that belongs in the well-respected pantheon of films involving animals that don't take too kindly on them humans. *Cujo* offers a great cinematic experience you shouldn't pass on, even though it still is "a fucking Saint Bernard."

Maxim Stollenwerk

Maxim Stollenwerk is a young director and screenwriter, living in Brussels, Belgium.

He made two short films – *Karkas* (2011) and *Lilith* (2013) - both of which won the Grand Prix and Meliès D'argent at the Brussels International Fantastic Film Festival (BIFFF).

For a long time, he was the clumsy assistant in the art department of a multitude of movies and TV series. He now works as a screenwriter for several TV projects, amongst which a prison series for Marmalade Films, while working on several feature film projects in different genres.

Maxim is also one of the programmers for the Offscreen Film Festival.

CURSE II: THE BITE (1989)

By Justin McKinney

"I hate snakes, Jock! I hate 'em!" Those seven immortal words were uttered by the otherwise pretty unflappable Indiana Jones upon his discovery of a giant Burmese Python named Reggie resting in his lap aboard a seaplane in *Raiders of the Lost Ark* (1984). Like Indy, I have never been a fan of snakes myself. The scales. The hissing. The fluid yet unpredictable way in which they move. The poisonous fangs. The way they dislocate their jaw to swallow prey whole while their beady eyes show about as much emotion as Keanu Reeves on Xanax. But I'm certainly not alone in this sentiment. According to the National Institute of Mental Health, ophidiophobia, or, the abnormal fear of snakes, is one of the ten most commonly reported phobias. If someone ever gives you hell about it, though, rest assured you can be like me and whip out your Indiana Jones card. "Yeah, I'm scared of snakes... but so what? So is Indiana Jones, and he's much more of a bad ass than you'll ever be, Bob!" If the wriggling reptiles happen to give you the willies, and you're one of those masochists who actually *enjoy* getting the willies, *Curse II* is a film that directly plays up that fear to the hilt... and then some!

While on a road trip through Southwest America, young lovers Lisa (Jill Schoelen, who'd gotten some attention a few years earlier for the minor classic *The Stepfather*) and Clark (soap opera regular J. Eddie Peck) decide to take a shortcut through the Yellow Sands area of Arizona where government nuclear testing has been taking place. Said testing has had an adverse affect on the local snake population, and the slithering serpents are literally all over the place; weaving their way through chain length fences, driving away the local animal population, and amassing by the hundreds in the middle of the road. One of the snakes manages to hitch a ride inside the back of Lisa and Clark's jeep and eventually bites Clark on the hand. He's given an antidote of venom extract by Harry Morton (*M*A*S*H* cross-dresser Jamie Farr), who they initially assume is a doctor but soon learn is actually a traveling salesman who just *wanted* to be a doctor. After the couple head out the following morning, Harry discovers he's given Clark the wrong antidote. Facing possible criminal manslaughter charges for dispensing medicine without a license, he then tries to track the

duo down with help from some of his trucker buddies.

Meanwhile, Clark begins showing signs of change. He becomes sick, moody and violent, keeps blacking out and convulsing and gets on the bad side of redneck sheriff Bo Svenson. Even more worrisome, the infection on his hand isn't healing. Actually, it's only getting worse. It all has to do with the radioactive snake bite and the venom injection, which have combined to mutate his hand and arm into a large snake with a mind of its own! As if the prospect of snakes being all over the place isn't bad enough as is for us ophidiophobes, just imagine the horror and revulsion of part of your body actually *becoming* a snake and then having no control over it! By using this inventive concept, devised by writer/director Frederico Prosperi (billed as Fred Goodwin) and co-writer Susan Zelouf, the filmmakers try every which way they can to wiggle their way under our irrational snake-fearing skin. More often than not, they're successful.

Previous killer snake films from the 1970s and 1980s almost always fell into two distinct camps. The first were films about snakes attacking on their own accord, whether driven by instinct, science, the supernatural, or man's disregard for them or their environment, such as in *Rattlers* (1976), *Venom* (1981), *Copperhead* (1983) and the unbelievably grisly Hong Kong effort *Calamity of Snakes* (1983), which featured hundreds of real snakes actually being smashed, burned, butchered, and chopped to pieces. The second were films involving humans using regular snakes as instruments for revenge, like in *Stanley* (1972), *Fangs* (1974), or *Jennifer* (1977). *Curse II* however goes a more Cronenberg-esque "body horror" route with something odd and alien actually taking over and completely altering one's body.

While far from a perfect film (the acting is uneven, the photography is a bit flat and unimaginative, and there's some unneeded filler here and there), this really starts letting loose in the second half. Though the buildup is a slow one, there's more than adequate payoff here in the form of some inventive, amazingly disgusting Screaming Mad George special effects. During one scene, Clark attempts to chop off his killer appendage with an axe, but it ends up growing back. He's not only unable to remove it from his body, but he's also unable to control it or keep it from killing people in gruesome ways as it proceeds to rip a deputy's heart out of his chest *through his mouth*, tear off a female doctor's jawbone, strangle a farmer with its tongue and spit venom directly into someone's eyes. Once the infection has completely taken over Clark's body, his eyeballs and tongue fall out, he vomits up a translucent sack filled with little baby snakes and then yacks up snakes of all sizes (right on top of our poor leading lady's head!) on his way to becoming a large snake monster himself.

Made with Italian, Japanese and American backing and filmed on location in New Mexico, this was originally titled simply *The Bite* but was given the misleading sequel re-title of *Curse II* for home video distribution in America. It has nothing at all to do with the first *The Curse* (1987), an adaptation of H.P. Lovecraft's short story *The Color Out of Space,* nor with the later *Curse III: Blood Sacrifice* (1991), which was filmed under the title *Panga* in South Africa and involved a witch doctor cursing a family, nor *Curse IV: The Ultimate Sacrifice,* which was filmed in Italy, involved a demon haunting a monastery and was filmed way back in 1987 under the name *Catacombs.* Under whatever title, *Curse II* is a film that knows exactly how to freak out all of us card-carrying members of the "I Hate Snakes!" club. Seldom have I come across a snake movie that's made my skin crawl quite like this one does.

Justin McKinney

Ohio native Justin McKinney was coerced over to the dark side by a late night viewing of *Night of the Living Dead* as a child.

He's worked on and appeared in a number of low-budget horror films (*Descend into Darkness* 1 and 2, *Brain Drain*, *Loonies*, *Dance of the Dead*, *Fatal Delusions*, *Witch Graveyard*, *Chubby Killer*, *Slice N Dice*, *Phantom Limb*, *Day of 1000 Screams*, and others) and contributed reviews to numerous websites, magazines and books, including *Horror 101*, *Hidden Horror*, *Seminal Cinema*, *Horrorpedia* and his own blog, *The Bloody Pit of Horror*, which recently celebrated its millionth hit.

His original screenplay *One Last Photo* will be part of the upcoming horror anthology *Screams of a Summer Day*.

DAY OF THE ANIMALS (1977)

By Erich Kuersten

No one saw *Day of the Animals* until it became the Movie of the week in 1979. God bless network TV, for it fit perfectly in with our prime time network anxiety about the next day back to school.

There's three trends from the 1970s you need to know about how to appreciate the perfection that's *Day of the Animals*:

1.   The *Jaws* craze (all things natural with teeth to bite were "in");

2.   The *Airport/Poseidon Adventure* multi-generational cast facing some heavy disaster and getting offed one by one theme;

3.   The back to nature trend, especially us kids, The Cub scouts, Indian Guides, Ranger Rick, The Wilderness Family, etc. as part of a new eco-awareness (the Native America crying on the side of the highway reminding us just how OK it used to be to throw your trash out the window while driving); the first realization of scientists that there was a hole forming in the ozone layer — leading to a ban on aerosol deodorant — the ban on the peel away pull tab rings of beer cans in favor of the now ubiquitous pull tab, etc.

Add these elements all together in the mind of William Girdler, and you're off and running (or rather walking), for the desperate group in the mountains is poorly prepared for both walking and self-defense, especially now that the animals (and some lesser humans) have gone "loco" due to the giant ozone hole, the close proximity to the sun and the thin mountain air.

As the hike staggers on we see: one hawk, three vultures, a carload of rattlesnakes, a tarantula, flying mice, a wolf, three panthers, and a gang of German shepherds. Granite-jawed Christopher George leads the group. There's also: a TV reporter (played by Christopher George's real-life wife, Linda Day George); a Native American trekker, a divorced mother and her son; a scientist who expostulates on the ozone layer during downtime; an injured football pro wondering what to do now; an attractive but really poor young couple reeling from news she's pregnant, another pair trying to mend their failing marriage; and if that wasn't enough, in the constant challenger to George's leadership role, the great Leslie Nielsen as one of the few humans who goes insane from the ozone and who, in the film's *pièce de resistance*, goes in shirtless to fight a giant grizzly. In town, there's a fat sheriff roused out of bed in the middle of the night, government agents in silver hazmat suits, and a traumatized little girl wandering around alone in a daze.

Like all its devotees, I was the right age to remember the night *Day of the Animals* premiered on CBS, but I missed their whole dog attack climax because it came after my bedtime. I missed the end of a horde of great films that way: *The Poseidon Adventure, Telefon, Day of the Dolphin, Orca, The Cassandra Crossing* – I still don't know how some of them end. I would be in bed furious and crushed, but I dreamt my own wilder crazier endings. For *Day of the Animals,* when I heard at next Monday's recess that the humans had survived by riding a raft down the rapids with rabid dogs snapping at their hands every yard of the way, I envisioned a pretty wild ride.

Naturally it's not that wild in reality, but "naturally" is the key word here, that's what saves it. *Day of the Animals* was filmed as far away from the age of CGI, mentally and spiritually, as film would ever get. The key to the guiltless pleasure of *Day of the Animals* lies in the relative benign treatment of these animals. The animal attacks are created in the same manner that Hitchcock did the shower scene in *Psycho:* sharp jagged cuts of different sights, tacky pink foamy blood dripping from a dog's jaw as it tries to growl and not wag its tail in anticipation of its handler's off-camera treat, quick edits between what is clearly just play wrestling with tame animals, close-ups of baring teeth, an animal's teeth resting on someone's arm, and then the hawk looking down signaling an end to the scrimmage with his cry resembling a gym coach's whistle.

Girdler's films aren't meant to be great gore pieces, but they'*re* great for sick freaks in search of Cecil B. DeMille-levels of under-direction. Actors stand around in a "funeral processions and snakes" kind of Cinemascope chorus line and wonder what to do, receive no guidance, and improvise. If that's not enough, there's an amazing near-Morricone-level cacophonous percussion score by Lalo Schifrin.

But take a knee, and let me tell you one last story. There was this friend's dog I knew when I lived up in Syracuse, a mutt of medium height; he was super smart and sweet, a brilliant actor and almost psychic. When I was filthy drunk in the Syracuse snow some nights, this dog and I would roll around in the snow in some random front yard, and I'd scream like he was tearing me apart while he jumped all over me making these terrifying growls. We'd go on and on, rolling around growling and screaming, the dog managing to seem like he was tearing my arm off while barely even getting fang marks on my coat. We sounded, I thought, like I was being torn apart. Then, one night, someone finally yelled out a window: "Hey, you and the dog: please keep it down!" I was like, *How the hell can that guy tell I'm not really being hurt? Why isn't he calling an ambulance, the cops, animal control? How can we as humans, even as children, just instinctively tell when someone is really being hurt vs. just pretending?* The dog and I froze in mid attack, looked up at the window, and resumed our attack, *quietly*. *Day of the Animals* is the same way, it attacks *quietly*.

Erich Kuersten

Erich Kuersten is the gonzo-theorist behind the *Acidemic Journal of Film and Media* as well as a freelance film and music critic whose work can be found in *Bright Lights*, *The Weeklings*, *Slant*, *Modern Drunkard*, *McSweeney's*, *Scarlet Street*, *VHJ*, *Daily Om*, *Muze*, *Divinorum Psychonauticus*, and *Midnight Marquee*.

Films include the award-skipping *Queen of Disks*, *The Lacan Hour*, *Drunkards of Borneo*, and the *Shortcuts to Enlightenment* series.

He lives in Brooklyn. Write him at erichk9@aol.com.

DEADLY EYES (1982)

By Jay Clarke

The horror genre is a beast of many colors, fragmented into countless subgenres. Having been an avid fan since I was a wee lad, my bread and butter has always been slasher and zombie flicks, but if you really want to get my attention, put a killer rat in your movie! I love these little critters and have always been fascinated by how reviled they are by the masses. Rats are right up there with spiders and roaches as public enemy number one, thus making them perfect horror movie subjects, right?

Killer rat movies generally come in three varieties. The first variety features large numbers of actual rodents being dumped on actors by the bucketful, as in Bruno Mattei's 1984 post-apocalyptic *Rats: Night of Terror*. The second employs some sort of rat-human hybrid like in Jim Mickle's 2006 debut *Mulberry Street*. The third and hardest to pull off, is the giant rat flick.

My favorite remains Robert Clouse's 1982 effort *Deadly Eyes*. It's one of the crown jewels of this small subgenre known as "ratsploitation." I love this movie not only for its ingenious representation of their antagonists but also for its treatment of the source material, the 1974 James Herbert novel *The Rats*. Since the movie was shot in Toronto, it comes with an extra level of familiarity.

Deadly Eyes opens with a university professor (Canadian icon Cec Linder) lecturing to a visiting high school class. He foreshadows the events of the film by talking about how man's carelessness with the environment threatens our delicate ecosystem. After the lecture, we meet high school teacher Paul

Harris (Sam Groom) and two students, Martha (Lesleh Donaldson) and Trudy (Lisa Langlois), the latter of which is crushing on her teacher. Across town, Health Inspector Kelly Leonard (Sara Botsford) is busy confiscating a shipment of grain due to vermin contamination. Much to the chagrin of the owner, she has it burned and the rats, now enlarged from having engorged themselves on the steroid-infused grain, flee into the city's sewer system. People are being attacked, but the Department of Health doesn't take notice until one of their own, Foskins (played by the inimitable Scatman Crothers) is ripped to pieces. When they attempt to gas the sewers, the rats then escape above ground, wreaking havoc on the populace, including a cinema attended by Martha, Trudy and her boy toy Matt (Joseph Kelly). When Harris hears of the ensuing chaos, he rushes to find Kelly, with whom he has recently struck up a relationship, and his son Tim (Lee-Max Walton) at the opening ceremony of the new subway line. Will he get there in time, or will his loved ones become rat food?

As you can imagine, making a low-budget film about giant rats in the early 1980s was ambitious. It had been done with some success six years previous, using a combination of puppetry, compositing and forced perspective, in Bert I. Gordon's *The Food of the Gods*, but shots that involved giant rats actually interacting with their human counterparts often proved problematic. This was before the advent of visual effects and stop-motion animation would have been too costly and time-consuming, so a new approach needed to be employed.

Head effects artist Allan Apone came up

with the brilliant idea of dressing dachshunds in rat costumes. It seems crazy, but you'll be amazed by how convincing it looks to see several dozen of them scrambling around in unison. Going this route was not without challenges as all of the dogs had to be individually fitted for their rat costumes, for which they had problems seeing out of and moving around in. It was rumored that one or more dogs perished from either suffocation or exposure, but that has since been discredited. In total, they called in 35 dachshunds, as well as five terriers for the more physical moments when jumping was required. Puppets were used when characters were actually being chomped on. I think there are only two shots in *Deadly Eyes* where they show an actual rat. I have seen this movie about 10 times now, including a few times projected on 16mm, and I never tire of the creature effects. I hold them up as one of the premiere examples of low-budget problem solving when faced with the difficult challenge of visualizing something that does not exist in real life.

By the time I came across *Deadly Eyes* in the video store I worked at in the early 1990s, I was already a big fan of the book it was based on. After discovering the work of James Herbert in the late 1980s, *The Rats* was one of the first I read. Being a British author, his books weren't easily accessible in Canada, so I made sure to stock up every time I was visiting relatives in England. The film largely differs from the book, but there are still similarities. Charles Eglee (who now works on popular TV shows like *Dexter* and *The Walking Dead*) wrote the screenplay and used not the book, but Joe Dante's *Piranha*, on which he worked as an assistant director, as a template. However, his script did refer to an earlier draft by Lonon Smith that was more in line with the source material, and those resemblances carried over. The book does feature a teacher named Harris, but there's no suggested love triangle between him and two women. I expect Eglee added that in to pad the running time and set up the final set piece. One of Harris' students is bit by a rat, but he expunged the book's device of the rats carrying an infection that kills within 24 hours. As for set pieces, left intact were the kitchen scene where a baby is mauled and the subway attack. In both mediums, the gas proved effective at first, only to have the rats subsequently come back stronger.

In addition to my love of the effects and the source material, I also appreciate that *Deadly Eyes* was shot in Toronto. It's always fun to watch a movie and see places you recognize. Within five minutes, characters are walking out of the Old City Hall building while the 501 streetcar barrels by. The Toronto subway is used so well that, on those rare occasions I use the service, I'm always scanning the shadows for signs of you-know-what. Perhaps the best landmark in the movie, though, is the Crest Theater (now called The Regent) on Mt. Pleasant Rd. It makes for a great sequence, and that the movie playing is one of the director's earlier films, the Bruce Lee vehicle *Game of Death*, is a nice little in-joke when that kind of thing wasn't yet commonplace.

In researching this movie, I came across a lot of negative comments online and find it sad that some don't appreciate this movie as much as I do. Clouse clearly knew what he was making here; a fun creature feature. To take it as anything else is sheer folly. *Deadly Eyes* does touch on environmental themes but doesn't

When Animals Attack

110

hit you over the head with them. If anything, it's merely used as an excuse to make rats seem more nefarious than they actually are, with scare tactic statistics like they outnumber humans 24 to one and that given enough time can chew through steel. Herbert's novel was initially called out as an extremist for his portrayal of the government's treatment of the lower class, so perhaps Smith and Eglee were taking a cue from him. After all, we do continue to destroy our planet and will have to eventually deal with the consequences, for just like Cec Linder states at the beginning of *Deadly Eyes*, "It isn't nice to fool Mother Nature."

Jay Clarke

Jay Clarke is a writer and filmmaker based out of Oakville, Ontario. He has been involved in the Toronto indie horror scene for over a decade, and his short films *Lively* and *The Monitor* have screened at several film festivals in North America.

Jay is also curator of *The Horror Section*, a horror media blog and VHS archive. But all of these activities are a mere distraction while he awaits the uprising of his giant rat overlords.

DEEP BLUE SEA (1999)

By Nick Meece

In the summer of 1999, shark attack movies were scarce. In fact, my only memory of a shark movie at that time of my life was Steven Spielberg's *Jaws*. I had become a full-fledged Great White nut, and that entire franchise is to thank for that. But 1999 was a different time. A new generation. And, late one night, I caught a trailer for *Deep Blue Sea* on the television, and everything changed.

I don't remember the specifics of that fateful night - or that trailer viewing, in particular - but what I took away from it was this: *there's a new shark movie coming out!* Not only was a new shark flick on the horizon, but judging from the trailer, it featured not one, not two, but *three* killer sharks. How cool is that?

The film's release date of July 30 came and went, and a week later I was finally in the theater to see *Deep Blue Sea*. A parent dropped me and a friend off at the theater, and 105 minutes later

we came out absolutely loving the movie. I remember racing through my front door to tell my mom all about it. I rambled on about a full-on blood fountain at the end of *Deep Blue Sea*, still processing it all.

My love for *Deep Blue Sea* diminished quite a bit after that initial viewing. It just didn't hold up very well. But in preparation for this essay, I revisited the film to get a fresh grasp on the material, and now I'm taking a complete one-eighty again.

I love *Deep Blue Sea*. I love it for all the opposite reasons for my love of *Jaws*. I used to view it as a *Jaws* rip-off. But not now. And not ever. *Deep Blue Sea* has its own merits. The movie even goes out of its way to separate itself from *Jaws*. Speaking to the Los Angeles Times, screenwriter Duncan Kennedy revealed that in *Jaws*, the shark was 25 feet long, so director Renny Harlin set out to do one better by making the main shark in *Deep Blue Sea* 26 feet long.

The film also gave a nod in the direction of *Jaws*. When Thomas Jane's character pulls a license plate out of the mouth of one of the Tiger sharks, it's the same plate that Hooper pulls from the belly of a Tiger shark in *Jaws*. That was a pretty neat Easter egg.

I also appreciate the science behind the film. Though not technically feasible, using genetically-altered sharks for an Alzheimer cure is a concept that initially aims to better mankind. Of course, there's a sinister consequence. The basic plot of *Rise of the Planet of the Apes* is pretty much the same: the main scientist has a family member suffering from some sort of terminal illness, and the goal of the animal experiments is to find or create a cure. With larger brain capacities, the animals begin to think and act for themselves. That, in turn, is an immediate threat to human beings. We'll just chock these similarities up to being a homage.

When looking at a shark attack movie, you also expect a certain level of shock value. Therefore, Renny Harlin attaches a big name star, only for him to die – just like Janet Leigh being killed

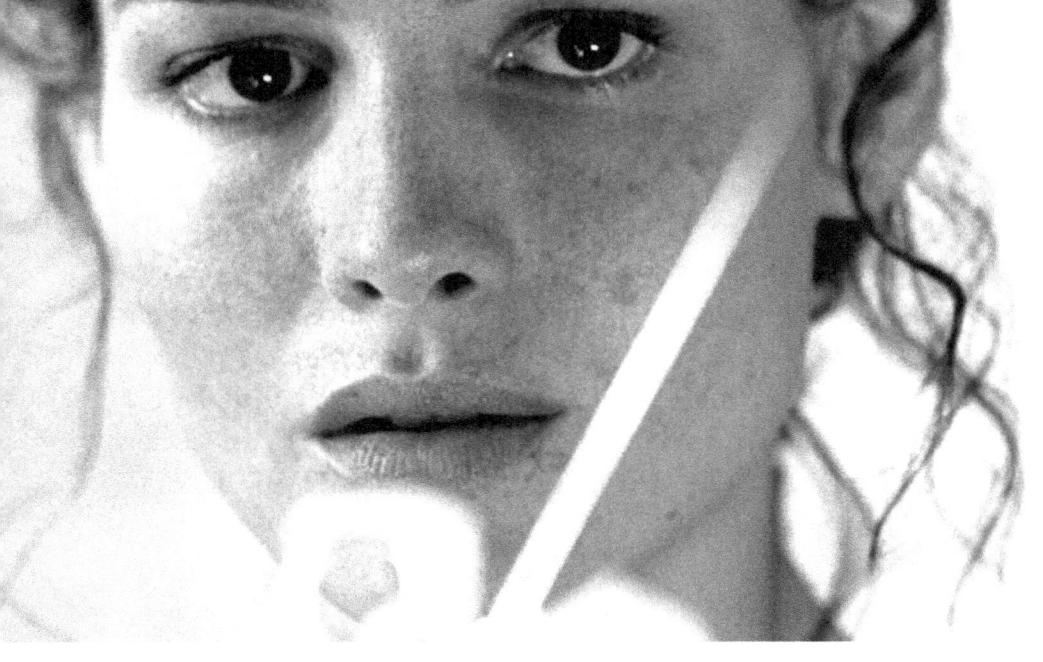

halfway through *Psycho*, or Drew Barrymore within the first eighteen minutes of *Scream*. In *Deep Blue Sea*, it's Samuel L. Jackson in the beginning of the third act. When someone dies in a shark attack movie, there's really only one way to die and that's to be eaten. That's not the shocking part. What was shocking is that it came in a moment in the film where Jackson is giving a highly inspirational survival speech, attempting to keep the spirits of the remaining crew high. Right as he's getting into the meat of the speech, a shark pops out of the small retaining pool behind him, biting him and dragging him back into the water. Holy shit! No one saw that coming. I sure didn't.

A stand out performance comes from rapper-turned-actor L.L. Cool J. (*Halloween H20*). He plays a character who goes by the name Preacher. He's a foul-mouthed chef with a deep knowledge of the bible, and talks to his pet parrot that hangs out in the kitchen with him. Speaking of the bird, there's a moment in the film when one of the sharks eats the bird. After the kitchen fills with gas fumes, Preacher lights up his Zippo and tosses it to the shark, but not before spouting the awesome one-liner, "You ate my bird." An instant classic and one that I still hear mocked to this day.

So let's move on to the climax of the film. There's one shark left, the giant Mako. Using a large battery, a harpoon gun, and the metal cable for the spear, the plan is to essentially shoot the shark and attach the other end of the cable to the battery, electrocuting the animal to death, a homage to *Jaws 2*. It doesn't go as planned, and the main scientist decides to sacrifice herself by cutting her hands and jumping into the water with the shark. Her new scheme works. L.L.'s Preacher attaches the cable, and the shark is blown to pieces.

And that's *Deep Blue Sea*, a tale about what can happen if you tamper with nature. Man may be at the top of the food chain now, but all it would take is just a slight evolutionary process to dethrone us. The film makes no attempt to set up a sequel, and that's probably for the best. As far as shark attack movies go, *Deep Blue Sea* is up there near the top. The sharks of *Deep Blue Sea* promised to be bigger, meaner and deadlier, and they deliver on all three.

Nick Meece

Nick Meece is an avid horror movie fan in his late 20s, residing in Indianapolis with his wife and two kids. He spends his free time writing about teen slasher movies of years past and collecting odd movie memorabilia. In the late summer of 2014, Nick began shooting his first feature-length horror film – one that's still in development.

Nick has also published a teen murder-mystery book, *Grim Volume I: Teen Spirit* and has two follow-ups planned. You can learn more about the books and Nick's film by visiting his blog at NickMeece.com, which he updates frequently with all the nonsense listed above.

DOGS (1976)

By Gert Verbeeck

Don't pet them... Fear them!

By the time the second half of the 1970s came around, it were the animals who had built up an unstoppable reign of terror in fright cinema. Naturally, man's best friend could not escape this transformation to onscreen malignity, hence the year 1976 saw the release of *Dogs*. Capably helmed by director Burt Brinckerhoff (as his one and only venture into independent horror cinema), this first effort from production company Mar Vista Productions turned out to be the forerunner of more murderous dog adventures to come. To name only two, in that same year Warner Bros. did things a little bigger and better with *The Pack*, and in 1984 a whole vicious horde of military trained Rottweilers would be unleashed on a peaceful mountain village in *Rottweiler* aka *Dogs of Hell*. It's hard to believe that killer dogs didn't surface in a horror film any time sooner, but *Dogs* does have the novelty angle for being the first. Granted, in 1972 James Brolin was up against half a dozen Doberman guard dogs in *Trapped*, but that particular film was made for television and can't even be branded as a full-blooded horror effort.

The premise of *Dogs* remains effectively simple. A pack of dogs goes on a killing spree. Or, as mentioned in the film, something is causing domestic dogs to pack and attack people. It all happens in the sleepy outskirts of desert city Chula Vista (San Diego, California, USA), where the Southwestern College is located. There we meet professor Harlan Thompson, head of the biology department, played with a healthy dosage of cynicism by David McCallum (from the hit TV series *The Man from U.N.C.L.E.*). McCallum provided the necessary star power for a validly questionable fright flick about ravenous dogs to secure theatrical distribution and was also appropriately cast, with his native Scottish accent lending his character credibility as an outsider rebel with a cause amongst his fellow American

English speaking colleagues. The dusty locations used in *Dogs*, blessed with cinematographer Robert Steadman's vintage grainy photography look, give us an interesting juxtaposed view on the setting of Chula Vista during the 1970s. On the one hand, both the suburban and college infrastructures appear all neat and civilized. But once we get outside these parameters, we encounter unfinished roads and inhospitable, rock-laden fields. As if progress stopped expanding its wings when it realized there's no use in trying to curb or restrain nature. As though the landscapes serve an underlying allegory to the central theme of our titular animals rising up against human civilization. For it are those barren fields and rocky hills where the dogs first decide to roam, commencing their group attacks on livestock and farmers, before later on invading the town, on the hunt for its inhabitants.

At the film's opening garden party of Dr. Martin Koppelman (Sterling Swanson), head of the faculty, Thompson gets introduced to Southwestern's newest faculty member Michael Fitzgerald (George Wyner). Thompson's inherent sarcastic nature almost instantly turns Fitzgerald into a possible adversary – be prepared for Thompson's splendid "parallel lines are not supposed to meet" reply — but ironically the two will find themselves soon enough joining forces to fight the town's collectively rising menace. Thompson inarguably is the best-written character. He's a typical anti-hero you love to root for, not ashamed to admit he prefers drinking a good beer in solitude or fine female company instead of mingling with the shallow small-talkers and not too shy to give so-called established authorities and undermining kick in the butt. By the time we have the film's exposition of characters out of the way, we've already learned all about Thompson's misgivings with the current state of the educational system he's forced to function within and his gripes with the squandering of grants going to the wrong kind of people. Yet he's determined in his attempts to change the system rather than dropping out. Not bad for a character running around in a film about deadly dogs. And he even comes with a love interest, Caroline Donoghue (Sandra McCabe) of the English department.

Linda Gray, who would later on see her career as a TV actress flourish and become big in *Dallas*, portrays one of her first roles in *Dogs*. Though she's clearly also a faculty teacher, what exactly her field of expertise might be remains a bit of a mystery, since she's

simply introduced as Ms. Engle, without further ado. Well, that's beside the fact that she also serves as a possible love interest for the obnoxious Dr. Aintry (Dean Santoro), a theoretical physicist. But that subplot soon fizzles when Ms. Engle cleverly puts Aintry in his place, on the front porch no less, by gracefully yet loud and clear declining his rather bluntly indecent proposals. Yes, *Dogs* even has its funny moments. And Linda Gray has a shower scene. Now, what happens when a woman gets a role in a film about blood-craving dogs, and her character enters a shower? Yes, we get to see a tribute to Alfred Hitchcock. All this should have you noticing that every female character in the script is severely underwritten. This film basically boils down to men fighting dogs. All women can pretty much just run away screaming.

Some blackly humorous social criticism aside, *Dogs* takes itself very seriously and for the most part succeeds in making the animals feel like a tangible threat. Even if we don't see them, we know they're out there, their group howls in the dead of night sounding downright sinister. Not much time is wasted with presenting us dog attacks with a certain regularity and increased ferocity in scenes of slaughter that mostly play out at night. All for the better of course, as we could witness during the film's opening credits already that a group of dogs running around in the streets on a sunny day to a wonderfully cheesy soundtrack just doesn't set the right tone for dread and dismay. First time composer Alan Oldfield's keenly orchestrated score does stick, though, and later on he'll even incorporate some classic sounding "horror horns" at the right moments.

The attacking dogs turn out to be persistent and can look reasonably imposing, depending on the specimen. A big, black, mean canine may look threatening while sitting still in a desolate street at night, seconds before he'll strike; a fluffy lapdog frolicking through the grass or hopping down the stairs looks considerably less scary. But these are just minor misfires. A bigger flaw is that the attacks often happen very sudden, so the film does suffer from a palpable lack of tension buildup. To make up for all that, in the third act we're treated to a decent double climax, with on one location a whole group of students being trapped and massacred in the campus library. In the other scene Thompson and Donoghue are locked in a garage, attempting to hotwire their car while dogs are running amok in the house, trying to get to them. Having those climactic scenes take place simultaneously, editor John Wright's cross-cutting between the two locations strongly enhances the impact of the film's finale.

The very ending of the film is one for the books. Remember those disturbed endings, particularly popular during the 1970s and 1980s, in which the ultimate shock or twist is revealed in the final shot? And that shot would freeze in a foreboding manner? Well, *Dogs* ends with one of those. One that tells us, as we could have guessed, that things are far from over. There's a different kind of threat that we, pitiful humans, might not have anticipated. A tacky terror that's such a hoot, it just might put a grin on your face which will last throughout the remaining end credits.

Whether it's been exaggerated or not, there exists a funny fact about *Dogs'* promotional campaign for its then scheduled TV run. After a week of broadcasting the TV spots, David Miller, head of distribution on *Dogs*, received a phone call from some very upset TV station representatives. Miller was informed that the spots had to be pulled off the air and was urged to reschedule them not to be shown before 10pm. Supposedly, TV stations were receiving a number of complaints from frightened viewers claiming that, since those spots had been running, they've had an increase of dog attacks throughout their neighborhood. The simple thought that those initial viewer calls might have been bogus didn't even occur to the television studio executives and the preposterous notion of domestic dogs watching the trailers, then decidedly go out and chase people, clearly didn't catch on with them either. No such thing as bad publicity, of course.

The whole crew behind *Dogs* – many of them all newcomers to the world of filmmaking – really gave it all their efforts to deliver the best film they could. Not to mention all this with very limited budget and means, a production period of seven weeks and allegedly 38 dogs running around on set, not always doing what they were told to. Shortly after the film's midway point, *Dogs* shifts into gear and goes for sheer entertainment right up until the very end, boosting a pretty high body count and a fair amount of bloodshed. Safe to say that the filmmakers knew what kind of film they were making all along. To this date *Dogs* could still use some additional exposure and really deserves to be a little more than a mere footnote in the history of "man vs. animal" eco-horror cinema.

Gert Verbeeck

Gert Verbeeck hails from Belgium, where he currently continues to hone his skills as a musician, writer and director.

Finding his way behind a drum kit at the age of ten, metal act Molest stands out as one of his bands having done the most damage so far. That all happened during high school. More bands and projects followed.

Starting his film education at the Sint-Lukas School of Arts, he left his hometown for the city of Brussels, from where he made the transition to onset work and editing room hours for various television production companies.

He produced and co-directed *Cinematek* (2010), a micro-budget docu-reportage on the renowned former Royal Belgian Film Archive. With British director Alex Cox and American actor Lance Henriksen he made the short documentaries *Shoot If You Live* (2011) and *Facts and Fiction in the Life of Mr. Henriksen* (2012). Irish producer Declan Lynch invited him to handle script consultant duties on the Ghent-based anthology film *Follow: Tall Tales from a Small City* (2014).

Co-founder of genre film website *Cult Reviews*, he published film essays in the reference books *Horror 101* and *Hidden Horror* and contributed articles to the bi-monthly printed *HorrorHound Magazine*.

Being a devoted attendant of the Brussels International Fantastic Film Festival since his teen horror fan days, Gert was recently welcomed by the BIFFF crew to conduct Q&A sessions.

EIGHT LEGGED FREAKS (2002)

By Chelseaa Benwell

Eight Legged Freaks is the story of a small American town that's overrun by a selection of mutated spiders after a large amount of toxic waste is spilled near a spider farm.

I had first seen *Eight Legged Freaks* when I had just turned 12. It was around 2008, and the film had already gotten quite old (it was a 2002 release). I wasn't the biggest fan of spiders. In fact, I was probably the biggest arachnophobe you'd ever come across. I couldn't even look at one printed on paper for fear it'd jump off and come to life. Naturally, this wasn't a movie I expected to sit through, alone in my bedroom. But I did, and I admit that I thoroughly enjoyed it. I won't say that I was ready to own a pet spider after seeing *Eight Legged Freaks* - I was still scared of finding one in the bath - but I didn't have a problem with fictional spiders anymore.

Since first watching the movie in 2008, I have developed a deep interest in horror movies, b-movies, and psychological thrillers. I love watching out for the newest releases, but I'd always kept those old, classic b-movies close to my heart. They were awful in production value and nearly equally as awful in story, but they were entertaining because they were so unreal and so bad. Like a guilty pleasure, I suppose.

I have watched *Eight Legged Freaks* a few more times as an easy-watching Sunday afternoon flick, but recently, I sat down and I thought, I'm going to seriously watch it this time. I wanted to watch it like I did the first time I'd seen it, but with my new knowledge of horror and b-movies. I grew to love spiders; I find them to be some of the most interesting species on the planet. I'd also since seen the cast in other movies, so I was able to compare how far they've come since starring in it. I thought to myself that a good modern b-movie can be made. It doesn't have to take itself too seriously, but at the same time it doesn't have to nearly mock the audience by coming across as a parody. That's what *Eight Legged Freaks* did; it took the atmosphere and the tone of a movie like *Tarantula* and *Earth vs. The Spider,* and it remastered it into how the modern world reacts to seeing a scenario like that.

I would say that I have grown to love this movie more over the years as I have slowly developed an admiration for the horror and sci-fi genres. The entertainment I got from tacky, yet memorable b-movies and found footage horror gave me a burst of nostalgia, which encouraged my experience all the more. It was reassuring to see that modern cinema could replicate the atmosphere and the "cringe" inducing monsters that made these kind of movies so popular back in the 1960s. Even down to the odd choices of sound effects used on the spiders themselves, it's all cleverly worked into a re-imagining of the genre.

The movie itself got a lot of backlash from critics but a lot of praise from movie-goers. It was as if half the viewers understood what they were trying to do, and the others just weren't impressed with it. I can understand the mixed reaction, but I'm definitely the one giving praise. The movie is almost self-aware, and whilst it doesn't take itself too seriously, it continuously references other popular horror movies and pop culture classics. It also references other spider movies such as *Arachnophobia, Tarantula* and *The Giant Spider Invasion.* All three are great movies, and *Eight Legged Freaks* knows that, which made their nod to similar works more interesting. It was great to also see the use of different spider kinds as opposed to generic spider types or a tarantula. From simple orb weavers to trapdoor spiders, whereas some may not be factually accurate, they've still done a very good job on including some more

interesting species.

Upon looking into the various spiders used, I have found that the film has kept a few truths about our arachnid friends. For example, the trapdoor spiders look quite similar to the real thing, despite actual trapdoors being slightly rounded (the spiders in the movie have quite jagged pedipalps). The way in which they catch their food holds the closest similarity. They leap from their "trapdoor" above their burrow and latch onto whatever unfortunate "meal" lurks near. They've successfully mastered the speed and ferocious approach of the incredible species. Also used frequently are the jumping spiders. In *Eight Legged Freaks* they're thinner, longer and look much sharper than the average jumper. This, however, does not interfere with the fact that they have the same jumping capability and movements in the movie as in real life. I was also glad to see that the mix of tarantulas in the movie include a Mexican red knee, a pink foot goliath, and a goliath bird eater. The simple orb weavers used in *Eight Legged Freaks* are the ones whose sizes and appearances were modified the most for dramatic effect. Our main orb weaver female resembles a black widow more than its generic counterpart, but this is to make her more threatening. I think it works as she looks the most frightening out of the different species used.

Eight Legged Freaks is one of the main influences on my interest in the horror genre and why I started my blog *The Scream Review*. I wanted to be able to share my interest in movies. I wanted to be able to talk about how movies made me feel, why they could have been better, or why they were incredible. The experiences, opportunities and joys of the horror world have been kind to me, and, essentially, this is all because I really enjoyed a modern b-movie such as *Eight Legged Freaks*.

Chelseaa Benwell

Chelseaa Benwell's blog *The Scream Review* shares news, reviews, and merchandise from all over the horror world. She predominantly reviews horror movies, but there will occasionally be games, books, music, and events thrown in, too.

She has also written for *Horrorville*, another horror-based review blog, and the paranormal hub *Paranormal Warehouse*.

She's a big fan of directors such as Quentin Tarantino, Eli Roth, Edgar Wright and Rob Zombie. Her favorite subgenres within horror are supernatural and serial killers. *Friday the 13th* is her most-cherished movie franchise to date.

EMPIRE OF THE ANTS (1977)

By Vanessa De Largie

For they shall inherit the earth…sooner than you think!

Some entertaining *ant-attack* films have been made over the years with a few dating back to 1954. But let's not forget the cheesy 1977 horror film directed by Bert I. Gordon (aka Mr. B.I.G.) titled - *Empire of The Ants.*

Glamorous Joan Collins plays a con-artist who attempts to sell dodgy real estate deals in the Florida Everglades. What she and her gullible prospective buyers don't know is that the land has been conquered by giant ants.

"EMPIRE OF THE ANTS" .... JOAN COLLINS · ROBERT LANSING · JOHN DAVID CARSON ....ROBERT PINE · EDWARD POWER · ALBERT SALMI · JACQUELINE SCOTT · PAMELA SHOOP

Bert I. Gordon was nicknamed "Mr. B.I.G." not only for the initials of his name but for his fondness for creating films in which protagonists have to deal with creatures that have been transformed into giants.

Gordon, who directed, produced, wrote, and provided the visual effects for his films had initial success with tales of giant people (*The Amazing Colossal Man* and its sequel, *War of the Colossal Beast*); giant dinosaurs (*King Dinosaur*: 1955); a giant spider (*Earth vs. the Spider*: 1958) and giant teenagers (*Village of the Giants*: 1965). He even reversed the trend with *Attack of the Puppet People* (1958), in which the protagonists are miniaturized.

Gordon's films of this period were typical entries in the short-lived phase of science fiction flicks that fed on the public's panic over the *possibility* of imminent Cold War destruction.

The sci-fi phase eventually fizzled out leaving Gordon to toil away in the less satisfying genres of horror and sex flicks. Just as the late 1950s had provided the atomic threat, the 1970s realized a concern for man's impact on the environment. Pollution in the skies, chemicals in the water, and the destruction of natural habitats were in the news. Add in the blockbuster success of *certain* shark movie in 1975, and the time was right for Mr. B.I.G. to open his primitive effects box and return to the science fiction fray.

Gordon claimed that *Empire of the Ants* was based on a story by H.G. Wells, although any resemblance is tenuous at best. Instead, the connection allowed the filmmaker to carry on the tradition of ants as film villains. The fear of what would happen when ant turned against man was perfectly distilled in the faux documentary *The Hellstrom Chronicle* (1971, Walon Green), which predicted that insects (and predominately ants) would soon take over the planet. Enter Bert I. Gordon with *Empire of the Ants*.

The film begins with a close-up of ants ripping apart an orchid flower. The visual is accompanied by a humorous voiceover discussing pheromones and how ants use them to communicate.

As the opening credits roll, we see drums of radioactive waste being dumped into the ocean. One drum of toxicity washes up on the shore, leaking its silvery contents which metamorphosizes the local ants into *giant* killer-ants.

Marilyn Fryser (Joan Collins) and her employees Dan (Robert Lansing) and Joe (John David Carson) take the group of unsuspecting buyers to view worthless ocean-front land. Her phony sales pitch comes to a halt when two members of the group are discovered dead. Minutes later they see a multitude of angry giant ants. The ants are totally  unbelievable; they make one's stomach cramp from laughter. The group's boat is destroyed, and the giant killer-ants chase them through the woods. Lives are lost. Clothes are wrecked. Relationships blossom and burn.

The survivors eventually arrive in town only to discover that the ants are feeding at the sugar refinery, and the queen ant is using her pheromones to keep the township under tight control. Will the survivors escape or be slaves to the ant-hood?

One could write a screenplay about the cast of *Empire of the Ants*. The actors' careers and personal lives are similar to a *Sirk* melodrama. The ageless Joan Collins appeared in 22 films in the 1970s including film adaptions of her sister's novels. Collins detested working on the *Empire of the Ants*, citing that she did not enjoy working with ant-props that bumped and scratched the actors. The audience may have hoped that Collins could shed her vanity whilst filming, but her self-consciousness of her own beauty is apparent from start to finish. Collins' accent switches from American to British haphazardly throughout the film – one expects more from a RADA graduate. In the 1996 television interview, John Hockenberry asks, "What about *Empire of The Ants?*" In which Joan replies, "I think that's one of the ones we'll forget. I'm a working actress. I act firstly because I love it, and secondly because I need to make a living. For some reason or another, some people have the impression that I don't need to make a living... that I'm rich, rich, rich but I'm not."

Robert Lansing has an understated presence as Captain Dan. He acts Collins off the screen with a look or a deep-voiced mumble. Lansing was an actor who started off on Broadway, before moving to California and being cast in popular sci-fi film *4D Man*. In the late 1960s, Lansing landed a guest role in a popular episode of *Star Trek*. His outstanding performance stole the show, and a spin-off series was on the cards. Unfortunately, around this time, the original series was on the verge of cancellation, and the project never eventuated.

John David Carson, who plays Joe, doesn't really shine in this film, but then the role doesn't really give him much to play with. It seems Carson's career was doomed from the get-go, when he starred in *Pretty Maids All in a Row*, directed by Roger Vadim, (also starring Rock Hudson). In interviews, Carson stated that refusing to work with homosexual directors cost him many great roles. Carson was married to actress Vicki Morgan, who was later murdered.

Albert Salmi played the sheriff role with great ease. Salmi always considered himself a theater actor and turned down many famous film roles, including the role of Bo Derek in *Bus Stop* with Marilyn Monroe, (the role eventually went to Don Murray). Aged 62, Salmi shot his estranged wife before turning the gun on himself.

Robert Pine plays the sleazy and cowardly Larry so well. His performance shines in this film. He's both irritating and agitating to the viewer.

In Summary, *Empire of the Ants* has a flavorsome combination of laughable killer-ants, bad acting, a plot that loses the plot, and endless continuity issues. It's one of those films that's so bad, it's good.

Vanessa De Largie

Vanessa de Largie is a multi-award-winning actress and author. She's also a writer and sex-blogger for *The Huffington Post*.

Vanessa has worked professionally in film, theater, TV, radio, voiceover, and as a photographic model. She has won two best female actor awards for her work in a feature film and a short film. In April 2015, Vanessa was crowned Most Promising Australian Actress by *Star Central Magazine*.

Nocturne Night of The Vampire (a film in which she stars) is distributed by Troma worldwide and screened at an array of European film festivals.

In 2009, Vanessa was one of twelve actors worldwide accepted into The New Actors Workshop in New York, where she trained with film director Mike Nichols (*The Graduate*).

Vanessa's most recent book *Don't Hit Me!* (published by Seattle publisher Booktrope) is a #1 Amazon Bestseller and has received five-star reviews from the Midwest Book Review, The San Francisco Book Review, and the #1 Amazon Hall of Fame Reviewer in the UK. It received the 2014 Global eBook Award (Bronze) for women's studies and an Honourable Mention Award at The 2014 London Book Festival.

Vanessa's memoir *Without my Consent* about her journey through rape at age 20, was released in 2015.

To learn more about Vanessa and her work, visit her website at www.vanessadelargie.net

FROGS (1972)

By Sven Soetemans

The opening credits take away all doubts straight from the beginning: George McGowan's *Frogs* is destined to become a prototypic "nature strikes back" classic! The stylish and relaxing, but nevertheless somewhat moody opening sequences introduce freelance photographer Pickett Smith (Sam Elliott) in his canoe, taking pictures in swampy rivers. The first pictures that he takes – each time illustrated through a lovely freeze-frame moment – are capturing the seemingly peaceful fauna & flora, but then the photo shoot unrelentingly focuses on floating garbage and polluted water being dumped into these exact same picturesque swampy rivers. It's a saddening sight to behold, and the experienced eco-horror fanatic knows that such appalling human behavior cannot (and will not) remain unpunished! Moments later, Pickett is nearly run over by a speedboat on a wider ranged lake, and we learn that he's

It's the day that Nature strikes back!

actually trespassing the private island resort of the wealthy Crockett family. Cousins, Clint and Karen Crockett, invite Pickett to their annual family reunion and escort him to the large mansion, where he's promptly introduced to the wheelchair-bound patriarch Jason Crockett (Ray Milland).

Even though it's Jason's birthday, and his entire family is there to celebrate this and the 4th of July together, Jason Crockett clearly is a grumpy and intolerant tyrant who reigns over his descendants with an iron fist. In spite of the breathtaking geographical location where he lives, Jason Crockett hates nature with a passion and proclaims that the superior human race shouldn't even live in harmony with trees and animals. While our detective/photographer Pickett gets to know the rest of the eccentric family and becomes aware of a menace coming from outdoors, abnormally large-sized bullfrogs venture dangerously close towards the house. The first victim is gardener/handyman Grover. While Jason Crockett is still convinced that he went back to party on the mainland, he actually lies dead with his face down in a puddle of mud. His cause of death remains unknown, but Pickett, who discovered the body and only informed old man Jason about it, senses that it's a bad omen. But then the actual Crockett family members are getting picked off one *Ten Little Indians* style by a wide variety of ill-natured island critters. For example, after shooting some ducks out of the sky, grandson Michael gets ambushed by nasty and hairy tarantulas that crawl into his mouth and ears. Cousin Kenneth is deliberately asphyxiated in the greenhouse when an army of funny-faced lizards throw his bottles of poison and pesticides on the floor, uncle Charles loses a swamp-wrestling match with an alligator, and then there's poor Auntie Iris… When she heads into the woods for catching butterflies, she's pushed off the path and welcomed by rattlesnakes and blood-sucking leeches. And what about the frogs? They silently stare and symbolically declare war when they jump on the Stars & Stripes birthday cake…

Oh, and by the way, did you notice how every victim committed his/her final crime against nature moments before they meet their end? Now that's pure and utterly cool 1970s eco-horror for you!

In all honesty, the absolute greatest thing about *Frogs* remains its legendary tagline: "Today the pond! Tomorrow the world." I never actually found out if the tagline was intended to be ironic or serious, but it sure is one of the most fabulous horror movie catch-phrases in the history of cinema. Luckily, however, the fun doesn't stop there! Unlike most of its contemporary eco-horror colleagues, *Frogs* still stands as one of the most straightforward and unscrupulously entertaining "animal attack" movies of the entire 1970s. Back then, uninspired but over-enthusiast directors were turning harmless animal species into ravenous monsters, even the most unlikely ones like worms (*Squirm*), rabbits (*Night of the Lepus*), and – well – frogs. One of the inventive aspects about Robert Hutchison and Robert Blees' script is that the croakers aren't just vicious avengers but also strategic army generals that mobilize the whole Crockett Island's ecosystem to commit nasty murders! Very much like in Alfred Hitchcock's *The Birds* – the granddaddy of all nature strikes back movies - the titular animals are merely the silently staring judges and relentless juries, while the executioners

are a variety of other critters like spiders, lizards, snakes, alligators, and even a turtle! Come to think of it, *Frogs* actually borrows a whole lot of elements from Hitchcock's *The Birds*, but you look

past that when you're into b-movies. *Frogs* also benefices from its geographically isolated island setting. The Crockett family are a bunch of inhuman bastards and deserve what's coming to them, but how can we be really sure that the  animal revolution only takes place here and not in the rest of the world? The film also doesn't feature a soundtrack but exclusively animal sounds, specifically lots and lots of eerie croaking!

So yes, the story is silly and hardly ever scary, but it's praiseworthy how director George McGowan attempts to build up an atmosphere of tension. He simply zooms in on the frogs and puts the emphasis on their stoic eyes and rhythmic croaking, so even though they're just everyday frogs, they look extremely ominous and psychopathic.

One of the best aspects of the film unquestionably is Mario Tosi's colorful camera-work that shows the beautiful environment from many creative viewpoints. The filming of *Frogs* took place in the damp and torrid Eden Park, Florida, where they probably still suffered from a frog-infestation for several more years, since many of the specially imported amphibians escaped and permanently settled themselves in the humid swamps. The director's name, George McGowan, perhaps doesn't ring a bell, but he's a very competent and sure-footed "leader" with a couple of interesting titles on his repertoire, like a sequel in the *Magnificent Seven* franchise (part 4, starring Lee Van Cleef and the second best in the series) and the curiously compelling *Shadow of the Hawk*, starring Jan -Michael Vincent and dealing with original themes like Shaman mythologies. The acting performances in *Frogs* are fair enough. The young Sam Elliot is quite good in his heroic role, but Ray Milland steals the show as the grumpy and bossy millionaire who thinks he can afford himself everything. Elliot was still in the earliest phase of his career, whereas for Milland this film marked the beginning of the last straight line in his long and versatile life in front of the cameras. After *Frogs*, the former Oscar winner and leading man in Hitchcock's *Dial M for Murder*, starred in several more questionably epic horror/trash magnum opuses like *The Thing With Two Heads*, *Terror in the Wax Museum* and *The Girl in the Yellow Pajamas*. Milland continued to make movies until he literally dropped dead. His last accomplishment was the imbecilic *Hydra: The Sea Serpent*, a zero-budgeted Italian monster flick with an adorably ridiculous sock-puppet who likes to twist itself around cardboard lighthouses and swallows entire mannequin dolls without even chewing. Milland, in his late 70s by then, traveled to Europe and completed his filming duties, but he was already terminally ill from cancer.

But let's not end with this sad and depressing note, because 12 years earlier, in the year that the wondrous *Frogs* was released, Milland was still very much his natural born grumpy self. *Frogs* is a delightfully entertaining horror that epitomes so many styles and trademarks that make this decade the absolute glory days of the genre.

Sven Soetemans

Sven Soetemans was born in Leuven, Belgium, and now lives with his wife and two children in rural Herzele.

Before family life took over his world, Sven was a fanatical horror viewer and review writer. It all started as a young teenager, when he rented VHS movies chosen solely for their distasteful covers. He got addicted to movies such as *Hellraiser*, *C.H.U.D.*, *Rawhead Rex*, and *From Beyond*, which he has seen 50 times and counting. His absolute favorites are the colorful Italian gialli from the 1970s and early 1980s.

Sven has written over 3,500 movie reviews for IMDB under the pseudonym Coventry. He has also contributed essays for the books *Hidden Horror: a Celebration of 101 Underrated and Overlooked Fright Flicks* and *Horror 101: The A-list of Horror Films and Monster Movies*.

GRIZZLY (1976)

By Steve De Roover

In this digital age, it seems almost impossible that a film slips under your personal radar. Especially with all the detailed websites, forums filled to the brim with rabid movie aficionados and impressive online databases. And, of course, let's not forget specialized books, like this puppy that you have now clinched in your hands! But funny enough, this *Grizzly* did...

Because I'm quite a fan of the "nature run amok" subgenre in horror cinema. For me a small little flick about a certain white shark started not only my love for the horror genre but also movies in general. I became a junkie for everything that could give me the same adrenaline rush as Steven Spielberg's *Jaws*. But still, I completely missed William Girdler's *Jaws* rip-off with a grizzly bear.

Life's little ironies, right?

But the universe is right again.

Grizzly opens when the horrible death of two female hikers shake up an unnamed National Park. When the National Park's chief ranger Michael Kelly (Christopher George) discovers that the two unsuspecting girls were brutally maligned by a bear, he tries to persuade Park supervisor Charley Kittridge (Joe Dorsey) to close down the Park. However, Kittridge, in turn, blames ranger Kelly about not following up on the bear population. While we get a couple of typical arguing scenes that would perfectly fit in the first act of *Jaws*, Park naturalist Arthur Scott (Richard Jaeckel) discovers that this specific grizzly bear is a complete newbie in the woods of

the park. While everybody gets their act together in how to proceed in the matter of catching or killing the titular monster, the huge grizzly leaves a bloody trail of mutilated bodies.

As legend goes, it was screenwriter Harvey Flaxman (known for the Troma distributed comical sex-romp *Preacherman* and its sequel) who came up with the story after he had an unpleasant encounter with a bear during a family camping trip. This was around 1975, the year that Spielberg's *Jaws* ripped open the global box office in a way that nobody knew before and probably never will. To "blaxploitation"-producer David Sheldon (*Sheba Baby*) this idea about a killer grizzly sounded like the perfect way to steal some of that coveted white shark-money, so together with

Flaxman, he wrote the screenplay for *Grizzly*. Sheldon wanted to direct, but all of that changed when director Willam Girdler discovered the script on the desk of David Sheldon. The two had previously worked together on *The Zebra Killer*, *Abby* and *Sheba Baby*, and when Girdler proposed to personally search for funding if he could direct the flick, Sheldon agreed. In less than a week, Girdler - with the help of associate producer Lee S. Jones - obtained the required budget of $750,000 through Edward L. Montoro's Film Ventures International. *Grizzly* was shot in Clayton, Georgia, with most of the town officials and people acting as extras in the film.

A case of the right man at the right job. Because director William Girdler made quite a quality "killer animal" film. Of course, a blind guy can see from space that *Grizzly* is a shameless *Jaws* rip-off from start to finish, but this never puts a dent in the absolute fun of watching this little shocker. The atmosphere is all over the place to begin with. The film feels sometimes like a classic Disney adventure film, which happens to have bloody kills thrown into the mix, and in other instances Girdler goes for real down and dirty horror (kids are not safe). While the special effects budget was quite low, Girdler pulls out the maximum of its cheap creature effects (read: a guy walking in bear paws) for a couple of tense POV-shots. After more than an hour you see the titular grizzly for the first time in its full glory, and what a beast it is! Besides the aforementioned crude trickery, Girdler and company made good use of the aptly named Teddy, an eleven foot tall Kodiak bear.

Besides Teddy, we see the acting chops of genre-favorite Christopher George (*City of the Living Dead*, *Graduation Day*) as the Roy Scheider of the film while character actor Richard Jaeckel (*The Dirty Dozen*, *Walking Tall Part II*) is always good as a tough-guy. The rest of the cast is at least serviceable in bringing some of the ridiculous dialogues with a straight face. But you will never see a film called *Grizzly* for that, right? But you probably will see it for the explosive ending, which involves helicopters and bazookas!

Grizzly became a huge box office hit in 1976 and grossed more than $30 million worldwide. It actually became the most successful

independent film of all time, until John Carpenter's *Halloween* blew that record out of the water two years later. However, the film's distributor, Edward L. Montoro, decided to keep all the profits, which led to director William Girdler and the film's writers/co-producers, Harvey Flaxman and David Sheldon, to file a lawsuit. The federal court forced Montoro to pay out Girdler and company. Surprisingly, after all these troubles they all still worked together like nothing happened, which led to *Day of the Animals* in 1977 - again funded and distributed by Montoro. This other "killer animal" flick also features Christopher George and Richard Jaeckel and is not surprisingly considered by many fans a sequel in tone.

But the real sequel, aptly called *Grizzly II: The Concert*, went into production five years later in Hungary, Budapest, again written by Joan McCall and David Sheldon, but this time under the inept direction of local producer/actor turned director André Szöts. The sequel - which also goes by the weird title *Predator: The Concert* – was never finished because the production went into financial troubles, and the Hungarian government seized most of the production's equipment. At least it's one of the explanations. The other one is that it's just a bad film.

A faded work print of the unfinished version with none of the necessary bear-action to be called a grizzly-movie and a temp-score featuring Michael Jackson songs got illegally released online in 2007. Before that *Grizzly II: The Concert* was already the holy grail of unreleased movies, but when it was readily available to the horror crowd the sequel became something of a cult film in its own right. And rightfully so. Because there's no better drinking game than "spot the stars." *Grizzly II: The Concert* features the talents of non-other than A-list stars like George Clooney, Charlie Sheen, Laura Dern, Timothy Spall, John Rhys-Davies, and Louise Fletcher but also has starring roles of loved genre talent like Charles Cyphers, Jack Starrett, Deborah Raffin, Ian McNeice, and Barbie Wilde. Do I hear a roar of hairy excitement?

Steve De Roover

Steve De Roover was born in Bonheiden, Belgium, in the holy year of 1981. He quickly garnered much love for the 7th art, especially the world of the macabre. At the age of 20, he started working as a movie critic for several respected film websites like *DVD Info*, *MovieGids*, and *Friday the 13th Franchise*, as well as for printed publications like *Publicity Magazine*.

In 2010, Steve De Roover started working behind the scenes on various feature films and television shows. He made a name for himself as a location manager and script supervisor. Three years later, Steve directed and co-produced the horror short *Un Homme Bien* (based on a story by author Vanessa Morgan), which received positive notices at a wide selection of film festivals around the world. In 2015, Steve co-founded Skladanowsky, a production company specialized in edgy shorts, documentaries, music videos, corporate films, and low-budget genre features.

IN THE SHADOW OF KILIMANJARO (1986)

By Charles M. Kline

Having seen quite a few horror films over the years, starting with a theatrical viewing of *The Beast Within* at age five, I'm not the least bit hesitant to admit the majority of my personal movie library falls into this particular genre. Although the demons, ghosts, and various monsters from these features provided me with their fair share of scares, I sometimes thought the most frightening premise of all would be to find myself in a situation where I was no longer at the top of the food chain, but rather a step-down, serving as a meal for something else. This idea, that I could easily become chow or a chew toy to an animal under the wrong circumstances, was terrifying to me because it could actually happen. However, the fear of such a scenario pales in comparison to the sheer palpable terror I'd feel if I were surrounded by savage creatures with a hankering for living flesh. No, I'm not referring to zombies. Try starved baboons driven to desperation due to environmental factors out of human control, which brings me to the subject of this essay.

I first discovered the horror film *In the Shadow of Kilimanjaro* (released in 1986) back when I was serving a tour as a U.S. Navy sailor in Misawa, Japan from 1996-98. I would spend my off-duty time checking out movies from various video stores on the base and also one in town, where the only English word the proprietor of the place knew was "tomorrow." One day, while at a video rental place on base I rarely got to since it wasn't within reasonable walking distance from my barracks building, I let my friend, Ken

Richter (a trained archeologist turned sailor who also introduced me to H.P. Lovecraft and Guinness) pick the movies, and he grabbed two: *The Unnamable* and *In the Shadow of Kilimanjaro*. Although I must confess that I recall very little of either film, probably on account of too much snake sake, something about the latter one stuck with me during the inaugural viewing. It was also the first film that came to mind when I was asked to contribute to this project.

Flashing forward to 2015, I was quite surprised to discover my attempt to track down a digital version of *In the Shadow of Kilimanjaro* on iTunes, Netflix, or even YouTube was like embarking on a quest for the Holy Grail. In fact, I ended up ordering the tape from Amazon and was thankful I still had a working VHS player in my house when a clean copy arrived in the mail a few days later. I eagerly fired up the popcorn machine, turned down the lights, and took a trip down nostalgia lane as I popped in the tape to view it the same way I had originally done about 17 years earlier. Bring on the raging monkeys.

The movie opens at dawn in what is probably Amboseli National Park (formerly the Maasai Amboseli Game Reserve), and we see a Maasai child out walking the brush alone. After stopping to retrieve a handful of earthworms from a hole in the ground, the child is suddenly confronted by a cobra that snaps into action with a hiss and bares its venomous fangs. The child is startled at first but quickly assumes a razor-like focus while pulling back on a loaded slingshot. Then the cobra closes in and the child fires, hitting the deadly snake with a skilled hunter's marksmanship. The danger has passed - or so we're led to believe until something even more threatening (unseen by the viewer) stalks the child with a predatory purpose and strikes, thus setting the tone of the entire picture in those first few minutes.

Shot entirely on location in Kenya, at least according to the credits, *In the Shadow of Kilimanjaro* (written by producer Jeffrey

Frygtindgydende og dødsens farlige. 90.000 desperate aber – sult og tørst tvinger dem til angreb på alt og alle.

S.O.S. KILIMANJARO

SHARAD PATEL PRÆSENTERER JOHN RHYS-DAVIES & TIMOTHY BOTTOMS I EN FILM AF RAJU PATEL
– IN THE SHADOW OF KILIMANJARO –
MED MICHELE CAREY · IRENE MIRACLE · CALVIN JUNG · DON BLAKELY · PATTY FOLEY
MANUSKRIPT AF JEFFREY M. SNELLER & MICHAEL HARRY · MUSIK AF ARLON OBER
EXECUTIVE PRODUCENT BACHU PATEL PRODUCERET AF JEFFREY M. SNELLER & GAUTAM DAS INSTRUERET AF RAJU PATEL
EN INTERMEDIA PRODUKTION · UDLEJNING OBEL FILM

Sneller and Michael Harry) is a fictionalized account of a supposedly true event that took place in the country during the drought of 1984 when baboons attacked humans once the natural resources upon which they subsisted grew scarce. After three fresh viewings prior to scribing this essay, I would say Raju Patel's debut feature (the Kenyan-born producer's only turn in the director's chair) is more akin to *Planet of the Apes* meets *Jaws* than anything else. The film's premise revolves around the consequences of the drought, which has turned 90,000 hungry baboons into carnivorous primates after most of the other animals on the reserve have migrated elsewhere - meaning bad news for the townspeople of Namanga, who are looking quite tasty to these furry foragers in the face of famine.

Jack Ringtree (Timothy Bottoms), whom we first see playing bumper cars with a couple of rhinos, is the game warden of the reserve (known to the locals as "The Great White Hunter"), and it's his job to take care of the animals in his jurisdiction. He pays a visit to Chris Tucker (John Rhys-Davies), who is on a government contract to operate a mine there in Namanga, and warns him to watch out for predators seeking food after a young girl's mother has probably been killed by such an animal due to the droughts. Ringtree also advises Tucker to pull his crew out until there's a break in the weather, but Tucker replies that he still has another 51 days on his contract and needs to meet his quota there at the mine, or he's through. Although each of these two men has a conflicting goal, which will collide as the baboon attacks become bolder and more frequent (Ringtree wants Namanga evacuated while Tucker wants to keep the mine running), the nemesis they both share will eventually override their differences and serve to unite them in a common cause to protect the people of Namanga.

Other notable characters include the following: Jack's wife, Lee (Irene Miracle), who arrives from California to tell him she's filed for a divorce; Ginny Hansen (Michele Carey), the proprietress of a local hotel that turns into a well-stocked pantry for the baboons at the film's climax; Emerson Maitland (Leonard Trolley), an old and eccentric British colonel with a seemingly unquenchable thirst for gin; and District Officer Tshombe (Carl Vundla), the head law enforcement figure in Namanga. A couple of Tucker's men, Julius X. Odom (Don Blakely) and Mitsuko Uto (Calvin Jung), provide a bit of comedy relief. Human casting aside, the real stars of this horror show are the baboons – the mechanical ones created by Bob Wasson but also the live ones, which were apparently captured under the supervision of the Kenyan Ministry of Tourism and Wildlife from areas where they had been a nuisance to the local population (can we say irony?) and rehabilitated upon the film's completion to their natural surroundings. Honorable mention also goes out to Percy Edwards for the "baboon voices," which makes me wonder what the recording sessions for that must have been like.

In spite of the film's many flaws – weak characterization (with the exception of Bottoms and Rhys-Davies), absurd plot elements (like the prop plane calamity), laughable baboon puppet moments, or an anticlimactic denouement – *In the Shadow of Kilimanjaro* makes up for what it lacks with style and visual flair. There's also plenty of blood in the span of 94 minutes to keep gore-hounds like myself entertained, including some severed limbs and chewed faces. One of the best (if not the most harrowing) scenes occurs about half an hour in when the baboons launch an attack against a miner who's changing a tire after getting a flat. All in all, this is an animal attack feature that deserves to be resurrected from obscurity. I'm also willing to bet the band Toto indeed misses the rains in Africa… especially when there are massive droughts, and the baboons start looking for something to eat.

Charles M. Kline

Charles M. Kline only recently discovered wolves had raised him until the age of two and that his "real parents" found him while camping in Montana.

As an aspiring author and illustrator, Charles M. Kline earned a BFA in Creative Writing for from Full Sail University and contributed an essay to the 2014 Rondo award-winning book *Hidden Horror: A Celebration of 101 Underrated and Overlooked Fright Flicks.*

He also enjoys drawing cartoons and longs to live in a Charles Addams house in the Midwest.

Visit his blog: chasmkline.wordpress.com.

JAWS (1975)

By Warren Fahy

In the summer of 1975, the trajectory of my life changed forever. Not only did I acquire a Sheriff Brody-like fear of the water along with millions of other movie-goers around the world, but, along with thousands of other impressionable young movie fans, I was bitten by the bug for telling stories through writing or film. The impact of *Jaws* would turn out to be lifelong. That summer I began writing my first novel, an epic ocean voyage about battling sea monsters. I made a *Jaws*-sized shark head out of foam-rubber and chicken wire, which was used in a Super 8 backyard movie with my friends. I carved a miniature shark, painted it and coated it with silicone just like the famous "Bruce" shark used in the movie. I devoured the plethora of paperbacks that soon came out about sharks and listened incessantly to John Williams' Oscar-winning soundtrack, much to my twin sister's chagrin. I got an aquarium, sketched Quint from Jaws, and even wrote a screenplay adapting the story of Gregor Mendel, the Moravian friar who discovered the laws of heredity by studying his pea garden, into a parody of *Jaws* – the shark was replaced with a giant man-eating pea.

And, of course, I saw *Jaws* again every chance I got. When my family took a vacation the next summer to Mexico City, *Jaws* was playing in the biggest movie theater I had ever seen. My parents dropped me off on the way to a tourist attraction after my insistence on seeing it for the sixth time. I bought a "TIBURON" chocolate bar with the famous *Jaws* movie poster on it and munched away as I watched the subtitled print. I was outraged when the projectionist adlibbed censorship with a piece of cardboard he lowered over the screen whenever one of the best parts, the gory ones, was approaching. I still resent that shadowy hand inching the cardboard over the projector's lens, then backing away as he realized he was a little too soon, then plunging the screen into darkness just as something scary happened.

The year after that, I accompanied my stepfather on a trip to Martha's Vineyard, the Amity Island of the movie, to visit his elderly aunts, and I was in paradise as around every corner was a familiar filming location. In the Gulf of California, my sister and I paddled far out on rafts into the warm shallow waters and noticed after a while that a dozen little shark fins were circling us. We kicked furiously back to the beach expecting to lose our toes to the tiny carnivores at any moment. Later, on a trip to Catalina, I watched for an hour as a shark swam in the bevel of water parted by the boat's prow, its toothy frown unmoving as I swore its emotionless eyes were glaring back at me. It knew; I was obsessed with *Jaws*.

Jaws permanently changed other things: summer movies would never be the same, Steven Spielberg became a household name, people developed a largely unrealistic fear of these primitive monsters of the deep, and doubtlessly a wave of future marine biologists were launched into universities around the world. Many modern filmmakers cite *Jaws* among their seminal inspirations. Certainly, many authors like myself can do the same. When I published my first novel, *Fragment*, the president of Bantam/Dell at Random House, Irwyn Applebaum (who never spoke to authors), summoned me into his New York office. He told me that he had published *Jaws* and *Jurassic Park* and that every once in a while a novel like those came along. *Fragment* was one of them. Well, I was overwhelmed, of course. But those two books and films were part of my own DNA; I was the monster those monsters had created.

One of the great lessons all of us learned from *Jaws* was, of course, a happy accident. The mechanical shark didn't work very well. So the writers and young director were forced to infer the existence of the beast lurking beneath the surface for as long as possible. The music score often substituted for the menace in the murk; our brains did the rest. The reveal of the denizens of Henders Island from my novel was patterned after that progression, paying out clues stingily so that the reader's mind would have done most of the work before the final unveiling of the Henders ecosystem in all it gory glory. I had learned from the

best. *Jurassic Park*, of course, followed the same formula-all because the mechanical "Bruce" was a cantankerous contraption, and Steven Spielberg was a cagey conjurer who knew how to tap into the primal fear swimming in our collective subconscious.

Of course, a worldwide campaign against sharks ensued in the wake of *Jaws* and led in subsequent years to a plea from the bestseller's author, Peter Benchley, to stop attacking them figuratively and physically. Bans on fishing them were instituted; there was no need to panic. Even great whites did not relentlessly hunt down humans with the ferocious obsession of Freddy or Jason. We don't taste that good, apparently. The focus on sharks would shift from fear to wonder over time, and today they're celebrated by Shark Week and other annual television traditions.

JAWS
At sea, no one can hear you scream.

Shark tourism has become an institution for those who visit Australia's Great Barrier Reef. Scientists have attached tracking devices to sharks much like the one the young shark aficionado Matt Hooper used in the film, and they have been astonished to see the incredibly wide range of their annual migrations across the world's oceans. New species of sharks have been discovered, like the nightmarish mega-mouth, resembling a recurring nightmare of the most primitive and Hieronymus Bosch-like ancestors that unfold in the lithographs of the fossil record. As a result of *Jaws*, we now know more about this group of animals than we ever would have otherwise; and we actually take steps to protect them from us.

After publishing *Fragment*, I took my first vacation in 14 years, traveling to the island of Kauai. When I was walking back to our lodging from Poipu Beach with a friend's young son in tow, there was a reminder that sharks are not to be taken lightly, either. A teenager in crutches was being interviewed by a TV news crew overlooking a small inlet favored by local body surfers. His leg had been bitten off below the knee by a tiger shark a few weeks earlier, and he was describing the encounter for the news team. These creatures that evoke such horror, eating machines that treat everything, including us, like food, still and always will strike an uneasy balance of dread and wonder. They're the stuff that nightmares are made of and will inspire the hearts of filmmakers, storytellers, and fish tales forever more.

Warren Fahy

New York Times bestselling author Warren Fahy was a bookseller, editor, database designer, and lead writer for Rock Star Games' *Red Dead Revolver* and *WowWee Robotics*. He also helped the Beastie Boys coin the word "mullet" to refer to the notorious hairstyle, a word recently inducted into the Oxford English Dictionary.

Having started writing novels when he was 12, his first published novel, the science thriller *Fragment*, was published by Random House. About an island isolated for half a billion years on which evolution created an alien ecosystem of lethal species, *Fragment* charts the discovery of this last piece of a lost supercontinent by the hapless crew of a reality TV show in the middle of the Southern Pacific Ocean. The Navy closes in as the chance some species might make it off the island threatens to destroy the world. *Fragment* was nominated for a BSFA and an International Thriller Award and is published in 19 languages. The sequel, *Pandemonium*, examines what would happen if those species were smuggled off the island... and weaponized.

Fahy resides in San Diego.

JERSEY SHORE SHARK ATTACK (2012)

By Katelyn Rushe

We can all say what we want about the quality of Syfy's Shark Week made-for-TV movies, but one thing we can agree on is that the studios producing those pictures know how to name them. In the era of titles like *Cloverfield*, *Lucy*, and *Pacific Rim*, it's so refreshing to tune into a movie called *Jersey Shore Shark Attack* and know precisely what you're in for.

Another thing that should be taken into account is that the filmmakers behind such pictures usually know full well how

ridiculous those movies are, and they're usually proud to show it. It's pointless to make fun of movies like *Sharknado*, *Sharktopus*, and *Hammerhead: Shark Frenzy* because they're already making fun of themselves. That leaves us with nothing to do but sit back and enjoy those features for the laughable, beefed up self-parodies that they are, which is quite easy to do with *Jersey Shore Shark Attack*.

Made during the run of the highly popular MTV reality show *Jersey Shore*, the film has a pretty simple premise: offshore construction drilling draws a school of angry CGI sharks to the

coast of New Jersey as the Fourth of July weekend kicks off, and beachgoers with gold chains and washboard abs start getting picked off like meatballs left and right. The only people who can stop the predators are local partier Tino "The Complication" Moretti, his ex-girlfriend, Nooki, and their band of other Italian-American friends with obvious knock-off nicknames. It sounds like a cheesy boatload of clichés and stereotypes, which it largely is, but since the filmmakers are aware of that, we get a lot of jokes and sight gags that are actually pretty clever.

We see the men stop to fix their gelled hair after every other gunshot they fire at the sharks. We see them throwing protein bars into the water as bait. We get a running gag where they get their friends confused with each other because so many of them are named Vinny. We even get a moment where Nooki calls out one of the gaudier male leads for not really being Italian — a common criticism of the MTV show's cast members. What's more, just to prove once and for all how tongue-in-cheek it is, the film throws in scenes and elements clearly borrowed from *Jaws* for no other reason than to poke fun at them for being borrowed. It's just great.

There's also a built up cameo from N'Sync's Joey Fatone that leads to probably the biggest laugh in the whole movie. I won't say

what happens, but when this film premiered on Syfy, it went to a commercial break right after that scene, and I spent every second of the break cracking up over what I had just witnessed. I recommend that DVD and Blu-Ray viewers pause it after that part.

Believe it or not though, *Jersey Shore Shark Attack* does have more to offer than comedy. There's more than one instance where it slows down to give itself substance, and a lot of those instances can be, I dare say, thoughtful and heartfelt.

For example, anyone familiar with *Jersey Shore* knows that the cast wasn't an easy group to sympathize with, let alone root for. This film could have gone the slasher movie route by just making the characters loathsome jerks that we want to see get killed, and while it does introduce them as such, it goes on to peel back more of their layers and show a surprisingly relatable side to them. They're not trying to get rid of the sharks just so they can go back to partying on the beaches. They're doing it to avenge one of their friends who was eaten near the start of the film, and his death is played a lot more seriously than you'd expect. We actually see the dread that they go through after his disappearance, and the sadness they feel after realizing that he's dead.

Another way the film gets us to like the heroes is by bringing in a group of snobby, rich (non-Italian) yacht club kids to pit against them. After a few minutes of seeing Tino and his pals get talked down to and covered in slurs, not only do we want them to survive the sharks, but we also want them to put those uptight bigots in their place.

That brings me to what is by far the film's most surprising element: the theme of prejudice against modern-day Italian-Americans. Yes, a Shark Week TV movie spoofing a reality show actually tackles the subject of racism, and it tackles it well. Okay, it's no *Glory* or *Dances with Wolves*, but the film does give us an interesting reminder of how wrong it is to frown on a certain group of people because of the way pop culture depicts them. If *Jersey Shore* is the misdemeanor, then *Jersey Shore Shark Attack* is the apology for it.

I also have to give serious credit to Jack Scalia, the actor who plays Tino's father, Sheriff Moretti, in the film. Scalia turns out such a phenomenal performance that I'm not entirely sure he knew what kind of a movie he was in at the time. If you watched his scenes on their own, you'd swear you were seeing clips from a serious drama; his whole arc centers around his conflict between being a better father to his screw-up son and being a better police officer even though he's aware that the people whose rules he enforces secretly despise his kind. He's the only cast member who seems to be playing a genuine person instead of a caricature, and that really makes you empathize with him.

Overall, *Jersey Shore Shark Attack* is a much better film than it ever needed to be. It's funny and satirical while also having heart, and it maintains a natural balance of those ingredients. Best of all, you don't need to know anything about the show it's mocking in order to find it entertaining. The fact that something so pleasantly amusing could come from something so brainless and pointless is a breath of fresh air in and of itself, and it's more than enough to keep shark movie fanatics afloat for an hour and a half.

Just beware of bad CGI in the water.

Katelyn Rushe

Katelyn Rushe is an independent author, illustrator, and filmmaker from Pennsylvania. She published her first novel, *Deer Lake,* at age 17 and has written numerous books, short stories, essays, and screenplays since then. She's currently editing her first novel in a science fiction/fantasy series, which is due to be released later this year. She's also involved in the filming of an upcoming post-apocalyptic web series called *Beginnings.* Her current works are available on Amazon and Kindle, and her blog *What's New with K. Ru* can be found on Blogger.

Rushe is no stranger to writing about animal attacks. Her novel *Deer Lake* tells the story of an outbreak of deer attacks near a small Canadian town and the efforts of three unlucky visitors to try and uncover the cause. Delving into action, horror, and even the supernatural, the book explores the constant struggle between predator and prey and conveys how blurred the lines separating man from beast can often be.

KAW (2007)

By Paul Kane

When the "revenge of nature" films eventually petered out in the late 1970s, early 1980s – excepting a few stragglers, and the massive contribution of the *Jurassic Park* movies – who'd have thought that particular subgenre would see a resurgence in the early 21st Century? Thanks in no small part to the cheapness of CGI, that's exactly what happened, with folk once again battling killer-ants and giant spiders left and right. The Sci-Fi (subsequently Syfy) Channel, who would later strike pay dirt with the likes of *Sharknado*, were at the forefront of this resurrection with films like *Mammoth* (2006) and *Mega Snake* (2007), and it was only a matter of time before they looked to that granddaddy of all nature goes berserk movies, *The Birds*, for inspiration – hopefully with some intention of wiping out all memory of the terrible belated sequel that appeared in 1994, *Land's End*. On the surface of things, *Kaw* appeared to be just such a film. It even had an aging Rod Taylor in it (who sadly passed away in 2015) from Hitchcock's 1963 masterpiece – though, again, that only served to remind how much time had actually passed since the original... and the best.

Kaw begins with a vicious attack on a farmer by some ravens in his barn: after we get establishing shots of a lone, bare tree and miles of deserted fields. Small town sheriff Wayne Hayborne (Flanery, from *The Young Indiana Jones Chronicles* and *The Dead Zone*) – in a reversal of that famous newbie police chief from *Jaws* – is getting ready to throw in the towel and move away with his beautiful wife Cynthia (Kristin Booth, who would go on to star in *Orphan Black*); to start a new life away from the place where he grew up. "I've had my fair share of speed traps and parking tickets!" he tells her, just as he gets to the call to go and investigate the mysterious death. And, if he thought things weren't exciting enough there, he's about to get a big surprise – because the ravens aren't about to quit with just one corpse under their feathery belts.

Local crackpot Clyde MacKenzie (Stephen McHattie, probably best known for his later portrayal of Rev. Driscoll in *Haven*) has been noticing the birds massing too. However, being the archetypal crazy old man that nobody listens to until it's too late, he's promptly ignored. Not even Wayne is sympathetic to his plight: "You have a reputation, Clyde. Whoever replaces me might not cut you as much slack." As more and more incidents are reported, and roads are blocked off by vehicles that have crashed due to the ravens, Wayne suddenly has to confront the fact that our flying friends have it in for the population of the town. With Cynthia in danger and members of the girls' basketball team trapped on a school bus driven by Clyde, it begins to look like a community under siege. But what does this have to do with the nearby Mennonite population? All is finally revealed when the remaining survivors seek cover in the local diner, Betty's Cookhouse, and try to figure out just how they're going to survive.

If it didn't have such big boots to fill, *Kaw* might have been remembered as a pretty decent little chiller. There are some very effective set pieces, such as the bus attack and subsequent chase through the cornfields at night (which, granted, do smack of *Jeepers Creepers 2*); plus there's just enough bloodletting to give you a shiver but not leave you feeling cold. One scene in particular is quite disturbing, involving radio operator Luanne (played by *Prom Night II*'s Wendy Lyon) having her face pecked at by ravens after her demise. And director Sheldon Wilson knows how to both crank up the suspense and handle the bird attack sequences, balancing out the CG with physical effects. The performances are all of a good standard too, something you don't always see in low-budget creature features of this ilk. Flanery, as usual, doesn't disappoint and plays the vulnerable hero part to a tee. However, the film is hampered by a number of stock characters who seemingly have little to do other than be fodder for the birds – a lost couple driving through town for instance, Deputy Stan (Gary Powell), who is channelling David Arquette's Dewey from the *Scream* franchise, or Coach Emma (Amanda Brugel), who has her brains pecked out before even having a chance to justify why her basketball team only consists of three girls.

The explanation for why the ravens have suddenly gone nuts, leaving aside the cries of Mennonites Jacob (Vladimir Bondarenko) and Oskar (John Ralston) that they're being punished by God for mixing with the "English," is credible enough. But it's also a bit of an anti-climax and is massively hinted at way too early. It does, however, throw out another potential hazard in the form of the madness spreading to the humans and creating a *Walking Dead*-type scenario. The real beauty of Hitchcock's movie, though, came from the fact that no explanation was given at all; one day the birds had simply had enough of us blasting them out of the skies or frightening them off with scarecrows and decided to turn. That ambiguity – which extended to the ending as well, here replaced by a silly shock twist – is what made them so creepy. No matter how many "menacing" close-ups of ravens' black orbs we get in *Kaw* – enforcing the notion that they're the "eyes of the devil" as Betty (Michelle Duqhet) claims – there just isn't the same level of terror. Not even Clyde's heroics with the petrol pumps – a nod to that suspenseful scene in *The Birds*, only this time intentional (and also recalling movies like *Independence Day* where the mad person no one believes saves the day) – can save the film itself.

In short, *Kaw* is a film with great aspirations and very nearly achieves them – making it worth an hour and a half of your time – but don't expect it to be a patch on what's already been done with this subject matter before.

Paul Kane

Paul Kane is the award-winning, bestselling author and editor of over 50 books – including the *Arrowhead* trilogy, *The Butterfly Man and Other Stories*, *Hellbound Hearts*, *The Mammoth Book of Body Horror and Monsters*. His non-fiction books include *The Hellraiser Films and Their Legacy* and *Voices in the Dark*, and his genre journalism has appeared in the likes of *SFX*, *Rue Morgue* and *DeathRay*. His latest novels are *Lunar* (set to be turned into a feature film) and the Y.A. story *The Rainbow Man* (as P.B. Kane). Forthcoming from him is the sequel to *RED*: *Blood RED*. His work has been optioned and adapted for the big and small screen, including for network US television.

He has been a Guest at Alt.Fiction, SFX Weekender, Thought Bubble, Derbyshire Literary Festival, Off the Shelf, Monster Mash, Event Horizon, Edge-Lit and HorrorCon, as well as being a panelist at FantasyCon and the World Fantasy Convention.

He lives in Derbyshire, UK, with his wife Marie O'Regan, his family and a black cat called Mina.

Find out more at Paul's site www.shadow-writer.co.uk which has featured guest writers such as Stephen King, Neil Gaiman, Charlaine Harris, Dean Koontz and Guillermo del Toro.

KILLER CROCODILE (1989)

By Jonas Govaerts

What would Alfred Hitchcock do?

Steven Spielberg must have asked himself this question 40 years ago when it turned out the rubber shark for *Jaws* was a complete failure. The answer: Hide your monster as long as possible. The horror lies in what you *don't* see.

The question is if Fabrizio De Angelis, the director of the amusing *Killer Crocodile* (also known as *Murder Alligator*), ever even heard of Alfred Hitchcock. From the first scene onwards, his beefy "coccodrillo" saunters happily through the frame in all its plastic glory. *Take that, Master of Suspense!*

Jaws is a movie the Italian director obviously DID see: his film starts in exactly the same way, with a young couple arriving at the

beach. Bored of her bossy, inattentive boyfriend who takes up all the place on the towel and let her sit in the mud, the girl decides to go swimming. Alas, what happens to her next is less clear: it could be a crocodile attack; it could be a strong piece of interpretative dance; or it could be nothing but a mighty case of menstrual cramps.

No problemo, Fabrizio De Angelis must have thought. *We can begin all over again, can't we?* Cut to – indeed - a second opening scene in which two men on a boat blame pollution for the lack of fish in the area. Then the crocodile jumps up, complete with freeze-frame on the monster's gaping mouth and a big yellow title: KILLER CROCODILE! Hmm... I wonder what this film will be about.

Afterwards, the viewer's patience is being tested for a while. The heroes of the story appear to be a group of drowsy, constantly argumentative eco-warriors that ask themselves aloud what in God's name is in these floating, steaming barrels deep in the swamps – barrels that have the words TOXIC WASTE written on them in big fat letters. By the way, their leader (played by Richard Anthony Crenna, son of Richard Crenna) is called Kevin. Really: *Kevin*.

Luckily, not long after the introduction of Kev and company, follows one of the film's high points: a croc offensive on a few black kids hanging from a collapsed scaffolding (again a glaring *Jaws* imitation). Fake or not, the gigantic smacking jaws of Signor Scaleman are a *sight to behold*, especially when they close in on the legs of a panicky daddy, who, for unclear reasons, has fallen partly through the scaffolding as well. When the titular reptile choses a little later another half-caste as a victim, you begin to wonder: is this a rip-off of *Jaws* or *White Dog*?

However, the most dangerous creature in the film is not the killer crocodile but a doddering crocodile hunter named Joe (played by Ennio Girolami): imagine Quint from *Jaws* talking like a pimp from Harlem in the 1980s. "Don't lose your cool, boy," he

ANTHONY CRENNA
ANN DOUGLAS
THOMAS MOORE
WORHMAN WILLIAM
VAN JOHNSON

Dirigida por
LARRY LUDMAN

COCODRILO Asesino

barks at Kevin when he voices one of his many idiotic eco-statements. Joe is also extremely knowledgeable about crocodiles: "They get really angry when you insult them," knows Joe, after which he says aloud to the gurgling water: "Pollywog!" (meaning "tadpole," apparently the insult of choice for crocodiles). Hey, if Joe says so, it must be true.

During the last half hour, *Killer Crocodile* treats us to two more unforgettable animal attack scenes.

In the first one, our deadly water-acrobat rises almost vertically out of the water and scares an unsuspecting boat driver straight into the plunge, ready to be eaten (biologically very suspect, to say the least, but nevertheless really impressive).

And the finale, too, is something you *must* have seen: Joe stands as some sort of Ahab on the squamous back of his arch-enemy, stabbing it with his harpoon. Just before he goes under water, he shouts at Kevin: "The motor! Use the motor!" At that point, Kevin gets a stroke of genius: why doesn't he use the outboard motor of his boat to eradicate the monster? An ingenious plan, or so it seems. When the former animal lover places the whistling screw duly in the muzzle of his forthcoming antagonist, Crocy does not only explode, but his carcass bursts into flames as well... in the water. Because... science.

In other words, *Killer Crocodile* is *croc shlock* of the highest order.

And if you can't get enough of the underwater adventures of Kevin and his friends: the simultaneously shot *Killer Crocodile II* contains not only even more croc-tastic action sequences (this time, creature designer Giannetto De Rossi was promoted as director) but also the best pick-up line of all time: "Don't you know fear and near death experiences heighten and stimulate a man's reproductive organs?"

Jonas Govaerts

In 2014, Jonas Govaerts directed the most popular horror movie in Belgian history: *Cub* (original Flemish title, *Welp*).

Before breaking through with *Cub*, Jonas made the short films *Abused*, *Of Cats and Women*, *Forever*, and *Mobius*. He also worked as a director on the TV series *Monster!* and *Super 8*.

He lives in Antwerp, Belgium.

KINGDOM OF THE SPIDERS (1977)

By BJ Colangelo

In popular culture, William Shatner is a man of many iconic names. The titular role on *T.J. Hooker*, Captain James T. Kirk from *Star Trek*, and Bob Wilson in *The Twilight Zone* are all characters that have cemented his residency in an unfortunately inevitable spot during Award Season "In Memoriam" segments, but Shatner's greatest performance lies in the underrated and underappreciated animal attack film, *Kingdom of the Spiders*.

Directed by John "Bud" Cardos, *Kingdom of the Spiders* is arguably one of the better known animal attack films of the late 1970s and early 1980s. Due in large part to the cultural influence of William Shatner, cable television stations often ran *Kingdom of the Spiders* on late night programming including USA's *Up All Night*. Although the film was given a pretty wide circulation after its completion, there are many that dismiss this hidden gem as nothing more than a forgotten b-movie.

Kingdom of the Spiders opens with glaring grind house title credits as Dorsey Burnette's *Peaceful Verde Valley* plays. The juxtaposition of the song is presented when the camera shoots to a dry and dusty desert landscape. The song choice was clearly intentional and downright spectacular. As the song subsides, we're introduced to quite possibly the greatest inciting incident in cinematic history. While on the farm of Will Colby and his wife, Birch (Woody Strode and Altovise Davis), we're introduced to a lonely cow grazing in the fields. The camera angles drop extremely low as if to give the audience the POV of something small and nimble. Unless someone walked into the film at that moment and had missed the glorious credits sequence and somehow wasn't sure what the title of the film is, it's safe to assume that we're seeing this cow through the eyes of a spider. Regardless, the camera stalks its prey as the cow turns its head in a deliberate fashion. This is not an exaggeration. The film opens with a cow capable of delivering dramatic tension. Eventually, the cow tightly closes its eyes and lets out a loud cry before the camera freezes on its pained expression. The same freeze-frame tactic used on the screaming counselor four years later in the opening sequence of *Friday the 13th* is used in *Kingdom of the Spiders* on a cow. While it would be easy to dismiss this opening as silly, this is precisely the moment the entire tone of the film is set. This is a film that (on paper) should be nothing more than b-movie garbage, but *Kingdom of the Spiders* is a film the director is genuinely taking seriously.

Predictably, the cow dies, and there's no other choice than to call in our hero, cowboy/veterinarian "Rack" Hansen (William Shatner), to solve the mysterious death. As expected, animal doctors with a penchant for lasso tricks apparently aren't great at solving deadly spider bite deaths, so city-girl entomologist, Diane Ashley (Tiffany Bolling), is called in to help solve the mystery while sporting around in her freshly feathered hair and sexy bell bottom

pants. Ashley discovers the cow died from an abundance of spider venom, and Hansen quickly dismisses her claims as impossible. Despite her PhD education (she's an entomologist, Rack!), it takes a few more dead animals for Rack to finally listen to her findings. Not only is there a dangerous spider roaming the land, but there are also dozens of spider mounds filled with thousands of poisonous eight legged creepies popping up all over Verde Valley. The townsfolk continue to make stupid decisions instead of

listening to Ms. Ashley (because why would desert farmers listen to a city-slickin' learned lady in 1977?) and completely exacerbate their spider problem. Suddenly we have people shooting their hands simply because a spider is on it, people being trapped inescapable webs, and an entire town taking the "kill it with fire" mentality seriously and destroying their city.

Shatner delivers a performance that's surprisingly convincing. Granted, his character is pretty unlikable, but he hadn't evolved yet into the walking parody of "Shatner-esque" acting style. He definitely chews the scenery every time he's onscreen, but there's a slight level of John Wayne swagger to his role that almost makes his undeserving confidence somewhat palatable.

Kingdom of the Spiders is completely deserving of attention because it's a film that simply cannot exist anywhere outside of itself. For one thing, the film was made during the primetime of practical effects. Meaning, the spiders crawling all over William Shatner's beautiful face were 100% real. The filmmakers reportedly spent $50,000 of the film's $500,000 budget on real tarantulas. Tarantulas as a species are actually pretty terrified of humans, so these actors not only had creepy crawlies all over their bodies, but they often had wind or water sprayed at them to force the spiders towards the humans. On a somewhat depressing note, this also means a lot of real life spiders were slaughtered during the making of this film. This was long before animal rights committees were involved in film production, so spiders were authentically squashed, thrown, run over with a car, and set on fire. *Kingdom of the Spiders* isn't a great film because it killed real animals, but it will make your skin crawl trying to watch people being covered by live spiders.

Horror films are often hailed as the proverbial breeding ground for young talent, and *Kingdom of the Spiders* was no exception. William Shatner had already become a household name, but the film's makeup artist was a young Ve Neill, who went on to win Academy Awards for her work on *Mrs. Doubtfire* and *Ed Wood* in addition to her role as a judge on the special effects makeup competition *FACE/OFF*. The film's co-editor, Steven Zaillan also went on to win an Academy award for writing the screenplay for *Schindler's List*. Historically, *Kingdom of the Spiders* cast two of the most important African-American actors in cinematic history; Sammy Davis Jr.'s wife as Birch Colby and Walter Colby's Woody Strode. For those unaware, Strode was one of the first two men to break the color barrier for the National Football League in the

1940s and played college football with Jackie Robinson.

History aside, *Kingdom of the Spiders* is a genuinely fun film. It's guaranteed to give you the heebie-jeebies, while also eliciting some laughter from the public domain available sound design. All of the "tense" moments use the same repeating three chords as made popular in *The Twilight Zone* and later in films like *Dumb and Dumber.*

Kingdom of the Spiders truly is the godfather of many of our favorites. When discussing the film *Arachnophobia,* the producer of *Kingdom of the Spiders,* Igo Kantor said in an interview with Fangoria Magazine, "I thought it was a copy, but you don't go and sue Spielberg!" Perhaps the film wasn't made under the most humane of conditions; its bleak ending, powerhouse cast, and unintentional hilarity allows it to stand above the rest of most animals attack films.

BJ Colangelo

BJ Colangelo is special. Not in a "please don't give her chocolate or knives" kind of special but pretty close. A recovering toddlers & tiaras alumna, BJ is a seasoned musical theater performer, filmmaker, and freelance writer. With a B.A. in Theater and English Literature from Western Illinois University, BJ is passionate about examining female representation within horror films.

In addition to her writing, BJ is one of the co-founders of Sickening Pictures and is proud to be one of the youngest survivors of pancreatic cancer on record.

You can find her work online at *Day of the Woman* and *Icons of Fright*. Follow her on twitter @bjcolangelo.

LAKE PLACID (1999)

By Alex J. Cavanaugh

This 1999 film makes no apologies for what it is – a b-movie laced with snarky, sarcastic humor. The storyline involves a giant, man-eating crocodile that terrorizes a lake in Maine. So, what sets this apart from every other nature run amok film? It certainly isn't the plot, which runs through all the familiar tropes of the genre as if the director had a monster movie checklist. No, what sets this film apart is its stellar cast, quirky characters, and a lake full of hilarious dialogue.

While the movie's title implies the body of water is Lake Placid, it actually takes place at a fictional Black Lake. (As one of the main characters sarcastically replies, "Yeah, we wanted to call it Lake Placid, but someone said that name was taken.")

From the opening sequence, we're treated to a *Jaws*-inspired attack in the lake. While far from original, it's still tense and sets up the ensuing investigation to discover what lurks in the water. Every genre of film has its clichés, so the question isn't *Have I seen this before?* But *Am I enjoying the ride?*

What makes this film is the director's flair for humor and the cast's ability to deliver the rapid-fire lines with snark. The pacing is perfect, and the 82-minute film feels neither too short nor too long. There are echoes of several monster movies, including *Tremors*. While not as imaginative as that film, it clearly establishes an identity through its quirky characters.

Brendan Gleeson is the first main cast member we meet. He's perfect as the sarcastic and weary sheriff, Hank Keough. He's the brunt of many jokes, but he knows how to dish it out as well.

Gleeson's calm demeanor and droll sense of wit elevate the character from back country sheriff to someone who's a keen observer and an asset to the team.

Bridget Fonda plays Kelly Scott, a paleontologist who works for a museum. She's sent to Maine to look at the tooth pulled from the body of the first attack. It's not by choice, though, as her boss is sending her out to cool off after terminating their inter-office romance. Kelly is someone who hates the outdoors and equates camping with a hotel room. It's this aversion to all things natural that places her in many funny situations, and Fonda keeps the

character from going over the top. Although she has her moments: "I will NOT calm down! This is the second time I have been hit with a severed head, and I don't like it!"

Bill Pullman is the Fish and Game officer, Jack Wells. He's a good "every man" and approaches his role with a smirk to let us know he's in on the joke. While he does have his sarcastic moments, he's the straight man in a sea of comedians.

Joining the group unannounced is Hector Cyr, played to the fullest by Oliver Platt. He's a rich, eccentric professor who swims with crocodiles and claims they're God-like. His social skills leave much to be desired, which is to say he's sarcastic and rude. The character is abrasive, but Platt plays him with just enough humor and charm that it doesn't grate on the viewer's nerves. The unpredictability of the character breathes new life into the film.

He does manage to grate on the other characters' nerves though, with the exception of Kelly and the female deputy he enchants. This adds to the tension and the biting snark. The banter between Hector and the sheriff is priceless as they go after each other verbally and sometimes physically:

Sheriff: "I never heard of a crocodile crossing an ocean."
Hector: "Well, they conceal information like that in books."

Rounding out the cast is Betty White as Mrs. Bickerman, the crazy old lady living on the lake. She's no Golden Girl, though. Older fans of White will recall her language-laced comedy, and here she's allowed to slip into that role, spewing obscenities left and right. Foul or clean, everything she says is dripping with sarcasm: "I'm rooting for the crocodile. I hope he swallows your friends whole. You might want to arrest me for that, too. Is that a crime? To wish the chewing of law enforcement?"

The special effects were done by Stan Winston Studios, who also co-produced the film with Fox 2000 Pictures. Some of the

CGI shows its age, especially with the land animals. During the crocodile's attack on a bear, you can see the mesh doesn't quite move right. However, the crocodile effects are excellent, utilizing both CGI and life-sized animatronics. The scene where Hector and the crocodile confront each other in the lake is chilling and tense. At that point, you believe there really is a giant crocodile in the water.

There's irony within the movie that touches upon real life. The sheriff muses how PETA would feel about Mrs. Bickerman feeding her cows to the crocodile. I'm sure while watching the film, viewers wonder how PETA felt about the cow dangling from the helicopter as well. In addition, White herself is a major spokesperson for PETA.

Steve Minor directed the film, and his credits range from movies such as *Friday the 13th Part III*, *House*, and *Forever Young*, to television shows such as *The Wonder Years* and *Switched at Birth*. His style of directing *Lake Placid* is similar to *House*, only more polished and refined. He knows how to lighten a tense scene with humor while reigning in some of the more over-the-top situations. Another director might've played it straight, forgoing the crass humor that is the movie's charm.

The film was a financial success, grossing almost $57 million worldwide. It spawned three, made-for-video sequels. A few stars turn up in the sequels, but none of the original cast returned, and the subsequent movies were not as well rated.

Although set in Maine, it was actually filmed in British Columbia, Canada. Buntzen Lake made a perfect substitute for the fictional Black Lake, and the outdoor scenes are very lush and beautiful.

Lake Placid is one of those rare gems. It's not an Oscar winner, nor is it a straight to video bottom feeder. It's just a fun guilty pleasure, one that will tickle your funny bone even as it satisfies your monster animal gone wild craving.

Alex J. Cavanaugh

Alex J. Cavanaugh has a Bachelor of Fine Arts degree and works in web design, graphics and technical editing. A fan of all things science fiction, his interests range from books and movies to music and games. He plays guitar in a Christian rock band and lives in the Carolinas with his wife.

Online he's the Ninja Captain and founder of the *Insecure Writer's Support Group*.

He's the author of Amazon Best Sellers *CassaStar*, *CassaFire*, and *CassaStorm*. The science fiction-space opera trilogy follows the adventures of a pilot named Byron. His latest book, *Dragon of the Stars*, focuses on a quest to find a legendary ship.

Visit his blog: alexjcavanaugh.blogspot.com.

LOCUSTS (1974)

By Amanda Reyes

During the heyday of the made for television movie (roughly 1969-1979), these telefilms piggybacked on, borrowed, and sometimes outright stole images and ideas from their big screen counterparts. So, it's probably no surprise that TV movies embraced the popular horror genre, even when it seemed impossible to work around budgets, restrictions (no nudity or violence!), and reduced shooting schedules. Classic horror and traditional shocks were often the

names of the small screen game, but the telefilm was certainly not above capitalizing on the most popular subgenre tropes of the day, and eco-horror was a popular go to blueprint during this era.

On the face of it, and much like the disaster films from the same period, nature run amok movies were perfect for the small screen in that they offered lurid titles, the promise of action-packed set pieces (without always delivering), and recognizable actors in a centralized location. *Locusts* was one of the first of the somewhat short-lived small screen "insects attack" films, predating both the well-remembered *It Happened at Lakewood Manor* (aka *Ants*), and *Tarantulas: The Deadly Cargo* (both 1977). But unlike those fun, fluffy time wasters, *Locusts* was something different. It may be that because prolific small screen director Richard T. Heffron was not generally a horror filmmaker and seemed more interested in intense family dramas (*The Morning After* (1974), *A Killer in the Family* (1983)) that this telefilm, which originally aired on October 9th, 1974, comes across as a curious and absorbing amalgamation of a critique on World War II era credos and eco-horror. Whatever the reason, this ABC Movie of the Week gives the goods in the bug invasion scenes but constantly pulls back the grasshopper plague to explore the dynamics of a family attempting to save their rundown farm.

Set during the Second World War, the rolling, brown prairies of Southern Alberta, Canada, stand-in for Anytown, USA. *Locusts* feature a teenaged Ron Howard as Donny Fletcher, a soldier who has been discharged before he can cross the pond and bomb the enemy as a fighter pilot. A horrible flight training accident that killed Donny's friend has left the young man traumatized, and he's forced to return to a small town that is currently building itself on the bravery of their young men fighting in the war. Humiliated and

ostracized, Donny has to face his disgraced father, Amos (Ben Johnson in a hard-nosed performance), who is determined to isolate Donny even more. Further stress is added to a family already in crisis when an immense horde of locusts is seen making their way towards the Fletcher's small town. For these down on their luck ranchers, total destruction also means absolute destitution.

World War II is an obvious stand-in for the disenchantment of Vietnam – Donny is shunned and/or harassed the moment he arrives home. Shrugging off all of the ideological descriptions of a barrel-chested war hero, Howard brings an immense amount of compassion to his character, who is simply a kid longing for his father's acceptance. Ben Johnson is frustrating as Amos, but he personifies a faux bravado that the men of the previous generation were raised on. He can't accept that Donny suffered a real trauma, instead focusing on the symbol of weakness he now represents to society.

Tearing apart the sentimental virtues of the stereotyped swagger of war films, *Locusts* possibly has more in common with *The Ballad of Andy Crocker* (1969) and *Tribes* (1970), than, say, *Maneater* (1973) or *The Beasts are on the Streets* (1978). Even Howard admitted in an interview that the screenplay was not what he was expecting: "I said yes right away, without even reading the script. I pictured myself in the cockpit of a Wildcat fighter plane, strafing island positions while a zillion US Marines were landing, slashing my way through flak to attack an enemy carrier, or knocking four Zeros out of the sky while thinking about mom, apple pie, and the right to boo the umpire. The character is just the opposite of what I had imagined. I portrayed a Navy pilot, but one who has just been medically discharged out of flight school as unfit to fly for psychological reasons. I return home to be branded a coward by my family and the rest of the community."

Also, anyone casually versed in biblical literature will quickly spot the metaphoric locusts as the massive military force that Donny had thought he'd avoided. Seen as an emblem of judgment and moral catastrophe, Donny's passage towards self-redemption hits the right dramatic beats, but unfortunately, this journey leads to a predictable endpoint, and inevitably (and frustratingly), holds firm to the idea that personal salvation can be found through gung -ho tactics.

So, while *Locusts* capitalizes on the glut of the animals run amok films that were in full force by the 1970s, it's armed with a fistful of metaphors, making this one of the quietest features to arise from the zenith of environmentally inspired terror flicks. It's probably, in fact, not often considered part of the animals run amok subgenre. This is an intense drama where grasshoppers may plague certain scenes, creating nightmarish cinematic scenarios, but, thanks to Heffron's top-notch direction, a focused script by Robert M. Young and forceful acting by the main cast, those creepy critters never overshadow the more intimate family dynamics.

Yet, while the locust attacks are methodically spread throughout the film, they're uniformly intense and showcase how genuinely game the actors were in making the set-pieces excruciating viewing. Nicknamed the "Hopper Honcho," special effects guru John Burke gathered 500,000 grasshoppers for the invasion scenes and used a centrifugal blower to hurl them onto the brave cast members (he also added some faux insects made of shredded paper and puffed wheat to give the apocalyptic effect of raining bugs). Young Lisa Gerritsen's screams of horror do not feel like acting at all, as the cast members scrape bugs out of their ears and hair and even pick them out from under their clothes.

And certainly, watching the bugs engulf Donny's home, farm and family is harrowing, but despite the admittedly exciting mayhem, *Locusts* refuses to reduce the quieter domestic turbulence to filler. Unfortunately, I have a feeling some audiences will be disappointed by this *Movie of the Week* because of what it lacks. And that's unfortunate because that means those viewers do not completely understand all that *Locusts* has.

Amanda Reyes

Amanda Reyes is a student working towards her masters in library science. She sometimes works as a freelance writer and runs the popular blog *Made for TV Mayhem*, which gives her an excuse to watch everything from *Snowbeast* to *Danielle Steel's Daddy*.

Amanda also loves soap operas, *Hart to Hart*, her husband, and two cats (but not always in that order).

Currently residing in Austin, TX, Amanda does her best to catch the *Terror Tuesday* screenings at the Alamo Drafthouse Ritz. But she's more often found writing papers on archival theory. She also thinks Peter Scolari needs to be more famous.

LONG WEEKEND (1978)

By Ingrid Dendievel

A recurring theme in horror movies is the battle between man and nature, usually in the form of formidable animals such as sharks, snakes, monkeys, wolves, and so on. The stereotypical hero will endure losses at first; the bitch and the unfortunate black man or woman die, as do a lot of innocent victims. However, at the end, man prevails, and nature is the big loser. Given the recent success of movies such as *Sharknado* – which now has already a fourth sequel – we can easily say that the public still loves this kind of horror.

But what if things were different? What if man was not the winner of the conflict? What if there were no big animals, and nature took revenge in a more subtle way? This is the premise of *Long Weekend*, an Australian movie from 1978. The director, Colin Eggleston, and writer, Everett De Roche, thus tackled the subgenre of environmental horror. According to an interview with

Spectacular Optical, De Roche got his idea for the movie from a long Easter weekend. He saw nature as having her own auto-immune system, fighting off humans behaving like cancer cells.

Unlike many American horror movies, *Long Weekend* doesn't rely on the typical "jump scenes." The creepiness of the movie relies heavily on the atmosphere. Right from the beginning there's a tense feeling. The relationship between the two main characters, Peter and Marcia, has seen better days. It's immediately clear that Marcia has a lover and is not looking forward to the camping trip Peter has planned. Once they get in the camper, the atmosphere becomes even more unpleasant. Marcia would like to spend the weekend in a hotel, but all that Peter can dream about is the isolated beach.

Before getting at the point of their destination though, the couple has to traverse a thick bush. With hardly visible, confusing signs, they soon become lost, and the bush seems to become impenetrable. In the end, Peter and Marcia decide to stop the camper and sleep in it. Not really a nice welcome.

The morning seems to bring a short positive change. The weather is beautiful, and now that the sun has come out they can orientate themselves. It turns out that they're actually close to the beach. Even Marcia's mood improves, and she helps with the tent and the cooking. Peter couldn't be happier; soon he goes swimming, surfing, and hunting.

Marcia becomes bored and frustrated and vents it off on Peter. Not only are they disrespectful towards each other but also towards nature. They throw away cigarette butts, spray insecticide, litter the camping place, and even kill an animal. Last but not least, both start to feel increasingly uneasy because of the creepy atmosphere; there's something in the air, ranging from strange noises to seemingly random attacks by animals.

Things rapidly escalate. A blue van mysteriously disappears in the sea and after a fight between Peter and Marcia, the former disappears from their camp and gets lost in the bush again. He's shocked when he finds an empty tent with an abandoned dog in it. When Peter reaches camp again, he finds Marcia harpooned to death. In a complete state of panic, he runs away to his early demise.

Long Weekend belongs to the category of "Ozploitation" movies. The word originated from a documentary called *Not Quite Hollywood: The Wild, Untold Story of Ozploitation!* by director Mark Hartley. Oz refers to Australia, whereas exploitation movies are low-budget horror, action, and horror movies. "Ozploitation" movies were popular between the early 1970s and late 1980s, and some of its most famous examples were *Mad Max* and *Razorback*. The introduction of this genre of films coincided with the introduction of the R-rating which allowed directors more onscreen nudity and violence. According to the documentary, "Ozploitation" movies were thought to be vulgar by the critics and film historians and were even overlooked by the official Australian cinema.

Long Weekend was made in 1978 but was only released in 1979. Although the writer, director, and two main actors were household names, the movie was a flop in Australia. Elsewhere, the movie was a commercial success. Apparently, the Australians were not ready (yet) for this kind of horror. Movie critics were quite positive, however, about *Long Weekend*, which even won a couple of prizes at movie festivals.

In 2008 – exactly 30 years later – Jamie Blanks remade the movie with Jim Caviezel and Claudia Karvan. This was Jamie Blanks' second Australian horror movie. Prior to this, he had worked on two American horror movies, *Urban Legend* (1998) and *Valentine* (2001). The differences between the two movies are minimal. The remake also follows a married couple during a long weekend to an isolated beach. The two main characters quarrel all the time, pollute the camping place, and are punished by Mother

Nature.

There are references to the original movie. In the end credits it's clear that the movie is made "In memory of Colin Eggleston," the original director. A pub in the movie is also named after the director (Hotel Eggleston). The cinematographer of the original movie, Vincent Monton, works as this movie's Second Unit Director. The original producer and main actress also worked as advisors.

Although a big name like Jim Caviezel was connected to the movie, the 2008 version of *Long Weekend* was a huge flop, with audiences and critics alike. In Australia the movie wasn't even released in the movie theaters.

In the meantime, the original *Long Weekend* has become a cult movie. If you're looking for a non-mainstream horror movie, this is it. It's quite astonishing, to say the least, how a movie can creep you out without the use of big animals or special effects. Let the creepy crawlies finish the job in 92 minutes. And let Mother Nature have the last laugh.

Ingrid Dendievel

Ingrid Dendievel has been a movie fan from the moment she could watch television. For 10 years, she worked as a movie critic for the Belgian online movie magazine *Moviegids*, where she specialized in author movies and foreign films. Nowadays, she has become addicted to YouTube and Netflix and is still a devout Oscar fan.

When she's not watching movies or teaching languages, she and her fiancé travel all over Europe to off the beaten track destinations. She likes to hug cows in Belgium, photograph wild horses in Denmark, enjoy a beer spa in the Czech Republic, climb dead volcanoes in Hungary, enjoy fine dining in Estonia and Albania and encounter bears in Germany. Sometimes, movies inspire her choice of destination; she has been to the Potemkin Stairs in Odessa and the Wolf's Lair in Poland. She hasn't stopped writing, since she pens down all her travel adventures on her own website: road-tripping-europe.com.

MONKEY SHINES (1988)

By Megan Fisher

Monkey Shines is an American movie from 1988 written and directed by George Romero. Some of Romero's other notable works include *Night of the Living Dead, The Crazies, Creepshow,* and many other famous films.

Monkey Shines depicts the life of Allan Mann, a promising young athlete who's crippled when he's hit by a car whilst running with cinderblocks in his backpack. Paralyzed from the neck down, he can no longer perform basic functions such as turning the pages of his law textbooks, climbing the stairs in his house, or calling someone on the telephone without the support of someone else. Allan's life goes from a dream to a nightmare as his girlfriend leaves him for his doctor, his overbearing mom tries to become a bigger part in his life, and his friends begin tiptoeing around him and treating him differently. To help him cope with his new life, Allan's friend Geoffrey lends him a monkey from his lab, Ella, whom he has secretly injected with a mysterious serum to make monkeys more human and intelligent. The relationship between the two rapidly grows stronger, and as Ella is continuously injected with the serum, she and Allan connect on a telepathic level. Ella begins acting out his most animalistic wishes and even attempts to kill his new romantic interest, Melanie.

Monkey Shines is heavy on themes of love, animal vs. human, jealousy, and many more. The audience is taken on a tumultuous ride as the relationship between Allan and Ella intensifies, she becomes his new best friend, his companion, and the only one who can understand him, and suddenly Ella begins killing off the people

Allan wishes ill on during fits of animalistic rage. Allan is forced to rip her from his heart and his home, and she's sent away. However, Ella loves Allan. She's a piece of him just as much as he's a piece of her and she won't let him leave her that easily. She finds her way back into his home and tries to take everyone he has left away from him. Once she has taken him hostage, Allan is left with no choice but to deceive her and play the songs they used to enjoy together. As soon as Ella is comfortable and hugging Allan, he bites into her throat and ends her life. The love that Ella held in her heart for Allan ended up being her downfall. She was too trusting, too loving, and too chemically altered for their relationship to really last. Her human emotions are what blinded her and his human intellect is what killed her.

On the other side, Allan was trying his hardest to detach himself from Ella. He no longer had a need for his animal

companion. He had other humans to help care for him, other humans that he loved. He was ready to move on, and Ella wouldn't allow that. He was forced into a battle of animals vs. human. Whether he was on the human side or the animal side was never clearly defined. Whenever Allan was around Ella he became enraged, spiteful, and angry. She brought out the beast inside of him that most humans can keep locked away. It was because they understood each other so well that he was able to end her, and it was also because they understood each other so well that her death affected him the way it did as seen through his sobs. He exploited the humanness within her, the piece of her that loved him and got her to trust him again. No matter how intelligent that monkey may have been, emotions are what killed her and humanity is what won the battle of man vs. wild.

Another huge aspect of the film is the monkeys, from the ones playing Ella to the others in the background. The first monkey cast to play Ella was named Emelia. She was trained to perform the necessary tricks and actions required of Ella, but when it was time to shoot, she froze and refused to act. Luckily, one of the trainers had her own monkey, Boo. The pair was described by director George Romero as being, "completely one." Boo turned out to be just what they needed; she performed the tricks, and she was quite the character. While trying to film the scene where Ella is feeding Allan grapes, Boo would fake out Jason Beghe, who played Allan, and pretend to feed him grapes and at the last minute would either eat them herself or throw them. However, one time, it appeared as though she was going to follow through and quit the games, but right before Jason's mouth closed, Boo swapped the grape for some of her poop and put it right in his mouth. The rest of the monkeys were uncooperative and had to be coaxed into following cues. The cameramen would dress up in crazy outfits and try and distract them. The monkeys would do things right only once, and then they would become wise to the intentions of the crew and would refuse to do them again.

Tom Savini and Greg Nicotero created monkey hands, monkey replicas, robotic monkeys, monkeys that could fly around, rubber monkeys, etc. They looked incredibly realistic, and perhaps this is why the special effects are so unnoticeable. Savini and Nicotero were so dedicated to making things look as real as possible that they even purchased a dead cat from a biology lab so that when Allan throws Ella from his mouth and she lands on the floor, her dead body looks realistic. Dead Ella is actually a lifeless

cat; that's how far they went for this movie.

Monkey Shines received mediocre reviews at the time of its release and is still not widely known today. I went into the film not expecting much, as my older brother told me how *Monkey Shines* was one of the more wacky and fun animal attack movies. This statement seems ludicrous after having watched the film a few times. The story of Ella and Allan is tragic. It's a story of loving someone so much it kills you. The love between Ella and Allan is real, and having Ella played by such an adorable monkey made it that much more tragic. We all knew Allan had to win, but if there were any other way the scenario could have played out, I would have wanted it that way. With its various themes, astounding acting from the monkeys, and notable special effects, *Monkey Shines* is not only a movie that casual watchers can enjoy, but film critics and connoisseurs as well. Even today, *Monkey Shines* has the potential to reach so many more audiences and to become a beloved classic.

Megan Fisher

Megan Fisher is an English major studying at her local community college while working part-time at In-n-Out Burger.

She's an avid cat and animal lover, and watching animal attack movies is a tricky thing for her to do because of that. She guesses that can be seen as a nod to the special effects departments for making animal deaths look so realistic and also to the storytellers for making the stories so touching.

Her brother, Russell Fisher, runs a blog called *The Overlook Theater* where she's featured as a reviewer and editor. She watches underrated horror movies and also new movies coming out and reviews them for fun.

NIGHT OF THE LEPUS (1972)

By Michael McCarty and Mark McLaughlin

Mark: In the words of Bela Lugosi in his starring role as Dracula, "I bid you welcome" ... to our movie review. I'm Mark McLaughlin, author of *Best Little Witch-House In Arkham*, *The Slime Of Our Lives*, and *Hideous Faces, Beautiful Skulls*.

Mike: And I'm Mark's partner in horror, Michael McCarty. We often collaborate on projects, but we each have our solo projects. I'm the author of *I Kissed A Ghoul*, *Liquid Diet & Midnight Snack: 2 Vampire Satires* and *Modern Mythmakers: 35 Interviews With Horror & Science Fiction Writers and Filmmakers*.

Mark: Together, we've written the novel *Monster Behind The Wheel* and the poetry collections, *Revenge Of The Two-Headed Poetry Monster* and *Bride Of The Two-Headed Poetry Monster*.

Mike: We'll write any book together, so long as we can put "monster" in the title.

Mark: We're here at an abandoned movie theater in Quigley Falls with some cheap Canadian beer–

Mike: And a big box of jerky in three different flavors!

Mark: Tonight, we're going to talk about the 1972 low-budget horror movie, *Night of the Lepus*.

Mike: Lepers? That sounds scary – deformities and infected flesh! Bleechh!

Mark: No, *Lepus*. It's Latin for hare. Rabbits –

Mike: Oh, that's right. I must have been thinking about *The Fog* – that had lots of leper-ghosts in it. Rabbits aren't nearly as scary. They have such innocent eyes, cute long ears and fluffy tails.

Mark: Monty Python did have a killer rabbit in *Monty Python and the Holy Grail.* And there's a guy dressed up as a monstrous rabbit in *Donnie Darko.*

Mike: Still, it's next to impossible to make a bunny seem scary.

Mark: By the way, do we have any rabbit jerky? Is that one of the three flavors?

Mike: No way – my wife Cindy and I have a pet rabbit named Latte. Cindy and Latte would never forgive me!

Mark: Oops! Forget I asked! Anyway, back to *Night Of The Lepus.* At the beginning of the film, they have some faux documentary scenes about how a few dozen rabbits went astray in Australia, and the country was soon jumping with hordes of wascally wabbits.

Mike: They're the   mathematicians of the animal kingdom – experts at multiplying!

Mark: This ambitious b-movie had an interesting cast. The biggest name was Janet Leigh from the Hitchcock classic, *Psycho.* She's also Jamie Lee Curtis' real-life mom.

Mike: Also in the movie is DeForest Kelley, who plays the president of a college. He also starred in *Star Trek*, his most high-profile role. "Damn it, Jim, I'm a college president, not a rabbit exterminator."

Mark: Arizona rancher Rory Calhoun tells DeForest Kelley about an ecological imbalance that's ruining his business: namely, excess rabbits. Kelley recruits the assistance of scientists Stuart

Whitman and Janet Leigh. Whitman comes up with the cockamamie scheme of using an experimental hormone drug to disrupt the rabbit breeding cycle.

Mike: Wouldn't cold showers or "Honey, I have a headache" have worked better?

Mark: Before long, a rabbit that has been given the experimental drug gets away, thanks to a clueless little girl who is allowed to hang around in the lab unattended. It's soon discovered that the drug is a mutagen. The escaped rabbit rejoins his kind out in the wild, and before long, new bunnies start to become big.

Mike: Big? You mean, big stars like Bugs Bunny or Roger Rabbit?

Mark: No. I mean size-big, not career-big. In time, the rabbits are over four feet tall and 150 pounds.

Mike: Those big bunnies would have given the Easter Bunny nightmares.

Mark: These ginormous hopping terrors soon become carnivorous and start attacking animals and people.

Mike: I do like the fact that the rabbits roar like lions in the film. I thought that was very funny, in an unintentional sort of way. Nowadays, there's a new rabbit breed called Lionhead rabbits, but they don't actually roar. They just have more hair framing their faces. So, Mark, what did you like best about the film?

Mark: I smile at the memory of all those slow motion scenes of giant jumping rabbits. I guess they thought that slowing them down would make them seem more menacing.

Mike: The film does have its low-budget charms. Wouldn't you agree?

Mark: Yes, it's fun to see how they make the rabbits look huge by using extreme close-ups and having the rabbits hop around on miniature sets.

Mike: Also, actors in rabbit costumes were used for brief shots in some of the attack scenes. Right now, I'm shivering with horror!

Mark: Because of all the bloody – or rather, ketchup-splashed – attack scenes?

Mike: No, because we've already run out of beer! But as you mentioned, the attack scenes do get surprisingly bloody. Their intent was to make a horror movie, and the rabbits alone sure weren't cutting it.

Mark: That seems to be the logic of most horror movies: when in doubt, splash some blood around. They would have been better off if they'd made the movie as a horror spoof … it already had a wealth of comedic moments in it!

Mike: Some of the dialogue in the movie is unintentionally hilarious. I like it when Janet Leigh says, "Rabbits aren't your bag, Roy." I also laughed out loud at the announcement, "Attention! Attention! Ladies and gentlemen, attention! There's a herd of killer rabbits headed this way, and we desperately need help!" The movie is so over-the-top that's really enjoyable.

Mark: And, it sticks to its guns as a "serious" horror movie by employing a fairly traditional ending. At the end of the film they call in–

Mike: The Cavalry? Elmer Fudd? A dump truck filled with poisoned carrots?

Mark: I'm not saying! I don't want to spoil the shocking ending for folks who haven't seen it yet. And speaking of shockers, I just finished off the last of the jerky! We've reached the end of the movie, the beer and the snacks, so that's a wrap! I guess it's time to say good night, Mike.

Mike: Good night, Mike!

Michael McCarty and Mark McLaughlin

Michael McCarty is the author of numerous books of fiction and nonfiction, as well as hundreds of articles, short stories, and poems. He received the 2008 David R. Collins Literary Achievement Award from the Midwest Writing Center. He's a five time Bram Stoker Finalist from the Horror Writers Association and the author of over 35 books including *I Kissed a Ghoul*, *Modern Mythmakers: 35 Interviews with Horror and Science Fiction Writers and Filmmakers*, *Liquid Diet & Midnight Snack: 2 Vampire Satires*, *Laughing in the Dark*, *A Little Help From my Friends* and *Monster Behind the Wheel* (co-written with Mark McLaughlin). Michael lives in Rock Island, Illinois with his wife Cindy and pet rabbit Latte, and is a former stand-up comedian, musician, and managing editor of a music magazine. Learn more about Michael at his blog site: monstermikeyaauthor.wordpress.com

Mark McLaughlin's fiction, nonfiction, and poetry have appeared in more than 1,000 magazines, newspapers, websites, and anthologies, including *Galaxy*, *Living Dead 2*, *The Best of All Flesh*, *Writer's Digest*, *Cemetery Dance*, *Midnight Premiere*, *Dark Arts*, and two volumes each of *The Best Horrorfind* and *The Year's Best Horror Stories*. His latest trade paperback story collection features his darkest tales from over the years and is entitled *Hideous Faces, Beautiful Skulls*. Other collections of his fiction include *The Slime of our Lives*, *Best Little Witch-House in Arkham*, *Beach Blanket Zombie*, *Motivational Shrieker*, *Pickman's Motel*, and *At the Foothills of Frenzy* (with coauthors Shane Ryan Staley and Brian Knight). He also wrote the novel *Monster Behind the Wheel* with collaborator Michael McCarty. He won the Bram Stoker Award for Excellence in Poetry, along with coauthors Rain Graves and David Niall Wilson, for *The Gossamer Eye*.

OF UNKNOWN ORIGIN (1983)

By Russell Fisher

Career oriented family man, Bart Hughes, finds himself home alone; his family has gone on vacation, leaving him behind to work on a special project that should land him a promotion. However, Bart isn't alone for long, as his gorgeous house is soon invaded by an intelligent rodent of unknown origin. Starring Peter Weller (*RoboCop*, *Naked Lunch*) and directed by George P. Cosmatos (*Tombstone*, *Cobra*), *Of Unknown Origin* plays like a lost feature from Polanski's apartment trilogy mixed with the typical tropes of a slasher. The latter is the reason for *Of Unknown Origin*'s obscurity. The film is incredibly smart and delivers on multiple levels appealing to both categories of cinema fans. Movie lovers who don't enjoy pretentious filmmaking get *RoboCop* battling a giant rat and his wife, Meg (playmate of the previous year Shannon Tweed), appearing in a bathing suit, underwear, and naked (briefly). Film lovers who like to ponder about what they're watching and how they're processing it, get a narrative mystery since it's obvious Cosmatos is saying something with this film but figuring out exactly what demands some thought. Especially since Cosmatos sprinkled red herrings throughout the film, in what feels like an attempt to make the thoughtful crowd think.

The film opens on the front of a house that looks out of place for what should be New York; with stone walls, large double doors, and a tower-like corner, the building looks like a modern castle. This is an important observation to make and understand, since the two major themes of the film are warfare and history, both of which apply perfectly to the urban castle metaphor. The advent of the castle dates back to the 9th and 10th centuries. Nobles built castles to better their control of the surrounding lands; they helped in both offensive and defensive maneuvering and were incredibly intimidating, which made them the best status symbol a family could have. This is later used against Bart when the rat is shown crawling through chewed holes in the walls, which now form a dungeon-esque tunnel or secret passage, fully equipped with medieval nails sticking up like ornate spikes.

The title, *Of Unknown Origin,* is perhaps the best example of the importance of history within the story. Midway through the film, Bart heads to the library to research the evil entity invading his house. When he comes across the rat section of an encyclopedia we get a close-up of his screen and see that the name "rat" is much like the species and is of unknown origin. If you head to Wiktionary they say, "The word may go back to an unknown substrate language or be formed from a Proto-Indo-European root meaning, to gnaw." Cosmatos' point being, Bart is up against an ancient evil, and the magnitude of this hits Bart so hard he later obsessively shares uncomfortable factoids at a company dinner party, unsettling everyone. However, the true importance of this theme isn't about learning facts or gaining an advantage by acknowledging the past. What this film does that's so smart is it immortalizes the rat by using events like the black plague, the incident mentioned on the subway, or the nuclear test site, so that we actually feel like Bart may be in over his head while dealing with a singular rat.

The strategic warfare theme applies to how Bart Hughes approaches everything; if you listen to him, he constantly makes war references throughout the film. Early on, Peter (Leif Anderson) is in the kitchen making a mess with boxes of cereal, and Bart comes in and says, "Hey hey hey hey, who's been shelling the kitchen, huh?" Later in his office, speaking to his secretary Lorrie Wells, he asks her, "You know how I would go about revamping the network of commercial America branches?" "How?" she responds. "A volley of mortar fire, followed by a flamethrower." Bart answers. Later, Bart discovers his rat trap has been mangled in such a manner that it's almost like the rat is mocking him. This also marks the first time his attention begins to really shift from work to war as he ignores a phone call. Next, we find Bart seeking advice from the neighboring kingdom's handyman, Clete (Louis Del Grande aka the guy whose head explodes in *Scanners*). Clete offers up five ways to kill a rat: trap 'em, poison 'em, knock 'em on the head, gas 'em, or shoot at 'em. He then adds: "A rat is a survivor, the best there is." Clete continues: "The huge blast! Couple of seconds everything was dead: insects, reptiles, freak'n amoebas, plant life, they all croaked. Except for the rats; they survived."

Many parts of *Of Unknown Origin* may seem strange to the casual viewer and give the impression that the film is poorly made, when actually it has a very poignant message about this major theme. Bart is locked in combat for control of his home with a large rodent. This isn't exactly unexplored territory for storytellers, and Cosmatos is very aware. In fact, he throws out a couple of titles to keep you thinking about the film's actual message. We see the first one when Bart becomes enraged and uses the book he was reading to hit the ceiling; that book is *Moby Dick*. Later in the film he's also watching *The Old Man and The Sea*. The placement of these titles is obvious once you think of the man vs. animal struggle in both stories. Bart's battle has elements of each: the stubborn determination of man and the arrogance to go it alone. But unlike those tales, Bart's motives are family. This idea culminates during the final conflict when Bart takes his *Mad Max*-esque weapon to the scale model house, literally destroying it in an attempt to kill the rat. The implication isn't that he's given up on life, but that he's finally free of the material desires that blinded him of what's really important. In his moment of clarity, he realizes his dream house and job mean nothing without his family.

I have to admit I had an advantage analyzing this film since I actually had a mouse infestation not too long ago and found this film terrifyingly accurate. I, much like Bart Hughes, am a materialist, and the mice that invaded my house loved to eat my books. And much like the mutant rat, the mice seemed to select the books I loved most, nibbling on signed, limited/first printings, and personalized copies exclusively. But the worst part about the experience was that at night I could hear them chewing behind the

wall. When this started happening in the film I felt like it triggered some sort of PTSD in me, and I instantly felt violated angry.

I understand the descent Bart goes through as I myself began punching the wall wherever and whenever I thought I heard chewing. The helplessness at that time was reality shaking, much like the descent Polanski's characters go through in his trilogy. It doesn't seem like *Of Unknown Origin* belongs among *Rosemary's Baby*, *Repulsion*, and *The Tenant*, but it's something about the worlds we create in our private homes. They become our world that we control (or so it seems). When nature invades, the loss of said control can be traumatizing. I felt emasculated by a few little mice. In the end, I couldn't judge Bart for his actions, and after a second viewing and some reflection I actually understood even the stranger choices.

Russell Fisher

Russell Fisher was born in the San Francisco Bay Area in 1985. He lived through several earthquakes and struggled through school. He was convinced he'd play in the NFL until he took up guitar; this hobby was later abandoned for a deep love of film.

It wasn't until his mid 20s when he tagged along with a friend to community college that he was bit by the writing bug. He started projecting films in his garage and leading impromptu lectures about the genre films he felt deserved a serious look and never got one. These screenings were the start of *The Overlook Theater*, a blog he runs with a group of his friends that catalogs their screenings and promotes local events.

ORCA: THE KILLER WHALE (1977)

By Brody Rossiter

"It is the sprouting whale that gets the harpoon." - Norwegian Proverb

The history between man and whale is both storied and deeply troubling. For millennia, mankind has devastated and devoured various species of whale for our own means, gouging the great beings from their ocean habitats and dissecting their lifeless forms for various purposes. Prehistoric coastal dwellers beached whales with primitive barricades before consuming their flesh. The early Basque peoples utilized soaring watchtowers to spot mammals before hunting them and stockpiling commodities stripped from their carcasses. The English and Dutch whaled extensively during the 17th century, sending countless expeditions to fish for the creatures, crippling the whale populous and triggering lethal ship battles between the nations in the process. Whether to survive, collect prized trinkets or source blubber for oil refinement, for centuries, whaling has been one of our greatest crimes against

nature.

It would be easy to assume that since the late 20th century we have shared a much more tender relationship with these marine wonders. Underwater wildlife parks and family-friendly movie fare such as *Free Willy*, have subdued the perceptions of these mighty predators, presenting them as gentle giants that would rather save the day than devour several seals for breakfast. Yet despite the cuddly toys and blockbuster branding, in reality, man and whale are still not at peace.

In spite of widespread condemnation and illegality since the 1986 commercial whaling ban, many countries, including Japan, Norway and Iceland, still hunt these majestic lifeforms thanks to legal loopholes and while acting under the pretense of scientific research – when have a few pesky laws ever stopped us from eradicating nature before? One of cinema's most potent portrayals of killer whales came in the form of the revelatory 2013 documentary *Blackfish,* a film that revealed you can take a predator out of the ocean and teach it some clever tricks - in this case, within the confines of SeaWorld - but you can only cage its innate ferocity for so long before it breaks free with truly horrifying results. The picture endeavored to reveal that man and whale aren't too dissimilar when it comes to our emotions and their fragility.

Orca: The Killer Whale serves up a schlocky seafood chowder comprised of grizzled fisherman, sinew ripping gore and most importantly, revenge. Starring Richard Harris as the reckless Captain Nolan, alongside Charlotte Rampling's scornful Dr. Rachel Bedford, *Orca* follows one man's battle against the force of nature he wronged in the name of cold-hearted profiteering.

Director, Michael Anderson's complex yet action-packed tale of man vs. beast opens with an affecting depiction of two Orcas breaching the bluest of waves. Ennio Morricone's wistful, siren song score punctuates this beautiful moment of nature at play, as blistering sunshine bounces off the water's crystalline surface and underwater shots capture the playful closeness of the two mates. The scene acts as an archetypal calm before the storm, an idyllic overture to the imminent opera of death and destruction.

Though *Jaws* and several other animal attack movies star creatures that display an innate aptitude for hunting their human prey, *Orca* introduces a killer that's not only highly intelligent, but also driven by emotions that are not purely animalistic, but distinctly human, namely, love, grief, and fury. After being tasked by a local aquarium to procure a killer whale for a new exhibit, Nolan and his crew set sail with the promise of a big payday. Upon discovering the whales, Nolan mistakenly harpoons a female. The scene conjures visions of road safety videos that warn of the perils of crossing before looking both ways. Instead of a speeding vehicle careering towards an oblivious child in slow motion, we witness one man's hubris and callous agenda turn a beautiful day at sea into a nightmarish crisis that floods the ocean with blood. In a shockingly grotesque sequence, the captured female whale aborts her fetus on the deck of Nolan's ship. Captain and crew are vilified.

This brutal act, all of which is witnessed by the orca's mate, casts them into an inescapable moral limbo and a war of attrition with the crazed male orca.

Despite its status today as a cult (but not particularly accomplished) "revenge of nature" genre classic, upon its release, *Orca* was widely accused of being an uninspired knockoff of Steven Spielberg's *Jaws* by both scornful moviegoers and bemused critics. And as exhibited by the film's early footage of a whale effortlessly dispatching a great white shark, *Orca* strives to present itself as an entirely different filmic beast of burden from *Jaws'* premise of an unsuspecting tourist trap held hostage by terrifying animal attacks. Whereas *Jaws* provided a summer blockbuster fueled on the rampant paranoia and distrust of a nation still stricken by the open wounds of Watergate and The Vietnam War, *Orca* employs a much more morbid, revenge thriller template, forming a picture that also carries with it a distinct and cautionary environmental message.

Instead of installing a wronged human as its emotionally broken but physically unbowed hero, it trawls the seas for a whale counterpart – distilling thousands of years of pain and suffering due to human wrongdoing within one humungous, unforgiving cetacean in the process. This choice to encourage the viewer to sympathize and side with a wronged hero is not unusual. Charles Bronson's *Death Wish* used such plotting conventions with great success in the summer of 1974 and is a much clearer precursor to *Orca's* vengeful storytelling origins than *Jaws*. However, what is unusual is the choice to turn a supposed sea monster into the hero of the piece.

If Orca is our hero, then Nolan is simultaneously a villain and anti-hero of sorts. He himself is tortured by the death of his own wife and unborn child at the hands of a drunk driver. He later reveals his empathy for the whale's plight to Bedford, while his remorse is often evident through his anguished expressions. The affinity between Nolan and the whale is an omnipresent theme, and one which is explicitly highlighted as Nolan attempts to translate Orca's whale song during a later scene. He states, "You're me, he said. I'm you, he said. You're my drunk driver, he said." However, Nolan is also a man ruled by circumstance, surviving in an environment buoyed by superstition. The potency of fishing village fables and folklore, and those who subscribe to its maritime mysticism, force Nolan into pursuing the unforgiving whale that now plagues the town in search of its new mortal enemy. The restless locals compel him to slay it before its fearsome quest for retribution further dismantles the town and its inhabitants' livelihoods.

After copious amounts of property damage and the death and dismemberment of his crew, the stage is set for the final nihilistic showdown as Nolan is led deep into freezing northern seas by his increasingly monstrous prey. With his ship dismantled after an iceberg collision, sole survivors, Nolan and Bedford, are left

stranded on the ice. Nolan has a clear opportunity to shoot the whale with his rifle but, left unable to emotionally detach from his rival, he hesitates; a momentary lapse that ultimately leads to his death as Orca flings his body against a giant wall of ice, instantly killing him. Moments later, we watch Orca swim off into the sunset as the vindicated hero. Nolan is dead and the whale's family avenged.

Decades prior to us learning of the true level of intelligence and emotional capacity present within whales, *Orca* presented such revelations in the form of a somewhat cheesy yet surprisingly poignant revenge thriller. It's a contemporary retelling of Melville's *Moby Dick* in which the roles of hunter and hunted are reversed, and man's compulsion to kill is adopted by his oceanic counterpart. In presenting such messages, *Orca* unfortunately becomes a lesser horror film when it comes to scares. Nevertheless, it remains a compelling remainder of the horrors that man has inflicted upon the wild and himself in the process.

Brody Rossiter

Brody Rossiter is a Falmouth University Film graduate and freelance journalist based in England. He's a features writer for the independent cinema magazine, *Onscreen*, and has contributed to several publications including *HeyUGuys* and *Bright Wall/Dark Room*. During his final year of study, he focused on discussing the depiction of masculinity in crisis within Mary Harron's *American Psycho*, and acted as editor-in-chief of *Rushes magazine*, Falmouth Film's online platform for emerging film journalists.

You can follow Brody on Twitter @BrodyRossiter or visit his website filminwords.com for more film and horror discussions.

PIG HUNT (2008)

By Bryan Schuessler

Fangoria FrightFest and Lightning Media released eight terrifying films back in the summer of 2010, one of the standouts being the low-budget *Pig Hunt* (2008), about a group of friends from San Francisco who join their buddy John Hickman and his attractive Asian girlfriend, Brooks, to go hunting on his Uncle's property. What Hickman neglects to tell is that his Uncle's shack is located in the deep backwoods of the forest where wild boars run around, including one that's so fierce, so big, and so mean the locals nickname him The Ripper and Hogzilla.

Pig Hunt continues, as one would think, with the city boys and gal getting hunted by the wild boar, picked off one by one in gorily

fashion. Those that don't get killed by animals run into a marijuana farming community of demented hippies that stops at nothing to preserve their crops and secret weapon, thus upping the ante of violence, gore, and creativity. They get into a scrap with them, making the enemies both human and animal.

Once I read the synopsis for this film, I immediately thought of the "Ozploitation" movie *Razorback*, directed by Russel Mulcahy. I loved that film, as I tend to enjoy over-the-top violent and gory "animals on the rampage" horror flicks, and I was hoping I would enjoy *Pig Hunt* just as much.

The film excels in pleasing its audience on many levels. The characters are unique. The film is edited with precision, creating tension and curiosity but also tosses in some ridiculously funny bits of humor. It works because 80% of the film goes along without showing the creature, which is killing off various characters in an ending I really was not predicting. The payoff packs more than a few surprises indeed with just enough blood and gore to satisfy both horror fans and animal-rampage fans equally.

One aspect that stands out is the unique soundtrack by ex-Primus/Sausage frontman and bassist Les Claypool, also recognized for *Robot Chicken, Barnyard* and *Zack and Miri Make a Porno*. His heavy, funky bass twangs fit in perfectly with the hillbilly, redneck region where the film takes place. Claypool also plays one of the characters, Preacher, who's the head of a family whose members don't look like they bathe regularly and get out to the city much, if at all.

Pig Hunt was directed by James Isaac *(Jason X, Skinwalkers, The Horror Show)*, who passed away in 2012 from Multiple Myeloma, and written by Robert Mailer Anderson (author of the novel *Boonville*) and Zack Anderson.

The film stars Travis Aaron Wade *(War of the Worlds)* as the young John Hickman, Tina Huang as his girlfriend, and Howard Johnson Jr., Trevor Bullock, and Rajiv Shah as his buddies. Musician Charlie Musselwhite has a cameo as the harmonica playing store proprietor, Charlie. He had a gig in San Diego at midnight, drove all night to show up for the shooting of his scene, and received his dialogue the very last second. The real challenge, however, was reserved for headliner Travis Aaron Wade. He did a tremendous job, considering he replaced the original lead just two days before filming. Talk about performance pressure. The rest of the acting was rounded out nicely with some decent performances by the two hillbilly brothers Jake (Jason Foster) and Ricky (Nick Tagas), who, back in the days, were quasi-buddies with Hickman.

Viewers are led to believe that all three, at one time or another, used to hunt together. However, some performances could have been more polished (Howard Johnson Jr.) or less ridiculous (Bryonn Bain). Overall, though, the acting had a quirky charm, added realism, and kept things serious when needed (like when characters are injured or killed off). And, even more importantly, they reacted in the correct manner to the news that a huge, flesh-eating wild boar that rivaled in size to a giant elephant was hunting them down and not vice versa.

The filmmakers originally wanted genuine wolf dogs for the scenes in which the cast hunted the massive boar, but due to budgetary constraints (the film cost $6 million), the dogs and their handlers were too expensive. In the end, they used only one dog that has to track down the boar and serve as suspense device as it senses the carnivore nearby.

The film not only is filled with violence, gore, and a bit of suspense, but there's also some decent nudity, making *Pig Hunt* a horror film that could be categorized in both the horror and exploitation genre but ultimately the subgenre of "animals on the rampage." Porky Pig and Babe would be highly offended at how their older and much more aggressive and violent cousin is portrayed.

It comes as a surprise that director James Isaac cites David Cronenberg as his idol and mentor. Isaac said that Cronenberg let him into his world and that he could ask him any questions he wanted. "Cronenberg really allowed me to pick his brain," he said. The plot of *Pig Hunt* is indeed not as simple as one would imagine. Fortunately, for fans of simpler horror films, *Pig Hunt* does not have any psychological underlying themes or bizarre scenes like in *Naked Lunch*. It's just a fun film about a wild boar ripping apart anyone that gets in its way.

The film has been the recipient of the Bronze Audience Award at the Fantasia Film Festival and the Gold Remi Award at the

Worldfest International Film Festival. It's the strongest entry bearing the Fangoria FrightFest banner by quite a large margin, and deserves a spot on the "pigsploitation" shelf (if a genre of such name existed) right next to *Razorback* (1984), the French *Prey* (2010), and South Korean *Chaw* (2009).

Bryan Schuessler

Bryan "Shu" Schuessler has a blog, Shu-izmz, where he writes reviews of movies, books, comics, and metal and rock albums, as well as coverage of various comic book, horror, cult, and exploitation conventions.

Hailing from Chicago,IL and living there and the surrounding suburbs his whole life, he has a distinct Midwestern attitude and flavor to his writing and activities but generally is interested in Blood, Boobs, and Bush.

Aside from focusing his attention on his website, he also conducts a podcast, airing on *Blog Talk Radio* and *Core of Destruction Radio*. He has written for *Kilter Magazine*, Killer *Film*, *Cult Reviews*, *DVD Resurrections*, *Luke is Back*, *Horror 101*, and *Horror Society*. He was also the movie critic on Annie Christ's *Metal Mondays* and made it on the television show *Mark at the Movies* on the REELZ Network.

PIRANHA (1978)

By Beverly Gray

In spring of 1993, people everywhere were buzzing about *Jurassic Park*. Michael Crichton's best selling 1990 novel about dinosaurs alive and kicking in the modern world, was being brought to the screen by Steven Spielberg, on a reported budget of over $60 million. The film had been in production since August, and excitement was mounting. That's when my boss, Roger Corman, called a meeting.

Roger, always one to sniff out a trend, recognized how badly the moviegoing public wanted to see dinosaurs run amok. Yes, *Jurassic Park* would open in June. But why shouldn't we tempt the impatient with our own dinosaur movie in May? That's how *Carnosaur* came to be. Roger bought the rights to a bad British novel by the pseudonymous Harry Adam Knight, then scrapped everything but the title. He hired a bright young film school graduate, Adam Simon, to write and direct on a budget not close to

a tenth of what Spielberg had to work with. Sophisticated CGI was out of the question, so we at Concorde-New Horizons banked all our hopes on a single large pneumatically-controlled tyrannosaurus rex. Roger decreed that it loom 18 feet high, taller than Spielberg's creation. Only problem: the ceiling at our dilapidated studio in Venice, California, only reached 17 feet. Oops!

Though Roger was foiled in that regard, he did meet his ultimate goal. *Carnosaur* showed up in theaters a full three weeks before *Jurassic Park*, garnering some marginally good press along the way. It even earned one thumb up on Siskel and Ebert's program, largely for the effective performance of Diane Ladd as a thoroughly mad scientist responsible for injecting dinosaur DNA into chickens. (Ladd, a Corman veteran and three-time Oscar nominee, was also the mother of *Jurassic Park*'s Laura Dern, a delicious semi-coincidence.) We didn't take in nearly as much money as *Jurassic Park*, but so little was spent on production that who's to say Roger didn't come out the winner?

I suspect that the making of *Piranha* at Roger Corman's New World Pictures felt very much the same. In 1975, the film *Jaws*, directed by Spielberg, turned Hollywood upside down. This was the moment when a-movies and b-movies switched places, with most budgeting dollars suddenly being pumped into thrillers and action flicks that had formerly gotten little love on studio rosters. My former boss still delights in a *New York Times* reference to *Jaws* as "a Roger Corman movie on a big budget." Characteristically, when *Jaws* was the talk of the town, Roger grew impatient to climb on board with his own monster-from-the-deep movie. The surprise is that it took so long. It wasn't until 1978 that *Piranha* made its appearance. Always practical, Roger had replaced Spielberg's great big scary fish with a lot of smallish scary fish.

I wasn't working for Roger in that era, but I knew several of the major players. *Piranha* was initially brought to New World by a Japanese actress with the unlikely name of Chako van Leeuwen, who owned a script she hoped to produce. Roger soon threatened to cancel the project, but she rushed into his office, where she cried and cried. Never able to withstand sobbing women, Roger quickly reconsidered. I met Chako a decade later, when she once again had a project to pitch. Somewhere along the line, she'd become a devout Christian, and the new film she hoped to make involved heavenly supernatural beings. As a token of good will, she presented Roger with a small ceramic statue of an angel. He solemnly placed it on a high shelf in his office, where it gathered dust for years to come. She then insisted that all of us involved in the scripting process — Roger, herself, the writer, and me — join hands and pray for the success of our endeavor. And so we did. Ironically, that film was never made.

I don't think there was any praying over the page-one rewrite of *Piranha*. But fortunately Roger's story editor, Frances Doel, had located a talented fiction writer who was eager to try his first screenplay. His name was John Sayles, and in 1999 he told me how Roger and Frances had taught him story structure: "When do you need suspense rather than action? When do you need comedy to give people a break from the suspense? That's what I found that Roger and Frances were very good at." Aspiring to make his own movies, Sayles paid close attention to the New World way of doing things. He learned, first of all, about

Roger's fondness for plots that came down hard on the military and on other authority figures. He also learned that it's sometimes expedient to crank out a second version of the script, for the purpose of winning over the powers that be. When *Piranha* was shot in Texas, it had access to trucks and other equipment from the local National Guard, thanks to a specially-doctored Sayles

draft in which the military characters look like heroes instead of the warmongers and bunglers they are.

In the time-honored tradition of Cormanites, Sayles got his own cameo, as a stern-faced National Guard trooper trying to prevent our heroes from escaping arrest. It's a classic Corman T&A moment: the female lead (Heather Menzies-Urich) distracts her captor with a quick flash of her bare breasts. At the last minute, she refused to be filmed topless, and so the bazooms of a local waitress had to be pressed into service. As someone who's worked on 170 Corman movies, I know that breast-replacement is an ongoing tradition. Either the star demands a body double, or

Roger, in his wisdom, decides that the breasts on view in the rough cut are not adequate to buoy his suspension of disbelief. Often the substitution is clumsily done. See Sayles' own memory of Roger's *Humanoids from the Deep:* "There's a blonde woman who's attacked in a tent, and there's a brunette woman with much larger breasts who runs out of the tent after she's attacked."

Every film needs a director, and Roger elevated Joe Dante from the editing room for this project. I knew Joe back when he was cutting trailers and found him amiable but very quiet. For Joe, the *Piranha* assignment was a gift in more ways than one because it taught him to relate to others in a more outgoing manner. Ultimately, Joe told me, "That was very liberating for me. Because I found a personality I didn't know I had." After *Piranha*, Joe of course went on to a major directing career. He's by no means uncritical of his former boss but will forever be grateful to Roger for widening his world.

Though *Piranha* contains genuine scares, its true fans also appreciate its tongue-in-cheek elements. Spielberg himself enjoyed it as a savvy parody of *Jaws*. The film's satirical edge shines through even in its official press kit, which reveals the hand of future big league producer Jon Davison (*Airplane, Robocop*). Jon's tips for exhibitors include creating "exciting prepublicity" by leaving dead piranhas on the banks of local lakes and streams: "Promote community interest and fear by organizing groups (Boy Scouts, citizen volunteers, etc.) to guard against the 'coming onslaught.' Give enterprising kids in your area a few bucks to make themselves scarce for a few days. Watch your grosses soar!"

The self-aware humor and political consciousness of *Piranha* have long made it a critical favorite. Back in the day, a Canadian critic named Bruce Kawin quipped that "Brecht would have loved it." Sadly, Roger Corman has a penchant for recycling his successes. In 1995, he launched a series for Showtime that included quickie remakes of several of his classics. Joe Dante laments the way this new *Piranha* was handled: "[Roger] simply took the exact same script, word for word, hired a kid to shoot it, used all the special effects from the old movie, and the only thing he didn't do is he didn't remind them it was supposed to be funny. And so it's a totally straight version of a movie that was done tongue-in-cheek originally. And it's unwatchable."

Fortunately for all of us, the original *Piranha* — which also boasts hilarious turns by Corman stalwarts Dick Miller and Paul Bartel — is very watchable indeed.

Beverly Gray

Beverly Gray has spent her career fluctuating between the world of the intellect and showbiz. As she was completing her doctorate in Contemporary American Fiction at UCLA, she surprised everyone (including herself) by taking a job with b-movie maven Roger Corman at the legendary New World Pictures. There she wrote publicity material, cast voice actors, supervised a looping session, tried her hand at production, and thought up the twist ending to *Death Race 2000*. Later, as Corman's story editor at Concorde-New Horizons, she developed 170 low-budget features. Along the way she earned six screenwriting credits and played several cameo roles, in all of which she kept her clothes on.

Beverly is the author of the bestselling *Roger Corman: An Unauthorized Biography of the Godfather of Indie Filmmaking*. Tastefully retitled *Roger Corman: Blood-Sucking Vampires, Flesh-Eating Cockroaches, and Driller Killers*, it's now available (as both ebook and paperback) in an updated and unexpurgated 3rd edition. Beverly has also published *Ron Howard: From Mayberry to the Moon... and Beyond*. She teaches online screenwriting workshops for UCLA Extension's renowned Writers' Program, and her popular blog, Beverly in Movieland, covers movies, moviemaking, and growing up Hollywood-adjacent. Join the conversation at www.beverlyinmovieland.com

PREY (2007)

By Christine Hadden

First things first: this is no *Born Free*. It's also no *Cujo* - to many considered the ultimate "trapped in a car" survival film. I also wouldn't call it "so bad it's good." But *Prey* does have enough moments of suspense and tension, and let's face it, beautiful scenery, to earn a place here.

While it's not entirely unusual to hear of lions killing people in the wild, it's not an everyday occurrence unless you're living in the African savanna. You're more inclined to hear about captive lions

injuring or killing their trainers, owners, or keepers. Regardless, to hear of a lion stalking and viciously killing someone will always be something that strikes fear in even the bravest soul. Let's face it, lions help put the graphic in National Geographic.

Thousands upon thousands of people trek to Africa to go on safari, where witnessing the beauty of the animal kingdom in its glorious natural habitat gives a thrill like no other. But what if something went wrong?

In the 2007 thriller *Prey*, one family experiences this reality in graphic, harrowing detail - giving its audience second thoughts about a trip overseas and making them much more likely to book that trip to Orlando to see the lions at Disney's Animal Kingdom instead.

When Tom Newman (Peter Weller from *Robocop*) takes his family with him on a business trip to Africa, the family decides to take a tour of the grasslands to see the sights while Tom gets to work as an engineer overseeing the building of a new dam. Tom's wife Amy (Bridget Moynahan) is burdened with babysitting her new step-children, Jessica (Carly Schroeder) and David (Conner Dowds). Jess is an angst-ridden annoying teenager who wants nothing to do with her new stepmom and holds a grudge the size of the savanna against her for breaking up their happy home. David is much more affable but still tests the nerves with his immaturity.

When their search for wildlife comes up empty, the tour guide Brian takes it upon himself to go off-road. Soon, David whines that he has to go to the bathroom. The ranger pulls over, and the two disembark from the Jeep and head away from the vehicle, rifle in tow. You know, just in case... Just as David is complaining about there not being any Charmin, Brian sees an ominous sight just behind David. The eyes of a predatory lioness raise just above the high grass.

And that's when the action begins. While *Prey* won't win any awards for having a compelling screenplay, it makes up for this with some remarkably tense moments and graphic deaths sure to make audiences cringe. There's just something about people being pulled apart by animal teeth, no matter what the species.

The first attack is terrifying. And this is because it reaches to our most primal fear of being eaten alive. With the obligatory death of Brian the ranger guide, it plunges our family trio into dire circumstances. Both the rifle and the keys to the Jeep are outside the vehicle. In the realm of the lions. Leaving them trapped in the confines of a sweltering, claustrophobic deathtrap while they're relentlessly pursued by a species that normally sleeps 20 hours of the day.

The inevitable attacks continue, and the storyline adds a red (no pun intended) herring by throwing a pair of poachers into the mix. We can see straightaway that they're only there to add to the body count, but the few moments of suspense that they provide - and the gore that ensues - make them a pertinent part of the story. Lions are insidious hunters, often not seen at all until it's too late. This is made all too clear when the hunters become the hunted.

The film as a whole, works on a very basic level, but there remains some unbelievable moments of incredulous foolishness. If

you can suspend your disbelief and just take it for the fun film it's attempting to be, you'll be fine. The teenage daughter is beyond irritating, jagging Amy's last nerve with constant barbs about how stupid she is and bringing family drama into places where most people would be much more worried about starting the damn car. And David starts asking moronic questions that are more age-appropriate to a five year old instead of the prepubescent he's. And in probably the most preposterous of sequences, Amy finally gets the car keys and takes off across the savannah at full speed, carelessly putting all their lives in further danger by crashing the Jeep into a massive ditch.

Lions are beautiful creatures, certainly to be respected in any and all situations. They're one of the most feared predatory animals in the world and second in size only to tigers in the big cat family, weighing in excess of 500 pounds. Hunting (both legal and illegal) has led these regal beasts to be added to endangered species lists, and populations have dwindled, particularly in West Africa.

Even at the zoo one can't help but think about the possibility of one of those majestic cats escaping its confines and charging the crowd. It's just human nature. In *Prey*, however, they're almost delegated to mindless hunting machines. The filmmakers thought it prudent to give us the "lion's eye view," with blurring images of what we're supposed to think is the lion surveying its prey, "thinking" of what the best way to eat them would be. It falls flat but still isn't enough to ease the fear of these patient creatures and the havoc they wreak.

Back in 1898, a series of animal attacks made headlines all over Africa and the world. A group of British workers were in Kenya building a railway bridge and ended up getting stalked and eaten alive by a pair of Tsavo lions. Responsible for the grisly deaths of upwards of an estimated 100 people, the two man-eaters were eventually hunted down and killed by John Patterson.

This story of man-eating lions is supposedly based on the Tsavo lions tragedy, but *Prey* bears very little resemblance to the actual events of the era. Another film, *The Ghost and the Darkness*, tackled the Patterson story with varying degrees of success, though it was much closer to the supposed events.

The production value of *Prey* was above average, and I was impressed with how excellent the film looked on my HD television. As stated, lions are one of the most stunning animals in the world and seeing them up close and personal - being able to count every whisker - makes up for any flaws the film may have. The ferocity of the attacks appeared real enough, though I'm certain every precaution was taken on the South African set.

While I can't claim *Prey* is the best film ever made about lion attacks, it would certainly be on a short list of competitors. The film moved at a good pace, with equal amounts of quiet tension and all-out graphic savagery. I enjoyed it for the entertaining little piece of horror it was without losing any brain cells in the process.

Christine Hadden

Christine Hadden is the creator, editor, and head writer of the Rondo-nominated blog *Fascination with Fear* and has been an obsessed horror fan for longer than many of her readers have been alive. She can overlook movie plot holes in exchange for style and atmosphere, generally rejects both the 3D and found footage phenomenons, values high gore content when done right, always prefers practical effects over CGI, and has an undying love of vampires and ghost stories. She considers Norman Bates her homeboy and claims *Jaws*, *Battle Royale*, *Alien*, *Ghost Story*, *Don't Look Now*, *The Woman in Black* (1989), and *Psycho*, as a few of her favorite films. She reads equal parts Poe and King, and she has written for *Fangoria*, *Paracinema Magazine*, *MoviePilot*, and Eli Roth's horror app *The Crypt*. She enjoys Kentucky bourbon and red, red wine. But not together.

PROPHECY (1979)

By Bob Ignizio

1979 was a watershed year for horror films, giving us *Alien*, *The Brood*, *Dawn of the Dead*, *Dracula*, *The Legacy*, *Love at First Bite*, *Nightwing*, *Nosferatu*, *Phantasm*, and *When a Stranger Calls*, just to name some of the more notable titles. It also gave us *Prophecy*. I didn't get to see *Prophecy* during its theatrical run, but I did catch up with it the following year when it debuted on The Movie Channel. I was only nine or 10 at the time, but since it was rated PG my parents agreed to let me watch it. Woo hoo!

I was excited to see *Prophecy* because, like any respectable horror flick of the 1970s, it had a promotional campaign that made it sound like the most terrifying film ever. The poster showed some sort of hideous creature curled up inside an egg, possibly in an attempt to draw comparisons to the previous month's sci-fi/horror hit *Alien*. "She lives. Don't Move. Don't breathe. There's nowhere to run. She will find you," it warned ominously. The film's teaser trailer ratcheted up the hype even further, the narrator serving notice of a creature that, "will mindlessly, mercilessly, kill every living thing it meets." Sure sounded cool to me.

On paper, at least, *Prophecy* seems capable of living up to its hype. The script, by *The Omen* scribe David Seltzer, is full of monster mayhem. There's head chomping, a guy being ripped in half, a kid being thrown into a tree, and multiple people getting clawed in the face by a creature that manages to combine Native American mythology and eco-horror mutation into one ferocious bear monster. To make sure this terrifying vision was put on the screen properly, respected filmmaker John Frankenheimer *(Seconds, The Manchurian Candidate, The French Connection II)* was hired to direct. What could go wrong?

After a prologue in which a search and rescue team are mysteriously killed by an unseen terror, we meet Dr. Robert Verne (Robert Foxworth), a burnt-out liberal crusader looking for a chance to make a real difference. He thinks he's found it in a job mediating between a lumber mill and a tribe of Native Americans (called "Original People" or "Opies"). Dr. Verne sets off for the woods of Maine (depicted by British Columbia) accompanied by his wife Maggie (Talia Shire), who, unbeknownst to him, is pregnant.

Guided by the mill's head honcho Bethel Isely (Richard Dysart) and some of his men, the party doesn't get very far before finding their path blocked by a group of Native American activists led by John Hawks (Armand Assante) and his wife Ramona (Victoria Racimo). Bethel blames drunk "Opies" for the disappearance of the search team from the prologue, while Hawks blames the mill for poisoning the water and his people, so the prospects of the two sides talking it out are slim. Instead we get a ludicrous confrontation in which Bethel's goons go after the protesters with chainsaws. Dr. Verne manages to defuse the situation, but clearly he has his work cut out for him.

Aside from the tensions between the two sides, there are disturbing portents like the unnaturally large salmon Dr. Verne sees while fishing. More dramatically, a deranged raccoon attacks Dr. Verne and Maggie in their cabin. Ok, maybe more comedically than dramatically, but at least it's some much needed action in this slow moving film. And, of course, there's the seemingly crazy tribal elder from central casting (George Clutesi, also in the same year's *Nightwing*) going on about some mystical defender of his people

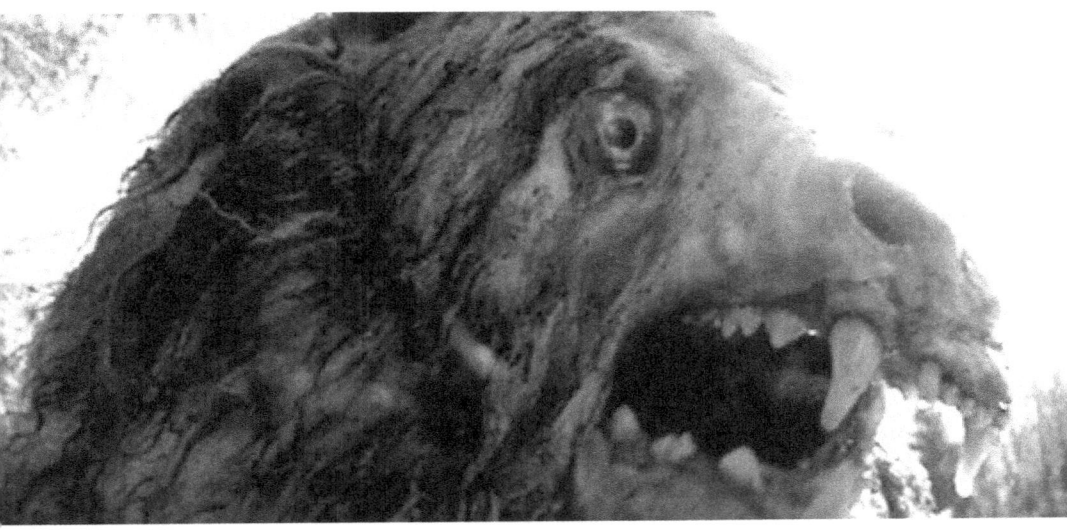

called Katahdin. He also shows Dr. Verne a really big tadpole for added effect. Then it's time for Dr. Verne and Maggie to visit the mill where we learn how wood gets turned into paper, and Isley denies any possibility of his mill polluting the water. Riiight.

Almost an hour into the film we finally get some monster action. A family is sleeping at their campsite when the pink bear thing (played by Kevin Peter Hall of *Predator* and *Harry and the Hendersons*) makes its big entrance, and it's a doozy of a scene. Where most horror films generally try to avoid killing kids, *Prophecy* shows no mercy. Its monster backhands a young boy into a tree while he's still in his sleeping bag, a cloud of feathers absurdly exploding from the impact in a scene that manages to make the horror of a child's death unintentionally hilarious.

In its final 30 minutes, *Prophecy* gets down to business. A number of disposable supporting characters (helicopter pilot, police officer, random tribe members, etc.) are brought in to the mix so the pink monstrosity can rack up a respectable body count, and even some of the major players get taken out. There's also a subplot about how Maggie is worried her unborn child will be a mutant, which is tied in with the discovery of a pair of mutant bear cubs. Ultimately, mama bear is defeated, but in true post-*Carrie* fashion there's a stinger at the end implying that the horror still goes on.

The main problem with *Prophecy* is that it takes itself too seriously. That simply makes no sense in a film whose plot reads like a William Girdler *(Grizzly, The Manitou, Day of the Animals)* grab bag of goofy ideas. But Frankenheimer plays up the drama and the social message aspects and tones down the violence and gore. That means the head chomping I mentioned earlier is more heard than seen, and the guy getting ripped in half takes place offscreen. Bummer. But I guess I should be grateful since the lack of gore helped secure the film a PG rating, which in turn led to me being able to see it at such a young age.

Regardless of one's feelings on gore, the monster is a major disappointment that has little resemblance to the cool poster art. Frankenheimer evidently wanted it to look more bearlike, but what he got is more like a giant hairless Shar-Pei drizzled in slime. You can tell the filmmakers are embarrassed, too, as whenever the "bear" shows up, there are lots of quick edits. Frankenheimer is on record blaming his alcoholism at the time for many of the film's shortcomings, but he may just have been the wrong guy to helm an exploitation movie about a killer mutant bear.

They say you can only polish a turd so much, but if there's one thing that can imbue even the drabbest pile of cinematic excrement with a golden sheen, it's nostalgia. Watching *Prophecy* as an adult, it's clearly a terrible movie, and its flaws are many and glaring. Still, the film's final act possesses a certain loopy charm, and maybe that, as much as nostalgia, is why it holds a special place in my heart.

Bob Ignizio

Bob Ignizio is a freelance writer living in Cleveland, Ohio. At the age of six his parents allowed him to stay up late to watch *Frankenstein Meets the Wolfman* on local horror host program *The Hoolihan and Big Chuck Show*, and it was all downhill from there.

Bob has written about music and movies for numerous alternative entertainment publications since 1991 including *Cleveland Scene Magazine* and the *Cleveland Free Times*. Now that almost all print media in the town has died off, he runs the *Cleveland Movie Blog* (www.clevelandmovieblog.com) where he has no editors to mess with his exquisite prose. Of course he also has no one to pay him for it, but you take the good with the bad.

RATS: NIGHT OF TERROR (1984)

By Chris Hewson

In the 1980s, there was a lot going on in the Italian exploitation film industry. Not only were there already heaps of quality horror films from the likes of Mario Bava, Dario Argento, Lucio Fulci, and more, but the more lower-budget knockoff fare was also popular, with people like Joe D'Amato making dozens of movies. The king of this subgenre was Bruno Mattei, alongside his collaborator Claudio Fragasso (of *Troll II "fame"*). The two would make movies like the "nazisploitation" *SS Girls* (a *Salon Kitty* rip-off), *Robowar* (a scene-for-scene copy of *Predator*), *Strike Commando* (a *Rambo* copy), *Jaws 5: Cruel Jaws* (which uses the *Star Wars* theme), and *Hell of the Living Dead* (a zombie movie which went as far as using *Dawn of the Dead*'s score, with no authorization). *Rats: Night of Terror*, is one of their more original films.

The year is 215 A.B (After the Bomb). Due to "the insensitivity of man," a nuclear holocaust devastated the Earth's surface, and humanity was driven underground. A long while later, many people who were unsatisfied with the laws of the underground fled back to the now habitable surface and lived as nomad scavengers. Now, in the "present," a group of survivors are roaming the desolated cities, in search for food. They find a large building, which has food and supplies in abundance, but the gang's joy is short-lived when they start discovering the corpses that litter the place. At first, they believe that the food is being guarded by whoever owns it, and the dead bodies are scavengers like themselves, but it soon becomes apparent that nothing human lives in this area. Here, the rats are in control. Strong, carnivorous, and intelligent, they start hunting everyone down, and no one may escape before dawn comes...

Rats: Night of Terror is a film that most will definitely find unintentionally hilarious, and some will find terrible. I understand those who dislike it, but I myself like this movie a lot! It's never boring, it's got many suspenseful scenes, and the funereal electro score sets the mood really well! Some movies that take half an hour to get going can get a bit boring, but many are able to use that length of time to build up the tension, and *Rats* does successfully!

Rats is still a pretty unintentionally funny movie despite the tension, due to the hilarious acting! The dub actors overact a lot, and their delivery cracked me up at times. They're not great actors, but certainly entertaining and never wooden! With actors like Geretta Geretta, Massimo Vanni, and Ottaviano Dell'Acqua (most under English pseudonyms in the film's credits), this also has a neat cast for the genre fans who are familiar with those people.

The dialogue in *Rats: Night of Terror* is a real treat! When Claudio Fragasso is writing, you're sure to get some amusing lines, which tended to come across as off due to the translation and language differences, resulting in lines like *Jaws 5*'s insult: "I want you to go find the tallest skyscraper you can, throw yourself off, and then go fuck yourself!" Ones on display in *Rats* are lines like, "This machine needs a good kick in the balls!" or, when the black character, Chocolate, has flour dumped on her, and she says, "Now I'm as white as all of you!"

The effects in this film are a mixed bag. The locale looks great and helps set the mood fantastically. Some of the effects are pretty good, like the first body the leads discover. The scene when a rat climbs out of the mouth of a recently killed group-member is a well-directed moment of creepiness. Everyone believe she was murdered by a person, but then her closed mouth starts contorting open, and a rat crawls out! Some effects are less than convincing, like one scene involving mannequins and invisible-yet-obvious wire! As for the rats, the same establishing shots are frequently re-used, and the effects of people being attacked are usually just of the animals dropping on top of them, but enough is left to the imagination that this doesn't come across as too shoddy.

The rats are all real, and they seem relatively well-off. At the midpoint of the film, the leads' flamethrower "conveniently" stops working. Despite the missed opportunity for badass rat destruction, I'm actually glad for this development, as this is an Italian exploitation film from the 1980s - I really don't think it would have used fake rats for flamethrower scenes! Maybe it was Bruno Mattei's conscious decision to cut the flamethrower from the action to spare the rats. Then again, it could have been a budgetary concern, but maybe not, because they already had the rats and the flamethrower.

Now onto the themes of this film. Be forewarned, this will be spoiler territory.

The building the leads discover is suspicious. It's got extensive machinery, including a hydroponic garden, and a purified water system, both of which aren't the thing regular people have after the apocalypse. Unbeknownst to the characters, this facility seems like a testing ground. The computer speaks of a test group being eliminated, so the building, even down to little details like the frantic recording warning of the carnivorous rats and their

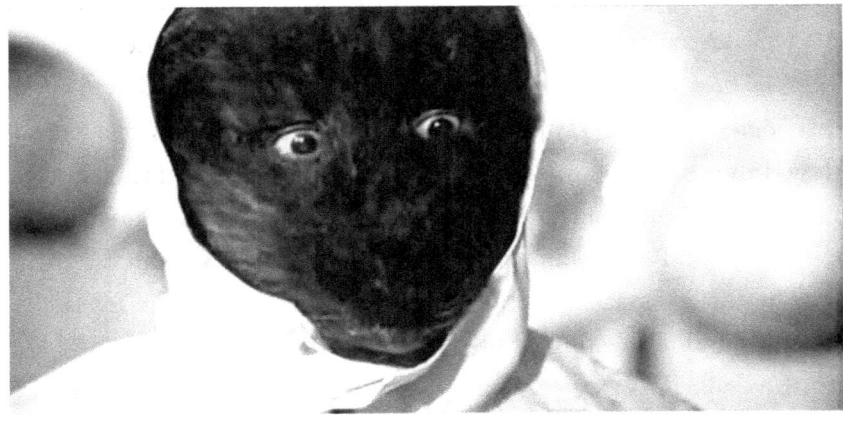

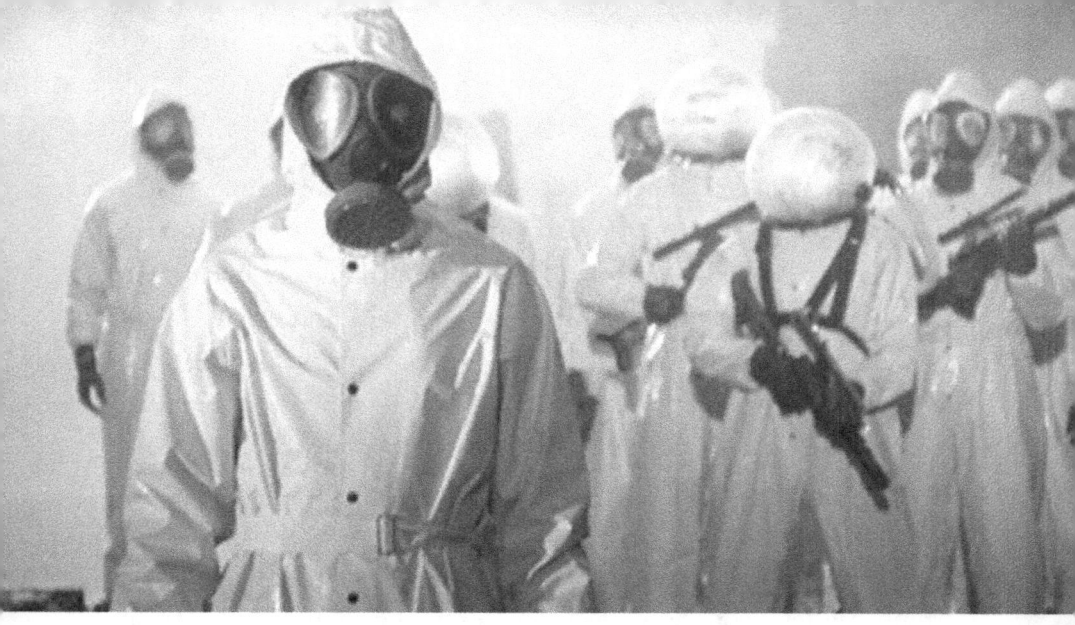

seemingly random nature, could be a mock-up, designed to see what regular people do in this situation and test their survival. The rats also seem to be controlled by something, with their aggression being activated and de-activated (seemingly by a high-pitched noise). Who's responsible for this, you wonder? Well, rat-people, of course!

The big twist at the end of the film is that the remnants from humanity's underground colonies have become rat-people, clad in protective suits and armed with gas pumps as they seemingly rescue the leads. The film ends on that note, so we never find out if their intentions are good or bad, but there's enough for one to make their own conclusions. Even the apparent evidence to them being good, such as the recording and them killing the rats and saving the surviving leads at the end, can be explained in the context of them being malevolent scientists. As a character says at one point: "Rats will freely kill their own kind, as long as they're killing rats from a different pack." I imagine that's the case here, and the rat-people only see their "cousins" as vermin that served their purpose for the test and have now outlived their usefulness.

This is all implied, and there's just as much to suggest that this isn't a testing ground at all, and the rat-people are benevolent. I like to think that because it's more upbeat, although the former theory is the more complex and interesting one.

Overall, *Rats: Night of Terror* is one of Bruno Mattei's most accessible films. It's fun, intentionally amusing (as well as unintentionally) and will most certainly provide you with an entertaining "animals attack" movie to wile away an afternoon with.

Chris Hewson

Chris Hewson is an Australian film buff who's been reviewing movies on his blog *Not This Time, Nayland Smith* for the past five years. An avid writer of both fiction and critiques, Chris has seen some of the craziest movies under the sun, including things like a Macedonian post-apocalyptic arthouse film about Santa bringing about Armageddon.

Current projects Chris is working on include a planned serialized graphic novel based on *The Cabinet of Dr. Caligari* and its 1989 successor, which should be out later in the year.

RAZORBACK (1984)

By Robert Hood

Mutated and fantastical monsters have always been present on my favorite movies list. Extreme size brings a certain unique, larger-than-life resonance to the animal attack/humanity vs. nature genre, not to mention offering images of apocalyptic destruction – a cathartic expression of humanity's ingrained existential angst.

Russell Mulcahy's *Razorback* — the *Highlander* director's first feature — belongs to a group of movies designated "Ozploitation" cinema that appeared in Australia in the late 1970s and 1980s. Horror flicks of local origin hadn't been all that common, but the late 1970s saw a concerted attempt to introduce genre-based, populist films with international appeal into the scene, resulting in such variable "classics" as the *Mad Max* trilogy, *Patrick*, *Turkey Shoot*, *Dead-End Drive-In*, and *Long Weekend*.

With an estimated budget of AUD$5.5 million, *Razorback* was

one of the "Ozploitation" films that didn't do well on initial release but have since become something of a cult favorite. Even big names in world cinema, such as Steven Spielberg, have expressed an admiration for it. It's easy to see why when you consider the film's inventive, music video-influenced visual artistry and the dynamic impact of Mulcahy's direction. The spectacular settings — it was filmed on location in the deserts around outback Broken Hill — play a big part in its appeal.

The titular antagonist is an unusually large boar, depicted in all its fanged, diseased ferocity as something hellish, primal and virtually unstoppable. Wild boars are an introduced species in Australia, thanks to the likes of Captain James Cook, who believed it was a good idea to "seed" the New Land with alien species — and now feral pigs have become a significant ecological problem. A sense of alien threat informs the thematic backbone of *Razorback*. Reports of monster wild pigs occur from time to time, though the largest seem to frequent parts of Eurasia (up to 330 kilograms apparently). Male razorbacks are bulky, with short legs, a head that takes up about a third of their body length and almost no neck, along with large teeth that sprout from the sides of their mouth. They can be extremely vicious, tearing prey apart without raising a sweat. As one character in *Razorback* says: "[a razorback] has two states of being - dangerous or dead."

The feral boar featured in *Razorback* is a bigger, even nastier version of this reality. It's about the size of a rhinoceros, only hairier and much uglier. Though director Russell Mulcahy has expressed regret that they hadn't made the monster even bigger, more mutated, and diseased, for me it works as is by confining what we see of the razorback to partials — especially its face, a superb animatronic construct (one of several designed by SFX makeup artist, Bob McCarron) — but also as a "blink-and-miss-it" mass of muscle and hair, a dimly seen shape in the mist, or a huge mass moving too fast and too obscured by shadows and random objects to be clearly seen. A fake razorback — a $1 million dollar animatronic beast on a trolley — is visible for barely 20 seconds, and even then, not clearly. Like Spielberg's animatronic shark in *Jaws*, it created problems.

Yet keeping the beast only peripherally visible throughout most of the film, albeit by necessity, contributes to the razorback's air of monstrous presence. It's like a violent, inexorable phantom. Scenes of its attacks are fast, bloody and horrific. The film begins with a sequence in which the isolated house of Jake Cullen (Bill Kerr) is invaded by the largely unseen razorback, which smashes through walls like an out of control freight train and snatches up Cullen's grandson, leaving Cullen with an obsession for revenge and his home burning spectacularly against a dark outback sky. Other brutal highlights include: the death of TV journalist Beth Winters (Judy Morris), gored in her car as the razorback relentlessly tears it and then her to pieces; and the chaotic but powerful climactic battle between man and beast that takes place in a huge abattoir — a setting that looks rather like some gothic torture chamber. Though the studio cut much of the film's graphic

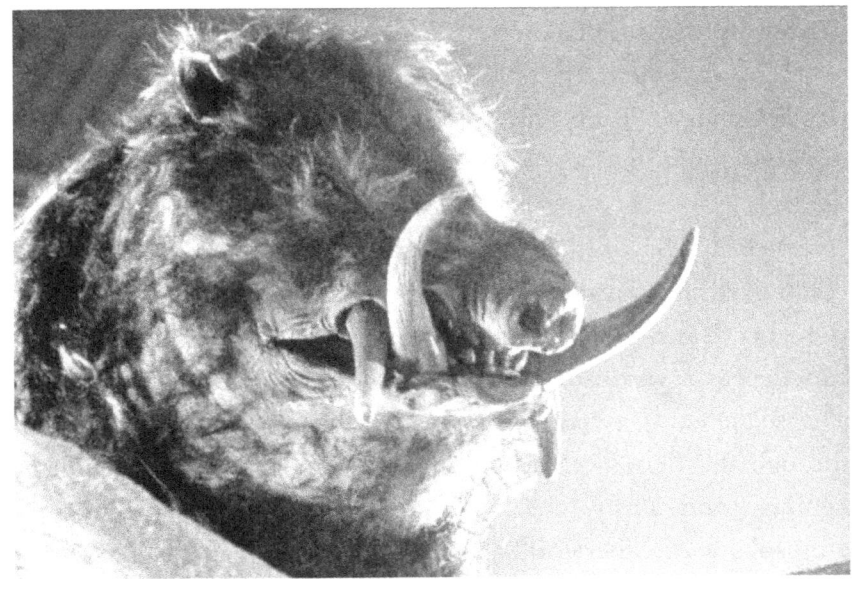

violence, enough is left to give it an ambiance of gore and violence.

Also illustrative of the razorback's power is a scene in which the Razorback grabs a dog chained to the outside wall of a house and races off, wrenching the place apart, while the inhabitant sits in what's left of his loungeroom as half the building, including the TV, disappears into the night. It's one of the most memorable set-pieces in animal attack cinema and not to be missed.

But not all of the film's horror is created through the sheer brutality of the titular boar; it's not just the razorback that's feral. *Razorback*'s monster exists in a version of outback Australia that is as feral, depraved and brutal as the beast itself — a manifestation of the worst aspects of the mythical town of Gamulla, its pub, wasteland environs and inhabitants. The film's outsider protagonists — doomed journalist Judy Morris, bereft fiancé US actor Gregory Harrison, and Arkie Whiteley as an unlikely researcher living among the psychos — have to deal with a diverse array of (to quote Mulcahy) "redneck, crazy people." As a result, the film has been described as "Ocker gothic," largely due to the spine-chilling performances of David Argue and Chris Haywood as Dicko and Benny Baker, the psychopathic proprietors of a derelict pet-food processing factory, which appears to be the town's main source of commercial activity (except for the archetypical outback pub, of course). Both Dicko and Benny are as frightening as the razorback and in fact do as much physical and psychological damage.

A highlight of the film is its startlingly beautiful imagery, epitomized in a dream sequence in which American Carl Winters (Gregory Harrison) is abandoned in the middle of the night and experiences a vision of desolation and surreal outback weirdness. The sequence is a *tour de force* that leaves its echoes reverberating through the film — in which unconventional camera placement, lighting, and misty chiaroscuro effects create a nightmarish atmosphere of otherworldliness. The bizarre White Cliffs region and its pockmarked landscape of opal mines are as alien as it gets.

I can't remember when I first saw *Razorback*. It wouldn't have been in a cinema, as the film was generally panned by critics and ignored by the public, getting minimal exposure. I suspect I first saw it in the early 1990s, when researching an article on Australian horror films — courtesy of a poor-quality, pan-and-scanned VHS cassette, which did it no favors. I was nevertheless stunned by the beautiful cinematography of Dean Semler (who would go on to win an Academy Award for *Dances with Wolves*), the film's hallucinatory imagery, and dynamic pacing. Seen now, on full HD widescreen Blu-ray, these aspects of it stand out even more. *Razorback* may be as detrimental to Australian tourism as John Boorman's *Deliverance* (1972) or any Rob Zombie movie is to American back country tourism, but it remains a grim joy to watch — an overblown, quintessentially Australian, yet universally resonant nightmare.

Robert Hood

Robert Hood is one of Australia's leading writers of horror, weird fiction and dark fantasy. He has also dabbled in crime and science fiction. His most recent publications are an epic fantasy novel *Fragments of a Broken Land: Valarl Undead* (Borgo/Wildside Press, 2013)and *Peripheral Visions: The Collected Ghost Stories* (IFWG Publishing, 2015).

His award-winning blog *Undead Backbrain* features news and commentary on genre cinema, especially giant monster, ghost and zombie films, plus other weird stuff.

Website: roberthood.net

SHAKMA (1990)

By Tenebrous Kate

You'd think that a movie about Roddy McDowall as a med school professor tampering in God's domain while a chemically altered baboon stalks LARP'ing med students would be a midnight movie slam dunk. Such is the promise of *Shakma*, a 1990 movie co-directed by Hugh Parks and Tom Logan. As with many offbeat features, the reality doesn't necessarily live up to the hype, and a more accurate pitch for this film might go something along the lines of, "there will never be a more thorough cinematic statement on people hiding from a baboon behind a dazzling variety of office building doors." This pitch would still be leaving out the seemingly endless scenes of people using walkie-talkies, but I'm getting ahead of myself.

Dr. Sorenson (genre stalwart Roddy McDowall) and his medical students are experimenting on animal subjects, using chemical injections to alter the aggression of primates. Student Sam is horrified to learn that Shakma, the baboon he had been training to be docile, has been transformed into a violent beast by these treatments. After Shakma attacks a group of Sam's colleagues, he's instructed to put the ape to sleep, a task to which he quite naturally objects. Sam is soon distracted from his grief, however, because the most popular students in Sorenson's Monkey Torture 101 class have scheduled a session of a *Dungeons and Dragons*-inspired game called (logically enough) *The Game*. *The Game* takes place after hours in the research institute where medical classes are held and consists of a bunch of kids wandering the halls with walkie-talkies while Sorenson monitors a computerized map of the building and hands out directions from his office. One gets the sense that the script writers have never actually played D&D, because unlike *Dungeons and Dragons*, this game has one monster, and the action consists entirely of solving riddles. Hardly worth a hard-working med student pulling an all-nighter to play! The large quantity of walkie-talkie action makes the "Shakma" drinking game an extremely efficient one - players would die if they took a shot every time someone says "over" into a hand-held device.

It turns out that *The Game* is one of the most needlessly complex McGuffins in film history, existing only as an excuse to separate our main players and leave them open to attack. Baboon attack, to be precise, because Shakma's euthanasia has not gone as planned, and he wakes up ready to kick the ass of any creature unfortunate to cross its path. A building peppered with the students who'd experimented on him, strolling around all alone

and unarmed, is a wonderful gift for the mad monkey, who starts to pluck off the kids one by one in frenzied, throat-ripping fashion.

If you're reading this and considering joining #TeamShakma, allow me to add more evidence to the case in the monkey's favor. Not to put too fine a point on it: this movie is entirely populated by assholes. Sam, who might have won some of your favor by being the only person in his class who's not enthused about gratuitous animal experimentation, is an arrogant sexist whose first lines of dialogue involve telling his girlfriend she'll have to abandon her engineering career in order to stay home, cook his meals, and raise "little Sams." He also flirts with Kim, a young lady of indeterminate age whose role as "princess" in *The Game* appears to consist of waiting for someone to find her at the end. Kim's brother Richard is an even bigger jerk, as he has invited himself into *The Game* and then sulks and refuses to play along when he finds out it takes more than two hours. He also makes out with his girlfriend while surrounded by animal test subjects, which is tacky at best and a precursor to a career in serial murder at worst. Then there's Bradley, a creepy nerd who speaks into his walkie-talkie in a tone of voice usually reserved for patrons of pay-by-the-minute phone sex lines. If the goal of the performers is to make you loathe them and root for the killer baboon, then they do a tremendous job. Christopher Atkins, perhaps best known as the heartthrob lead in *The Blue Lagoon*, brings such energetic smarm to his role as Sam that you pray he won't emerge unscathed.

The real star turn in this feature is put in by Typhoon, the baboon actor who plays Shakma. Typhoon is an animal actor with remarkable range, having appeared as a tank-driving, karate-chopping, spy sidekick in the tragically underappreciated b-movie adventures *Unmasking the Idol* and *Order of the Black Eagle*. Acting as a pissed off victim of torture only uses a fraction of his range, but the monkey gives it his all: running, leaping, and throwing himself against doors with all his might. Rumor has it that these attack scenes were prompted by placing a female baboon just out of range, a theory supported by the appearance of Typhoon's monkey erection in a number of shots.

It's clear that there's some kind of message intended in *Shakma*, dealing with the weighty subject of animal experimentation and concluding on an extremely dark note. What starts as a goofy stalk-and-slash has a final act that includes multiple lingering shots of dead characters being removed to locations where they can't be chewed-on by a vengeful animal — pretty heady stuff for something that started out so goofy. What are we left to conclude from this strange movie? Are the walkie-talkies a metaphor for how technology drives us further apart? Is the inclusion of the computer-powered *The Game* a critique of our reliance on and overwhelming faith in science? Maybe it's just a movie about a killer baboon on the loose that has some serious tone issues, and I'm just over-analyzing this whole thing. An odd entry in the animal attack canon, there's a darkness lurking in *Shakma* that makes it hard to dismiss.

Tenebrous Kate

Tenebrous Kate is a New Jersey-based writer and artist whose work explores her longstanding fascination with all things dark, fantastical and forbidden.

The creator of the web-comic *Super Coven* and the editor of various zines under her imprint *Heretical Sexts*, Kate has also written for publications including *Ultra Violent Magazine*, *I Love Bad Movies*, and *Occult Rock Magazine*.

She has appeared in New York-based comedy variety shows including *Kevin Geeks Out*, *Meet the Lady*, and *Bonnie and Maude*.

Love Train for the Tenebrous Empire is her long-running blog where she writes about psychedelic cult films, bizarro art, throwback forms of heavy metal, and all manner of other esoteric nonsense.

SHARKNADO (2013)

By Ben Daniels

Few horror films succeed in blending multiple sources of terror. The unlikely combination of destructive weather patterns with the ferocity of man's most feared ocean predator have given birth to what is now the tour de force we know as *Sharknado*.

This unlikely project from film studio The Asylum was originally created as another in a long line of low-budget made-for-TV movies for the Syfy Channel. Designed as a satirical combination of "natural disaster" and "animal attack" subgenres, it used the standard formula of combining two scary things in the attempt of creating a catchy title, similar to its brethren *Crocasaurus* or *Sharktopus*. Little did the studio and production team realize that *Sharknado* would soon swim its way into the consciousness of mainstream American media.

During its initial airing *Sharknado* had less than stellar viewership, but thanks to social media outlets such as Twitter subsequent runs captured the imagination of the television watching public who began to understand that meshing former *Beverly Hills 90210* stars with flying Carcharodons was a stroke of pure genius worthy of hash-tagging. This led to *Sharknado* becoming an underground success overnight. It steadily gained a larger audience with each showing, entrenching it into the annals of cult film history.

To understand the overwhelmingly positive reception to *Sharknado*, we need to examine the nature of American pop culture and modern media itself. What makes this film rise above so many similar releases from the same company? How did these airborne apex predators chew their way into the hearts and minds of the public? Why didn't people talk this much about *Megashark vs. Crocosaurus* starring a once beloved Jaleel White?

Sharknado became an overnight sensation and moved beyond its peers because it chose not to take itself seriously. Call it "self-awareness." *Sharknado's* inability to moderate anything from dialogue to action to its "Enough said!" tagline, made it a relentless and shamelessly over-the-top creation in a sea of shamelessly over-the-top movies. What Jaleel White got wrong that Ian Ziering got right was leaping into the mouth of a flying shark while wielding a chainsaw.

Speaking of Ian Ziering, another facet to *Sharknado's* success was undoubtedly the ironic genius of its casting. Ian Ziering, Tara Reid, and John Heard were an excellent ensemble and managed to deliver great performances with material that was clearly ridiculous on all levels. Horror films are a landscape littered with both rising and fading stars, but rarely actors and actresses at the peak of mainstream success. The genre simply doesn't support it due to lower box office incomes and narrower audience appeal. However, the horror movie community is fiercely loyal and will embrace honest attempts no matter how ridiculous the concept of a movie.

This is where the cast of *Sharknado* excelled, by completely embracing the insanity. Ziering and Reid are former teen icons, and this couldn't have been further from *Beverly Hills: 90210* or *American Pie*. They threw themselves completely into *Sharknado* understanding it was so absolutely ludicrous that they needed to have fun with it. In one scene, Ziering saves a school bus of children from a fiery demise after a tornado of sharks rips down the iconic Hollywood sign. In another, Reid screams in horror as the first floor of her house is flooded with sharks who then devour her boyfriend. Again, the self-awareness of how absurd this all is makes *Sharknado* work, in contrast to movies like *Mega Shark vs. Giant Octopus* where Debbie Gibson and Lorenzo Lamas act like they might truly be attempting to create legitimate art.

On a more subconscious level, *Sharknado* tapped into the zeitgeist of our troubled modern times. It's a metaphor combining multiple phobias woven into our current societal fabric. Climate change; much like *Twister* and *The Day After Tomorrow*, *Sharknado* displays the awesome power of nature by posing a "what if" scenario that plays on our current worries about a changing global climate causing extreme weather patterns. Add to this our fear of sharks that is annually recycled in the media and popularized by films like *Jaws,* and it creates a situation that capitalizes on our most visceral instincts: our population's fear of unforeseen dangers given form as a whirling airborne meat grinder.

The murderous sharks were covered, lampooned and adored in the news, social media, and merchandising tie-ins. It marked a huge, albeit unexpected, win for The Asylum and Syfy Channel and has since spawned an expected franchise including three sequels. It has also to an extent, rekindled the careers of those associated with the project. Additionally, the lure of the *Sharknado* has drawn in bigger name stars eager to make cameos and be part of the continuing Cinderella story as the franchise flies forward.

Sharknado is a must-watch film within its niche. It's a standout in a heavily overcrowded field and captured the imaginations of both horror fans and wider mainstream audiences alike. It achieved a perfect balance of horror, action, and summer popcorn action absurdity. For these reasons it should be held in high regards as one of the most popular disaster/animal attack horror films in recent history, in addition to its status as a pop culture talking point.

Ben Daniels

Ben Daniels is the owner and managing editor of *Terrorphoria*, a horror genre blog that takes a light-hearted, comedic approach. It's the goriest comedy blog on the Internet, or maybe just the horror blog with the lamest jokes around. Either way, Terrorphoria embraces all the things that make horror a hilarious genre. You'll find a unique take on everything from horror movie reviews, to info about survival horror games and horror-themed music.

Ben has also written for multiple music and video game sites for almost two decades, including outlets such as *Gaming Target*, *Evil Avatar*, and *Splitkick*. He has penned scripts for various shows including the Sayer science fiction podcast. He's an avid consumer of movies, video games, books, and music who is also self-righteous enough to think other people will read his opinions on those things. Narcissistic? Maybe, but you ARE reading this right now, so he might be onto something.

SHARKTOPUS (2010)

By Michael P. Spradlin

Roger Corman, a combo shark and octopus, a genetic engineering experiment that goes horribly awry, babes in bikinis, and Eric Roberts. Mix it all together, and what do you get? A giant piece of cheesy cinematic goodness called *Sharktopus*.

First of all, this is a made-for-TV movie. Somewhere out there is a former network TV executive who green-lighted *Sharktopus*. This person is now the assistant manager of lawn care products at Menards in Sherman Oaks.

Roger Corman is obviously a warlock.

Let's start with the film's basic premise - the genetic engineering of a shark and an octopus, which Eric Roberts' character, the evil Dr. Nathan Sands, describes as, "a giant leap forward in genetic engineering." The creature is called S-11, and we learn from one of the characters that sharks hunt while octopuses

are territorial. So apparently Sharktopus can only hunt in its own territory. So what if poor S-11's territory runs out of food and tasty things to eat?

Luckily for Sharktopus, its territory seems to be the entire West Coast of Mexico. In Puerto Vallarta and Playa del Sol he finds more bikini-clad women to eat than Clint Eastwood has liver spots. But not to worry, Sharktopus is indiscriminate in his eating habits. He eats men as well, including a couple of boat painters that he pulls right off of scaffolding, the last man screaming, "Not like this! Not like this!" which is interesting since at this point in the movie, no one is aware of what is happening or what this creature is. Yet boat painter guy figures it out right away (although he could have been referring to his acting career).

Then there's Sharktopus' penchant for killing in multiple ways. We're never quite sure how he will kill from scene to scene. In one, he rips a woman right off of a bungee jumping line. This happens directly after her boyfriend assures her that bungee jumping will cure her of her fear of heights. In several other scenes, he uses his tentacles to stab, rip apart, and pull his prey into his shark mouth. Is S-11 a thrill killer? Is he an adolescent giant leap forward in genetic engineering that can't stay out of the human refrigerator? We never know.

With this particular marriage of two disparate species of sea creatures, S-11 has also developed the ability to roar and growl. This is indeed among the biggest leaps forward since neither

species is known to have vocal chords. Perhaps, Dr. Nathan Sands implanted the vocal chords from the dying throat of a Conway Twitty impersonator for good measure.

One thing is certain: S-11 is mad. Really mad. He has been raised to be a weapon, and his brain is controlled by implants needed to control S-11. They have a red and green light that show us when they're working and when they aren't. Mostly Dr. Nathan Sand's daughter operates them with a video game joystick in the Blue Water Corporation Laboratory. When the Navy orders some tests that S-11 is not ready for, the implants are damaged, and now S-11 is no longer S-11. He's at last his natural self. He's Sharktopus.

Once free, Sharktopus swims from the coast of Los Angeles to Mexico in about five minutes. Dr. Sands, his daughter, and their team follow him in what must be the world's fastest private jet. They were lucky because there was no traffic in LA that day, and they were able to get to the airport and take off in a matter of minutes.

Also, Sharktopus hates cavorting. We see revelers, roller bladers, fishermen, boaters, and every single one of them is a cavorter. Don't they know the danger that awaits them?

Sharktopus also knows how to avoid the media. And, of course, the military can't chase after him because then their top-secret experiment would be exposed. Never once in the movie, not a single time, do we see any kind of civil authority. There's no Roy Scheider screaming for everyone to "get out of the water!" In the film there are 19 utterances of "Oh My God!" but zero of "Call 911!" In the first scene of *Sharktopus*, when the team tests S-11's implants by having him chase a bikini-clad swimmer, then veer off at the last second by turning on the implant's green light, we do get a brief glimpse of lifeguards on the beach. But even when the swimmers BFF (who refused to join her friend in the water because "there are fish in the ocean") screams for help, the lifeguards never appear. Perhaps they were on a cavorting break.

After that it's up to Dr. Sands' daughter, who, two-thirds through the movie, decides her father is evil, but she still loves him because he's her father. Of course, there's only one man who can stop Sharktopus: Andy Flynn, a former Blue Water employee that Dr. Sands fired because... he asked for a raise.

Flynn agrees to come back and capture S-11 for the tidy sum of $300,000. Their plan is to shoot a dart into Sharktopus' side. But they only have two darts (which later become four in the movie), and they must be shot from a grenade launcher because it's the only weapon accurate enough to hit S-11. Obviously, no one in the cast, crew or script department has ever fired a grenade launcher. They don't shoot. They launch. Shoot is not accurate. But, oh, well.

One of the other interesting facets of S-11's engineering marvels is his ability to occasionally come up onto land to eat someone. In addition, he apparently also has salmon DNA somewhere in there because he's able to go from the ocean to a freshwater river without missing a beat. Roger Corman is a genius. This is not up for debate.

Another trait S-11 has obtained in his petri dish emergence is an uncanny consistency for only eating women in bikinis. However, I may need to research this further because it might be there were no one-piece suits in the movie, and he's after all an opportunity predator. Even Liv Boughn, who plays Stacy Everheart, the tough as nails reporter for CNE, wears a mini-skirt and skimpy, ample cleavage showing top. It's a two-piece outfit, putting it in the bikini category. Poor Liv, she tries so hard, but alas, Sharktopus does not like the media and does not want his story told, so Stacy ends up as a Sharktopus kabob. Luckily, Liv did not stop her acting career with *Sharktopus*. She went on to give an unforgettable performance as "Concerned Mother #2" in *Cesar Chavez*.

There's only one thing I can't fathom about *Sharktopus*. It's Eric Roberts. Sure, he might be the biggest ham to appear on the big screen since Porky Pig. But he has done some credible work in some big films and TV series like *The Dark Knight* and *Heroes*. Besides money, what could convince him to appear in a film like *Sharktopus*?

So I keep going back to my original theory, which is that Roger Corman is really a warlock. Heck, in 1994 alone he executive produced 20 films!

Get busy Spielberg.

Slacker.

Michael P. Spradlin

Michael P. Spradlin is a New York Times Best Selling author of several books for children and adults. His *Killer Species* series from Scholastic is about a crazed environmentalist who genetically engineers animals to wipe out invasive species in the Florida Everglades. And things go horribly awry. In fact, something usually goes horribly awry in all of his books. Also writing *Killer Species* probably makes him the most qualified person to offer a critical assessment of *Sharktopus*.

His latest book, *Into the Killing Seas*, is a middle-grade novel set amidst the sinking of the U.S.S. Indianapolis in the waning days of World War II. The shipwreck was the worst human-shark encounter in human history. Over 600 men lost their lives, and only 317 of the original crew of 1196 ultimately survived.

SLUGS: THE MOVIE (1988)

By Danger_Slater

I was a teenager during the Golden Age of VHS. This was in the 1990s. There were no corporate video stores in my hometown. No Blockbuster Videos flying their flags of blue and gold; their impenetrable and sanitized castle walls constructed out of boxes of *Jerry Maguire* and *Forrest Gump*. There certainly were no streaming sites like Netflix or Hulu yet. There was barely an Internet.

All I had was a place called JMD Video, a sliver of a store jammed into a hole in the wall in between a pizza place and a nail salon.

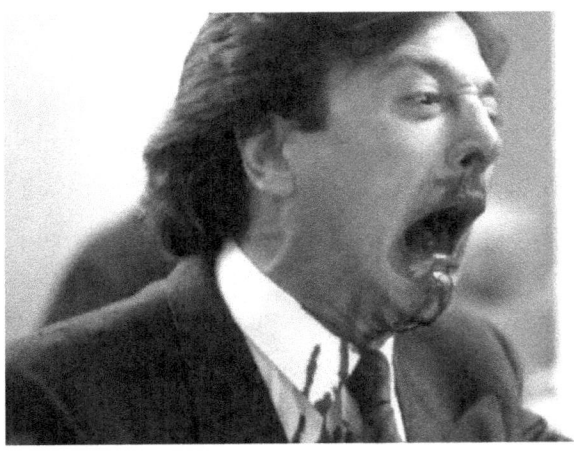
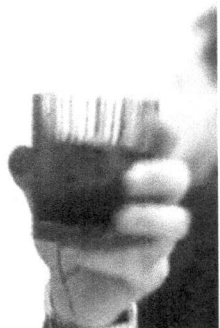

If it was a new release you wanted, JMD never had enough copies of it. They didn't rent out video games. They charged your account if you forgot to rewind your tape before returning it. Once the format switched to DVD, the tiny neighborhood video store defiantly refused to keep up with the demand. Not that they had the space or the capital to make the switch anyway. Around 2004,

JMD Video closed its doors forever. R.I.P.

Nevertheless, this essay takes place before all that.

The year is 1997, and I'm a sophomore in high school. By this time mom-and-pop video stores like JMD had amassed these massive collections of older movies from the prior decade or so of business. So while Blockbuster might have been able to guarantee you a copy of *Titanic* was in stock, JMD seemed to pride itself on the opposite. They had multiple copies of things like *TerrorVision* and *Rock n' Roll Nightmare*. The entire middle section of the store was a wellspring of old movies, and their horror section was huge! Not only that, but renting them was a bargain: three older releases for three days for three dollars. A big banner behind the cash register advertised it. It was locally known as the 3-3-3 Deal.

This was my home. My safe haven. My sanctuary. It was a crash course in cult cinema. It took me about two years to run through every horror movie in the store, and I loved every second of it.

Among the early gems I discovered in this time was a seemingly innocuous black-boxed VHS tape, simply entitled *Slugs: The Movie* (1988).

I wasn't expecting much. I mean, of all the animals that could possibly attack, there's none ostensibly more harmless than a slug. They're small. They're slow. They can be defeated with ordinary table salt for God's sake – a fact which no one in this movie ever thinks to use. *This is going to be awful*, I thought.

But. I. Was. Wrong.

The thing is, it's precisely *because* slugs are so unthreatening that they're truly nature's perfect predator. Shit, this movie might as well have been a documentary.

Let's use the "sex scene" that comes about halfway through the movie for an example: In the span of time these two teens finish getting it on (which, if you've ever been a teenager, you'd know is not very long) a horde of slugs have entered the house, climbed the staircase to the second story, and covered every inch of the floor. The naked woman gets out of bed and immediately slips and falls. The slugs attack. She writhes around in a pool of her own blood for about a minute before the slugs eat all of her skin off. Her boyfriend, reasonably horrified, tries to escape by attempting to open the window by the foot of the bed. The window is locked, of course. After the most minimal effort to fight for his own survival, he slowly acquiesces to his fate, and he too is eaten alive.

So why are these slugs so angry, you ask? Well, they've been 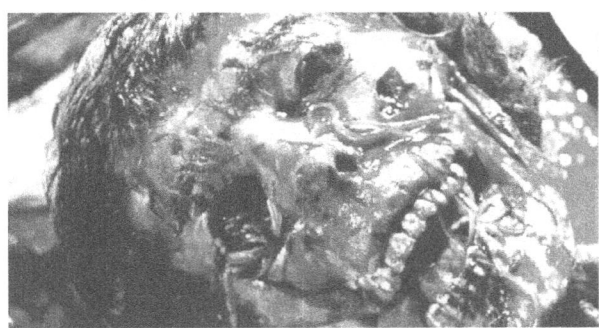 exposed to toxic waste, of course. And if movies taught us anything, it's that toxic waste pisses nature off and makes crazy unpredictable shit happen. But the slugs in this movie don't mutate into monsters. They're not gigantic or physically deformed in any way. No, the toxic waste only makes them hungry for human blood. Apparently they're able to metabolize superfast too because they can reduce a man to skeleton over the span of a night.

So enter Mike Brady, the local health inspector and the only person who can stop these bloodthirsty gastropods from literally eating everybody in the entire town (note: I believe this might be the first and only time a health inspector was a movie's protagonist. Feel free to fact check me and report your findings to danger_slater@yahoo.com).

Here's are a few stats I have compiled from the film:

- Death count: 12 people + one hamster
- Slug death count: millions (minus one because "The end, or

is it?")

- Real slug fact: 6th slowest animal in the world
- Fastest slug speed ever recorded: .19 MPH
- Best death in this movie: this is a tie between: a) The scene where the horticulturist has a slug climb into his glove and bite the tip of his finger, which prompts him to flail around like an idiot so that he bumps into a shelf which falls on him just before he's forced to hatchet chop his own hand off to escape the pain, during which a small fire starts, which then travels across the ground to a small gas can which obviously explodes the entire greenhouse with him and his wife trapped inside, or, b) The scene in which the man who ate slug-contaminated lettuce is now at a fancy restaurant when his nose starts bleeding into his Scotch and water, and as he gets up, his face and eyeballs suddenly explode with these wiggly slug-worm-thingies.

If all of this sounds ridiculous, it's because it is. This is not a movie to be taken seriously. But that's not to say there isn't a lot to like here: the over-the-top gore effects; the killer thriller synth soundtrack; the hokey dialogue, especially coming from the sheriff, whose inexplicable disdain for the protagonist still makes me laugh. What it may lack in realism, performance and writing, it more than makes up for by just being fun. At the end of the day, if you can ride your bicycle back to JMD Video and stick your copy of *Slugs: The Movie* in the return slot before riding off into the sunset feeling like you had spent your time well - that, my friends, is what it's all about! And much like a man-eating, toxic waste contaminated slug in the sewers beneath a rural town, my love for this film will never die!

Danger_Slater

Danger_Slater describes himself as "devastatingly handsome."

He's the bizarro author of *DangerAMA* – a collection of three science fiction novellas with walking penises and a homosexual Will Smith – and *Love Me*, about a guy in a Viking suit on a quest to figure out the meaning of life while encountering obstacles such as rabid gangs of disgruntled grannies, rival cults of pie-enthusiasts, toasters, and annoying celestial bodies.

His stories have appeared in the collections *Stranger Danger, Junk, Tall Tales with Short Cocks Vol. 2*, and *Tall Tales with Short Cocks Vol. 4*.

Talk to him on Facebook, Twitter, GoodReads, or at www.dangerslater.blogspot.com.

SNAKES (1974)

By Stuart R. West

In 1971, an apparently very eager cinemagoer audience turned the film *Willard* into a huge box office hit. The story of a socially awkward "boy" (relative in cinema-world terms) who befriends a bevy of rats and uses them to gain revenge on those who had wronged him, spewed out a legion of copycat films with a variety of animals running amok. Yep, even *Slugs* (1988, J.P. Simón). But forget about all of those pretenders. Let's talk the real deal, *Snakes!*

Snakes, a 1974 regional oddity, was made on a minuscule budget, far removed from Hollywood, and is possibly the worst film in this collection. Yet, cinematic masochist that I am, I have viewed *Snakes* four times. A bizarre black comedy, even if unintended (or was it?), it succeeds as a fascinating character study. *Snakes* is an exploitation/horror hybrid, the bastard perverted offspring of *Willard* on a budget.

The copy I viewed opens with a freeze-frame and the clearly computer-generated title, "*Snakes!*" This prompted research for possible original titles. I found two (unsubstantiated) alternates: *Fangs* and *Holy Wednesday*, both probably tougher to market to the drive-in crowd. I was particularly fond of the credit: "music by John Phillip Sousa." I'm fairly certain the late Mr. Sousa didn't write original music for this gem.

Snakes opens squarely in *Green Acres* territory. In a small, undisclosed, dusty town, Miss Williams' fourth-grade class is seen marching around what appears to be a rock quarry (teachers had more leeway back then), butchering Sousa's *The Stars and Stripes Forever*. It's Wednesday, better known as "snake-feeding day." The

BIGGEST BITE SINCE JAWS

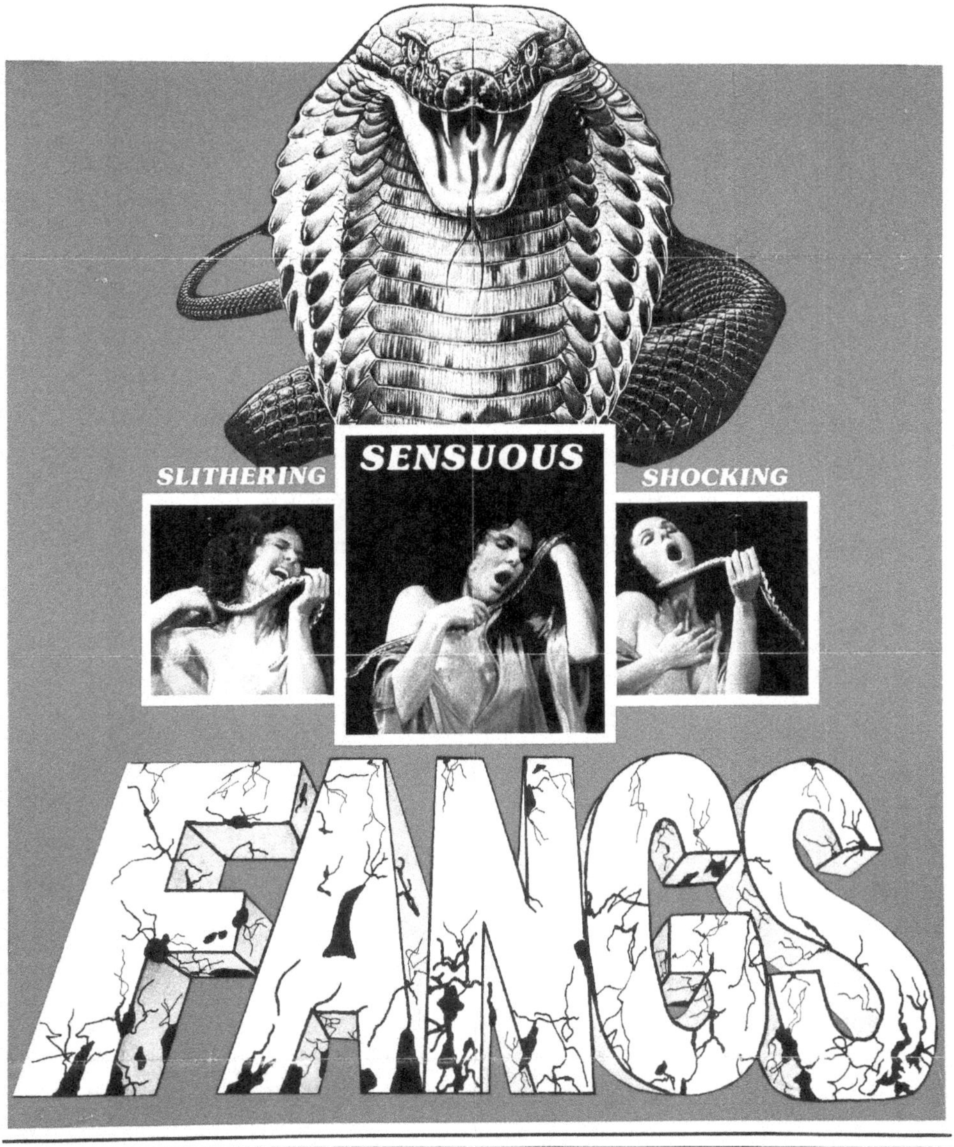

SLITHERING SENSUOUS SHOCKING

FANGS

STARRING
ALSO STARRING
LES TREMAYNE · JANET WOOD AS IVY · BEBE KELLY

Guest Star MARVIN KAPLAN · Special Guest Star ALICE NUNN

Screenplay By JOHN T. WILSON & ARTHUR A. NAMES

Directed By ARTHUR A. NAMES · Produced By ARTHUR A. NAMES & JOHN T. WILSON

Released By WORLD WIDE FILMS CORPORATION    RESTRICTED

children gather mice and lizards every Wednesday to feed Snakey Bender's snakes. Our hero, Snakey, loves his pets but is socially challenged and hangs around the school in his filthy, lived-in long-johns and overalls.

Brother Joy (sanctimonious town preacher) has deemed it the devil's work to destroy God's little creatures, thus railing against Snakey's pride and joy. A student asks Miss Williams if it's wrong to feed the snakes, and she says it's fine. He replies, "You're a real friend to snakes, Miss Williams." *Indeed* (more on that later).

Enter Burt Holden, Snakey's only human friend. For reasons never fully defined (as very little is), Burt lets Snakey live on his burnt down homestead. The BFFs conduct weekly "band concerts" where they get drunk, strip down to underwear and march around to Mr. Sousa's blaring soundtrack. Fun on a budget! Trouble arises, though, when Burt decides to go into town to get a wife.

Of course, no regional drama would be complete without the constant of an overweight sheriff. Constable Al fits the bill, upset over Snakey's driving on the wrong side of the road but too out-of-shape to get in his Mustang fast enough to do much about it.

Finally, and perhaps best of all, we're introduced to the brother and lesbian sister team of Bud and "Sis" (a great cartoonish, villainous performance by the incomparable Alice Nunn – forever immortalized as "Large Marge" from *Peewee's Big Adventure*), who run the local general store. The siblings paw and lear at Miss Williams in the store, enticing her with the promise of having "bedrooms and everything next door."

Director Art Names sets the stage, characters all comfortably slipping into stereotypical prototypes. Snakey is our hero, fighting the establishment. Burt's his best friend. The villains are despicable: religious hypocrites and sexual predators. And lovely Miss Williams is the virginal, sweet heroine. It's the *Andy Griffith Show*.

Except it's not. Far from it.

Snakey drops by to visit Miss Williams, who's none-too-happy to see him. "Lucifer is getting a bit anxious, Miss Williams," says Snakey. She reluctantly lets Snakey in, and he pulls Lucifer (a large snake) out of a bag. Miss Williams treats the snake to sexual favors.

Wait. *What?* Until this point, *Snakes* felt like a comfortable friend, a glimpse into what really happens on *Hee Haw* between commercial breaks. Harmless and comforting. But here we've reached the point of no return; cinematic madness has transformed a Horton Foote portrait of a broken, dusty small town into an insane fever dream.

Bud and Sis spy Snakey leaving Miss Williams' abode and move in for blackmail sex (making it a very busy night for Miss Williams). The next day, Miss Williams, in tandem with Brother Joy, releases the food for Snakey's harem (term seems sorta' appropriate now) and tells Snakey it's over.

This, of course, is the "Charles Bronson moment" when our protagonist's world crumbles, catapulting him straight over the top. Losing his food supply, Miss Williams' ending their "friendship," Burt's rejecting him, and finally, Bud's popping the head off a favorite pet just proves to be too much for Snakey. The standard ominous "no turning back" musical cue is there. A fight between Snakey and Burt escalates violently and ends tragically. Snakey realizes what *must* be done…

This is merely the halfway point; there're plenty more interesting details and set-pieces for the daring viewer to discover. But if you've seen any animal attack movies, you know what happens next.

So, what *are* we dealing with? Upon first viewing, I had no idea how to respond. The hero wasn't particularly likable or empathetic, a petulant man-child killing people because he couldn't have his way, the heroine was into bestiality. *Snakes* didn't fit any cinematic glove I have ever tried on. Research beckoned me (hello,

Google!). Director Art Names' credits didn't yield anything helpful as *Snakes* was the only film he directed. Interestingly enough, most of his credits were for sound; I'm disregarding that because Mr. Sousa did all the heavy lifting. I thought writer John T. Wilson's credits might shed some ligh... nope, he wrote scripts for Ted V. Mikels, a notorious schlockmeister who couldn't tell a coherent story.

I believe *Snakes* is an underrated and daring black comedy. Some may argue the comedy is unintentional, as I originally thought. But upon second viewing, I realized some comedic episodes are carefully set up. Trudging through dusty fields after his first murder, Snakey is a broken man, shuffling despairingly, accompanied by a somber drumbeat and dislocated voices. But the more people Snakey murders, the jauntier his step grows, marching exuberantly with the music rising into full orchestration.

Director Names also filled his film with many comedic character actors. Marvin Kaplan (Brother Joy) should be familiar to anyone who's ever watched a sitcom from the 1960s or 1970s. Bruce Kimball (Bud) portrayed comic relief characters in a slew of 1970 exploitation films. Les Tremayne's broad performance is zestfully played, an unlikely mix of pathos and psychopathy, yet he makes it work. If director Names didn't set out to make a comedy, he certainly cast for one.

Maybe I'm reaching, but Snakey's habit of driving victims' cars off a cliff and watching forlornly is similar to Norman Bates' favored method of body disposal in Hitchcock's *Psycho*. Bebe Kelley's Miss Williams is set up as the heroine we can root for in the midst of squalor, then, like Janet Leigh, she does something despicable and gets her comeuppance. There's even an end sequence with monolog-delivered exposition, à la Simon Oakland's *Psycho* character.

Snakes is daring and never dull; a funny, unsettling experience. Every character is unlikable and corrupt; I have to wonder who thought the bestiality angle was a good idea. While watching *Snakes*, I kept trying to pigeonhole it into my b-movie expectations, but it kept writhing in other directions. From the start, it lets you know things are different in this universe. *Snakes* doesn't care if you like the characters; it revels in the grotesqueries of these unsavory lives with sordid detail. While a "nature attacks" film, it also wallows in the pig-pen of mankind's ugliness.

Stuart R. West

Multi-published author, Stuart R. West explores the hidden underbelly of the Midwest with horror, heart and humor in YA and adult thrillers. His debut YA thriller, *Tex, the Witch Boy*, was released to acclaim; teens and adults alike suggesting it should be taught in schools. The *Tex, the Witch Boy* trilogy tackles contemporary issues teens face such as bullying, identity, drugs, religion, and alternate lifestyles in an entertaining manner. Supernatural allegories abound, but no preaching allowed. West's adult thrillers, *Godland, The Secret Society of Like-Minded Individuals, Zombie Rapture* and *Neighborhood Watch* depict a Midwest not usually seen, unpeeling layers off the Norman Rockwellian exterior to reveal the moral rot, corruption and hypocrisy that lay beneath.

West lives with his wife, a pharmacist, in a Kansas City suburb. They've also adopted a rescue dog, who harbors a pathological hatred toward the mailman. He imagines he'll let it ride, to the detriment of his furniture. Dog psychiatrists can be expensive.

West spent 25 years in the advertising/graphic arts field before turning his attention toward something he's passionate about, writing.

Read more about West's books at his blog, *Twisted Tales From Tornado Alley*: stuartrwest.blogspot.com. Find his books at Amazon and other booksellers.

SNAKES ON A PLANE (2006)

By Christine Rains

The hype drew people to the theaters, but it was more than just the hokey concept and Samuel L. Jackson that made *Snakes on a Plane* a cult classic. Okay, maybe a lot of it was Jackson, but proudly donning its b-movie skin, the film gave us exactly what we were expecting and more.

I was one of those thousands of people eager to see the flick on the big screen. The noise on the Internet was immense. The theater was packed, and someone had spilled soda under my seat. At least the sticky floor would keep any snakes from silently slithering over my feet.

It was a possibility. I'd heard about snakes being released in other theaters. Later I found it was all baloney. Only one rattler accidentally found its way into a popcorn perfumed lobby in Arizona, but it was released safely back in the desert. Yet there's always that little hissing nag in the back of your mind that it might happen.

The audience came with an attitude. They made catcalls at the previews and cheered when the film started. It began light and beachy, but it fast hit us with a gruesome mob killing. It was no *Rocky Horror Picture Show*

experience, but people seemed to feel it was their duty to shout things at the screen. Of course, Samuel L. Jackson received the most attention. I had the feeling some folks had seen the flick at least once before as they prompted and said lines with him.

It didn't ruin my enjoyment of the film. I giggled, cheered, held my breath, and jumped. The soundtrack was fitting, and Cobra Starship's *Bring It,* cheesy as it is, still gets stuck in my head whenever I listen to it. I reveled in all its b-movie glory, especially when we get to see through the eyes of the snakes.

We get to be lurking in the machinery and under the seats. Who's foot is that? Or hanging from the compartments. Who will be bit next? The green tinged and blurry vision really gave the viewers a feeling of the serpents' points of view, adding to the creepiness and tension. It helps to not to pay any attention to the fact snakes use scent to get around, and their vision isn't blurry or green.

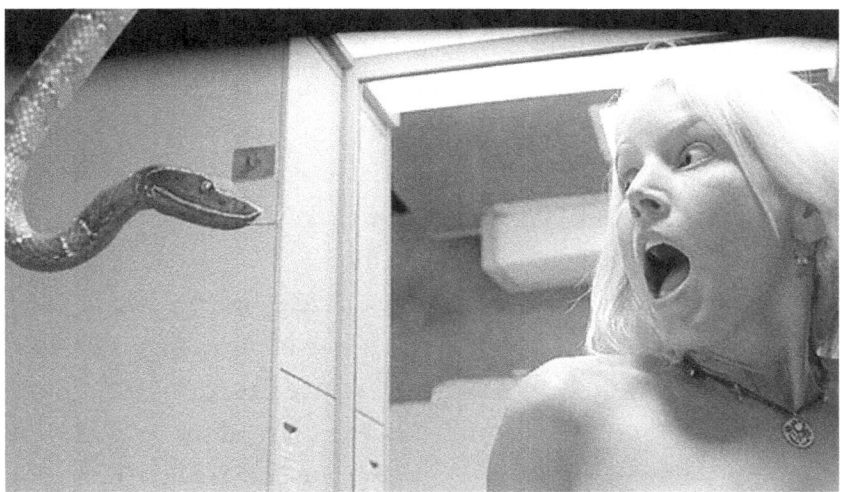

I have seen parts of the flick on television a few times over the years, but recently, I sat down by myself and watched it in its entirety. I laughed and wondered if snakes would really react that way to the pheromones sprayed on the leis. The thought one sliding over any part of my body still gives me goosebumps, but I know they don't attack unless provoked. Over-thinking is not good in helping the enjoyment of suspense and horror.

My curiosity drove me to look it up. Animal experts agree that the film is complete fiction. Snakes only react to the pheromones of their own species, so one scent would not affect them all. And it would not make them aggressive. The passengers on the plane would get some loving from the serpentine stowaways!

Even the aggressive actions of the snakes were not consistent with their natural behaviors. Rattlers wouldn't hang from things because they're ground dwellers. Pythons do not crush their prey, they constrict them, suffocating their meal. There's no snake that can swallow an average adult human either.

Besides, how could I feel afraid if Jackson didn't worry when he was filming? He didn't work with live snakes, but they were on set. He stated the animatronic snakes were much scarier because real ones were lazy and didn't like to be in the light.

As the movie played on, I felt as though I was missing something. I couldn't place my finger on it. Was it because I knew what would happen? Part of the thrill is guessing who will live and who will die. Or maybe my tolerance of snakes is a little better than it once was? The fact that most of the snakes in the film were CGI (computer-generated images) helped too.

Contrary to what everyone expected, the graphics were phenomenal. The film was made on a low-budget, but when New Line first saw it, they loved it. They allowed the producers more money to re-shoot scenes and create more realistic effects. The extremely enthusiastic animation team studied snakes, removing the shiny and sleek appearances, and simulated real serpentine movements. Plus, they added multiple snakes to several scenes to increase the chaos. (There are extras on the DVD that demonstrate how much work was put into the special effects. And the commentary is absolutely hilarious!)

When Jackson shouts out his famous line near the end, I said it with him: "I have had enough of these monkey-fighting snakes on this Monday-to-Friday plane!"

But, you know, I said the uncensored version.

Ah, that's what I was missing. The audience. Movie fans to share the experience with me. The laughter, the shouts, the yelps. The energy of a theater full of people all rooting for the good guys to defeat the monsters.

This is a film that needs to be watched with friends. Rowdy and hilarious buddies that can riff on it without missing a beat. I bet there's even a drinking game designed for it. Oh look! I googled it. There is one.

If you see a snake, take one swig (two swigs if the snake bites someone). You can also take a chug when someone says, "snakes on a plane," AND when Samuel L. Jackson swears. That means two chugs for his famous line!

Snakes on a Plane never pretended to be anything other than solid b-movie entertainment. That's the kind of fun you need to share. Next time I plan to watch the film, it will be in the company of fellow fans.

Christine Rains

Christine Rains is a writer, blogger, and geek mom. She has four degrees which help nothing with motherhood but make her a great Jeopardy player. When she's not reading or writing, she's going on adventures with her son or watching cheesy movies on Syfy Channel. She's a proud member of Untethered Realms and S.C.I.F.I. (South Central Indiana Fiction Interface).

She has several short stories published including ones in the *Indiana Horror Anthology 2011* and *Mortis Operandi*, a Harrow Press anthology of supernatural crimes. Be on the lookout for her latest short story, a science-fiction horror tale in *Mayhem in the Air* (An Untethered Realms anthology).

Christine has a well reviewed and readers' award nominated paranormal romance series of novellas called *The 13th Floor*. Early 2015, her first geeky erotic romance was released with Ellora's Cave. Two more in the Dice & Debauchery series are awaiting release. Her newest book is an urban fantasy novel, *Of Blood and Sorrow*. All her stories add a twist to existing tropes and make the ordinary into something extraordinary.

SQUIRM (1976)

By Jeff Lieberman

When I was a child, my brother read an article that taught how to free bait worms. Just attach two wires to an electric train transformer and tie them onto two metal rods, then place the rods in the ground, wet down the earth, and zap them with electricity. In seconds, they spring out in the hundreds. That's the basic idea of *Squirm*, only on a megawatt level.

Squirm was a spec script which I wrote from my own idea in about six weeks. I transitioned from fine art into filmmaking right after I saw the movie *Blow-Up*. It had a huge and lasting impact on me in that for the first time, I realized narrative moviemaking could be an art form. Also, I was thinking about *The Birds* (together with *Jaws* one of the best made animal attack movies) and the term "early bird gets the worm." It hit me that since I was already familiar with that biting species of salt water worm, masses of them could be as menacing as birds if it's shot right. My experience using that species of worms for fishing was all the research I needed. And, yes, these worms do bite. So when you use them for bait, you need to be mindful of holding them by the backs of their heads, just like snakes.

While most animal attack movies from the 1970s were basically "revenge of nature" stories, *Squirm* had nothing to do with revenge at all. It was just a freak phenomenon caused by the sudden surge of electricity into the muddy ground. Personally, I'm more impacted by the sci-fi from the 1950s, the "radiation scare" movies such as *Them!*, *It*, and *The Incredible Shrinking Man*, whose general structure I used later on in my first two movies. *The Incredible Shrinking Man* in particular had a lasting impact on my young psyche. I was very afraid of the atomic bomb and what it could do.

To test the idea for *Squirm*, I spread dozens of worms over my daughter's doll and filmed them in 8mm. I then sent the film in to be developed. A week later, I picked it up, I turned on the projector, and instead of worms it was a film of a child's birthday

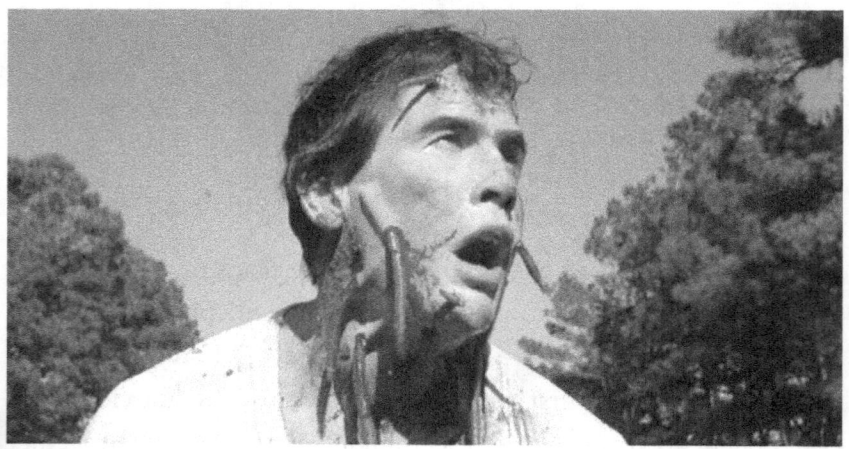

party, which, of course, meant that somewhere out there was a family who was expecting to see a little girl's party and saw a reel of gross out worms instead. I sure wish I could have seen their reactions. To this day, young boys see screen grabs from the movie

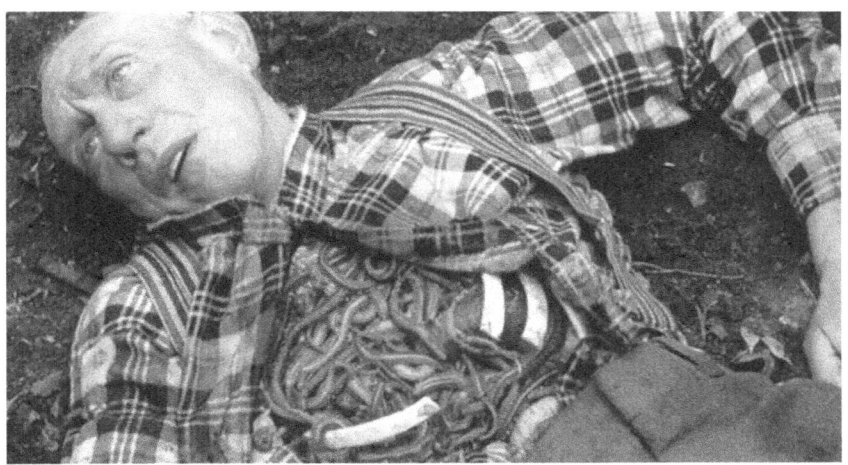

and say the same kinds of things they said back in 1976 - "Eww, gross!" and "Cool!" It's an evergreen. Sure can't beat that.

The biggest challenge with *Squirm* was making the fake worms look real. We used a quarter million real worms and another quarter million fake rubber ones. Getting the fake worms to be constantly animated was a great and constant challenge. We coated them with this ultra-slimy fluid and then had to always have them go downhill so gravity would move them along. As for the real worms, to get them to jump around like that, we had to electrocute them.

When dealing with any outrageous idea like *Squirm*, you need to play it straight, just like you do with an all-out comedy. The timing of the scare and gross out gags is very similar to comedic structure and timing – set up, gag, reaction. I think *Squirm* makes a good comedy because people laugh at the right places. A bad comedy would be when they laugh at the wrong places.

Was their comedy on set too? Absolutely. R.A. Dow, the actor who played Roger, had his full worm face makeup on and was standing around on set. I got the idea to go into the nearby neighborhood drug store and see if they had anything for this "rare skin condition." I wish I had filmed it. The druggist was speechless. Only recently, I also learned that there was a big bootlegging stall at the end of the block that was the main location. Had we known, I probably would've had a very drunk crew half the time.

We did a normal casting through a casting agent. The principals were all NY trained actors who we brought down to Georgia. Then we cast locals, mostly non-actors to play the lesser roles. I like the scenes in the luncheonette with the locals because they're so authentic and really ground the movie in the reality it needed to tell this total bullshit story.

We lensed *Squirm* on the coast of Georgia, more precisely in the town of Port Wentworth. We needed to shoot in November, and that's the only place where it was still green without being tropical, which I didn't want.

Would I recommend *Squirm* to an audience that doesn't yet know the film? Not if you ever want to eat spaghetti again. Honestly, anyone who's ever made a movie has some regrets about how certain things turned out as opposed to "on paper." But by and large, *Squirm* has really held up for being exactly what it is, and I think that's because the tone is spot on. A real Saturday matinee fun movie with a beginning, middle, and end. And, even more importantly, it got me a house and another movie. What more could I ask for?

Jeff Liebermann

Jeff Lieberman is an American film director best known for his movies *Squirm*, *Blue Sunshine*, *Just Before Dawn*, *Remote Control*, and *Satan's Little Helper*. He has also directed the TV movie *Doctor Franken*, an episode for the TV series *The Days and Nights of Molly Dodd*, and the TV documentaries *Sonny Liston: The Mysterious Life and Death of a Champion* and *But... Seriously?* He created and produced the TV series *'Til Death Do Us Part* for which he directed the pilot and wrote several episodes.

Apart from scripting his own movies, he has written screenplays for *Blade* (1973) and *The Never Ending Story III* (1994).

He also produces and directs TV commercials.

STRAYS (1991)

By Daniel Alves

For reasons that now escape me, the theme we decided to go for that night was animal attacks; out of several options, we chose *Strays*, a film that we believed would follow the slasher formula (as do many animal attack films). It became apparent almost immediately that this film would be an entirely different "animal."

The film opens with a crazy cat lady being killed by what seems to be a giant cat. We're then introduced to our victims: a professional couple with a young daughter. This initially perplexed me since a good slasher needs at least five potential victims, and those victims generally do not include children. However, we soon see that the couple is buying the home of the crazy cat lady from the opening. A young couple with a small child buying a suspicious new home; this isn't a slasher movie; it's a haunted house film!

The creators of this movie decided to take a haunted house narrative but replaced ghosts with feral cats. Fortunately it's a very good haunted house movie. The formula usually has a shocking/ mysterious intro, some jump scares

or deaths of minor characters to keep up suspense, and then the supernatural force reveals itself for the climax. Most of the story, however, is about the victim's day to day life while the ghost gears up for act three. The key to a successful haunted house story is to make that day to day almost as, if not more, interesting than the supernatural action, and *Strays* delivers.

We're introduced to the central conflict almost immediately as the realtor who sold our victims the house is revealed to the wife's younger, hotter sister, who the husband (a lawyer) is helping through a nasty divorce for free. It's quickly established that the wife feels threatened by her sister, who is a successful realtor while the wife herself is an unsuccessful author. She feels guilty for being supported by her husband and for convincing him to move to the country. The wife also fears that her sister is after her husband and that his reluctance to charge her for his legal services is due to his attraction to her rather than her status as his sister-in-law. Despite (or perhaps because of) her insecurities, the wife is clearly in charge of the relationship. It's made explicit that the move to the country is her idea, but this is also shown in other ways. For instance, the wife is the one that drives whenever they're in the car together (except once, which immediately leads to a car accident).

As the film progresses it becomes apparent that the wife's suspicions are half-justified: her sister is after her husband, but her husband is mostly oblivious. He's distracted by the divorce case and his cat allergy, an allergy which acts up despite there (initially) being no obvious signs of cats. The couple and their daughter go through their routine of settling in to the new home; dealing with a

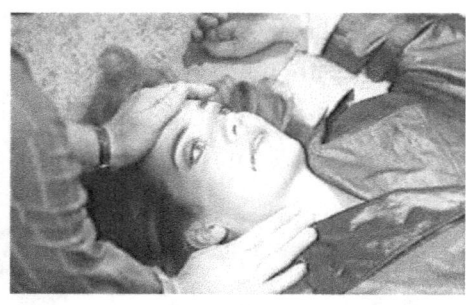

new much longer commute, not working on that new novel, having non-arguments about money, setting up utilities, not noticing that the electrician has been killed by feral cats and left in the basement; normal stuff. Also, the wife sees the husband giving her sister a hug and assumes the worst. During this time the feral cats increase their harassment of the family, so they call an expert.

The role of paranormal expert in haunted house films is a problematic one. The character can be interesting (like in *Poltergeist*), but they've been overused to the point of ridiculousness (I'm looking at you, *Sinister*). In this case, the condescending veterinarian called to deal with the felines explains that feral cats are territorial monsters that have no fear of humans and after some prodding gives the husband a squirt gun. Though worried that the problem is more serious than the vet believes, the family is determined to stay in their new house. Even if they wanted to leave at that point they can't afford to move. The aforementioned non-arguments about money mostly concerned the failure of the wife's previous book and how it was a terrible time to buy a new house.

The cats finally launch their attack, forcing the wife and daughter to hide in the tool shed/playhouse. The sister enters the house unaware of the murderous cats, and the wife rushes in to rescue her. When the wife returns to the shed/playhouse she finds her daughter is gone! Fade to black. Then the husband arrives, and the movie continues. After an exciting showdown, we fade to black. Then come back for an epilogue and fade to black again. Then come back for another epilogue and fade to black again. A fade out is not used for a scene transition anywhere else in the film, why it would be used four times during the film's climax is a mystery to me. Perhaps the filmmakers, having filmed multiple endings, decided to use as many as they could?

"Like herding cats" is used as a metaphor for an unfeasibly tedious task, yet the film features acting from a clowder of cats. They're mostly present for *The Birds*-style staring matches, but that in itself is impressive. The action mostly implies the cats are attacking, but it's always actions you'd believe cats could take. The cat leader (who, sadly, is not a giant cat) displays his ugly mug for numerous close-ups, making me wonder how they got the cat to hold still for makeup; or, alternately, how they found such an ugly animal.

For all the praise I have heaped on this film, it's not without flaws. The whole production gives off a noticeable "made-for-TV" vibe; the lack of recognizable actors is one factor, but the lack of sets is much more obvious. Other than driving scenes, there are only three scenes that do not take place in the house. These scenes nominally take place in different locations but are all obviously filmed in the same spot. The crew does a good job making use of the house itself, it feels like its own character; but the husband's office and the sister's apartment being the same set really hurts suspension of disbelief.

Despite, or perhaps because it features no ghosts or overt supernatural phenomena of any kind, this is an excellent example of a haunted house film. The filmmakers play with tropes just enough to make a unique and satisfying story while following a proven framework.

Daniel Alves

Daniel Alves is a Mathematics teacher at the Academy of San Francisco. His primary hobbies are tabletop role-playing (D&D), followed closely by shonen manga and anime. He also enjoys deconstructing genre films and analyzing the tropes and themes therein.

The worst sin a film can commit is to be boring. He especially dislikes Mary Sues (I'm looking at you Liam Neeson), as they rob a story of tension. However, even terrible things can be enjoyable, especially if you watch them with friends. Some of the best times he has had watching movies have been with truly horrible films (*The Beast of Yucca Flats* springs to mind).

Daniel writes movie reviews for *The Overlook Theater*.

THE BEASTS ARE ON THE STREETS (1978)

By Brian Saur

I'm an unapologetic fan of "animals attack" films. There's just something about the idea of this often normally safe environment suddenly becoming a treacherous and deadly place that I find appealing. In films, it's great to have a really solid bad guy. It drives a film forward and makes the drama richer if you have a villain that is sinister yet believable. Bad villains can really bring a film down. The trick is to make their motivations and goals fit the story or the level of drama already established. If they're too over the top in the wrong film it makes things laughable. The "animals attack" genre is great in that you have your villains as basically unpredictable terminators who are driven by pure instinct. They have no feelings about you or your family other than that they must make you dead as it's in their genetic material. I'm not saying that animals are evil in general (I'm a true animal lover at heart), but in the context of this genre they're generally the means by which people will die. And the other thing is, you can't blame them for dispatching people in these movies, so there's an odd imbalance of sympathies (on a subconscious level) at play that I like a lot.

I saw *The Beasts are on the Streets* via a bootleg, but it was quite tricky to track down at that time. I found that to be a bit of a shame as it has a solid cast and a great TV movie vibe. I love movies about institutions that don't really exist anymore. *The Beasts are on the Streets* is about animals getting loose from a safari park after a freak accident tears down a section of their fence line (the impetus for which is some rednecks menacing a tanker truck driver). This safari park happens to have one of its borders along a stretch of freeway, and as soon as the truck rips down the fence, the road is flooded with animals from the park. Camels, elephants, lions, tigers, zebras, panthers, and a bear stampede on and around the gridlocked traffic as the horrified passengers try to keep them out of their cars. There's one particularly stupid gentleman who leaves his vehicle to go check things out and finds himself run down and tackled by a tiger. Some elephants shake a few cars and crush them underfoot. A rhino bashes a sedan. The animals even fight with each other. A helicopter overhead repeatedly tells the people to stay in their cars. This is easily my favorite sequence in the film. Very enjoyable stuff. There's also a good scene where the animals go to a children's amusement park. I know it sounds a bit sadistic, but I have a fondness for scenes of children in peril as they seem kind of shocking today. It's just kind of cry to see some of the shots with the animals so close to real people. A good portion of the film's plot involves the safari park staff doing their best to round up and return the all of the animals. There are a few suspenseful moments as some of the big cats descend upon a suburban neighborhood. The main dramatic thrust has to do with the safari folks trying to contain the animals with tranquilizers whilst dealing with the threat of citizen hunters.

While safari parks still exist in some capacity, they have really all but disappeared, especially in the U.S. (as far as I know). The idea of a park where there are wild animals roaming free, and you tour it via a tram or in your own car seems like a bad idea in the litigious society we live in today. So many potential lawsuits! Anyway, it makes for an enjoyable TV movie.

Quick aside: There's an Italian film called *Wild Beasts* from 1984 that is similar to this movie. In the Italian version, a zoo's water supply is contaminated with PCP, and the animals go nuts and get loose. *The Beasts are on the Streets* is a bit tamer than that, but it still features lots of citizens being attacked by and fleeing from

ARCHIVE COLLECTION

CAROL LYNLEY   DALE ROBINETTE   BILLY GREEN BUSH
PHILIP MICHAEL THOMAS   CASEY BIGGS

THE BEASTS ARE ON THE STREETS

large live animals. It's hard not to bring up CGI when watching something like this. I probably harp on it a lot in my regular discussions of moviemaking, but it's just on my mind a lot watching as many older films as I do. *The Beasts are on the Streets* would have little to no live animals if it were to be made today. It's a sad thing. I love watching the way real animals move and behave on camera. It's extremely difficult to attempt to mimic the way they observe and react to things. You could watch hours and hours of footage to try to get some insights into the psychology behind their actions, but when it comes down to it, that instinct factor is like an unknowable chaos theory. It really does lend itself to a sense of genuine suspense when they're menacing actors (or stunt people/ trainers). Also, animals are just pretty to look at. Simple as that. Plus, my cinematically obsessed mind always goes to the first scene with Burl Ives in Sam Fuller's *White Dog*. His character runs a facility that trains and loans out animals to film productions. He's throwing darts at a cardboard version of R2-D2 and talking about how his business is basically dying because of movies like that.

As far as the main cast of *The Beasts are on the Streets* goes, it consists of Carol Lynley, Philip Michael Thomas, and Billy Green Bush, but there are lots of familiar faces to be seen as well. Interesting note about this film's director is that Peter R. Hunt has some big time ties to the *James Bond* franchise. Not only did he direct *On Her Majesty's Secret Service* (one of my favorites), but he was also the editor on several classic Bonds including *Dr. No*, *From Russia With Love* and *Goldfinger*. He even edited the great British spy thriller *The Ipcress File*. He also directed *Death Hunt* (with Charles Bronson and Lee Marvin), *Shout at the Devil* and *Gold*. All interesting films.

Oh, and I totally forgot to mention that *The Beasts are on the Streets* was produced by animation giants Hanna-Barbera, who have an interesting legacy of oddball TV movies such as *Kiss Meets the Phantom of the Park* and *The Legend of the Superheroes*. This movie isn't like those by any stretch (as both are off-the-wall insane in a lot of ways), but it's intriguing that they're behind this nonetheless. I mean, they made countless cartoons with talking animals, why not a live action movie with them running wild and attacking people? Seems like a bizarre choice, but I for one am glad they made it.

Who knows, maybe this film and Hanna-Barbera's cartoons inspired the *Madagascar* series. Okay, I'm just reaching there, but sometimes reaching is fun. And so is this movie.

Brian Saur

Brian Saur is the film blogger behind *Rupert Pupkin Speaks*, which he began focusing on seriously circa 2010. He has also written for *Paracinema Magazine*.

He attended the University of Wisconsin in Madison where he studied film. He worked in video stores for nearly a decade and became an even more voracious film viewer during all that time. During his college years, he discovered the books of film author Danny Peary. Peary was so inspirational to him that he's currently working on a documentary on the impact and influence of his writings.

THE BIRDS (1963)

By Chris Austin

If you've seen the movie, you know the scene. Even today, with advancements in visual effects, the scene retains its power to shock, repulse, unsettle. The bloody corpse of an old man, his eye-sockets black holes where his eyes should be. And we all know what happened to his eyes. If there's one shot from this film everyone remembers, this is it.

It may have been one of the highest grossing films of the year and regarded as a classic today, but Alfred Hitchcock's *The Birds* split the critics back in 1963. Some rallied against what they considered to be weak characterization and the haphazard coming together of suburban family drama with terrifying bird attacks. Others however, such as Andrew Sarris, described it as a "major work of cinematic art" and expressed appreciation for the shocking effects. Today the film is sometimes described as Hitchcock's last "great" film, pointing to a perceived decline that would begin with *Marnie* (1964) and would be all but complete by the time of *The Family Plot* (1976).

For those who have yet to see this wonderful piece of cinema, the premise is simple enough: small town America finds itself under attack by birds. Coming at a time when crazed animal attack movies had become a staple of drive-in theaters and b-movie presentations across the United States this might not sound particularly engaging and at worst rather cheesy. The nuclear age had brought with it a myriad of tales about large mutated spiders, rats, ants, etc. terrorizing small towns, yet *The Birds* stays comfortably away from such overdone tropes.

Hitchcock takes horror back to its very essence – mystery. He does not seek to provide any explanation for the sudden savagery of the feathered sky dwellers, and there's no mad scientist to conveniently explain the phenomena. What we're given instead is something that goes beyond the absurd premise and works because it happens to characters that feel like real people.

Any potential explanation for the events that unfurl seems more based on the movie's underlying symbolism – something that Hitchcock had become renowned for by this late stage of his career. In the first act of *The Birds*, we're introduced to Melanie Daniels (Tippi Hedren), who has traveled to the picturesque Bodega Bay to play a prank on a lawyer, Mitch (Rod Taylor). Hedren is the typical Hitchcock starlet, in the mold of Grace Kelly and Janet Leigh – she's blonde, she's beautiful, and she oozes sexuality. Having been unable to lure the aforementioned Grace Kelly out of retirement, Hitchcock spotted the model Tippi Hedren in a commercial and chose her for the role despite her complete lack of acting experience.

As this young bombshell storms into Bodega Bay, so too does the tornado of flying fury in the skies. Some have surmised that the birds represent Hitchcock's own rumored discomfort with female sexuality, and like a tidal wave of hormonal energy it's manifested in the onslaught wrought against this sleepy, conservative town. The most beautiful woman in the entire town, before Melanie rocks up, is a school teacher; hardly the epitome of 1960s glam.

Others have suggested that the birds are a physical manifestation of fear on the part of both Mitch's mother (Jessica Tandy) and his former lover, Annie (Suzanne Pleshette). Melanie, with her sex appeal and chic dress could be the poster child for 1960s sophistication. In her, Mitch's mother can see aspects of herself, of a former life that she has long since been forced to put away. Mitch's mother casts knowing looks in the direction of Melanie; she's aware of the way such a girl could turn a man's head. By extension, Annie can see a sexual challenger. It may be a gender reversal from the stags that lock antlers to prove themselves worthy of the pick of the does, but there's a sense that Annie and Melanie are challenging one another for the same mate, and the way in which the birds swoop to attack Melanie's face seems more than a touch symbolic.

A blunt accusation cast in Melanie's direction, associating her arrival with the attack of the birds, is as close as we come to an explanation. This ambiguity would continue all the way to the end. Hitchcock reportedly spent many sleepless nights trying to come up with a suitable conclusion to the film. Although an ending existed in the screenplay, he felt it too neat and favored an approach that could leave the audience in a state of fear long after the film's conclusion. Hitchcock wanted viewers to cast wary looks to the sky as they walked or drove home and, finally, after much deliberation, drew upon a drunk character's throwaway line about the end of the world and opted to cast aside the traditional "The End" card, feeling this would signify a terror without end thus creating the desired effect.

Originally Hitchcock courted Joseph Stefano, his screenwriter for *Psycho*, to pen this picture, but Stefano passed, citing no interest in the Daphne Du Maurier story on which the film is based. Hitchcock went on to hire Evan Hunter, a crime novelist published under the pseudonym Ed McBain, although Hunter would later make several public complaints about Hitchcock's handling

of his material and the number of revisions by other parties. Hunter would later write several versions of the script for *Marnie* but was even more annoyed when Hitchcock eventually opted to use a script penned by Jay Presson Allen.

Hitchcock had become renowned for his dictatorial style of making motion pictures, and *The Birds* was no different. In order to attract the trained birds to the actors, Hitchcock would have their hands and arms smeared in ground meat or anchovies, and during the movie's standout attic scene, he insisted that real gulls be used and attached to Tippi Hedren's costume via elastic bands. During the week-long shooting of this scene, which accounts for scarcely a minute of screen time, Hedren suffered a scratched eyeball, causing her to break down in tears. Cary Grant, a long-time leading man in Hitchcock's movies, happened to be visiting the set that day and comforted the young actress, pointing out that she was "one brave lady."

Although many real birds were used during shooting, prolific Disney animator Ub Iwerks was the man responsible for the larger scenes. He blended trained birds with animated birds to create convincing swarms of birds, most obviously during the movie's ambiguous ending, and received an Oscar nomination for his efforts. The Oscar would eventually go to *Cleopatra* and *The Birds* itself received no further recognition from the academy. For the early scene in the playground, puppet crows were used while the children ran on a treadmill to create the illusion of running from the attacking birds.

One further point of note is the soundtrack, or lack thereof. Hitchcock again dispensed with convention, a nod to the power he yielded over studios at this point in his career. Most studios would be very protective when handing directors expansive budgets, but Hitchcock was given free rein to do as he pleased. The soundtrack was produced on an electro-acoustic device, a predecessor to the synthesizer, and consisted of various bird calls countered with calculated silence. A little source music exists, such as when Melanie plays *Deux arabesques* on the piano, but there's no traditional scoring, further adding to the ominous tone throughout the film.

The Birds is a film that every horror fan has to watch at least once. Whether it's Alfred Hitchcock's final "great" film is a matter for discussion, but it's a "great" film that would go on to inspire a slew of horror filmmakers over the next few decades. John Carpenter, for example, cited the elements of mystery and the lack of safety within the home as an inspiration for his 1978 slasher masterpiece, *Halloween*, while Xan Cassavetes has described it as one of the most profound influences on her own work. If *Psycho* is Hitchcock's horror masterpiece, then *The Birds* is his terror masterpiece.

Chris Austin

Chris Austin is a freelance writer from England. He has seen work published on a variety of subjects, including film, sports and politics, both in print and online, and was the writer of the 2014 short drama film *Long Lost Father,* which premiered at the Flanders International Film Festival Ghent. Chris is currently working on several book projects, including *Dawn's Light*, a grimdark futuristic science-fiction saga.

When he isn't writing, he enjoys horror movies, video games, trying to get his dog to behave and studies for fun. He holds diplomas in sociology and humanities, a degree in social sciences and is currently studying creative writing, part time, with the Open University. His proudest achievement is managing to quit smoking and his biggest regret is starting in the first place. You can follow Chris on Twitter @TheVacantPage or visit his personal site www.vacantpage.co.uk.

THE DEADLY MANTIS (1957)

By Christopher Robinson

The promotional trailer for *The Deadly Mantis* pledges, "a thousand tons of beastly fury." This 1957 science fiction classic from Universal-International Pictures joins *Night of the Lepus, The Birds, The Fly and Them!* in the elite pantheon of man vs. beast. Although their quality varied, no classic horror fan can dispute Universal's place in setting a high standard for the genre.

A volcanic eruption in the North Pole results in the surfacing of an enormous frozen prehistoric insect. Col. Joe Parkman (Craig Stevens) arrives on the scene of a wrecked military post in Northern Canada to discover clues of a mysterious attack which

occurs again in another region. Flying to the second site, Joe brings back a long green object appearing to be a hunk of innocuous vegetable matter. Paleontologist Ned Jackson (William Hopper) deduces that it's part of an impossibly large insect (probably a praying mantis) which is somehow a throwback to prehistoric ages. The rest of the mantis, now sporting ample screen time, attacks an Inuit tribe, sending Ned and his photographer, Marge Blaine (Alix Talton), to the adjacent outpost. Ned, Marge, and Joe get an up-close look at the marauding bug as it smashes through their compound's ceiling, forcing them to take cover and sending all available units into defensive action. The mantis is first undeterred by their firepower but eventually retreats. After attacking a few fishermen, the creature now makes its way to the nation's capital, scaling the Washington Monument. Fighter pilots, with Joe among them, forge an offensive attack to bring the bug down and barricade it in the Manhattan Tunnel. A barrage of bombs and gunfire only agitate the mantis, but soon a grounded Joe makes his way toward the stubborn critter with a line drive bomb, exterminating the menacing mantis once and for all. Ned and Marge now enter the tunnel and, as is the case with much of the classic horror/sci-fi genre, a quick exchange and some closure on the romantic angle (Marge, in between smooches, finally takes that big photo she's been waiting for) is all that needs to play out before a series of title cards begin flashing away. Nothin' will be buggin' *them* for a while!

Nathan Juran directed *The Deadly Mantis*, though without cooperation from stop-motion pioneer Ray Harryhausen, with whom he created the enduring fantasy features *20 Million Miles to Earth* (1957) and *The 7th Voyage of Sinbad* (1958). Production values in *The Deadly Mantis*, however, are far superior to those of Juran's embarrassingly schlocky *Attack of the 50 Foot Woman* (1958).

Martin Berkeley, previously a co-writer of *Revenge of the Creature* and *Tarantula* (both 1955), penned the script. Berkeley's reputation, however, lingers in Hollywood lore for his part in the infamous House Un-American Activities investigations. A named former party member, Berkeley outed over a hundred fellow members in his testimonies. This may explain the downward global trek of the mantis, conquering societies in a domino effect until reaching iconic American landmarks such as Washington, D.C. and New York. Presumably, subtle allusions were safer commentary than any movie that could have been adapted from his 1953 propaganda piece, *Reds in Your Living Room*. The inherent cold war anxieties which Berkeley brought to the script might seem ironic in light of the undertones of *High Noon*, for example, long rumored to be an allegory of the very threat Berkeley himself represented to Hollywood. One wonders if the paranoia that spawned the giant creature features actually inspired conversation and debate among everyday Americans, dominating water coolers and playgrounds across the land.

A capable cast also brings their specialized styles and genre experience to the proceedings. Craig Stevens would later portray Peter Gunn, and William Hopper was already a ubiquitous

presence on 1950s screens, large and small. Hopper even starred in Columbia Pictures' *20 Million Miles to Earth,* in a role not unlike Stevens' in *The Deadly Mantis.*

Nathan Juran's economical approach is evident. Acquired film clips were used as needed (was that *Nanook of the North*?). Further cost-cutting measures are particularly obviated during a scene where Ned tosses an attaché case at Marge. He aims a bit too high, nearly clocking her in the jaw, and their incredulous expressions are ostensibly unscripted. In the very same shot, a boom microphone shadow takes center stage as they leave the room, all signs of a rushed director's penchant for single-take shooting.

Typical for Universal is the inexplicable calm of the characters in the face of terror. In *The Deadly Mantis,* Joe and Marge's flirtatious affair is unmitigated even as the entire country is plainly informed they're in the path of a 200-ft. killer insect. They really aren't any different from the 3 billion other people across the world who manage not to show even the slightest sign of stress. The notion that young love will trump any emotions triggered by world crisis suggests that director Juran is more the romantic than we would have taken him for.

Ned Jackson declares: "In all the kingdom of the living, there's no more deadly or voracious creature than the praying mantis." An overlooked, underestimated specimen in nature, the praying mantis possesses quite an arsenal. Spiked legs trap its prey, which often includes larger animals or insects. They're masters at the art of survival, with exceptional skill in speed, vision, camouflage, and flight. Yet, who sympathizes with the Deadly Mantis? It's the creature everyone looks down on, pointing: "Check out that weird bug!" "He's gross!" One can only take it for so long. Was its rampage simply payback for centuries of enduring humiliation at the hands of those intimidating humans?

It wasn't even enough that it got "no respect," its timing was wrong, too. Arriving as it did in 1957, it made the scene too early for model kits, Halloween masks, and lunchbox posterity. Concurrently, it was too late to duke it out with Abbott and Costello. One can only imagine those possibilities:

Bud: "I told ya, Lou. Pull it together. There's just no such thing as a giant praying mantis!"

Lou: "Oh, I wish I could agree wit ya, but either you're wrong, or dat thing up there is the *ugliest* piñata this side of the border!"

But despite its undervalued status, the deadly mantis succeeds in stealing scenes from its co-stars, with its most iconic moment being when he attacks the station outpost and Marge's one and only scream is sounded. Acknowledgment is simply giving credit where it's due. *The Deadly Mantis* is a fun and entertaining film with a fantastic giant bug from one of the finest and most fastidious studios of Hollywood's golden age. That's the truth, not a just a *big* story.

Christopher Robinson

Christopher Robinson is a writer and filmmaker who has also worked as a cameraman, videographer, and teacher.

He produced, directed and hosted a cable access TV show in Princeton, NJ. Other credits include directing a legal video deposition of singer Jon Bon Jovi and a music video featuring revolutionary war sites, which is on file in the library of the Princeton Battlefield.

He has contributed to several websites, among them, *Cult Reviews* and *Rare Cult Cinema*. A lifelong resident of North Jersey, he currently resides there with his two dogs, Lon and Lon Jr.

He believes the significance of movies is that they all reflect the attitudes of some portion of society.

THE DEVIL BAT (1940)

By Sven Daems

"All Heathville loved Paul Carruthers, their kindly village doctor. No one suspected that in his home laboratory on a hillside overlooking the magnificent estate of Martin Heath, the doctor found time to conduct certain private experiments – weird, terrifying experiments."

No one could guess how consistent bitterness overwhelmed the ever-smiling company chemist Dr. Carruthers (Bela Lugosi). Being considered one of the finest men in Heathville, the doctor feels betrayed for being denied his share of the success of the  Heath and Morton imperium. After all, their fortunes are based on a greaseless cold-cream "formula" that he invented. It's not the most subtle move of Henry Morton (Guy Usher) to rub it in quite abundantly:

Henry Morton: "A net profit of over a million dollars! Not bad, eh? – when you remember what we built on: a mere ten thousand dollars for your formula!"

Dr. Carruthers: "'Formula! That's but child's play for a great scientist. Your brain is too feeble to conceive what I accomplished in the world of science!"

Even a fat bonus check of 5000 dollars in return for countless years of creating bestselling colognes and perfumes felt like an insult. By seeing the company getting richer every day on his account, things started to get ugly inside the frustrated genius' mind. Plotting his revenge, Dr. Carruthers creates a new fragrance with a "slightly deadly" side-effect. The secret of this after-shave lotion lies in an intoxicating Tibetan ingredient, used by Lamas during their religious rites. Not the shaving lotion on its own will kill its bearer, but the scientist also breeds a vicious mutant species of oversized vampire bats that detect and attack anyone who wears this lotion. By handing out "test-samples" to the members and relatives of the Heath and Morton family, each one will experience the wrath of Dr. Carruthers.

Of course, these enigmatic assassinations will not pass unnoticed. The national media smells a big scoop and send their

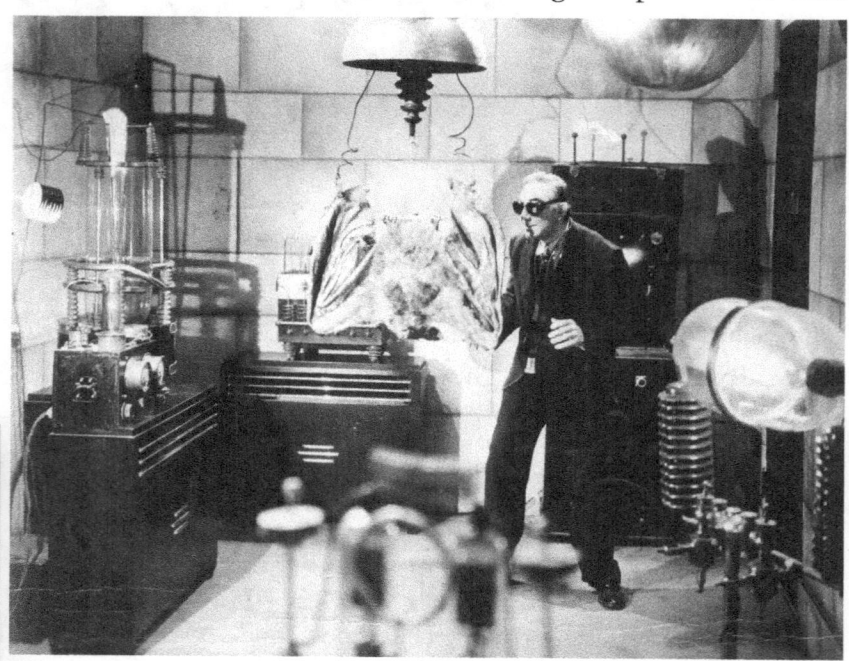

big city newspaper journalist Johnny Layton (Dave O'Brian) and cameraman "One-Shot" McGuire (Donald Kerr) to find clues and proof. Henry Morton calls upon his fellow companions with his own elementary deductions, but before Morton has the chance to share his findings, Dr. Carruthers sets loose one of his hematophagous monsters, which causes the lotion-wearing Morton to die in the arms of his companions. In the meantime, Mary (Suzanne Kaaren) retires to her room and notices, after putting it on, that her perfume was not the same as usual. She goes to bed anyway, and, like clockwork, the sonic slaughter machine appears.

However, the beast fails in its attack because of the window being too small for his oversized shape. While the sinful doctor is attending to the traumatized Mary, Johnny discovers the dark secrets hidden in Dr. Carruthers well camouflaged basement. Now realizing the doctor is behind this scheme, Johnny knows he has to play his cards right. Therefore he invites the doctor to an experiment of his own.

A fatal one, so it seems…

Jean Yarborough's *The Devil Bat* was not only the first but also the most successful horror movie from Producers Releasing Corporation (PRC) after it was formed from the failed Producers Distributing Corporation (PDC). Much of this success had to do with the casting of Bela Lugosi, without a doubt the most famous vampire in cinema history. Launched in the 1940s, when filmmaking had to be done as cheaply as possible to yield maximum results, there was no budget to attract expensive Hollywood stars. Yet, despite having played Dracula both on the silver screen and on Broadway, Bela Lugosi had become affordable. He was suffering a physical downfall, living on a diet of morphine and methadone. In fact, he was the first celeb being a notorious drug addict in Tinseltown. As a result of taking any role possible, his reputation declined heavily, and he practically transformed into a pitiful caricature of his proud, handsome, and mysterious self. For *The Devil Bat*, however, casting this remaining "shadow" of the once superstar Bela Lugosi was a clever move. The script needed a strong character for Dr. Carruthers and Bela's firm Eastern Europe appearance and Hungarian accent seemed the ideal marriage. Because the film suffers from painfully bad special effects and the short timeframe that makes the movie look like an incoherent series of developments pressed into a small time bomb, it remains safe to say it was Bela Lugosi who turned *The Devil Bat* into a classic of the genre. Movie critic Tom Weaver even hailed *The Devil Bat* as one of Lugosi's best movies in his "poverty row horrors" (1993).

Because of the no budget atmosphere and bad special effects, a superficial viewer could easily mistake *The Devil Bat* for a second-rate b-movie horror film. At the core, however, *The Devil Bat* is about dissatisfaction and how far it can drive a poor man. A frustrated doctor wants to avenge the company that took advantage of his work. But what does that really mean? What is more evil? The mad doctor with his trained killing machines? Or could it be the socially accepted fiber of the "green fabric" that spreads greediness by those that are hopelessly addicted to it? Money, or, more to the point, the power-syndrome, is as old as mankind itself. Aztecs, Romans, Conquistadores, and so on, sacrificed countless amounts of people for the promised mountains of gold. On their quest to conquer the mythical golden city "El Dorado" thousands of people died in horrible circumstances. Or what to say of the gold rush, which was perhaps less violent but drove so many people simply stark raving mad? Of course, in this tale, money took the place of gold, but the effect is the same.

The Devil Bat, which had a 1946 sequel titled *Devil Bat's Daughter,* is a must for people who can see beyond what's buried beneath the obvious. It's this layered undertone that is both critical and pre-kitsch, together with Lugosi's shining performance what really makes *The Devil Bat* worth seeing.

Sven Daems

Based on his well acclaimed erudite musical knowledge, DJ SVN aka Sven Daems created his own spot on Soundslike.be, at that time one of the most significant Belgian digital music platforms. While regular channels didn't want to tackle "difficult" music, art, movies, and readings, Sven's goal was to place these in a broad, meaningful context and to seek out the highest quality possible.

Alas, the digital world moves fast, and the curtain fell. Artists and organizers persuaded him to launch a new digital platform: *Svn's Corky Corner*. The focus remains on stigmatized art forms to prevent them from getting lost into oblivion. Contradictory to its creator's passion for music, the actual shape or form has no consequence. To stay in the spirit of the medieval bishop of Bath and Wells: "Animal, vegetable or mineral, I'll do anything to anything."

THE FOOD OF THE GODS (1976)

By Aaron Christensen

For millions of monster kids, the gigantism craze of late 1950s sci-fi cinema represented a buffet of charm and chills. Every week, drive-in screens were awash with jumbo-sized beasts bearing down on helpless humans, only to be vanquished just as the soda and popcorn ran out. Perhaps the most celebrated purveyor of this brand of escapism was self-taught Wisconsin filmmaker Bert I. Gordon (dubbed "Mr. B.I.G." by *Famous Monsters of Filmland*'s Forrest Ackerman), who cranked out a strapping sextet of oversized odes between 1957 and 1958: *Beginning of the End*, *The Cyclops*, *The Amazing Colossal Man*, *War of the Colossal Beast*, *Earth vs.*

...for a taste of HELL!

H.G. WELLS' MASTERPIECE OF SCIENCE FICTION

SAMUEL Z. ARKOFF presents
a BERT I. GORDON film
H.G. WELLS' **FOOD OF THE GODS**

An American International Picture

MARJOE GORTNER · PAMELA FRANKLIN · RALPH MEEKER

the Spider, and *Attack of the Puppet People*.

Following this avalanche of capacious creativity, Gordon moved away from the subgenre he had helped create, expanding his oeuvre to include ghost stories, action thrillers, and sex comedies. But the 1970s ecological horror boom combined with the *Jaws*-inspired "animals attack" movement proved too alluring to pass up; when longtime producer and American International honcho Samuel Z. Arkoff approached in 1975, inquiring if he had any new projects, Gordon thought immediately of a certain book by H.G. Wells, one upon which he had already riffed with his 1965 romp, *Village of the Giants*. "I remembered the giant rats in *The Food of the Gods*, and, instantly, I knew we had a picture."

In addition to Volkswagen-sized rodents, our bipedal heroes are besieged by humongous wasps, grub worms, and chickens. Purists be warned: a faithful adaptation of Wells' novel this is not. (Note the credit: "Based on a portion of the novel by...") Rather than the lab-created *Herakleophorbia IV*, here the titular vittles bubble straight up out of the ground, resembling a particularly viscous batch of creamed-corn soup. Almost the entirety of the action takes place on a remote island (Gordon shot all his principal photography at Cowan's Point on Bowen Island, British Columbia, returning to Los Angeles to complete the special effects on miniature sets). The character of Bensington is changed from a bald, benevolent scientist to a scurrilous flim-flam artist (played to perfection by burly Ralph Meeker). And our main hero is a horseback-riding, shotgun-shooting, football-playing ideal of liberal pragmatism named Morgan (Marjoe Gortner), who kicks things off with a narrated reminiscence of his father prophesying, "One of these days the Earth will get even with Man for messing her up with his garbage."

While subtlety is not the first (or fifth) item on Gordon's priority list, the writer-producer-director-special effects artist and his committed ensemble take the opening speech's portentous tone to heart, playing every scene to the hilt without an ounce of camp. Gortner, with his curly blonde hair and Heston-sized teeth, is a terrific brains-and-brawn man of action, as comfortable setting a giant wasp nest ablaze as he's constructing a makeshift electric fence. He's matched ably by genre legend Pamela Franklin (*The Legend of Hell House*, Gordon's 1972 feature *Necromancy*) as Lorna Scott, a sharp and attractive bacteriologist working with Bensington. Franklin is unfortunately saddled with some of the clunkiest dialogue, but she sells it as best she can, even the notorious scene where she confesses to Morgan, "I want you to make love to me," during a brief lull in the rat attacks.

Ida Lupino, star of such classics as *High Sierra* and *The Devil's Rain*, and a trailblazing director in her own right, brings an enormous amount of humanity to her penultimate screen role of Mrs. Skinner, the simple God-fearing woman who discovers the mysterious substance and mixes it with chicken feed, thereby setting the hideous chain of events in motion. (She stores the tasty mixture in mason jars, helpfully labeled "F.O.T.G." in case anyone forgot the movie's title.) Belinda Balaski and Tom Stovall round out the main cast as an unmarried pregnant couple caught up in the voluminous vermin's wake.

One can only guess that Gordon assumed viewers wouldn't mind seeing rats get shot with red paint pellets. After all, they're *rats*, right? Even so, members of PETA would be well-advised to steer clear, as it's impossible not to have a modicum of sympathy for our four legged thespians getting blasted in the face, blown up, and/or held underwater by their tails. While Gordon insists that the ASPCA was in contact at all times, there's no doubt that *animals were definitely harmed during the making of this film*. (The director also asserts on Shout! Factory's 2015 Blu-ray commentary that – at the actor's request – it's none other than Gortner laying down the crimson fire on his rodent nemeses.) Thankfully, the rats are the only real-life creatures to take a beating, and FX wunderkind Tom

Burman lightens the load with his large bucktoothed puppet heads and chicken beaks savagely attacking from just out of frame and giant latex wasps strapped to people's backs. The Oscar-nominated artist also supplied the copious amounts of red blood dashed about – this is easily Gordon's goriest film to date – and the nasty makeup job on an unfortunate venom victim. But not all of the effects earn their "special" title, the biggest offenders being the optically printed see-through wasps. Franklin and Lupino's looks of disbelief and awe from the farmhouse window are textbook examples of "no acting required;" watching Meeker swinging wildly away at the air with a shovel, you can almost hear them thinking, "What is he doing? What are we doing? How did we end up here…?"

According to Balaski, the shoot was originally slated for 10 days but ballooned to six weeks due to an unforeseen snowstorm that blanketed the location. Refusing Arkoff's demands to return to California and shoot in Griffith Park ("A tree's a tree!"), Gordon ultimately resorted to using blowtorches to melt away patches of land to complete his exteriors, and rewrote the third act to accommodate the weather, substituting the novel's farmhouse conflagration with drowning the rodent menace via the explosion of a nearby dam (another lackluster effect). One interesting by-product of the delay, however, was Lupino's ingenious solution to getting herself back to civilization – one day, she approached Gordon, telling him, "I have written my death scene, and I'll be on the 4pm ferry today." When the director pointed out that her character was supposed to *live*, the screen veteran looked up at the sky, back to Gordon, and said, "Clock's ticking, Bert." Mrs. Skinner met her gruesome death, and Lupino caught her ferry shortly thereafter.

Food of the Gods was excoriated by critics upon release – *The Hollywood Reporter*'s Arthur Knight called it "…not only sick, but sickening" – but audiences dug in, making it AIP's biggest moneymaker of the year. The success led to Arkoff and AIP producing two more Wells adaptations the following year: John Frankenheimer's *The Island of Dr. Moreau* and Gordon's own *Empire of the Ants*, the director's final foray into the realm of bloated behemoths. (It's also the perfect double feature with The *Food of the Gods*, with mind-controlling insects terrorizing members of another secluded island community, including Joan Collins and Robert Lansing.) The film later became a late-night TV staple, where further generations – including this writer – first encountered it. Happily, in this day of instant access, the bulk of Mr. B.I.G.'s work is widely available on home video, so pour yourself an extra-tall glass of contaminated milk, switch off the lights, and let the good times *grow*.

Aaron Christensen

Aaron Christensen (aka "Dr. AC") is a Chicago-based actor/writer. As one of the Midwest's rising enthusiasts of horror films/monster movies, he has now born witness to over 3000 fright flick titles (and counting), scouring the mainstream, foreign markets, and fringe indies for that next big thrill.

In addition to serving on the writing staff of *HorrorHound Magazine* since 2009, he's the editor of the critically acclaimed film guidebooks, *Horror 101: The A-List of Horror Films and Monster Movies* and *Hidden Horror: A Celebration of 101 Underrated and Overlooked Fright Flicks*, available on Amazon and wherever tomes of ill repute are sold. He's also a founding member of WildClaw Theater, Chicago's only horror-centric theater.

Fellow fright fans are welcome to join in the fun at horror101withdrac.com or on Facebook.

THE GHOST AND THE DARKNESS (1996)

By Kajah Ram

The Ghost and The Darkness is a nod to classic safari adventures like *Mogambo* (1953). Despite being based on one of the most fascinating true-life accounts of an animal attack and featuring material ripe for thematic exploration, *The Ghost and the Darkness* is a straightforward African adventure film of the khaki-clad Great White Hunter variety. Val Kilmer and Michael Douglas play the men who must defend a colonial railroad project in Africa from two "man-eater" lions, respectively known as Ghost and Darkness. The lions maim, destroy and massacre their way through the film as our heroes frantically try to stop the malevolent leonine duo.

These two lions are known as *The Man Eaters of Tsavo,* based on the title of a memoir by Lt. Col. John Henry Patterson. In 1898, Patterson was commissioned to build a railway bridge over the River Tsavo in Kenya when two beasts attacked and killed some of his workers, halting construction, and generally disrupting the progress of the British colonial machine. Patterson, an experienced engineer and hunter, played the most dangerous game: laying fresh bait to lure the lions, he perched in a high place and waited for the lions with a rifle in hand. Patterson eventually managed to kill both Ghost and Darkness, whose maneless skins are now on display at the Chicago Field Museum of Natural history. *The Ghost and the Darkness* was not the first film to be made from this source material, but it's the most famous adaptation known today.

The film begins in a steamy *fin de siècle* London with narrator Samuel (John Kani) describing Col. Patterson as a "fine Irish Gentleman." Patterson meets with Sir Robert Beaumont (Tom Wilkinson), the railroad project's financier. Beaumont starts his introduction by remarking, "Look at me closely Colonel Patterson: I'm a monster," inviting the viewer to speculate on who the real antagonist of this film really is. Patterson is presented here as the man of civilization: educated, competent, curious, compassionate, and driven to complete his bridge-building task by any means necessary. Greeted by the pious and ineffectual Angus Sterling (Brian McCardie), Patterson forays through an African safari idyll of giraffes, zebras, and hippos, which promptly ends upon their arrival in Tsavo, juxtaposing idyllic Africa with the juggernaut of colonial domination: thousands of laborers industriously laying track amid steam engines and steel. The workers themselves are drawn from all parts of Africa, and interfaith kerfuffles among Muslims and Hindus are a problem that our intrepid hero must keep under control. Patterson learns that one of the workers has been attacked by a lion and decides to camp out with Sterling in order to kill it. He does this with one carefully measured rifle shot, showing how a "normal lion" is easily vanquished. The audience is primed to accept the hypothesis that the coming beasts are in fact "more than lions."

However, the real story begins when Mahina, the charismatic foreman and local lion-killer, is ripped from his bed screaming and dragged out to (by?) the darkness. When the resident physician Hawthorne (Bernard Hill) examines the corpse, he observes how the lion has skinned Mahina and drank his blood. "Lions don't eat this way. Are you sure it was a lion?" These savage animals are more than lions, they're "pure evil." The speculation among the camp is that they're demons or the ghosts of the men who have died working on the railroad come to revenge themselves and relieve the white man of his burden. Thus the man of civilization is

once again put to the test against the unbound forces of the dark continent. In order to save his railroad project and his professional reputation, our Great White Hunter must become the Great White Savior, but when his methods fail, many of the workers blame the curse of the lions on him. When lead Muslim worker, Abdullah (Om Puri) is convincing the workers to quit and return home,

Patterson confronts Abdullah, taunting him: "Well, then you go, too. You lack the courage to lead, but I will kill the lions, and I will build the bridge, and you, you must go home and tell the wives of the men who died working here that you fled with the others because you could not master your fear."

Controlling/mastering fear is a constant refrain echoed throughout the narrative, and this is later echoed back to Patterson as he begins to lose his confidence. After the notorious hunter Charles Remington (Michael Douglas) arrives, there's a welcome shift in tone for the film where the domineering and laughably rugged Douglas takes over the lion-killing lead from a humbled Patterson. Despite a number of truly hilarious scenes where Douglass is attempting to be intimidating, the chemistry between Patterson, Remington, and Samuel is surprisingly endearing. The nighttime campfire scenes where the trio commiserates and joke lend a sympathetic humanity to the leads that make the violent intrusions of Ghost and Darkness that much more otherworldly and jarring.

It's in fact the murderous antics of the lions that are the most memorable parts of the film. One cannot help but laugh with glee as characters are dragged to their doom a way reminiscent of *Jaws* on land. The film score is aware of this: some scenes have the music mimic the iconic "dah-dun, dah-dun" refrain of that legendary shark attack film. The animal work becomes increasingly effective at portraying these maned scamps as preternatural monsters, and it's their ominous, violent charisma that gives the film an aura of eldritch strangeness. One of the best scenes in the film is where the hunters, after everyone has left, decide to journey into the heart of darkness and happen upon the man-eater lair, a cave strewn with human torsos and clavicles. Remington breaks steely-eyed character and realizes with a gulp "They kill for the pleasure." This journey into the lion's den forces the representatives of civilization to truly confront the possibility of death. Worries over whether the bridge or one's reputation must be put aside if Patterson ever wants to make it back home to his family. Indeed, while Kilmer and Douglas manage to present sympathetic characters, we can't help but admire the lions for checking colonial arrogance and dispelling the grandeur that many of the characters share.

Though based on an interesting story, the overall execution of this film makes it an ambitious but ultimately uninspired studio project. There are far better films about colonialism and Africa, and, certainly, there are more entertaining safari adventure films. So what in the end endures about *The Ghost and The Darkness*? The tone and imagery of the lion encounters and a powerful story. I had seen this film at age 11, but my only memories were images of Kilmer waiting in the dark, perspiring and gripping his rifle in terror. The mysterious charisma of these lions and the idea of facing them in the dark remained while everything else about the movie gradually drifted from my memory. When watching the film for this essay it felt as if I were watching a film I'd never seen before, and I wondered why I had assigned such gravitas to it. Then the lions showed up.

Kajah Ram

Kajah Ram is a bearded twenty-something who resides in a sleepy seaside burg of the San Francisco Bay Area and cohabitates with two fierce Yorkshire Terriers known as Jimmy and Ginger.

A recent graduate of linguistics from U.C. Berkeley, Kajah now makes his living at a public library slanging books and information, occasionally helping senior citizens use the Internet.

His free time is divided between playing video games and hacking out faux-erudite essays/reviews for the horror blog *The Overlook Theater*. Having recently attended his first Renaissance fair, Kajah has already begun compiling leather for next year's costume while writing embarrassingly accurate historical short fiction about the love lives of ducal handmaidens in 14th century Provence.

THE GIANT CLAW (1957)

By Jon Kitley

In the 1950s, Hollywood had left the gothic horror films behind and moved into science fiction pictures, with flying saucers carrying alien visitors and/or invaders, and all sorts of science-gone -wrong themes. Of course, one of the biggest subgenres of that time was the giant monsters. With an abundance of enormous spiders, grasshoppers, scorpions, squids, and prehistoric beasties, there weren't too many creatures or ideas that weren't being blown up to outrageous proportions and exploited for our drive-in entertainment. No matter how good or bad, I've always found plenty to enjoy with these oversized cinematic monstrosities.

The most engaging of the bunch usually employ a plethora of stock footage and/or opening narration telling us about how the world was created or changing, or something to do with science, or some fascinating "science talk," presented with such conviction that as a viewer, especially if you were a youngster, you'd be tempted to believe it.

Now there are giant monsters, and there are giant monsters... and then there's *The Giant Claw*, which is like no other you'll ever come across. Ever. There are a lot of cheesy creature features out there, but if ever a movie deserved to be credited as being the biggest Turkey out there, it's probably this 1957 epic. But even so, it's still one of the most entertaining Turkeys ever made. The term originated with the 1980 book, *The Golden Turkey Awards*, written by film critic Michael Medved and his brother Harry to "honor" monuments of cinematic ineptitude. But for me, a true Turkey is when filmmakers are trying their hardest, giving all they got, and just coming up short. You often wonder how *The Giant Claw* got made in the first place, much less *released*. For most, the taste for Turkey is an acquired one, but die hard crazy cinephiles eat it up.

Our story starts out with... narration, of course! This "helpful" device clues the audience into what's going on without anyone having to figure it out for themselves. Even in scenes where the actors are obviously speaking, we still get our disembodied voice feeding us details, almost like an episode of the TV series *Dragnet*. Everyone approaches their roles with Shakespearean seriousness, which aids in viewers (almost) buying into the fantastic tale unfolding before them. Until the titular creature shows up, that is.

But, before we get to that, a little history. Famous low-budget producer Sam Katzman, who produced close to 250 films in just under 40 years – an average of over six films a year! – worked in just about every film genre imaginable. But he's probably best known for some of the wonderful titles in the 1950s, such as *It Came from Beneath the Sea* (1955), *Earth vs. the Flying Saucers* and *The Werewolf* (both 1956), and *The Night the World Exploded* (1957). The last three of these titles were directed by Fred F. Sears, who only worked as a director for 10 years before his life was cut short by a heart attack. He worked at Columbia Pictures his entire career, cranking out over 50 titles in that short decade, many of them for Katzman.

The prolific producer had worked with Ray Harryhausen on *It Came from Beneath the Sea* and wanted to hire him again to create a stop-motion beastie for his latest project. But, due to monetary reasons or personal tastes, Harryhausen opted out of the picture, forcing Katzman to find someone else to build his flying terror. While Ralph Hammeras, George Teague, and an unbilled Lawrence Butler are credited for the special effects, the story goes that Katzman actually hired someone down in Mexico to handle the chore of creating the film's star. The resulting creature turned out

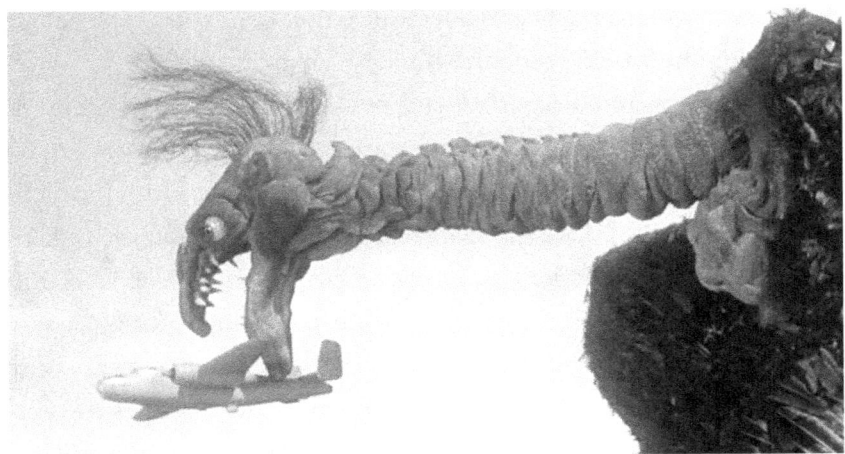

to be a marionette that resembles a cross between a very angry, sickly turkey and maybe a grumpy old ancestor of Big Bird. The strings holding up the bird are clearly apparent, as are the ones on some of the airplanes it attacks. I'm assuming that, south of the border, they were attempting to make its face look terrifying, but instead it just looks kind of old and wrinkly. We see this monstrosity destroy a few planes, a moving train, and even take out a hot rod full of teenage delinquents out on the road for a joyride! In the spirit of full disclosure, however, I admit that when I first saw the film, the shot of the creature eating some unfortunate passengers parachuting of an airplane still had a discomfiting effect. Yes, it's a silly looking monster, but that particular scene tapped into my deep-rooted terror of being eaten alive, a phobia I have had ever since seeing *Jaws* as a kid.

During filming, none of the actors or crew actually saw the mysterious creature, since all of the special effects were added after principal photography was completed. In fact, most of them didn't see it until they were sitting in the theater at the premiere, whereupon they immediately found themselves wondering if they might need to seek out a new line of work. Jeff Morrow, best known for his performance as the alien Exeter in *This Island Earth* (1955), probably caught the worse of it; the actor reportedly sunk down in his seat and eventually snuck out during the screening, hoping no one would recognize him.

Delivering credible performances in a wide variety of movies and TV shows throughout his long career, Morrow is always fun to watch. One of his last film appearances was *Octaman* (1971), which, thanks to a young Rick Baker, at least made a step up in the quality of the monster. In *The Giant Claw*, he plays Mitch MacAfee, the scientist who first witnesses this "flying battleship" during a test flight, though he has a hard time convincing anyone because it never showed up on any radar. He also somehow manages to keep a straight face while spilling out lines of dialogue such as, "That makes me chief cook-and-bottle washer in a one-man bird-watching society!" The scene where Mitch and his cohorts are trying to figure out why the military's weapons have no effect on the creature and conclude that it must emit "a field of anti-matter" is some seriously classic scientific gobbledygook guaranteed to make you cross-eyed. (We know this anti-matter exists because, well, they mention it several times during the discussion.)

Mara Corday, playing Sally Caldwell, a mathematician working with Mitch, is a favorite of mine from this era, even though she only performed in two other sci-fi/horror titles, *Tarantula* (1955) and *The Black Scorpion* (1957). She also appeared in *Playboy* magazine as October's Playmate of the Month in 1958, but unfortunately, it was when the centerfolds still had clothes on. Genre mainstay actor Morris Ankrum shows up in his usual role as the military brass in charge of taking the bird down. Ankrum can be seen in a ton of this type of fare, including *Rocketship X-M* (1950), *Invaders from Mars* (1953), *Earth vs. the Flying Saucers* (1956), and *Curse of the Faceless Man* (1958), usually playing a figure of authority, though his career extended to all manner of characters in film and television.

Prior to his death in 1993, Morrow often dismissed the film in interviews. "The less said about *The Giant Claw*, the better." With all due respect, I strongly disagree. Sure, it may be a Turkey, and it may showcase one of the most laughable giant monsters on film, but it's still around and still being discussed, inherently memorable and undeniably entertaining almost 60 years later. And, at the end of the day, isn't that what really matters?

Jon Kitley

Jon Kitley has been a life long fan of the horror genre and has made it his life's journey to not only seek out as much as he can but also passing that onto other fans. To do this, he started the website *Kitley's Krypt* in 1998, which he continues to run today, making it one of the oldest horror sites on the web. Through *The Krypt*, he channels his passion for the genre into news and information that he feels is important, trying to keep the history of horror alive and well.

Besides running the Krypt, he's one of the staff writers for *Evilspeak Magazine* and *HorrorHound Magazine*, the later featuring his Rondo Award-winning column, *They Came from the Krypt*. His work has also appeared in the books *Horror 101: The A-List of Horror Films and Monster Movies* and *Hidden Horror* (another Rondo winner for Best Book 2013), and he has appeared on several different documentaries, such as *Monster Madness: The Golden Age of the Horror Film*, *Monster Madness: The Gothic Revival Of Horror*, and *Fanex Files: Hammer Films*. When he has some free time, he attends about a half dozen or so horror conventions a year, hoping to spread his love of horror reference books to other like-minded fans, trying to help them to "discover the horror."

THE KILLER SNAKES (1974)

By Wim Castermans

Let's first get this out of the way: while other films in this book may decidedly go for an ecological "nature strikes back" theme, the snakes in this lurid entry stand for nothing but phallic symbolism.

The Killer Snakes is a production of the legendary Hong Kong-based Shaw Brothers film studio, famous for martial arts classics like *The 36th Chamber of Shaolin* and *Five Deadly Venoms*, but also occasionally dabbling in horror movies. The most outrageous of these were made by director Kuei Chih-Hung. Kuei started out under the wings of Chang Cheh in the early 1970s, to later emerge as one of the most promising of the studio's new filmmakers. However, despite huge critical acclaim for his entry in the omnibus film series *The Criminals*, he stubbornly stuck to churning out lowly-regarded exploitation and horror flicks. Luckily most of these are

standouts of the genre, with the colorful and trippy *The Boxer's Omen* as a high point. Known for his eccentricity and rage on as well as off set, Kuei got fed up with cinema in the 1980s and moved to the US where he started a pizzeria.

The film opens in black and white, with Chen as a young boy sitting alone in the living room, doing his homework. Nothing but a cardboard-thin wall separates him from his mother's excited cries next door, "Hit me. Hit me!", as she's slapped around the bedroom in a wild S&M session. The boy gets his pet snake out of its cage and gently strokes the serpent, listening to her moaning. Less than one minute in the movie, we've already been served sadomasochism topped off by hints of masturbation, child sexuality, and oedipal issues. Yay!

Chen grows up into a skinny young man, a timid loner who's despised and ridiculed by all that surround him. He tries to earn his living doing menial jobs while staying in a ramshackle hut next to a filthy open-air market. The pretty stallholder Xiujiang seems to be the only one who takes pity in the miserable outcast. When she seeks him out in his rundown shack, she catches him masturbating to pictures of naked girls in bondage that he has ripped out of porn magazines. Surprised by her sudden appearance, Chen throws over a milk bottle, the white liquid spilling over the dirt floor as in a cumshot. Kuei Chih-Hung was never one for subtlety.

That night Chen discovers an escaped cobra as it crawls

THE **KILLER SNAKES**

WARNING! CONTAINS EXTREMELY SICK AND DISTURBING SCENES. NOT SUITABLE FOR MOST PEOPLE.

through the cracks of the wall from the snake medicine shop next door. When he talks to the reptile, it seems to react to everything he says, swaying left and right as if agreeing to his words. After being stood up by Xiujiang on a date, robbed by the thugs that control the market and mocked by the prostitutes prowling the area, Chen decides to strike back, using an ever-growing army of deadly snakes as his tool of revenge.

The Killer Snakes is a deliciously dark and cynical movie, filling the wide Shawscope frame in cramped and claustrophobic compositions. You're left gasping for air by its constant use of skewed camera angles and hard diagonal shadows, reflecting the protagonist's deranged mental state. Frames are placed within the frame, cutting Chen loose and isolating him from his surroundings. Scenes bathe in vivid green and purple light, accompanied by pounding music, stolen from the soundtrack of the Italian spaghetti western *Death rides a Horse* by Ennio Morricone. Unusual for a Shaw production, everything is shot on location, offering a fascinating view of the slums and rundown areas of Hong Kong in the 1970s.

Humanity is shown at its worst. When Xiujiang's ailing father draws his last breath, the owner of her dilapidated one-room apartment stands next to his death bed, oblivious to her sorrow, only to complain it's no reason for her to be late on the payment of the rent. Meanwhile poor Chen is abused by literally everyone he meets. Not that you'll look on with sympathy when he later seeks vengeance by tying up prostitutes and penetrating them with his pet cobra, you sort of get where he comes from. In some way. Perhaps.

When Celestial Pictures bought the Shaw Brothers catalog and started to release the films on DVD in 2002, I first focused solely on the kung fu classics, overjoyed to finally watch them in widescreen with original dubs. But when I started to dig into the non-martial arts titles, these turned out to be where my real fascination would lie. Next to Ho Meng Hua's work, Kuei Chih-Hung's horror films quickly became a sure bet, with titles like *Hex*, *Bewitched*, *Corpse Mania*, and *The Boxer's Omen*. Even when it comes to martial arts films he holds his own, as his *Killer Constable* might count as the best the wuxia genre has to offer.

The Killer Snakes may not be the most acclaimed of Kuei's work, perhaps due to its unrelentingly dark tone. While definitely an unpleasant film that may inverse its title into *The Snake Killer* due to all the real snakes that are hacked to bits and burned alive on camera, it's an expertly shot and uniquely atmospheric sickie that deserves a look. If you can stomach it, that is. If not - there's always Kuei's pizzeria to check out.

Wim Castermans

Wim Castermans works as a programmer for the Offscreen Film Festival in Brussels. The three-week-long festival features a careful selection of the best and weirdest of new unreleased films, labeling them as "the cult films of tomorrow." Its specialty, however, is retrospectives for which it prides itself in mainly showing rare vintage 35mm prints. Over the years, the festival has welcomed guests such as John Waters, Radley Metzger, Tobe Hooper, Umberto Lenzi, Jess Franco, Jack Hill, Ruggero Deodato, Monte Hellman, and others. Thematic retrospectives have included the Italian giallo, Shaw Brothers productions, Pinky Violence, home invasion films, British cult cinema, the Nikkatsu studio, spaghetti westerns, post-apocalyptic cinema, and more.

Wim's Dutch-language writings include reviews and interviews, which appeared on the now defunct website *Cultfilms en Kutfilms* but also in *Schokkend Nieuws*, the sole Dutch glossy magazine devoted to genre cinema.

THE LAST SHARK (1981)

By Stephan Jankovic

The early 1980s were the heydays of the rip-off. Following the box office successes of some major films in the US, cashing attempts went from lame to very lame. Italy in particular managed to squeeze the genre to the bone like no other country did (or will probably ever do). Sometimes teaming up with France or Spain, the European boot-shaped country was firing on all possible fronts with varying degrees of inspiration, following in the footsteps of *Conan the Barbarian*, *Mad Max*, *Star Wars*, *Dawn of the Dead*, and *Rambo*. The big sellers were post nukes, heroic fantasy, and science fiction.

But in 1981 the success of *Jaws* led them to some of the most enjoyable shark flicks ever: *L'ultimo squalo* aka *The Last Shark*!

The rip-off tactic proved diabolically effective: follow the script of the original film as much as possible, add some American not too faded glories, and find a great title. Mix this together and what you'll get is James "Brody" Franciscus (*The Amazing Dobermann, Killer Fish, Nightkill*) and Vic "Quint" Morrow (*Dirty Mary Crazy Larry, The Bronx Warriors, The Twilight Zone*) hunting down a great white inflatable shark, "the last shark" or "Great White."

Port Harbor, a peaceful seaside community in the likes of Amity, has just lost one of its windsurfers. A large bite on the later found board drives Dr. Peter Benton (Franciscus) and old fisherman friend Ron Hamer (Morrow) to suspect a Great White to be responsible. The city mayor obviously refuses to cancel the windsurf regatta, which results in several deadly and unintentionally funny shark appearances. The mayor's son and his friends decide to hunt down the shark using his dad's boat and a big piece of meat. A chopped off leg later, they're back at Port Harbor. Daddy mayor, who is now looking for revenge (and electors), decides to hunt the beast himself. Using the city's chopper and his rifle, he falls into the water and gets bitten in two in one of the most memorable scenes of the movie.

The rest of the story is just as good. I won't spoil the ending for you, but the shark dies.

Enzo G. Castellari is not new in the business. At the time *The Last Shark* was released, he had already directed several movies, including the western classic *Keoma*. Therefore, despite the film's budgetary constraints, the movie works. *The Last Shark* is never boring.

A clever approach to hide the budget limits was the use of three different techniques for the special effects: (1) a pretty convincing dummy shark head for close-ups and body chewing scenes, (2) real shark images from shark documentaries, and, (3) a miniature shark for underwater scenes.

Not all these special effects are convincing. In a scene that takes place during the windsurfing race, a red buoy gets tangled onto the shark's body. After knocking several windsurfers into the

water, the red buoy heads into the direction of a small boat where a man is commenting on the race and sends it exploding into the air by three or four meters. The guy in the boat is obviously a dummy, but it hardly looks as fake as the "shark" who sticks its head out of the water looking like a motionless inflatable toy.

The miniature shark, too, is an epic failure. There's a scene in which the shark knocks down rocks with its head in order to deliberately trap Peter and Ron in an underwater cave. The figurine used in this scene looks like a sick dolphin instead of a shark. It's pitiful. Luckily it's not used in many scenes, and the remaining effects are pretty decent.

Most of all, though, *The Last Shark* has a great soundtrack. Guido and Mauricio De Angelis' music is efficient and easily reaches the same level of quality as many other catchy 1980 songs. It's very much like the scores of Claudio Simonetti and other horror movie soundtracks of that era. *The Last Shark* is also one of the rare genre films to feature a "shark tune." For many people, the *Jaws* theme may still hold its place as the number one most visceral tune of the last 40 years, one that has the capacity to give you goosebumps, but while the theme of *The Last Shark* may not have the same effect, it deserves a good second place of best shark tune ever after *Jaws*.

Speaking of which, at the time *The Last Shark* was released, Universal sued the filmmakers due to the many references to the plot of *Jaws* and *Jaws 2*. The windsurfing regatta in *The Last Shark* obviously takes its cue from the catamaran race in *Jaws 2* whereas the characters of Vic Morrow and Joshua Sinclair are almost identical copies of the characters in Spielberg's movie. Several countries even cashed in on this by giving the film alternate titles like *Jaws 81* (Hong Kong), *Jaws Returns* (Japan), *The Last Jaws* (Netherlands, Norway), and *Son Jaws* (Turkey). However, due to the lawsuit from Universal, the theatrical release of *The Last Shark* was blocked.

Thinking about present day productions from studios like The Asylum, that releases titles like *Atlantic Rim, Transmorphers,* or *Paranormal Entity,* we regret that *The Last Shark* never had a normal theatrical run where it could have become a commercial success.

Stephan Jankovic

Stephan Jankovic belongs to the generation that discovered *Jaws* and *The Last Shark* on early rental VHS. The result is that now at 42, he's still not comfortable to go swimming in the sea.

He's also lucky to live in Belgium where, unlike other countries, the majority of the horror films of that time were released theatrically. Even the French went to Belgium to see genre films. Some of his favorites are *The Exorcist*, *The Omen*, *The Thing*, *The Return of the Living Dead*, *The Evil Dead*, *The Beyond*, and *The Children of Ravensback*. These days Stephan finds it difficult to come across horror movies he really likes. Maybe they stopped making good ones. Or maybe he's getting too old.

He has a little girl of five whom he tries to keep away from horror. However, she always asks her father to show her "things that scare her." This proves that adoring horror movies is not the result of education; it's genetic.

THE PACK (1977)

By Joel Warren

Seal Island is a popular summer tourist spot for families, but the summer is winding down, and people are returning home as the residents settle in for the quiet time of year. The problem is, some of those families brought dogs with them, dogs that they don't intend to take back home. These dogs form a pack and forage for food at the junkyard and elsewhere, eventually resorting to attacking domesticated animals before turning on humans. In a terrible parody of the usual situation, the residents of the island have to clean up the mess left by the tourists. They have no way to communicate with the outside world. There's only a single rowboat and a limited number of shotgun shells.

Dogs don't normally go wild when abandoned, but when they do, it's a serious problem. Like wolves, wild dogs claim a territory and defend it from interlopers. However, these feral dogs aren't

particularly afraid of humans as they were only recently abandoned, which means they will attack with very little provocation. These animals have banded together under an alpha, a slavering beast that strikes out against people with a homicidal rage born of his likely abandonment. This alpha has quite possibly been on his own for a while as he's smart and vicious, and with the support of the pack he's even more dangerous. The situation here is dire because the island is small, and the dogs quickly tear through the little wildlife and few domesticated animals before their hunger causes them to turn on humans.

The humans on the menu are mostly rural fishermen as well as a group of vacationers that the filmmakers take great pride to characterize. There's a banker and his strange adult son, who he's trying to set up with his braless secretary (who actually finds the young man charming), a pair of widowed parents with children (the father played by Joe Don Baker), an old coot and his dog, and others. These interesting characters give the film a sense of realism often lacking in horror films.

Fans of the cinema of the 1970s will recognize many of the faces, which is a boon to this movie. Most of them are experienced character actors who make the people seem a lot more genuine than usual; even Joe Don Baker is good. The script helps these journeymen actors as it doesn't make them behave stupidly – each action taken seems reasonable given the situation, and there's never a moment where I sputtered "Oh, come on now!" Ultimately, this is a film about average people's heroism under extraordinary circumstances as most rise to the challenge and do the best they can.

Interestingly, *The Pack* is similar in structure to *Night of the Living Dead*. The people are faced with a threat that seems surreal at first – neither dogs attacking nor the dead walking seems normal - and have to find a way to escape, first by trying to hide, then by trying to flee, and finally by fighting back.

There are also parallels with *Jaws*. It's unlikely that this film would have been made without *Jaws* as it takes place on an island, and the animals are acting in an unnatural fashion as man finds himself lower on the food chain.

The island itself – which is actually Bodega Bay, where *The Birds* was made – is small and wild, and the dogs have the advantage because the lush foliage and lack of good trails and roads means they can outpace the humans and disappear easily. It cannot be emphasized enough that having normal harmless dogs as vicious killers make this film even worse than *Jaws*; after all, a person can stay out of the water, but the dogs aren't afraid of breaking into a house.

I'll be the first to admit that I'm not particularly fond of dogs. Now, it's taken me years to realize that it's not dogs that I dislike but dog owners. Dog owners have the same annoying attitude toward their dogs that parents have toward their children, that idea that their particular dog is wonderful and magical and can do no wrong. I know a woman whose dog is vicious, and she knows it, but she lives in denial and always blames other people when they get bitten for provoking her sweet little baby. Like parents, some dog owners take great care to teach and have a more realistic outlook. Another couple I know, who runs a day-care center, have an Irish wolfhound that is smart and well-trained but takes his shepherding duties so seriously he will sometimes growl at parents who come to take "his" children (which is solved by taking him for a walk at pick-up time every day). People are very sentimental about dogs, which is why the tourists abandoned them in the first place, choosing to believe that someone would adopt the stray. This was a serious problem in the United States in the past – and is still occurring when people leave dogs at properties that have been repossessed by banks, giving those checking on the property a horrible surprise (usually of the dead dog variety, rather than the vicious dog variety) – but has been reduced a lot over the years as society's attitudes toward animals have softened.

The Pack is very 1970s, from the clothing to the abandoned dogs and the techniques used. Veteran cinematographer Ralph Woolsey shoots the film well and makes good, moody use of the foggy woods. The score by Lee Holdridge sounds good and is also moody. The thing that makes this stand out as a product of the 1970s more than anything though, and the film's biggest weakness, is the reliance on slow-motion during the action scenes.

Joel Warren

Joel Warren is a mathematics teacher who has watched and enjoyed horror for nearly 30 years, though he has disliked dogs longer still.

When not watching films, playing video games, or teaching math, he's sleeping; sometimes he drags himself out of laziness to write, most often for *Cult Reviews*.

He attributes his love of horror to years of his parents telling him that those movies were terrible, and he shouldn't watch them, coupled with teenage rebellion. There was also the added benefit that many of the slashers of the 1980s had lots of bare breasts, a subject that he still finds as viscerally fascinating as the way that horror is a medium that has less to risk when it comes to creating transgressive art that can lay the human experience as exposed as those same bosoms.

THE SWARM (1978)

By Adam Artruc

Around the age of six, I developed an irrational fear of African killer bees. There are two reasons for this. The first was a television special focused on the migration of Africanized killer bees into the South. The program focused on how the bees had arrived in North America and could eventually infest additional segments of The United States. This was really bad news as these bees were overly aggressive and stung to kill. Second was *The Swarm,* a film directed by Irwin Allen, which reinforced everything that television special had warned of and embedded a fear in me that I still remember 26

years later.

    The Swarm was originally released in 1978 and directed and produced by Irwin Allen, who was best known at the time for producing the hit disaster movies *The Towering Inferno* and *The Poseidon Adventure.* The film featured an all-star cast including

Michael Caine, Katharine Ross, Richard Chamberlain, and Henry Fonda and was backed by a generous budget. It was also produced at a time when nature run amok was a popular movie topic. It seemed like a guaranteed success.

Unfortunately, for Allen and everyone involved, the film was a major failure both critically and financially. Variety referred to *The Swarm* as a "disappointing and tired non-thriller." Janet Maslin wrote in The New York Times that the film "could be... the surprise comedy hit of the season." Even everyone involved in the making of *The Swarm* seem to have distanced themselves from it with little to be found in the way of interviews or comments. Internet rumors abound that Allen allowed no one to speak of the film after its release (though I can't find any actual evidence to support these claims). Even the DVD contains only a single feature, and it's a short documentary which was put together during production to help promote the film before anyone knew it was going to bomb.

Considering the overwhelmingly negative reception, I now have the interesting task of explaining why I love the film. So I'll start at the beginning. I first saw *The Swarm* in the late 1980s on cable television. I spent many of my weekend afternoons stowed away in the family room scouring through the cable channels searching for horror films. I would watch anything that even remotely resembled a genre movie. It was a guarantee that a film about a giant swarm of killer bees would catch my attention. What I didn't expect was for it to affect me as much as it did. This was a film that portrayed bees as relentless killing machines that would not only kill men and women but would take out an entire schoolyard of children. These bees were also smart. They derailed a train, knew to avoid poisonous pellets and could find their way into the most protected of places. These are images that have stuck with me for 26 years.

Nostalgia, however, isn't all that *The Swarm* has in its favor.

Most obvious is the cast. Despite the dialogue being downright laughable at times, the actors appear to be completely committed to their roles. There aren't many actors who could deliver lines like, "I never dreamed that it would turn out to be the bees. They've always been our friend" without their tongue firmly in their cheek, but Michael Caine does it with ease. It's the straightforward delivery of awful lines like these that add to the film's overall charm. The best b-movies are often the ones where those involved commit completely to the material no matter how ridiculous it may be.

Then there's the set pieces. This is an Irwin Allen disaster film, so if there's one thing a viewer should expect it's over the top scenes of mayhem and destruction. Sure, there are a few too many downbeat moments where pointless dialogue is slung back and forth, but when things go bad they go really bad. For example, the bees attack the small town of Maryville and kill off a large portion

of the population including an entire schoolyard of children breaking one of the cardinal rules of horror films. If there's one thing I was sure of it was that kids didn't die in movies. Allen even goes so far as to have one kid survive an attack only to die later after we believe he's going to be okay. There's also a train derailment that kills off even more of the Maryville survivors, and the entire city of Houston is set on fire.

Unfortunately, these bees are so tough that not even a city on fire can take them out, which brings me to the one single element that makes *The Swarm* a must see of the nature run amok genre. Even if expert acting of badly written dialogue and over the top disaster set pieces don't do it for you, there's always the bees. There are 20 million bees in this movie, and when they attack they're menacing. Of course, they're using honey bees, but even 20 million honey bees is a pretty terrifying sight. I don't think I'd be running into that swarm if I saw it flying into my town. There are scenes where actors are covered from head to toe in live bees, and the visuals of the bees flying through Maryville are really pretty amazing. I don't know how these effects would be achieved today, but I doubt that many studios would be willing to put up the money to deal with the headache that 20 million live bees would cause. It seems like a logistical nightmare that *The Swarm* actually pulled off.

In the end, these things boil down to personal taste. I often love the things that conventional critics hate. *The Swarm* is technically not a good movie. It's poorly written and unintentionally funny. It's filled with clichés and ridiculous set pieces. It delivers everything one would expect in a b-movie but on a big budget. But that's also why lovers of drive-in and b-movie fare would eat it up. Of course I can't ignore that nostalgia, as with much of the entertainment I love, plays a large part in my admiration. The lasting impression this movie has left on me since the age of six still amazes me. Maybe anyone viewing *The Swarm* for the first time should try to see it through the eyes of a 6-year-old. That might be all it takes to really appreciate it.

Adam Artruc

Adam Artruc is co-host and contributor to the *Midnight Triple Feature* podcast and blog. Started in 2013 this bi-weekly podcast features reviews from Adam and co-host Mike on a variety of genre films as well as discussions on current news, events, and releases. They also regularly review and discuss new independent horror releases and attend conventions and other genre-related events.

Adam has been a fan of movies for as long as he can remember. Some of his earliest memories are of endlessly re-watching films like *Gremlins, Back to the Future, Indiana Jones and the Temple of Doom,* and *The Wizard of Oz.* This all eventually led to a full-blown obsession with genre movies resulting in weekly visits to the video store to consume as many titles as possible. He began writing about the genre regularly at the age of 14 and has never looked back.

While Adam is a graphic designer by profession he still spends much of his free time watching, discussing and writing about films as often as possible. Today some of his favorite films include *Jaws, The Return of the Living Dead, The Texas Chainsaw Massacre, The Beyond,* and many more.

THE WHITE BUFFALO (1977)

By Peter Braidis

After the amazing success of *Jaws (1975)*, any creature was fair game to hit the screens munching on unsuspecting humans. What a wonderful world. That world would include the oddball 1977 flick *The White Buffalo, directed by J. Lee Thompson (Cape Fear, Happy Birthday to Me, 10 to Midnight, King Solomon's Mines) and* starring Charles Bronson, whose character, Wild Bill Hickok, is haunted by - you guessed it - a giant white buffalo.

I knew I had to beg my dad to take me to the cinema after seeing the poster and the TV trailers. And he did just that. Also starring Clint Walker, Slim Pickens, Stuart Whitman, Jack Warden, Will Sampson, and Kim Novak, *The White Buffalo* was a strange little movie for sure. It was *based* on Richard Sale's novel *The White Buffalo* and produced by Dino De Laurentiis, who was also responsible for that year's *Orca: The Killer Whale* and the 1976 remake of *King Kong*.

The year is 1874. Wild Bill Hickok's life is fading. He's having a *Moby Dick*-style meltdown as he suspects that the albino buffalo that haunts his recurring nightmares isn't just a myth. Traveling under the alias of James Otis, he returns to an area of the country where he has made numerous enemies to search for a creature that may or may not exist.

Together with his sort-of trusty sidekick, Charlie Zane (played by Jack Warden from *Shampoo* and *All the President's Men*), Wild Bill Hickok ventures into the Black Hills to look for clues. On the way, the pair encounters an American Indian known as Crazy Horse, played here very well by Will Sampson from One Flew over the

Cuckoo's Nest, *Orca: The Killer Whale, and Poltergeist II: The Other Side*. Crazy Horse seeks revenge because the white buffalo has steamrolled through his encampment and killed his daughter. Until he slays the beast and wraps his daughter's corpse in its pelt, he's to be referred to as Worm. Wild Bill Hickok and Charlie Zane form an alliance with Crazy Horse, though it's fraught with tension as Charlie is a racist and doesn't like his new pal too much. Of course, Crazy Horse and Wild Bill Hickok prevail.

Thrown in this mix are some awful scenes in a saloon, some gunfights, as well as a pointless romantic interest in Kim Novak's cameo character, Mrs. Poker Jenny Schermerhorn. But it's all about that big-ass buffalo, which Novak still proudly had at that point.

Some of the scenes in the film are awkward, especially when Wild Bill Hickok and Crazy Horse use sign language to communicate all the while speaking English out loud at one another.

Bronson also spouts off a bunch of pretentious lines of New Age nonsense that he doesn't seem very convinced by (and neither would I). But you know what? He's Charles Bronson, so who cares? His screen presence still works, and he does fairly well of playing a legendary, violent outlaw coming to the end of his life

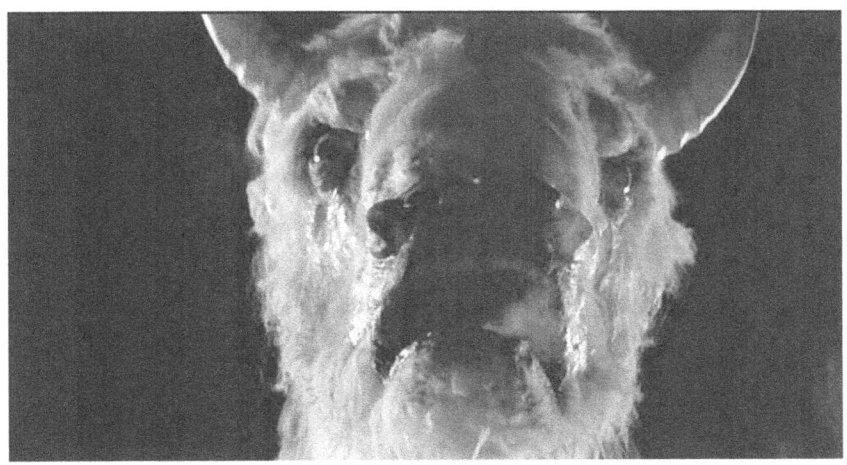

with failing vision and other signs of age.

Anyway, when the buffalo starts appearing, he seems to be in full attack mode. Unfortunately, the buffalo scenes are an example of ineptitude. The creature looks like a pissed-off lamb, either hopping and skipping along or sliding around on tracks in only one direction - straight. At other times, the close-ups of the buffalo (especially the eyes and snout) work rather well, as does the menacing score by John Barry of *James Bond* fame.

The film never reaches that scary level, but the buildup to the final battle is pretty good. The climax, however, leaves one unfulfilled, as it feels things got a bit rushed and/or trimmed down due to budget constraints. But I will always dug the buffalo charging like a steam-train (was that the intent?), barreling through the snow with steam coming from the snout. That was pretty kick-ass.

The White Buffalo misses whatever mark it was going for, but it's a highly unique cinematic experience that is part western, part horror, part fantasy, part adventure, part drama, equaling all weird. Due to the oddity of *The White Buffalo* and the strange mix of styles, it's a worthy film, if only because it has no idea what the hell it wants to be. We really don't know what we just watched. I do know that if I had Kim Novak waiting for me, my spurs would be jangling with her and not chasing some giant monster in the snow.

The movie bombed, both with critics and at the box office, and ended a long-running relationship between Charles Bronson and United Artists Pictures.

Should you see *The White Buffalo?*

You know, I have an affection for *The White Buffalo*, despite the numerous flaws. But, yes, it's weird, intriguing, poorly edited, and bizarre. Sounds like a good time to me. Also, it's finally on DVD and Blu-ray, and the transfer is nice, so saddle up and buy it.

Fun Facts:

- *The White Buffalo* had the ignominy of opening just two weeks before a little film called *Star Wars came out* in May 1977.
- Carlo Rambaldi designed the creature. He would later create a critter named *E.T.*
- The film was shot at both a soundstage (and looks it at times) and on location in California, New Mexico, and Colorado. The locale in California was called Bronson Canyon. Really.

Peter Braidis

Peter Raymond Braidis was born January 8, 1969, in Bristol, PA, and earned a B.A. in History and Journalism from Rutgers-State University of New Jersey-Camden. He has been published in *Metal Rules Magazine*, *Goldmine Magazine*, Indie-music.com, and *The Philadelphia Inquirer.*

He co-owned and operated *Watchdog Video* from 1995 to 2006 and the *Watchdog/Cool Beans Café* from 2006 until 2008. Currently, Pete is a part time teacher and also works for the Philadelphia Phillies Major League Baseball Club.

He also has a humor blog at chudbeagleblog.wordpress.com where he mocks cheesy monster movies from the 1970s and 1980s, awful album and book covers, and 1980s music videos.

Pete's first book, *Unstrung Heroes: 61 Underappreciated Guitar Greats,* featuring in-depth interviews with Steve Hackett (Genesis), Rik Emmett (Triumph), Vicki Peterson (The Bangles), Eric Bell (Thin Lizzy), Tony Hicks (The Hollies), and more will be released through Schiffer Publishing in 2016.

THEM! (1954)

By Barend de Voogd

"When man entered the atomic age he opened a door to a new world. What we'll eventually find in that new world nobody can predict." So says Professor Harold Medford at the end of one of the finest American creature features of the 1950s. Born in the same year as *Gojira*. 1954: the Japanese had their great Atomic destroyer of cities; the Americans had *Them!*

Warner Bros., following up on their 1953 smash hit *The Beast from 20,000 Fathoms*, tried to build up the suspense in their trailers. The pre-release publicity for *Them!* warned the public that the film would feature an "unknown terror," a "nameless horror," and a "fantastic invader." Its spectacular artwork, however, already gave

it away: *Them!* is about enormous ants, fantastic mutations caused by nuclear radiation. They're gigantic versions of the Camponotus Vicinus, identified by Professor Medford (Edmund Gwenn) with characteristic pseudo-scientific precision. In reality, this species of Formicidae doesn't grow beyond 11mm, but *Them!* features specimens that measure up to three-and-a-

half meters: menacingly crawling through the desert, threatening us with their jaws and injecting their victims with their deadly acid.

It's no wonder the little Ellinson girl looks completely traumatized. She's found in the desert, wandering aimlessly with her broken doll, by two kind policemen, Sergeant Ben Peterson (James Whitmore) and Trooper Ed Blackburn. Her parents are missing. Their trailer appears to have been viciously attacked, just like Johnsons' general store and, I'm sorry to report, poor Mr. Johnson himself.

These are my favorite scenes because they're beautifully shot, kind of sweet, yet still run a chill down your spine. Director Gordon Douglas treats the first act of *Them!* as a mystery. The little girl doesn't utter a word about what happened, her eyes and sun burnt face completely blank. Still, the policemen get their first clues: the caravan and the store have been destroyed *from the inside*, and the only thing stolen seems to be *sugar*. Only when Professor Medford tests his suspicion by holding a bottle of formic acid in front of the girl's nose, her apathy breaks: "Them!", she screams. "Them!"

Like *The Thing From Another World* (1951, Christian Nyby and Howard Hawks), *Invaders from Mars* (1953, William Cameron Menzies), and *The War of the Worlds* (1953, Byron Haskin) before, *Them!* appealed to the fears of the Cold War. But to interpret the gigantic worker ants as symbols of communist subversion, as some film historians have, is stretching it a bit - even for a film that was made by the director of the extremely right-wing (but Oscar-nominated!) *I was a Communist for the FBI* (1951). *Them!* simply doesn't feature the paranoia that is so typical of the Red Scare sci-fi movies of the period. The case has even been made that the ants do not represent the Soviets but the American people: blindly running amok in their insatiable desire for "sugar," i.e. materialism.

Whatever the intended symbolism, the political logic of *Them!* is deeply authoritarian. All the protagonists are authority figures:

policemen, FBI-agents, scientists, or military. The few civilians we get to meet, are flawed: a possibly corrupt night watch, a few alcoholics and a woman arrested for speeding after she spent the night with a man that wasn't her husband! In the finale, when the ants have nested in the storm drains of Los Angeles, the

filmmakers seem only too happy to declare Martial Law on Los Angeles, imposing a six o'clock curfew and demanding absolute obedience to the military authorities. They will restore status quo, using everything from guns, bazookas and flamethrowers to – *gulp!* - phosphorus bombs and even cyanide gas.

Thus, contrary to the Nature Strikes Back movies of the 1970s, it would be very hard to talk of *Them!* as a "green" film. There's a lengthy lecture by the Professor in which he expresses admiration for the strength and organizational skills of the ant colony, and he does state that the mutations are caused by "lingering radiation from the first atomic bomb," but the concerns of the movie are not ecological. They're moral. "We may be witnesses to a Biblical prophecy come true," says Medford. And he quotes: "And there shall be destruction and darkness come upon creation. And the Beasts shall reign over the earth." The ants are not caused by nuclear testing in general; the film specifies that they're caused by the first atomic bomb. It's hard to not think of the traumatized little girl, blinded and sun burnt, as a victim - not of gigantic ants but of the nuclear flash. A Pandora's Box was opened in Hiroshima en Nagasaki, and for many Americans it contained a sense of guilt and fear of the future.

Them! has a thematic depth, while still presenting a very entertaining and exciting adventure. The story was written by George Worthing Yates, who would later write *Earth vs. the Flying Saucers* (1956, Fred F. Sears) and *The Amazing Colossal Man* (1957, Bert I Gordon), amongst others. Its simple structure provided the template for films like *Tarantula* (1955, Jack Arnold), *The Deadly Mantis* (1957, Nathan Juran) and many, more recent creature features. Gordon Douglas, a filmmaker who died in 1993 with almost a hundred movies under his belt (*The Detective* with Frank Sinatra, for instance), gave the film a semi-documentary feel.

One of the other highlights is the discovery of the first ant in the midst of a fierce sandstorm. The policemen and the scientists, all wearing futuristic-looking goggles; the howling wind and obstructed view; the desert, looking like an inhospitable planet; the eerie sounds of the approaching creatures... It kind of reminds you of a certain, more recent film.

Them! loses some of its thrust and tension in the second half, when the top brass discusses what to do in a long series of meetings, lectures, and interrogations. Still there's plenty to enjoy in dialogue ("We haven't seen the end of them. We only had a close look at what might be the beginning of the end of us.") and comedy. British-born actor Edmund Gwenn plays a great absentminded professor, battling with goggles and radio equipment. The male leads, Whitmore and James Arness as FBI-agent Robert Graham, are pretty standard. Joan Weldon, however, is interesting as Dr. Patricia Medford. "Pat" is obviously written as a love interest but comes off strong and emancipated.

Partly filmed in the famous LA River Basin (also featured in *Terminator 2: Judgment Day*, *Chinatown* and *Grease*), *Them!* was nominated for an Oscar for Special Effects. The award went to Disney's *20,000 Leagues under the Sea* (1954, *Richard Fleischer*). Deservedly so, I guess. Set photos reveal that Ralph Ayes constructed an impressively large mechanical ant for *Them!*, but it's hairy skin, lifeless eyes and clumsy claws didn't really stand the test of time.

But upon enjoying *Them!* once more for the sake of this article, I'm again struck by the scene in which our heroes enter the subterranean chamber where the Queen Ant laid all her eggs. They ready their flamethrowers. You can even see the creatures twitch inside the transparent eggs. Remember the landing of the Nostromo in the midst of a sandstorm? Remember traumatized little Newt and her doll on planet LV-426? I guess Ridley Scott and James Cameron liked *Them!* too.

Barend de Voogd

Barend de Voogd is the editor of *Schokkend Nieuws*, the only Dutch film magazine dealing exclusively with horror, sci-fi, fantasy, and cult movies. *Schokkend Nieuws* has been around since 1992 and is published bi-monthly and distributed in The Netherlands and Belgium. www.schokkendnieuws.nl.

Barend also writes for a variety of non-genre film publications, and is a programmer for the Imagine Film Festival in Amsterdam. He directed three short horror movies and is currently developing a film script called *Bijlmer Voodoo* for *House of Netherhorror*.

Website: barenddevoogd.wordpress.com

TICKS (1993)

By Matthew House

Animal attack movies can go in any number of directions. Whether it's your average everyday animal such as a bear or dog taking a bite out of their victims' behinds, or a swarm of animals such as birds or wasps using the power of numbers to wreak havoc, nature can run amok in an endless variety of ways. They can come big; they can come small; there can be many; there can be few; heck, they can even be mutated, too, and that is exactly the direction that is taken with *Ticks*, a direct-to-video horror film that proves you can always up the ante, even at the expense of dignity.

Shot in five weeks with a budget estimated at 1 million dollars, *Ticks* takes a simplistic approach in putting its protagonists in danger. The film follows a group of troubled inner-city teens who partake in a wilderness project meant to set them straight by building campfires and being bored. While wiping with leaves and singing Kumbaya is a bit of a challenge for any teenager, the group find themselves faced with far bigger problems, one of them being

a pair of dangerous and territorial marijuana farmers who are using an herbal steroid to jack up their dope supply. This herbal steroid system leaks and somehow leads to the movie's most worrisome antagonists: overgrown mutated ticks.

Outside of its off-the-wall premise, *Ticks* is significant for boasting some serious horror clout both behind the camera and in front. Doug Beswick, who is a bona fide special effects guru, wrote the original screenplay for *Ticks* two decades earlier under the title *Cycle of Blood*. Also notable, long-time Stuart Gordon collaborator Brian Yuzna is the film's executive producer, while makeup effects are provided by special effects powerhouse K.N.B. EFX Group (the special effects, however, were spearheaded by Doug Beswick).

Leading the splat pack is director Tony Randel, who is certainly no slouch when it comes to the horror genre. At the time *Ticks* was made, Randel was a bit of a hot horror commodity, having helmed direct-to-video features such as the Fangoria produced vampire film, *Children of the Night*, in 1991 as well as the sixth installment in *The Amityville Horror* franchise, *Amityville 1992: It's About Time*, in 1992. Those films (*Ticks* included), however, might be considered disappointments in comparison to Randel's most recognizable directorial accomplishment, the 1988 sequel to

Clive Barker's *Hellraiser* (which Randel was an editor on), *Hellbound: Hellraiser II*, a film that some consider to be on par with its predecessor. While that is certainly a debatable topic, there's no doubt that *Hellbound* is the best sequel of the mostly abysmal *Hellraiser* series as well as one of the rare sequels that is able to somewhat sustain what was created with its forefather.

In front of the camera, *Ticks* features an interesting mix of character actors, some more recognizable than others. The wilderness group is led by Holly and Charles, who are played by veteran TV and film actors, Rosalind Allen and Peter Scolari. Outside of being the film's VHS cover girl, the beautiful Ami Dolenz doesn't get much to do with her role as Dee Dee Davenport, as she's mainly relegated to playing the typical blonde bimbo. On the more recognizable end of things, Seth Green plays Tyler, a somewhat awkward teen who suffers from panic attacks, but, in truly original form, is able to step up and be the hero when the time calls for it.

One of the most notable actors in *Ticks* – at least in terms of genre recognizability and film presence – comes in the form of legendary cult film actor Clint Howard. Howard plays Jarvis, a backwoods hillbilly whose storyline runs parallel to that of the teens in the wilderness group. Being the character in charge of running the herbal steroid system that eventually leads to the mutated ticks, Jarvis is the first person to come into contact with the overgrown creatures. This results in some genuinely entertaining and often humorous moments that are strewn throughout the movie, most specifically during his death scene, in which he hysterically yells, "I'm infested!" as a number of ticks are bursting out of his skin. While Jarvis plays a fairly large role in the film, the character was not featured in the original cut of *Ticks*. In fact, it wasn't until Randel and the producers found the rough cut to be a little anemic – only focusing on the teens in peril – that, months later, they re-scripted and created the character of Jarvis and his over-the-top interactions with the titular creatures. On an interesting side note, the film also features Clint Howard's father, Rance Howard, in a small role as the town sheriff.

Alfonso Ribeiro is also memorable. For anyone unfamiliar, Ribeiro is best known for portraying Carlton Banks on *The Fresh Prince of Bel-Air.* Carlton is best described as a happy-go-lucky, Ivy League preppy who takes great joy in dancing to the Tom Jones song *It's Not Unusual,* which would eventually become famously known as *The Carlton Dance.* In *Ticks,* Ribeiro plays Panic, a tough kid from the hard streets of LA. "See, they call me Panic... 'cause I never do," he says. In any event, despite the bad attitude, fingerless gloves and backwards hat, it's extremely difficult to take Ribeiro seriously as Panic. Regardless, however, it's not for a lack of trying, as Ribeiro's performance is actually not too bad, and the character also proves himself to be the most durable of the pack, despite being the only protagonist who dies.

But the meat and taters of this fiesta are, of course, the ticks. Classified as arachnids, ticks are closely related to spiders and scorpions. Ticks are small enough to sneak pretty much anywhere onto a person's or animal's body completely undetected, and when

they find a comfortable place to feed, they cut open the skin, insert a feeding tube and secrete a cement -like substance to ensure they have a good grip. At this point, a tick will enjoy a slow blood feast for up to two days, all the while possibly transmitting any number of pathogens that the tick may have picked up along the way.

The proper way to remove a tick – at least according to the CDC and any rational person who's taken the time to look it up – is to use tweezers. The common misconception, and one that is actually shared in the film, is that the only way to safely remove a tick is to burn it off. One would think that the fine people behind *Ticks* would've taken a moment to uncover this fact, though I suppose watching a bunch of characters killing ticks with tweezers is far less exciting than them using fire, so disbelief can be suspended in this case.

The ticks featured here – which are about as big as the average human hand – are not as silly as one would expect from a 1990s low-budget direct-to-video horror film. They're effectively creepy. Despite their large size and the film's small budget, the special effects used to bring the ticks to life are impressive, mainly consisting of a mixture of animatronics and wonderfully executed stop-motion animation. One of the film's highlights comes in the finale, where Panic – after barely making it back to the cabin to warn the others about the dope farmers – dies and becomes the vessel for what can only be described as The Super Tick. Giant tick legs tear out of each appendage just before Panic's lifeless corpse is ripped in half, only to reveal a massive, human-sized tick.

Ticks is likely considered by most everyone to be a forgettable 1990s direct-to-video horror movie due to its cheese factor; however, the movie is able to succeed because of how genuinely fun it is. The film fully embraces its b-movie qualities, which is exactly why it built up a small following as a cult film over the years. A following large enough, in fact, to warrant a 20th Anniversary Blu-ray release courtesy of Olive Films in 2013, complete with commentary from director Tony Randel and co-star Clint Howard. Good or bad, in the end, *Ticks* had enough staying power to entertain a segment of genre film fans for over 20 years and will likely be maintaining its cult status for many years to come.

Matthew House

Growing up with an unhealthy obsession with horror films and the Halloween season, Matthew "Matt-suzaka" House would come to love and appreciate all forms of cinema, from classic and foreign film to exploitation and martial arts.

This would lead him to his first blogging gig for *Paracinema... The Blog* in 2009. From there, Matthew would cut his teeth writing for websites such as *BThroughZ*, *Strange Kids Club*, *The LAMB*, and *The Gentlemen's Blog to Midnite Cinema* as well as eventually becoming a contributor to *Paracinema Magazine*, providing thought-provoking analytical pieces on a variety of genre films.

Matthew spends his days as a freelance writer and social media expert, having contributed content for businesses such as *Brides & Beyond*, *My Mercer County*, *Ohio*, *Preferred Insurance Center*, *Lady Who Travels*, *Revival Spa*, and *Community Sports and Therapy Center*.

His nights, however, belong to *Chuck Norris Ate My Baby*, a personal website which he started in 2009. At *Chuck Norris Ate My Baby*, Matthew focuses his efforts on writing introspective, honest, and sometimes humorous reviews and analytical pieces for genre cinema.

UNINVITED (1988)

By Justin Coote

For a monster kid like myself, meeting legendary writer/director Greydon Clark was like meeting Alfred Hitchcock. Although Clark is not as well known or praised for his cinematic achievements, he has left his mark in film history and has inspired countless generations of grindhouse enthusiasts, creature feature kids, and independent filmmakers. Sitting with Mr. Clark at Monsterpalooza, I experienced his love of the genre first hand as we went from discussing his film *It Came Without Warning* (1980), which was admittedly the inspiration for the film *Predator* (1987), to one of Greydon's lesser known creations, *Uninvited* (1988).

He placed a DVD in my hands with some of the worst cover

art - an airbrush profile of a cat hovering above a small yacht in the ocean. "The best monster cat on a boat movie ever made!" Mr. Clark said about it, and I challenge anyone to disagree.

The tagline - "Cats have nine lives. You only have one!" - lets the viewer know exactly what they're in for: entertainment. Sadly this killer cat classic has never been given the respect it deserves. Not only was it made in an insanely small amount of time on a shoestring budget, but you can tell a lot of love went into the making of this film.

Husband and wife team, Jim and Debi Bouldin, are the creators of the cat creature. Jim Bouldin had already worked on the film *Predator* in 1987, but for Debi Bouldin this was her first onscreen FX work but by no means her last as she later went on to work on yet another feline run amok film, *Strays* (1991). Both would become the top creators of animatronic animals for TV and blockbuster films. The creation of these much needed animatronic

and puppet animal effects allow for realistic yet cruelty-free action and stunts. It's through their artistic abilities and love of animals (they own a rabbit, five cats and a dog) that no killer cats were harmed during the filming of *Uninvited.*

The Bouldins were not the only noteworthy people involved in the creature feature. From *Faces of Death* and *Friday the 13th part 3* to *The Avengers* and *Django Unchained*, Allan A. Apone's resume would easily impress any sci-fi, action, or horror aficionado. Somewhere hidden amongst the classic and big budget titles lies *Uninvited* on which Allan was the makeup effects supervisor. Allan shows how to make a small budget count as his gore effects showcase creativity in a practical way without coming off as cheap. They even rival the bigger budget practical effects of its time.

A major part of the cast should not come off as strangers to fans of the horror genre either. Actress Toni Hudson went on to be in *Leatherface: Texas Chainsaw Massacre 3.* Acting veteran Clu

Gulager was one of the most recognizable characters in *The Return of the Living Dead,* A *Nightmare on Elm Street 2: Freddy's Revenge,* and most recently *Feast* and *Piranha 3DD.* Clare Carey, you will recognize from the classic 1980s horror romp *Wax Work.* If you look deep into the resume of most great actors, directors, producers and makeup artists, you will find more than a few skeletons, or in this case cheesy low-budget horror releases, in their closets. But let's get back to the killer cat.

The premise is this: a radioactive mutant cat escapes a lab and ends up on a yacht with some spring breakers and an eccentric murdering mafia boss/eccentric stockbroker with a taste for young women. The cat has obviously been through a lot seeing how it's in a rush to get out of the lab. The feline only mutates and attacks as self-protection and to protect those it cares about, much like most creatures found throughout Universal horror classics. To top it all off, if you're bitten or scratched by the cat you end up contracting a disease that makes your skin burst out with boils before you die. As if that weren't enough we have subplots involving old hit men questioning where they are in life, cheating girlfriends, embezzlement, and murder - not by the cat! Who is the real villain here?

This creature is the creation of man, this is not nature run amok. This is something to keep in mind throughout the film, that much like *Frankenstein* or *Jurassic Park,* it is humans with their God complexes and complete lack of understanding that are the antagonists. Murder, deceit, and greed all exist amongst these characters before the monster rears its ugly head. Taken from its home like King Kong, the cat is forced to survive by any means necessary.

The setting of a yacht allows for some beautiful and simultaneously bleak settings. The middle of the sea is a place of freedom and adventure but also of danger and solitude. Sailing out to sea allows our characters to be trapped by nature. Whatever troubles they're escaping from pale in comparison to the troubles ahead where the most basic primal instincts become their only options. The ocean places them at the mercy of nature and turns bravery into fear.

The transition of cat to mutant animal is not that unusual within this story as innocents turn to violence rather quickly with every character. "Fight or flight" is a commonly used human instinct in horror or suspense movies. Quick decisions must be made when our lives or those of the people we love are in jeopardy. Primal instinct kicks in, and everyone on the yacht has to fight for their lives, not only when confronted with the killer cat but with fellow humans as well. In true horror/science fiction form, people never seem to be able to work together and get past their petty greed or jealousy, not even if life is on the line.

All in all, Greydon Clark's *Uninvited* is a killer cat movie to be shared and enjoyed by the masses, a fun and cheesy creature run amok film that will have you loving how good bad movies can be. Clark pulls it off and gives the audience exactly what they paid for:

entertainment! Creature kids worldwide will keep this title near and dear to their hearts for decades. In a better world, Mr. Clark would receive an Academy Award for his achievements. Sometimes I guess it's just as good to have made "the best monster cat on a boat film ever."

Justin Coote

Justin Coote lives in San Francisco with his wife, Ruby, and his baby girl, Ellie Mae, who he hopes will grow into a beautiful horror nerd since she already has a plush Jason Voorhees in her crib.

His mother, Sonia, was a classic monster kid who showed her young son VHS rentals of *Night of the Living Dead* and described how it promoted civil rights. She then introduced him to classic Universal monsters like *Dracula*.

When not traveling to cemeteries, he and his family are seeking out classic film locations like the house from *The People Under The Stairs*. The Coote family can often be seen at the local classic car show, Monsterpalooza, or Disneyland.

Justin likes to think of himself as a musician playing both the upright bass and drums. He currently sings for the Hardcore band Alcatraz and is still proud of his Straight edge punk roots.

Justin reviews films for *The Overlook Theater* under the name XkilldozerX.

WHITE DOG (1982)

By J. Luis Rivera

To many people, it's hard to believe that racism is still an issue in 21st Century America. Sounds like something anachronistic, something that no longer happens, that's made irrelevant by contemporary society. And the fact is, that racism just has a new face, less visible perhaps than KKK rallies but still prevalent underneath. To think of it as nonexistent is naive at best, as it's deeply rooted in the American psyche, perhaps irremediably. That's precisely the point argued by one of the most interesting films of the 1980s: Samuel Fuller's *White Dog*.

The story is simple: a young actress named Julie (Kristy McNichol) accidentally runs over a white German Shepherd. Guilt-ridden, Julie takes it to a vet and then keeps it at home, in hopes of finding its owner. One night, the dog saves her from a rapist, so she decides to adopt him. After the dog attacks a friend of her, an actress on the set of her new job, Julie discovers that something is not right. Taking it to a training service, she discovers that her dog is a "white dog," an animal trained to attack African Americans. After it tries to kill Keys (Paul Winfield), a black dog trainer, his boss wants to kill the dog, but Keys insists that he's able to cure it.

What follows are Keys' attempts to break the dog's conditioning, in an attempt to prove that racism can be cured. A true battle of wills between the trainer and the dog, where the goal goes beyond making the dog a functional part of society, it's to demonstrate that racism is not inherent but something that can be taught. Something instrumental in Fuller's drama is the fact that the characters do not know to what extent the dog is dangerous, but the audiences do: on the days the dog escapes, it mercilessly kills African Americans. The audience knows the destructive power in the dog.

Written by director Samuel Fuller and Curtis Hanson (who would go on to direct *L.A. Confidential* in 1997), *White Dog* has its origin in a novel written by Romain Gray in 1970. The novel is a fictionalized memoir dealing with Gray and his wife Jean Seberg who accidentally adopt a white dog. While the novel finishes on a less than optimistic note (the black trainer makes the dog take revenge on white people), Fuller uses it as the basis for a greater message: that it's going to take a lot to "cure" racism in America. The dog, lovely and loyal with Julie, brutal and savage with the African Americans, is a metaphor for American society, as racism takes out the worst of it.

Despite not being the Studio's first choice to direct the film (Paramount wanted Polanski, until he fled the country), Sam Fuller makes the film his own (he wasn't a stranger to racial themes, as *The Crimson Kimono* shows), focusing less on the people and taking a special interest in the dog. The dog is no longer the tool of hateful individuals but a victim of its masters. This would be the key, as it's the dog's racism where the crux of the film is. Is it curable or not? Or more important, is the hatred inherent to its nature? America, like the dog, must walk a long and tortuous way to answer those questions. Hopefully, with much better results.

White Dog is not the first time Fuller employed Hollywood's traditional melodrama to convey strong messages: *The Naked Kiss* deals with child molestation and *Shock Corridor* with mental illness. However, *White Dog* is perhaps the film that most brutally hits, not only because of its controversial subject matter (even today, it seems as if racism can't be discussed), but also because of the emotional grip it has on the audience. *White Dog* is a film that aims to confront, to question its audience's moral values with intelligence and skill. The dog, a noble animal, becomes a terrifying demon in a matter of seconds, and this duality and what it represents can be unsettling. And that's because it's true.

The premise, a dangerous savage animal on the loose, puts *White Dog* in the terrain of genre films, and here's where the maverick director shows his skill. Filmmaker Sam Fuller employs the genre's classic elements to make a thrilling story come to life, but *White Dog* is more than a thrilling story, it's an analogy of the social injustices still present in America. With great intelligence and boldness, Fuller has made a thriller with a message deeply rooted at its core. And the film succeeds at being both. Often "films with a message" tend to become preachy and tedious thanks to its lack of subtlety, *White Dog* on the other hand, never forgets that the best way to convey its message is through drama, like the ancient Greeks used to do.

Technically, the film is impeccable. Fuller makes the most of his resources to tell a gripping story of hatred, creating an unforgettable character in the dog, an angel and a demon at the same time. The way Fuller gives a personality to the white dog is pure cinema language at its best. Scenes like the rapist's attack or the killing at the church are masterful in their elegance and power. Fuller puts us in the point of view of the dog, which is perhaps

why the movie is so unsettling: we are the white dog.

Bruce Surtees' work of cinematography is Fuller's greatest ally in this, as his sober and classicist style suits nicely the subtlety that Fuller's film requires. Most importantly, Surtees manages to portray the normality and realism of modern life, in the sense that *White Dog* is not a fantasy horror film, the horror is real and closer to home than one would wish it to be. Ennio Morricone's score echoes the subtlety that seems to be the mark of the film and delivers a fantastic work that suits the movie nicely.

It's impossible to discuss *White Dog* without mentioning its troubled release. Unfortunately, at the time of the release rumors were spread about the film's theme (probably founded more on fears regarding its source novel), and Paramount felt the movie was potentially racist and controversial. The solution, as incredible as it seems now, was to shelve it. The film only saw the light in the UK and France, and later was forgotten, appearing occasionally on cable TV. To Fuller, this was a disgrace and the trigger that prompted his moving to France. The film saw finally an American release in 2008.

Can the white dog change? Can America change? This nature vs. nurture argument is the core theme in Sam Fuller's film. A question that Fuller suggests is more complex and disturbing because racism is still a reality. As written above, racism seems to be swept under the rug in modern America, but it's still present even today, rearing its ugly head more often than not. Sam Fuller's question is sadly, still relevant.

J. Luis Rivera

J. Luis Rivera was born in Monterrey, Nuevo León, Mexico. An engineer and a filmmaker, J. Luis has been writing about cinema since his days in college, but his love for movies dates from his childhood, when he accidentally watched David Cronenberg's *The Fly*. It was love at first fright. His reviews can be occasionally found in local newspapers and on a couple of websites. He also collaborated in Aaron Christensen's books *Horror 101* and *Hidden Horror*.

Living in Mexico City, J. Luis works in the Mexican film industry while plotting to conquer the world. Recently, he's preparing his feature length debut.

WHITE GOD (2014)

By Oksana Osachiy

White God is a powerfully shot film about a girl and her dog. It depicts a fear that stems from what is impossible to know and what can quickly spin out of control in our minds: the fate of our animal companions if we're forced to part with them. Although for most the worst case scenario is death, survival can prove to be infinitely more unthinkable.

The opening scene of this Hungarian drama/horror-thriller is

set on the streets of present day Budapest. The streets are deserted except for one young girl who is bicycling in the middle of the road. She appears to be looking for something in the emptiness but only finds abandoned cars and boarded up windows, until her solitude is trampled through by a wave of savage, barking dogs.

The story begins with a young girl, Lili (Zsófia Psotta), laughing and playing affectionately with her dog, Hagen. Her

mother calls her over to inform that she's leaving the country for several months and that Lili has to go live with her father.

Next, we see two men standing before a dead cow that is hanging by two legs, skinned in several places. Blood is dripping and flowing on a tile floor. This is where we meet our other main character, Lili's father, Daniel (Sándor Zsótér). Although he has no part in the slaughtering of the animal and is actually inspecting it for disease, these images of death are the first the audience has to associate with him. A slaughterhouse employee calls him "professor," and Daniel sounds awkward when he remarks, after the fact, that he's no longer exerting that profession. There's no clear reason for his uneasiness until moments later, when he refers to his ex-wife's new man with the same title, hinting that she left him for someone with the same background but higher regard.

It's obvious that Lili does not respect her father; when Daniel asks for a kiss from his daughter, all he gets is a split second of cheek contact, followed by an obvious lie about chewing gum. Lili does not appreciate her father's attempt to break the ice and is continuously rude to him. But when it comes to Hagen, she's all smiles and sweetness, which her father counters by treating him like an unruly stray. My instinctual reaction was to hate this man based on his harsh treatment of such a sweet dog, but I realized that his whole life must have changed after what I suspect was a one-sided divorce, and that this dog was just a walking reminder of the whole situation. While his resentment may be misdirected, he becomes much easier to sympathize with under those conditions.

The conflict in *White God* stems from a political McGuffin that states all mixed breed dogs must either be put in a shelter or registered at a price. Since Hagen is not a pure breed but the target of Daniel's hostility, he ends up getting left on the street in a fit of rage. There, Hagen looks like any other stray. However, he does not act like one. Hagen has a naive innocence about the world; he recognizes another dog and tries to nuzzle it awake, not realizing it's dead rather than asleep. He jumps at every sharp noise and licks

the hand of a dogcatcher who's trying to capture him. He cannot distinguish what is and isn't a threat to him, since he never experienced the difference.

During his time on the street, Hagen finds a sort of stray dog paradise, a semi-secluded vacant lot filled with strays and a giant puddle perfect for a dip or a drink. He befriends one of these dogs, and she helps him out of several situations. But Hagen still has some lessons to learn. Lacking this knowledge leads to Hagen getting trapped, sold, and transformed into a vicious fighter, a life that he manages to escape, and he seeks revenge for everything he had to endure. And Hagen is not alone in this. Now, he has an entire army of discarded dogs rallying behind him.

White God takes great strides to show how similar and yet complimentary Lili and Hagen are. After the two are separated, there are several instances when the camera cuts from one to the other, and they're sharing the same expression, even though they're nowhere near each other. Although their separate stories are very different, their reactions to certain uncomfortable, overpowering situations are alike. These traits are paralleled in many ways throughout the film, from the company that Lili and Hagen find

themselves around to the situations they wind up in, and they allow the audience to compare the changes that each are going through. One of these parallels can be seen when Lili is looking for Hagen and unknowingly retraces almost every place where he had previously been, staring at the same passing cars and down the same corridors. There's also a scene where both are running away from their unjust masters, one being legitimately abused while the other just perceived things as such. Running away was a turning point for both Lili and Hagen but in opposite ways. While the former was finally acknowledged as a young adult by her father and realized how much she was hurting him with her outbursts, the latter was entirely fed up with people and decided to discard his passive ways.

This story could have been told in many ways and director Kornél Mundruczó definitely chose the most effective option. The dog end of the film was told in long, mute sequences, where the camera angle, soundtrack, and canine expression took the place of verbal exposition. Despite seeming like an impossible feat to every dog trainer, the entire film was made without the use of computer-generated effects. Trainer after trainer telling him that this hurdle could not be overcome the way he wanted it to be, didn't discourage Mundruczó. Instead, he found Teresa Miller and Árpád Halász, two ambitious dog trainers who were up to the challenge. They used positive reinforcement training and gave the dogs a lot of freedom, which kept them in good spirits. That, paired with a three month period of building a relationship between canine and human actors, added authenticity to the film.

On the surface, *White God* is the story of an impending uprising, but the film communicates a lot of its messages in a more subtle language. In order to calm and sooth Hagen, Lili plays her trumpet. Early in the film, it's used to calm him down in order to go to sleep and also let him know that she was there with him. This tune follows Hagen during his brief stay at the pound, reminding him of his previous life and taunting him to fighting back. When Lili attempts to use the melody to convey the same message after both have gone through their trials, it seems to say that, although she's here now, they cannot re-enter their lost paradise.

Oksana Osachiy

This lean, mean killing machine is one of the best Street Samurai to walk the concrete wastelands. In fact, the only time this dystopian lioness isn't stalking her pray, is when she enjoys a good film. Why she travels to a haunted theater in a past time to enjoy such things, is beyond anyone among the living.

The genre Oksana enjoys the most is horror-comedy, and her top five favorite movies are *Vertigo* (1958), *The Excorcist* (1973), *The Rocky Horror Picture Show* (1975), *Predator* (1987), and *Hatchet* (2006).

She writes movie reviews for *The Overlook Theater*.

WILD BEASTS (1984)

By Vanessa Morgan

I first came across *Wild Beasts* (original Italian title: *Belve Feroci*) at a flea market. At the beginning of the century, flea markets were the best places to discover obscure horror movies and forgotten classics. Video stores were closing, and several of them were selling their stock at these markets for a few cents each. For that price, I bought every horror film I hadn't seen. With a bit of luck, the film was as grimy as its mold-covered VHS jacket.

Wild Beasts was one of those films. I wasn't sure what to expect, but the blurb and the French dubbed title *Les bêtes féroces attaquent* (translating as *The Ferocious Beasts Attack*) were enough to wet my appetite. As it turned out, the film affected my love for the animal attack genre in ways I couldn't have predicted beforehand.

In *Wild Beasts* - also known as *Zoo Terror, Night of the Beast, The*

Wild Beasts Will Get You, *Wild Beast*, and *Savage Beasts* - a veterinarian at the Frankfurt Zoo, Dr. Rupert Berner (played by animal specialist John Aldrich), and his scientist girlfriend, Laura Schwarz (Lauraine De Selle from *Cannibal Ferox* and *House on the Edge of the Park*), investigate the causes of the zoo animals' sudden restless and aggressive behavior. Before they know what's going on, an electrical malfunctioning of the zoo's security system does the rest. The wild beasts escape from their unprotected cages and set out for the city. It's then upon Dr. Rupert Berner and Inspector Nat Braun (Ugo Bologna from Fulci's *Zombi 2*), to hunt down the animals with a tranquilizer gun. Meanwhile, Laura tries to get to her daughter, Suzy (Louisa Lloyd).

The film showcases one of the most diverse varieties of animals ever to creep, rampage, and stampede across the screen. A

mischief of rats gnaws away at an amorous couple that makes out in a car. A cheetah chases after a vehicle and causes it to burst into flames. Tigers, lions, and hyenas escape from the zoo and devour everyone on their path. A polar bear targets the children of a dance school. A guide dog for the blind turns on its master. And a drove of horses and cattle attacks a diner. The most memorable scenes, however, involve the elephants. They break iron fences and walk through brick walls before setting out for the town's main street where they crush human heads and strangle people with their trunks. They even head to the airport's runway on which an airplane crashes as its pilots try to avoid the herd.

Like so many other horrors from the 1970s and 1980s, there's an ecological and societal component tied to the animals' behavior. Starting with images of factory discharges and used syringes in public spaces, the film underlines the slow degradation of society. The animals turn violent because they've been accidentally exposed to the man-made dissociative drug phencyclidine (also known as angel dust or PCP), which is often used in science to mimic schizophrenia. Phencyclidine brings out effects such as hallucinations, aggression, depression, agitation, and memory disorders.

Though Italian director Franco E. Prosperi exaggerated the effects of phencyclidine to facilitate an engaging storytelling, he knows what he's talking about. He graduated in natural sciences, agronomy and ichthyology (the study of fishes) and spent the majority of his career participating in various submarine expeditions and conducting ethnological and ethological research through the Institute of Zoology at the University of Rome. He also made several nature documentaries and travel features.

Prosperi's fascination with zoology is clearly present in *Wild Beasts*. However, *it mostly* takes its cue from a rare American made-for-TV movie, *The Beasts are on the Streets* (1978, Peter R. Hunt) in which a bunch of animals (zebras, bisons, dromedaries, ostriches, rhinos, etc.) are unleashed on the streets after a careening tanker truck rips through the fence of a drive-through wildlife park. Yet *Wild Beasts* swims above its derivative origin because it flirts heavily with the Euro exploitation genre. The animal attack scenes in *Wild Beasts* are elaborate and bloody. Director Prosperi wants you to live your fear and doesn't shy away from confronting its viewers with

the world's atrocities. That, unfortunately, involves real suffering of animals. In the film's first animal attack scene, a black cat desperately puts up a defense against a mischief of rats by biting them in the neck and tossing them around. Later, the fire department sets the rats on fire. In yet another scene, Prosperi unleashes mountain lions and hyenas on defenseless cows, pigs, and horses and films them as they put their fangs into the animals' necks.

Contrary to what you might expect, *Wild Beasts* is Prosperi's most "user-friendly" movie. He became known for his documentary *Mondo Cane* (1962) in which he featured shocking cultural practices around the world, including sharks being choked with sea urchins, dogs being cooked and eaten, pigs being beaten to death, and bulls being beheaded. Thanks to *Mondo Cane*'s box-office success and numerous awards (such as the Palme d'or at Cannes, and Grammy and Oscar nominations for its soundtrack), Prosperi, together with his co-directors Gualtiero Jacopetti and Paolo Cavara, continued on the same track with titles as *La donna nel mondo* aka *Women of the World* (1963), *Mondo Pazzo* aka *Mondo Cane 2* (1963), and *Africa Addio* aka *Africa Blood and Guts* (1966). The Mondo film - documentaries made for the sole purpose of shocking viewers - became a genre all of its own. After wrapping *Wild Beasts* (which was meant to take place in Africa but had to be relocated because of a terrorist attack), Prosperi returned to his first area of expertise: zoology and ethnological activities in Africa.

It's neither the gore nor the abuse of animals that makes *Wild Beasts* shocking, though. Prosperi is far more sneaky in his approach of confronting our fears. In the final scene, we discover that the animals weren't the only ones exposed to phencyclidine. Children, too, have been drinking water containing this chemical, and now they have turned into killer kids. Animals, just like children, offer respite from the act of random violence. We use their cuteness and purity to remind us of the good things in life. Bereaving them from their goodness is like taking away our last bit of hope. *Wild Beasts* not only eliminates our belief in innocence, but it also makes us realize that we're the cause of this absence. Or, like the Francis Thrive quote states in the beginning of *Wild Beasts,* "Our madness engulfs everything and infects innocent victims such as children or animals."

Vanessa Morgan

Vanessa Morgan is known as the "female version of Stephen King." She's the author of *Drowned Sorrow*, *The Strangers Outside*, *A Good Man*, *GPS With Benefits*, *Next to Her*, and *Avalon*. Three of her stories have been turned into movies.

She has also written for numerous Belgian magazines and newspapers, and introduces movies at Offscreen, the Brussels International Fantastic Film Festival, and Razor Reel Fantastic Film Festival.

If she's not working on her latest book or screenplay, you can find her reading, attending film festivals, digging through flea markets, or photographing felines for her blog *Traveling Cats*.

She lives in Oudergem, Belgium.

WILLARD (2003)

By David Royce

"Willard! There are rats in the basement!" With that line, the 2003 remake of Willard begins.

Rats have a bad reputation. We call someone a rat when they reveal too much information; James Cagney's famous line, "You dirty rat," is still used to this day. And, in any given situation where things are not going the way we'd like, we yell out, "Rats!" Well, that is if you're in the presence of young children or your church group.

Despite this visceral reaction, horror films haven't really capitalized on our fear of these four legged germ carriers.

> RAT FACT: Rats are extremely clean animals, spending
> several hours every day grooming themselves and their group
> members. They're less likely than cats or dogs to catch and
> transmit parasites and viruses.

I tried to figure out why I love this particular movie so much. It certainly wasn't very popular when it was released (the reviews weren't very kind), but I had an affection for it nonetheless. After some thought (and more than a few beers), a realization came to me.

While on the surface *Willard* could be considered an "animal attack" horror film, it's much more. It's, in fact, a slasher movie in disguise. Jason had his machete, Michael had his knife, and Freddy had his claw gloves. Willard has his rats.

A very basic synopsis of *Willard* would be as follows: A put-upon meek, awkward man is taken to his breaking point by his overbearing mother, an insulting and abusive boss, and being the office laughing stock at his place of employment. When he realizes he has the ability to communicate mentally with the rats that have infested his mother's house he plots his revenge against his tormentors. Ultimately, he discovers that he doesn't control them as much as he believed after all.

RAT FACT: A rat can go longer than a camel without having a drink of water.

If the thought of seeing a gaggle of rats climbing over human flesh and slowly devouring a person bite by bite is unsettling to you, well, that makes you pretty normal, actually. But it's a gloriously gruesome thing in this film. However, it's not all blood and gore here. This is a story of revenge and the consequences thereof, a story of the bullied becoming the hunter and, in doing so, making himself a worse specimen than his former enemies. I like a movie that can make me hate someone and raise my fist at them but turn it around and make me feel sorry for them later. At first, you'll feel a certain bit of righteous vindication as Willard tasks his new friends with the disposal of those who make his life miserable. After all, haven't we all wanted at some point to make some insufferable jackass squirm and beg just a little bit? It's okay to admit it. I have those thoughts on most days waiting in line or driving to work. However, once you see the writhing mass of legs, fur, teeth, and tail taking its flesh, you feel sorry for the jackass in question.

Willard is loosely based on the novel *Ratman's Notebooks* (later re-released as *Willard*) by Stephen Gilbert. Another movie was made in 1971, but this is more of a reimagining.

This version is superior for two reasons: R. Lee Ermey and Crispin Glover. These two actors are better known for their respective roles in other films. In the case of R. Lee Ermey, that movie is *Full Metal Jacket* (for which he received a Golden Globe nomination for his portrayal of a drill instructor). And I think we all will recognize Crispin Glover as the mousy, awkward, meek father of Marty McFly in *Back To The Future*. Whether by choice or circumstance, these two play their roles in *Willard* with the same intensity as they played their more famous roles. The differences are almost nonexistent - R. Lee Ermey playing a tough boss who lives to verbally torture Willard, and Crispin Glover playing the man who takes it without sticking up for himself. Until, of course, the rats start talking to him.

> RAT FACT: Baltimore's rat problem is bad enough that at one point, rats tunneled so intensely beneath a particular area of pavement that when garbage collectors drove over it, their truck sunk up to its axles. Rats in the vicinity took full advantage of the mishap and swarmed the truck, gorging on the garbage inside.

To give you some idea of the relationship between Willard and his boss, I refer you to a scene when Willard confronts his boss with his newly found friends:

Willard: "They'll do anything I tell them."

Frank Martin: "Then tell them to get the fuck out of my office!"

Even facing the wrath of hundreds of sharp teeth gnawing at his flesh, Willard's boss won't give him an ounce of respect. These interactions truly make *Willard* a unique and awesome viewing experience.

For the intensity and emotion involved in the more volatile and verbally abusive scenes, it was not all business on set. Crispin actually found the monologs and rantings of R. Lee Ermey hilarious and would often be laughing behind the camera as they were being filmed. Much to the chagrin of the director, I'm sure.

RAT FACT: A female rat can mate as many as 500 times with various males during a six-hour period of receptivity — a state she experiences about 15 times per year. Thus a pair of brown rats can produce as many as 2,000 descendants in a year if left to breed unchecked.

Joaquin Phoenix and Macaulay Culkin both turned down the lead role of Willard, thus allowing Crispin Glover to jump in and give a phenomenal performance. He also had a certain look that appealed to the director, Glen Morgan. He wanted to make Crispin appear as more of a "rat man," so the makeup people would put dark circles under his eyes, and they would film certain scenes to accentuate the profound shape and length of his nose.

But the real star of *Willard* is Ben. He's the rats' rat, the main tail if you will. Since most rats here in the United States only average eight to 10 inches (which includes the tail), the filmmakers used a Gambian Pouched Rat. These can grow to almost two feet in length and weigh as much as six pounds! I guess that gives Dennis Quaid a run for his money as everyone's least favorite actor to work with.

And, yes, the rats in this film are real. In fact, over 500 rats were used here. They were trained for months before filming. The rats were like actors, except that they got lots of food .

The bottom line is this: If you're looking for some great acting, a creepy premise, and downright terrifying kill scenes, you could do a lot worse than *Willard*. And remember, the next time you get that feeling as if you're being watched, don't bother calling the Ghostbusters. Recent studies have suggested there may be as many as two rats for every one person in most major cities. It would be best to call an exterminator.

David Royce

David Royce is the founder of the website www.horrorcabin.com. The first movie he watched that scared him as a child was *The Exorcist*. He felt terrified but so alive at the same time. His heart was pounding. His mind was racing. But he loved it. After that, he would eat up anything having to do with the supernatural. From watching the TV series *Dark Shadows* to reading almost anything he could get his hands on that had a horror vibe to it.

He soon began writing his own original short stories about ghosts and creatures. They were crap, but at the time he thought he was a genius. His love for the genre never went away. Through good times and bad, hell or high water, he maintained his attraction to this dark twisted world of horror.

When he's not doing all this, he enjoys playing video games, collecting comic books, and generally getting his "nerd" on with his fellow geeks.

ZOLTAN: HOUND OF DRACULA (1978)

By Marvin the Macabre

In 1970s America, no dog breed was more feared and reviled than the Doberman Pinscher. Communities tried to ban them. Lowlifes lined up to buy them. They're rippled with muscles and sport cropped ears so long and sharp they could practically impale you. Their teeth could bisect a dachshund in one chomp. If Dracula, the Prince of Darkness, were to have a dog, it would definitely be a Doberman.

That's the concept behind *Zoltan: Hound of Dracula* (originally released as *Dracula's Dog*): you take the biggest, meanest, most feared dog in the country, and give it the powers of the undead. The end result is an unstoppable killing machine and the most terrifying movie monster this side of *Jaws*.

Here's the film in a nutshell: soldiers disturb Dracula's tomb and accidentally awaken Zoltan. The dog, who's not the biggest fan of his former master, opts to revive his half-vampire original

owner, Veidt Schmith, instead. Together they track down the last living descendant of the Dracula family so that they can turn him into a vampire and make him their new master (for some reason, neither of them can survive without a master to serve). Turns out, the last Dracula is living in California under the name Michael Drake. Drake and his family have just set out on a family camping trip when Veidt and Zoltan arrive in the U.S. Instead of outright attacking Drake, Zoltan instead goes for his German Shepherds plus another random hunting hound, transforming them into a small army of undead dogs. Fortunately for the Drakes, there's also a Van Helsing character, Inspector Branco (played with totally inappropriate gravitas by the great José Ferrer), who shows up to deliver exposition and help Michael Drake vanquish his ancestral family pet.

So, Zoltan is pretty simple in the story department. But where Zoltan's dumbness really shines is in the execution. The film is so ineptly crafted that it's impossible to suspend your disbelief. A killer dog movie works best on an audience that's terrified of dogs. Not this one. It's impossible to see Zoltan as a creature of evil when the pooch is so clearly a sweetheart. Every snarl makes you want to pat him on the head and tell him what a good boy he is. The dog attacks never look real. There's a simple reason for this: dogs are terrible actors. The answer to the dog's acting conundrum, "What's my motivation?" is always "Treats!" In each

scene, the viewer knows precisely where Zoltan's handler is positioned. Just follow the dog's eyeline, and you can practically smell the waving bacon. Also, even if you've never seen a dog fight, they're so familiar you can effortlessly recognize when Fido is faking it. We know how they move, how they behave. We can read their body language in a way we can't with less familiar animals. I have never personally seen a pissed off bear or recognized the signs it was about to charge, but I can damn sure tell the difference between a dog who's about to unleash Hell and one who's waiting for a Beggin' Strip.

That's why I prefer a killer dog movie that doesn't just fall short of reality, but that falls like frickin' Lucifer. One that falls so far it nearly burns up upon atmospheric re-entry. A movie that so spectacularly fails to live up to its premise that it transcends its own badness and becomes a metatextual commentary on itself.

At one point in the film, Drake and Branco are holed up in a cabin fending off Zoltan's pack when, honest to God, one of the dogs PUNCHES through a window. What I wouldn't give to have been the guy operating the paw on a stick prop for that shot. When they barricade the windows and doors, Zoltan jumps up on the roof and chews through it. After biting through live electrical wires without suffering any harm, Zoltan finally breaks through. To top it off, once Zoltan has the two men cornered, he decides that it's too close to daylight to finish the job and just runs off.

The sound design is equally amazing. In the scene where Michael is being attacked in the car, every bark sounds like a chorus of ten dogs with a hint of a chainsaw in the mix. As over-the-top as it sounds, it's unsettling. It also helps that the close-quarters animal attack is shot so you can't really tell what's going on, and so it doesn't look nearly as fake as the rest of the film.

But the true joy of Zoltan lies in the editing, where the filmmakers valiantly attempt to save what was always destined to be an incoherent mess. Nearly every scene in which Zoltan attacks

The Blood Lusting Killer...

ZOLTAN

...HOUND OF DRACULA

X

was shot with the dog isolated in front of a black background with no visual context. The editor intercuts Zoltan snarling or lunging unconvincingly at the camera with reaction shots from the equally unconvincing victims. In the film's only gore scene, Veidt commands Zoltan to destroy anyone nearby who might foil their plans. Zoltan finds a lone camper and does the deed. In what may be the highlight of the film, someone offscreen tosses Zoltan at the guy, then they play-fight on the ground for a while. Next comes the context-free lunging of Zoltan intercut with the camper's increasingly bloodied face. Each time they cut back to the camper, there's more blood, yet no apparent wounds. Finally, Zoltan attacks his legs, and we're treated to the special effects wizardry of a young Stan Winston, who apparently just tucked a bloody steak into a pair of ripped jeans, then washed his hands of the whole affair. Oh, and instead of the usual "bite-him-and-hold-still" approach, this attack features some actual head-shaking motion, albeit by a very fake-looking dog head prop.

Shall I spoil the ending for you? I can't resist. Michael Drake defeats Zoltan by flashing his cross necklace. Zoltan backs away from it and accidentally falls off a cliff. And when I say falls, I don't mean downward, like physics would dictate. He zings off the edge like someone has chucked him off, accompanied by the sound of a screaming woman. Dracula's dog is impaled on the metal fence below, and the world is once more safe from canine cadavers. Or is it? Just before the credits roll, we get the most adorable horror movie stinger of all time. One of the German Shepherd puppies the Drakes had lost is still wandering the woods. It turns to reveal its glowing eyes and vampire fangs, and it's just too damned cute for words.

As fun and ridiculous as Zoltan can be, you must remember that this is a truly bad movie that forces you to sit through long stretches of filler. Hopefully, you enjoy driving montages because they beat dog attack scenes for screen time by a 2:1 ratio. But the moments of sheer unspoiled glee more than make up for it. So if you're up for some bottom-notch killer dog action, invite a roomful of your goofiest friends, track down a copy of *Zoltan*, and drink yourselves half-retarded before hitting play. You're going to need it.

Marvin the Macabre

Marvin the Macabre watches an unhealthy number of horror films and sporadically blogs about them on his website *The Montana Mancave Massacre*. He's also a frequent contributor to *Dread Central*, the midnight movie blog *From Midnight with Love*, as well as to *the delinquency of minors*.

Marvin probably could have written a book-length essay about everything wrong and so very, very right about *Zoltan: Hound of Dracula*, but he'll spare you that. He would also be down for some beers later, if you're not doing anything.

www.ingramcontent.com/pod-product-compliance
Lightning Source LLC
Chambersburg PA
CBHW051058030726
47504CB00006B/1677